PROMISE
OF
DUSK

By Wrylie Parks

ISBN: 979-8-9918221-1-4

Cover illustration and design by Kyla Martinez.
Editing by White Willow editing.
Published by Apparition's Publishing.

To the people who dream of something *more*.

3

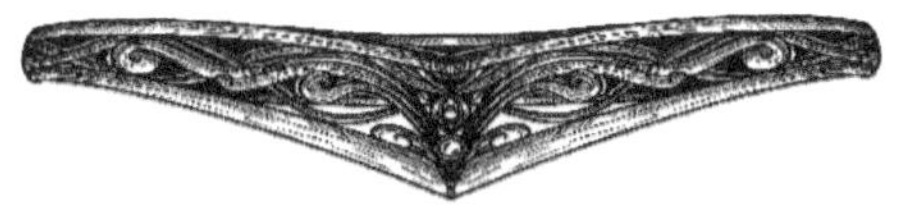

Chapter 1

Death chills the doorway. It hasn't come for the child laying in the bed yet, but it will. His final resting place is softly illuminated by window-filtered daylight. His sweat-dampened chestnut curls lay softly against his flushed forehead.

He looks angelic, really. Divine, even in the clutch of a reaper.

His mother clings to his hand beside him. Sara came to Diana's apothecary only a few days ago, her son still grinning, gap-toothed and flushed. She carried him in, frazzled and panting, claiming that he had fainted outside in the garden that morning. At first, we thought perhaps he was just malnourished or dehydrated, a common condition around the village of Comraich. But while the boy was definitely underweight compared to the plump, rotten children of the affluent neighborhoods in Raith, the blazing fever seemed to be ailing him most. No amount of fever-few could mellow the heat, and by dawn, he had fallen to delusions.

I've seen enough of life to know when to brace for death.

A tragedy. One I have become quite detached from, unfortunately.

There are only so many dead children, siblings, parents, and friends that I can muster up true devastation for. Now, the family's grief pounds at the walls I've built up around my soul; it's relentless but manageable. I leave the empty, soft smiles and wasted condolences to Diana. I cannot bear them anymore.

I chew on the rough skin around my thumbnail while I observe, a phantom in the shadows. A gross habit—one I can't be bothered to stop.

A voice, roughened by age, comes from beside the mother, soft and comforting. "He knows that you are here with him. A mother's strength is no small thing for a babe. He needs you." Wrinkled hands, which I know to be cold and soft, gently pat the back of the mother's hand melded to her child's. "We are going to do everything we can to break this fever and bring him back to you, dear. We have overcome worse odds than this."

The mother stares stone-faced at her son, memorizing every detail of his too-thin face, not acknowledging Diana's reassurances.

Cold disgust washes over me as I watch. Hope is a wretched thing; a friend peeling back armor, leaving you vulnerable.

Too often a friend betrays.

Diana is no fool. She knows that this boy is too hungry, too small, and was born with every single odd stacked against him.

Diana slowly—too dramatically—makes her way to her feet and hobbles over to where I loiter.

Closing the door, we silently pad down the hallway to our workspace. I swiftly go to the tea that is brewing over the fire, stirring the mixture, swallowing back the vitriol that I am predisposed to spill. Through the fogged-up windowpane, gray skies and drizzling rains are painting the town a dreary shade of despair.

"You'll need to go back to the clearing for some dandelion," Diana directs, glassware clinking as she putters about her workbench.

I stand slowly from my sullen vigil over the poppy tea, turn, and level Diana with a stare.

She glances up at me and sighs. "Oh don't give me that look, Alyx," she mumbles, pressing her lips together for a moment. She resumes carefully placing a bundle of sphagnum moss into a small woven basket. "You wouldn't make a weak old woman walk all the way through town and past all of those horrid Crows, would you?"

I almost let it go.

"This will not end well. Why lead her to believe otherwise?" My words come up like shards of glass. Flashes of my own silent vigil over a lifeless form harden my voice. "It's cruel."

"Are you a god? Because that would have been nice for you to say before I wasted all of these herbs trying to heal that poor boy." She flits around, moving into my space, flapping her hands to get me to move out of the way. "You should have just told me you could snap your fingers and make him healthy again—"

"—You know better." I cut her off before she can finish, my eyes rolling.

She grasps the pot of tea from over the fire and brings it over to the wooden countertop, shuffling in her old brown boots—there is a hole in the toe of the left one. "No. I don't.

And neither do you," Diana states. "Child, just because you're staring doom in the face does not give you the right to give up on that poor baby boy. We can be brave for him, if not for ourselves." Her face turns up at me, drawing my eyes from her boot. "You would be surprised…" She stops as if unsure of her words.

"What would surprise me?" I ask, sure to regret it.

"How far a little hope goes." She finishes her thought.

The sounds of hot tea hitting glass fill the silence as she looks away and pours a jar full.

I know my face betrays my thoughts. I'm glad she doesn't see it. How could one with so many years of experience still believe that? I have not, in my few years of apprenticeship for Diana, even once, seen hope do a damned thing to save anyone. Hope does not heal a broken body. Hope does not rid the mind of fever-ridden delusions. No amount of hope could save a life that was bound to go.

My eyes catch on the herbs hanging from the wall and my thumb goes to my mouth. There's a rough edge that is just barely too short for me to get with my teeth, no matter how I turn my finger. It's like an itch you can't scratch.

"Who's this for?" I ask, voice muffled by my hand.

My thumb starts to bleed. I suck on it to make it stop.

"Rhodri. You know, he's always banging himself up in that tavern on goodness knows what. That daughter of his is wilder than him. Clumsy, too. All bumps and bruises. I would think Rhodri was taking a beating to her if I didn't know him to be above all that." She arranges a few more supplies in the basket, along with the special tea I remember Rhodri's wife, Elena, favors. "They best watch out or she will set fire to this whole town one day."

Mariana *is* wild. Like fire licking across the ground, unbidden, and untethered. We used to be friends when we were little. Well, she forced us to be friends. If seven-year-old Alyx had known that asking to hold the ladybug Mariana had found in the dirt would make the little fireball stick to her like a thorn, she probably would have kept quiet. Maybe not. I was glad to have a friend then.

But then I grew sullen. And we grew apart. She still waves to me when she passes by in town, sometimes making idle chat whenever I visit the tavern to drop something off for Diana. I never wave back, and I give as little as possible in those conversations. I was a bad friend. She deserved better. Still does.

Desperate to get away from all of Diana's hopeful nonsense, I throw my cloak and hood on over my floor-length standard woollen dress, step out of Diana's place, and begin the trudge across town.

Keeping my head down is a natural instinct at this point. Like a ritual, practiced every day, whenever one moves from place to place. Don't stand out. Don't make eye contact. Walk amongst the rats that scurry along walls lining the streets. Be one with them.

Paranoia causes me to seek out the threats that haunt these streets. Out of the corner of my eye, I see two, standing outside the butcher shop. There are three more down an alleyway, questioning a drunk who's sprawled on the ground, against the wall of a tavern. At least ten are pacing the square at the center of town around Crow Stage, the rickety gallows that lord over the heart of town.

I keep up my brisk pace to the other side of town, the outskirts of which contain the meadow where I gather many of my medicinal herbs and roots. Some days, the energy in the streets drives me straight to the wood, where I circle around the circumference of town instead of passing through it. Today seems low-energy, the Crows calm, their depraved hungers well-fed. So I go the quick way, slinking through the middle of Comraich.

I've managed to stay unnoticed since the flock came. Still, I miss the days when no gleam of plated armor halted my steps; when raiders were a whisper in the wind. Back when a mother would occasionally abandon her family one rainy afternoon and we would all write her off as a rotten woman, even those of us who knew better. A child would be snatched from the edges of town in some rare but unfortunate happenstance. Men would be found dead in the woods, their bodies too brutalized to be brought back to town for a funeral. Still, I'm unsure if I would rather have the Pretty King's men-monsters in metal "guarding the populace" in plain sight, or monsters under a foreign king's sigil waiting to ambush me in the woods.

The hairs on the back of my neck stand up as I skirt around the edges of the main square, keeping as much in the shadows as possible. There is a body on Crow Stage, swaying in my periphery. There always is. They leave their carrion as a reminder. A reminder to those that would rebel. A reminder that there is no hope to those that oppose the Crown. I wish I could feel anything about it anymore.

My boots slosh in the mud puddles dotting the path, though I try to gently place them. The ever-present mist dampens my clothes and face as I travel the last stretch of pitted road, avoiding the drunks and addicts laid out on their sides, napping against the thatch roof and stone buildings. Few people are out and about, silently shuffling through alleyways or attaching themselves to groups as they pass through the square, trying to remain unremarkable. Sheep avoiding wolves.

As the buildings dwindle, the footpath becomes an animal path, scarcely traveled but for the creatures of the wild and darkness. Stepping into the brush, I let out a heavy breath, fidgeting with the emerald bracelet under my long sleeves, letting it see the light of day only in the solitude of the wood.

My mother gave it to me when I was too young to remember.

Once, when I was little, it dropped into the river bordering my property. I was washing off some treasures I found around the land—rocks mostly. It slipped right off my little wrist, too loose for my six-year-old lankiness. I remember desperately throwing myself into the river's rapid streams, uncaring that I could not reach the bottom or swim its rushing currents. I remember my mom pulling me out, frigid water drenching us both. I can still feel her harsh kisses raining down on my face as I sobbed my terror, bracelet clenched in my trembling fist.

I've never been able to part with it. Even in the darkest of days.

I melt into the shadows of trees and life. I can almost feel its hum that is dampened in the streets of Comraich. Like a song from the outside of a room versus when you are sitting amongst its vibrations. The evil of man cannot battle the harshness of the wild.

The glass panes of Diana's apothecary hold no light an hour later when I return, basket of dandelion and comfrey root in hand. She must have stepped out. Very occasionally she braves the streets for a good book when the traveling merchants come. But the merchants are certainly not in town, and she has no qualms about asking me to run her errands for her, so there must have been some sort of emergency.

The exhaustion of the day pulls at my shoulders and

makes my feet ache. All I want as I trudge up to the door is to lie down somewhere and fall into a dreamless sleep.

I try the front door, finding it unlocked. Hissing voices whisper from the darkness as I step in. I freeze, silently closing the door, mindful to stifle the light from outside before it reveals my presence.

The voices stop.

Damn it all.

I only get the door open a fraction of the way before a tanned hand the size of my face slams it closed.

I whip around to face what I'm sure will be my attacker.

What I find is a hulking stranger baring white teeth at me.

God. He. Is. Huge.

Twice as wide, at least a half a foot taller than my—already tall—form. His yellow eyes glare at me amidst his snarling face, molten. Hair curls around his face, shaggy to match the scruff of his face. The darkness hides the color.

"Did you never learn it's rude to eavesdrop?" His voice is thunder. Low and menacing.

I stare up into his vicious face, bracing myself. His hand firmly holds the door closed by my face. His presence is a storm in the room, bringing with it the promise of destruction, charging the air with an electric force so potent I struggle to think.

Raider.

Drug-seeker?

We generally only keep small batches of poppy tea on hand for this exact reason after that one time—

"She practically lives here too, Fionn. Stop scaring the piss out of her," Diana's voice comes, crotchety and annoyed, from the hallway behind him.

Fionn—which must be the giant's name—is blocking

my view as I try to turn incredulous eyes to Diana. Is she trying to get us killed? Does she not see this man for the threat he clearly is?

I keep my voice steady. "What do you want?"

"Oh look, the trembling little mouse has a voice. I do wish you were mute, maybe then I could have let you leave here." Threats glint in golden eyes.

Instinct kicks in.

I duck under the arm caging me in.

I get all of two steps away before he wraps an arm around me and yanks me back, slamming me back against the door so hard I lose my breath.

"Don't hurt her, she's my only help," Diana's exasperated voice comes from right behind Fionn this time. I see her little wrinkled hand slap his arm.

"I guess I will leave your help alive, Diana." He directs his next whispered comments at me, still trapped in his hard grip, "Though you should remember what this felt like. Remember how helpless and small you are. Because if my description appears on a posting, I'll know it was you. And I don't believe in giving the benefit of the doubt."

He turns away from me, meeting Diana's glare.

"I don't think that will be necessary. And I don't think we have any more to discuss, Fionn." Diana's voice is firm, daring to command this hulking threat taking up all of the air in the room.

An exasperated sigh comes from Fionn before he shakes his head at her. "I understand your protectiveness of your ward. I will behave." He holds up his hands, placating. "Would you deny somebody help just to prove a point to me? Armund is innocent in all of this. Would not hurt a worm. He deserves your help, even if I do not."

The look on his face says it all. He's an arrogant,

manipulative bastard.

"Well, it's very unfortunate that this Armund sent the most insufferable, condescending ambassador to ask for help for him," I say. "Maybe his poor judgment is crime enough." The cold words tumble out before I can stop them. Diana is too gentle, too willing to believe the best in others for her own good.

His smile, once smug, turns into a sneer. I can see venom gathering in his mouth as he spits it. "I don't recall asking for your feedback, bit—"

"No need to spew such vitriol in my home, Fionn," Diana snaps. "I know your mother would disapprove. Maybe you don't remember her, but I do."

Blood drains from Fionn's face.

Diana continues, "You're right about one thing. I would not deny help to someone out of spite. That is not our way."

It would be my way.

"I may need some special supplies for this specific… ailment. But you cannot linger here. There are too many eyes. I'll have to make a special errand tomorrow, but I should be able to get it to you…" She tosses her head side-to-side, considering. "…The sunset after next. I'll give you some things to keep the swelling down and the infection at bay for now. Keep him comfortable and hopefully alive until I can make the poultice he needs."

Fionn nods, his demeanor resigned since Diana's chastisement. Is that…*shame?* Maybe.

He should be.

My anger and residual fear war inside my body, their battle shaking my bones.

Diana dispatches me to assemble the dirty wound pack, the instruction clearly an offering to escape the glowering man. Or to keep us from each other's throats.

My movements are quick but trembling as I gather clean dressings, dandelion leaf paste, poppy tea, and comfrey root poultice. I sense tension coming from the other room, hearing nothing. I ignore it when I come back in the room, shoving the basket into Fionn's crossed arms. I want to dump the poppy tea right over his arrogant face, but then I would just need to brew another batch before I could be rid of him.

"Try not to let the Crows make you their next feast on the way out of town." The saccharine sweet smile on my face looks as unnatural as it feels, I'm sure. It's a muscle unused. When did I last smile? Real or otherwise?

Diana chortles under her breath behind me.

Fionn seems to need the last word. "Remember what I said. Don't turn into a rat, or I might have to make you *my* feast." Fionn gives me a smile that is more of a baring of teeth, turning silently, and slipping out the front door with a feline grace.

His absence brings relief that quickly transfigures into something far more consuming.

Rage and betrayal drown any residual fear. They warm my face, make my voice shrill and quaking.

Fists trembling at my sides, I hiss in my coldest voice, "*What were you thinking?*"

Diana sighs deeply, closing her eyes and holding them so. Weariness reveals her age. For a moment there is no teasing light in her eyes, nor smirk around her mouth.

"There is so much you don't know, Alyxara."

"Then enlighten me. Because to me it looks like you're aiding rebels, or worse, raiders." If I could scream I would, but there are Crows outside.

She meets my imploring eyes before turning to stare out the front window.

"They're... Those are our people. Fionn may be a chore,

but he and his friends don't deserve the stage." She runs her wrinkled hands over her white hair, smoothing it out of her face, eyes closed.

"Who does deserve it, Diana? I've yet to see anyone *deserving* hanging there. You know as well as I do that it doesn't matter. So, he's a traitor one way or another. And now we are too, by association."

Please tell me I'm wrong. Please tell me you didn't risk your life for some idiot who thinks they can overthrow an empire.

Silence.

I'm determined to make her give me a straight answer to at least *one* of my questions. "Who are you to endanger both of our lives because you're too righteous to do what everyone else does? *Nothing.* All you had to do was nothing at all. If they find out, we are feast for Crows. If Derren next door decides he needs money to buy more smoke, all he has to do is say he saw Fionn leave here. A lone, hooded figure, who does not match the description of *anyone* who lives here. Who met us in the dark of night? *Does* that *not* look suspicious to you? Doesn't that seem like something that would get you killed?"

Diana's expression becomes disappointed.

I can live with her disappointment. I can't live with her absence.

"We have a duty, Alyxara. A duty as healers, to heal people, regardless of who they are. I had hoped to instill this morality in you. It is what your parents would have wanted. Especially your mother."

Her last words drop the temperature of the room.

Ice crawls through my veins.

"My only duty is to myself. To stay alive. And *my* *mother* is dead. I don't care what she would have wanted." I suck in a quick, pained breath. "And *you.*" My finger points, and there it is, a tremble. "You act as if you even knew her. As if you gave a damn when she died. I don't remember seeing your face at our door. I don't remember your offer of help once she was gone. When my father was raising me alone. And my father. The father you didn't help when he was choking to death on his own blood." I hate the catch in my breath. "*Do not speak of them.* Do not pretend to be some holy healer. Not when all you are is a glorified nursemaid who makes teas and gives people false hope. You need to learn how to accept reality Diana, to temper your delusions, because they cause destruction to everyone around you. You do more harm than help.*"*

Diana's face loses all color.

If I look at her for one more moment, I fear I will be swallowed whole by this roaring, freezing, cacophony.

I fight my urge to throw things—to break them—to destroy her home as she has destroyed me. Destroyed me by doing too little too late—and then doing too much, at the worst time.

The door shuts quietly behind me.

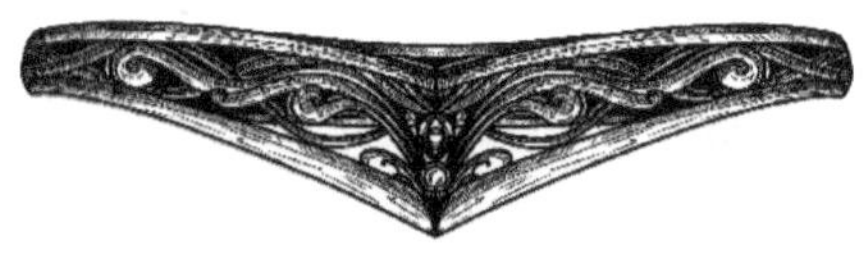

Chapter 2

The familiar numbness creeps over me as I tread across the worn muddy path towards my house. The interaction with Fionn and Diana plays out in a loop inside my head—promised violence and betrayal whirl. It's unbearable—the thought of all the things I should and shouldn't have said, and what I'm going to do if someone finds out. What is there to be done?

A small shack, the color of the gray stone of the mountains, comes into view through my panic. The winter has painted the brambles a deathly shade, overgrowing the farm that once flourished, their sharp thorns climbing over my childhood home; now a lifeless hull.

I know it's ghastly. I know I should try to restore it, as they would've wanted. I would feel ashamed of the state of my living quarters, but nobody ever visits me here anyways.

Except Diana, once. I had no idea she would come. She

hobbled up on me one day when I didn't show up for work. I had been stuck, staring at that lump in the yard. I had no idea the entire day had passed as I sat and fought with myself—trying to find a reason. She sat down next to me and started jabbering on about nothing. Once she grew tired of a one-way conversation, she had yanked me up and started guiding me up the road, murmuring something. "…not meant to be so alone, Alyx." I didn't understand what was happening. I just walked beside her up the road, thoughtless and floating. What really snapped me out of the haze was when she began talking of a room in her house that would be mine.

I have many regrets about the words we had next. I hated that. I hated spewing vitriol at the one person who gave a damn. That was the slam that caused my front door to tilt sideways a little. She left in a hurry after that—I'm glad she hasn't come back. We never talked about it. I don't look at the lump in the yard anymore.

I pick my way across the path to the door, gaze fixed straight ahead, avoiding the sight to my right. I'm holding my hem up, so it doesn't catch on sharp thorns. My exposed legs get the worst of it, but they're just a few small scratches. They overlap all of the others.

The wood on the door used to be a warm reddish-brown color, made from an old redwood. It's gray like the rest of the place now, worn down by the relentless elements of life. It creaks as I lift the splintered bar and push, struggling with the weight. I wouldn't know the first thing about how to build another door that was less troublesome, more pleasant to look at. So this one will have to do.

Closing it behind me, I step into the darkness. There is a small window over the kitchen area, though it brings in little light through the smudges and dust. I move through the house by memory. I know it by heart. If it were light enough, if I were to light a fire in the hearth, you would see the worn path I walk. The only places the dust hasn't rested. The path from the door to my bed on the floor. The path from my place on the floor to the back of the worn-in chair that I sling my spare clothes over. The path to the countertop in the kitchen where I will bring my bread from town, maybe the occasional stick of dried meat, berries Diana forces into my hands. If I leave anything there for long the mice get it. It's alright—they need to eat too, and it feels nice to have another living thing share my space again.

I shuffle towards my corner, feeling the weight of the day with these last few steps. My feet cry out in relief as I take my slight weight off of them and plop down on the cold ground. The threadbare blanket is chilled when I sling it over my body, kicking off my shoes beside me as I lay my head on my flat cushion. I rub my feet together, hoping it warms up quickly.

We were always poor, even when the farm produced what little it could, before the blight on the land and the Crows' descent. My parents got the bed. I used to have a cushion with chicken feather stuffing. That was a luxury. Mice needed the bedding one winter a year ago, though. I do miss the extra padding on my hard bones that press into the floor. I feel the pressure at my ankle bones and knees, my hip bones and ribs rubbing against hard ground with every breath.

The rain starts up, pattering against the wooden roof. I can see it splash against the ground in the slot under the door. I shut my eyes tightly, breathing deeply, finally letting that heavy weight drag me under. The rain begins to roar as loud as my thoughts, finally giving me respite.

Not seeing the emptiness helps. Not seeing the dust cling

to their bed, my father's pipe that he left on the table by his bedside. In the dark I can't even see the rust-colored stain on the wood floor next to the bed.

One night, soon after it happened, I had lit a candle. The sight of it—sitting still, right where he left it in the warm glow of flickering candlelight—made me want to burn it all to the ground. Me with it. So I don't light anything anymore. No fires in the hearth, no candles. One less chore I need to do anyway. I always hated chopping firewood. I'll take the chill over the screeching in my mind.

My stomach howls. I'm so tired. And there is nothing here for me. Nothing here to eat.

If I could move, if I could leave, I would. But I just stay here.

And let the dust settle over me too.

I feel that I'm awake before I can pry my eyes open. The sleepy hum in my bones only lasts as long as I don't move. So I lie there until enough light filters through the windows that I know it is time for me to do the responsible thing and get up. I could just not go in today. Not have to spend the day, waiting to be carried away by a Crow. Not listen to Diana drone on and on about thistles and teas and hope. She could run her own errands for once. Gather Fionn's precious medicines.

Opening my eyes is an exercise in self-control. They latch onto a burned spot along the gray wood grain in the floor near the door, maybe a finger length long. My hips, back, and shoulders creak far too much for my twenty-year-old bones as I push myself up from my curled position on the floor. My gaze is still trapped in a memory, on that little burn scar in the wood. I analyze it as I slip my shoes on, still sloppily discarded next to me on the floor. It's been there for a year, but I still can't help but stare at it.

Pushing myself up, shuffling stiffly across the space, I drag all of my clothes off the back of the wooden chair by the kitchen. I don't bother putting them on as I tromp outside, gaze forward, body still awkward from waking up. I take the worn path over to the river to wash. I do my daily hygienic things because Diana once complained that I stink. She may have been joking, but I won't take that chance. I can be a lot of things—homely, mousy, surly—but I refuse to stink.

The river flows gently, forming the border of my family's land. I keep my eyes on the shadows shifting in the woods, the forest of Wynedd. What sick raiders are hidden by its darkness, I have no clue. They've been pillaging the countryside since the new king was crowned a few years back. Burning villages, stealing food, all in the name of some foreign king, some heinous plot to make our fragile kingdom crumble. I can already see the cracks, the fissures of distrust, the deaths that quiet our communities. At any moment, your neighbor may let slip your "treasonous" acts or words murmured in the quiet of your own home. Everything belongs to the Crown: every morsel of food, every son or daughter. Every fire burning warms the seat of the king.

The Pretty King, they call him. No one knows if he is indeed as handsome as the name implies; he's never bothered setting foot in these parts. He came from seemingly nowhere; starting as the king's adviser from a court across the eastern Seas. He must have been more than pretty to charm the king into naming him heir to the throne of Suri on his deathbed.

I remember my father grumbling about "this serpent" bringing "war and famine" to our lands. He would accuse him of whispering half-truths and poison in the king's ear.

My father was mostly concerned about his farm falling victim to raiders and pests, but he was already too weak to tend to his dying land anyways. I waved his pessimism off at the time. Kings hold enough power to keep the food in their hands instead of ours, but they don't have the power to steal the life from the very ground. Even so, his reign has been worse than I ever would have imagined. The people of Suri have never known such fear, never been so firmly under thumb as when the king decreed the Crows would reside amongst the people for our safety. But I fear the bones that litter the wood are mostly of hard-working, gentle folks that were in the wrong place at the wrong time.

Bitingly cold waters jar me fully awake as I edge my way down, my body tensing further with every step past the knees. Dunking my head underneath, my mousy blonde hair turns brown with wetness. I feel alive again for a moment. The power of the river's current is a song in my blood as peace washes over me.

Once clean, I pull on an old, worn dress and braid my wet hair into one plait down my back. My boots have holes that fill with water as I trudge quickly back up the hill to town. The cold is the only thing that gives a semblance of energy to my steps. The backs of thatched roofed buildings grow closer as my mind wanders.

I have no hope. Not one ray of light warms my heart, that the boy from yesterday has made any progress. I dread looking his mother in the face, seeing my own reflection in her blank stare. How do you move through a loss so great? How does one live with a phantom lurking in the corner of every new memory? I still don't know.

My own phantom sings to me glimpses of the past—soil underneath fingernails, wet coughs, the scent of peppermint and mullein teas, rattled breaths. Memories stained with gray and crimson, freeze the ground beneath my feet.

Consumed in my reverie, I am unprepared when some force runs straight into me, knocking me almost off of my feet. A blaze of red hair tells me who it is before I see her face.

"What the hell is wrong with you?" I wheeze, getting my footing and my mind back in the present.

"You have to go!" Mariana pants out in between breaths. I take in her ragged appearance. Usually Mariana is a brilliant flame flitting from place to place, her smile warm, her freckles and smile always cheeky. This Mariana is frantic and fluttering. She is rattled. Her house is on the other end of town; she must have run all the way here. Her hem is splashed with mud up to her knees.

"What?"

"Diana…" she pants. "They think she's helping rebels…" More pants and gulping breaths. "She's gone." One trembling breath. "Dead." Her eyes are imploring me as her hands stay on my arms, pushing me off the road, into the woods. "You need to get out of here!"

My mind is unable to process what she is saying. Nothing but an echo-chamber, the word "dead" a cacophony. Our last words repeat in my mind, choking me, burying me—

No. Not now.

She died not knowing all I never said. Only knowing the worst of what I did.

"Who?" I feel my mouth repeating the word over and over. The world around me blurs as my eyes flit between Mariana's blue ones. I feel my feet following where she leads, back into the brush, into the shadows.

She'll never know now.

"They'll kill you! If she's a rebel, you're a rebel by association. You need to leave before they bring you to the stage, too." She finally stops, satisfied with our place amongst the shadows, but her hands stay digging into my bony arms, right in the bruises from the honey-eyed man from the night before.

The blood drains from my face and my breaths quicken. *It's over*. The figurative rope that has been around my neck for the past year is going to become real. My feet will sway just like all of those others.

There is no universe where I plead ignorance, and they acquit me. There is no mercy, no fairness to be had in this realm of death. We are all the Pretty King's carrion.

"Where do I go?" I whisper. I am the hunted—a mere prey animal. I'm a dumb lone deer in a wood made of shadows and predators, too afraid to run, frozen and attempting to blend into a tree.

I doubt the tactic ever has much success.

"Anywhere but here, for now. Maybe… maybe I can talk to my father, and we can try to get you off of the continent. He still has connections I'm sure…" Her voice trails off as her eyes take on a distant look and she slowly nods.

A shred of clarity slams into me as I realize how she and her family may be implicated.

"No." It's the first firm word to come out of my mouth.

She opens her mouth to protest but I cut her off. "You need to go. Now."

"Alyx, you can't be serious—"

"I am serious. Go. If they see you with me…" I don't need to finish. Twin corpses hanging from a parapet flash in my mind—bodies of two foolish girls who never learned when to stop loving each other.

I remember girlish shrieks echoing across valleys. The

kind of joy only children know. Water splashing as we played in the creek during the summer when the water was low. A friendship that gave me memories to cling to when my life was painted gray and crimson. When all I could hear was rattled breaths or nothing at all. Reminders that things are just this bad *now*. That I am capable of feeling joy. That I've felt it before and that if I hold on, just one more day, I could feel it again. The same memories that made her run across town, risking her own life to give me a head start. If only to give me a handful of minutes.

"You need to go," I whisper again. Numbness has crawled over my frigid bones of stone, like creeping thyme. "I'll just go west, to the coast, for now."

She searches my gaze.

I almost think she sees it.

"Fine," she finally relents, somewhat nervously. "Make it count!" she shouts over her shoulder, darting out of the brush, taking off at a sprint back home.

My gaze turns heavenward, at the canopy above, noticing the whispers between the trees as their leaves shuffle against one another. Their sparks of life are almost tangible when I actually pay attention. I can feel them, warming my frozen insides. I should have paid more attention.

I probably won't make it out. Without supplies, I'll be lucky to survive the elements for more than a few days. But going to town is a fool's errand and my house is the first place they'll look.

There's almost nothing there of use anyways. I'm wearing my only cloak and there's no food there.

But there is something there. Something I need to see.

My boots seemingly turn themselves around and begin walking back to the house. I just want to say goodbye to one more person. They'll come for me there soon enough. If they beat me there, I'll deserve what I get.

26

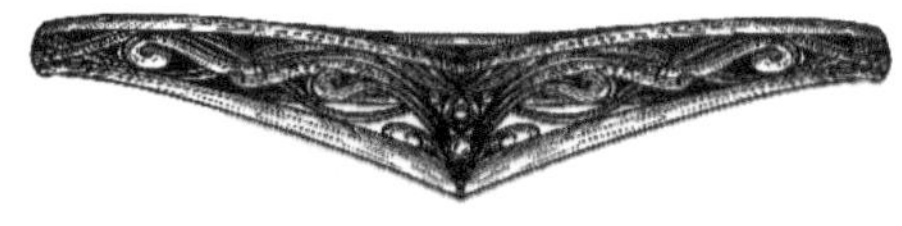

Chapter 3

Longing mingles with self-disgust in my throat as I stare down at my childhood home from atop the hill. Bitterness colors the lens I peer through at dilapidated ruins of a home left to rot, myself along with it. I have seen this view every day, but it looks different here, now.

I used to feel justified in my feelings, but I can't anymore.

People lose people every day. People move on. They still smile, make dinner, go to work, clean up their damned walkways. They can still light a fire in a hearth, go to sleep in a bed instead of on the floor. What is wrong with me? I must have been made of the weakest spirit to allow it to cripple me in such an all-consuming way. To be so stuck while everyone else continues on. I still can't grasp the feeling of fear that should be consuming me. I feel only a longing to *remember*—something I've spent many cold nights avoiding.

My boots carry me down the road, mud squelching beneath my feet. I can't see the trees lining the boundaries of our land without seeing my father, his body strong with youth, chopping wood to burn. My mother is a figure in blue beside him, her face containing no discernible features. I can no longer see the shape of her nose or mouth, the sound of her laughter. It burns. She's chasing a silver-haired toddler through the lush grass, little me squealing in delight.

When did I stop screaming my feelings? When did I start screaming in my head instead?

I've moved into the dead patch of herbs that line the walkway. I look down at my ten-year-old body, face devoid of emotion, plucking the rosemary to dry. She's gone somewhere deep in her head, maybe for the first time. My father hovers near me, steeped in painful confusion. A child should scream, cry at her mother disappearing. I should have been more normal, more outwardly broken, should have shown him that he was not so alone in his devastation. I remember feeling so far away from my body in that moment, unable to do anything but the motions, clinging to what I know. There was nothing to say. Nothing to be done but what needed doing. And maybe, if I just did that, my every raw nerve would stop *screaming*. He walked away eventually, leaving me to navigate my own grief while he wandered aimlessly through his. Maybe he felt like I had left him alone first. Maybe I did.

The dead plants crunch under my feet as I walk up the walkway and glance over at the lump in the yard. It is what he would have wanted, to be buried with his love—his garden that he loved more than me, the daughter he didn't know what to do with. Maybe he saw my mother in the irises. Smelled her in the rosemary. Felt the softness of her skin in the rose petals.

A love that just won't die.

He never had to say a word about it. I could see it in every line of his face as he took a deep pull of his pipe; the scent always clung to his skin. I could hear it in the silence whenever I passed him in his garden, his hands deep in the dirt. I could feel it hanging in the stale air during his last days, as he stared at the ceiling, seemingly at nothing, a slight smile on his face. I like to think she was talking to him, helping him be not so scared.

He was a man of few words. I could not take it personally that there were none of comfort, none of love, just a few of necessity here and there. What do you say to a daughter who doesn't grieve with you? Can I blame him for not giving comfort when he never received any from me either?

She loved us. I remember that much of her. Her love for my father and me was fierce, despite our shared aloofness and oddities.

She would not have wandered off without us.

I remember her sneaking me little fruit pies that she would bake whenever the weather began to turn. My grubby hands would grasp at her skirts, begging for one more.

She loved my father too; the pawing, the sweet smiles he only gave to her, his low whispering, and her giggles when they thought I was asleep.

She would not have left us.

That meant that the raiders, who had just started terrorizing Suri at the time, probably took her, or killed her. I try not to think about what brutality she faced in her end.

Glancing up at my childhood home I am faced with one blaring thought.

A home requires life.

I died here a long time ago.

It ended with a wet choke, bloody lips, and a weight

slumped over the side of a bed. Heaven and Hell could never contain me when my spirit longs to collect dust with the beams of my childhood.

Meaningless minutes, seconds, hours pass. I can't go inside. Just like I couldn't burn it to the ground the day it held nothing for me anymore.

They came, as I knew they would, no Banshee scream to preclude them, just rattles of armor cutting through the charged silence. I just stand there, staring at the door, offset from its hinges. It's too late to run anyways.

"Alyxara vch Seren?" The croaking voice makes me sick. Her name coming from his filthy beak. I don't deign to turn around. They are not worth seeing in my last moments, not worth turning away from my past.

Metallic clinks follow his voice as he approaches me. His darkness is the night falling during the twilight of my life.

I try not to focus on the feeling of him at my back, try to absorb the feeling that clings to this dead structure before me.

A needlessly rough hand grips me at the elbow—as if I was going anywhere. I'm yanked almost off of my feet, turned face-to-face with my executioner. These men crave violence, they don't need me to instigate it.

His face is almost too human to be the monster I know him to be. Although under his hood I can see it is gaunt, with soulless eyes—they're an inky black, twinkling with malice and nameless hunger.

I want to spit in his face—spit in the face of the Pretty King's Crows and spit directly in the face of the monarch himself. Though self-preservation starts to hum under my skin, keeping me from spurring on this man's ire. I hate that the fear is the sun burning off the clouds of my nostalgia.

Rough-gloved hands grip my cheeks, pulling me

forward, the other hand still gripping my arm. My hands fist at my sides, shaking in fury and fear already, even though I know this to be only the beginning.

He feels wrong, like he doesn't belong, even in this place that reeks of lives passed. His smirk turns into a leer as his gaze sweeps downward, hand still gripping my face. The three Crows behind him are chuckling and looking among themselves.

"Look at this one, boys. A little skinny for my tastes, but most of you rats are these days. Can't afford to be too picky."

It feels like insects crawling down my body. I try to rip my face out of his hands, but he holds on, his grip turning painful. He grows tired of my squirming and pushes me at the others.

Wandering hands of the other five Crows grip me everywhere.

Hindsight sickens me. I shouldn't have lingered here, not caring if I lived or died. If I had walked straight into town, to them, I would have had an audience. It would have encouraged them to maintain their stoic sense of duty. They represent the Crown after all. But here, in secret, they feel safe to let their monsters out. Here in the outskirts of town with no neighbors, no eyes to witness them, they feel brave. If you call this bravery.

Hands start to tear at my dress, pulling it off my shoulders. Chilled gloveless hands slide up my calf, smoothing past my knee. Brisk air, though warmer than his hand, breezes up my dress as it lifts.

A strange prickling sensation starts up in the back of my skull, like sharp talons drifting over its surface. Cold and wicked.

Terror claws its way up my throat. I had not thought this through. I had begun to feel relief that I would not have to live in my own head anymore.

But now, as I stand violated by the monsters that have been tearing apart my world, life by life, for their own gluttony and pleasure, I cannot.

I cannot bear it.

I thrash wildly, like a wildcat caught in a snare.

Some dormant force in me awakens. Writhing and starved.

The monster living beneath the ice bursts free, and my apathy turns to screams.

They can't be allowed to take, and take, and take.

Fury drives me to take something *from them*.

And so in the place I had died, I am born with a burst of power.

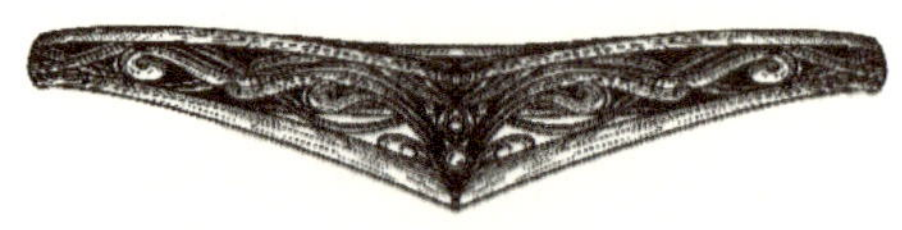

Chapter 4

I don't remember ever feeling this alive. Floating through nothingness. Nothing but a bodiless soul. Dying is more peaceful than I had ever imagined. So quick. More painless than I deserved. I don't know how long I sit in this peaceful space between realms, but I could stay here forever. In this chasm of endless life and death. A place of choice.

Whispers pull at the edge of my consciousness, caressing my soul, pulling me towards some understanding—some place that feels impossibly far, a journey of a lifetime away, but so familiar. The place calls to me, knowing my name, my heart. A mother, a lover, a sister, a friend. All four voices asking me to *stay.*

Visions flash in the emptiness. *A river of fire—red and white iridescent scales against a smoke-filled sky—red ink moving within tan skin—trees, endless, ageless, locked in a timeless dance with the winds—red stone—*

The peace is shattered. I'm pulled viciously back into my body. The grass, wet with dew, tickles my arms, legs, and the left side of my face. A shiver races down my spine and makes my eyes burst open. My body feels so oppressively heavy, like I'm being pulled into the ground by some force.

The world is sideways. I lift my head where it lies against the cold, damp grass, my hair sticking to the side of my head and face. My vision spins, making the world shift and turn. My head is the weight of a boulder. I let it fall to the ground again, closing my eyes to keep the bile in my throat from coming up.

How did I get here? There's a throbbing pain behind my eyes. I wiggle my toes, fearing paralysis. *Did I fall?* My fingers and toes move; I can feel them. I start to bend my knee, my joints protesting greatly. My muscles are useless, exhausted in a way I have never experienced before. Am I ill? I take a deep breath, sending shooting pains through my ribs and sternum. Did I get trampled by a horse?

I risk opening my eyes once more and see light start to peek over the hill, the road to my house down the hill barely visible. It's either the start of the light or the ending of it. I never realized how the beginnings and endings of the day look so indiscernible.

Taking a deep breath I try to remember. *Where was I last?* I remember dandelions, yellow even in the mist and fog. Walking into Diana's darkened house. A handsome, golden-eyed stranger. Rage and fear. Hissed accusation— words I'll never be able to take back. I remember waking up the morning after, going to work… Mariana nearly knocking me over, pushing me into the woods… The memory stops my heart in my chest.

My whole body screams as I roll over onto my front. I push myself onto my hands and knees, panting through searing pain in my chest. I distantly take note of my whole body being wet and chilled, but my mind is reeling, looking for the threat. Looking for something to defend myself with. My gaze darts around as remnants of terror crawl out of my stomach. Trembling starts in my shoulders and radiates from my spine. I look up, still unable to get to my feet. My house is many paces away. Darkened forms are scattered near the front walkway, many of them. They do not seem big enough to be men—not the hulking Crows that accosted me.

I haul myself onto two feet, my body and vision swaying. I have no idea how much time has passed. Hours or days, it could be either.

Stumbling towards the shapeless forms, I search for clarity. I approach slowly. There's no sound or movement. Not even the frogs croak from the river. Bile rises in my throat as pieces click together. The forms are… parts of them. Parts of the Crows.

My hand flies over my mouth, and whooshing begins in my ears. The first one is just a torso, lumpy and mangled. One armored arm, a glove removed, reaches away from the torso, reaching for something it will never touch. The skin is almost purple in death. The armor provided no aid to this male. The torso looks like it has been roughly torn off of the bottom half of the body, innards broken off as if made of stone.

I walk amongst the destroyed. An omen of death in a graveyard. Did I do this? I was the only person here, in my memory, of their final moments. How could I have done this? Even in my fear-addled state, thrashing and desperate, I have the muscle tone of a malnourished child. Who helped me?

I reach for more memories, grasping at wisps of smoke. Nothing.

None of the other Crows are in better shape than the first one. I see the one who first grabbed me. The hand covered in a leather glove is curled, the flesh underneath blackened. The plates of his armor, once shined silver, are now coated in ash, black as night. His corpse is pieces of shattered marble.

I should feel remorse for a life lost. But I stare into the fractured face of a monster who inflicts pain and suffering upon innocents. One who would have hurt me in ways he had probably hurt many other women.

Some people don't deserve to live.

Would he have re-dressed me before he hung my violated body off of the parapet? Would he have continued polluting the world with his greed? Terrorizing people? Turning neighbors against one another? Stealing food from the mouths of starving children for sport?

Nothing would have changed for him. If I would have died as he intended, it would have been just another day for him.

I have to go.

The others will come looking for their comrades.

I rest my eyes upon my house.

Whatever life I have ahead, I can't continue to sit in this ache. This loss. Holding onto the phantom of my mother's hand. Holding onto... what else exactly? The absence of something?

My hand moves from over my mouth to check I still have my bracelet. Even in the dim lighting, the green gem glistens in its silver inset, untarnished, more perfectly crafted than any piece I've ever laid eyes on. It grounds me. Reminds me that this is real: the mourning doves cooing in the distance, the ground beneath my feet, the Crow corpses strewn around me.

Maybe I will catch a barge across the salt sea, get away from this hopeless realm. Sheer my hair to my scalp, steal some clothes. It can't be that hard. I just have to get there. I look towards the woods, as if my eyes can see through it all the way to the port towns on the western coast. I look back down at my bracelet. *This may be worth enough to get me there.* But even as I think it, my whole being rejects the idea. Maybe this is why my father never suggested it, even in the worst of our poverty.

Sell this treasure, this one last line of attachment? She would want me to, to live—to get away from this place. There are many things my mother would have wanted for me. I have disappointed her in pretty much every way anyways.

I'll find a way. But not this way.

I walk up to the lump in the ground. My father's grave. I take it in for a long time—longer than I have been able to since that day Diana found me. Crouching down, I smooth my fingers over the damp grass crawling over the dirt. My flat, calm hand turns to a claw, tearing at the ground, ripping up clumps of dirt and grass, rocks bloodying my fingertips. Once I have a hole the size of my fist, I lay the bracelet down, gently, as if handling a delicate corpse. I cover it with the clumps I tore out.

Now we are all together. My mother in the rose petals and thorns, my father's body in the ground, and the last beautiful part of me. All in the ground together, in this empty place that was once full of strawberry pies, quiet giggles, and love.

God, I hope I never see it again.

Standing is easy. It's as if that bracelet carried the weight of a boulder in my pocket and I had never realized it. I turn away, not looking at the other corpses desecrating this holy ground.

Numbly, I take note of the ground where I awoke, as the

light of dawn begins to reveal truth. The grass that blanketed the ground is now dead. It is browned in a circle radiating out a house-length from where I arose. The corpse of a rabbit lies amidst the destruction. My steps are steadier than they should be as I make my escape over the footbridge, disregarding the dead frogs piling up on its lapping, shallow shores. I can feel the shroud of darkness hide me from seeking eyes as I step into the wood.

Chapter 5

The dense foliage keeps the light away, for it stays dark longer than it should. Then the damp leaves and moss are cast in an emerald glow as the morning rays of sunlight shine through, trying to force their way into the cracks in the canopy. I trudge my way through, seeking trails worn by animals that will hopefully lead to some water source that will hopefully lead to the sea.

Comraich is surrounded by the forest of Wynedd, nestled in a glade, expanded by human hands. The dense trees served as a sturdy defense against armies until the raiders started showing up. After the Pretty King sat himself on the throne, parties from Ashvynd—our enemies from an age-old war—began terrorizing towns, lurking in the outskirts, stealing people from their homes. Supposedly, they operate independently from their monarch, the Dragon King. They act out of sheer hatred bred into them from a dispute spanning decades. Now, the forest provides no protection, only a place for the raiders to hide.

I aim to stay silent enough that I will see them before they see me.

I just want to reach a port town, find some job working in an apothecary until I make enough money, then run. Run as far as I can. Board a ship to another continent and figure it out from there. What other option is there besides flight or death?

So lost in the labyrinth of my mind, I almost walk straight into a camp, catching myself mid-step. The small clearing, maybe the size of my house, is occupied by a small group of people. The dawn is still trickling pink light down upon the sleeping forms and smoking embers from the dead fire in the center. I count them. One, two, three, four, five, and a small one nestled in between two large ones. A child?

The question is: friend or foe? It is not a question I'm willing to stay and find out.

I don't dare breathe. Surely they've posted a watch? Would they dare to sleep completely unaware?

I wait for several minutes, shifting slowly to peer into the brush on the other side. Nothing. Are they really so confident? Without fear of the Crows, sleeping soundly.

I slip backwards, intending to give the camp a wide berth.

But they have food. They have food and cloaks.

In the midst of the massacre, my dress and cloak got singed by something, my dress eaten through, holes all about my bodice, allowing brisk air to easily pass through. I can probably last a few days without more food, but without proper gear? How long will it be until I come upon another village? The closest coastal town is several days away at this rate. Will I make it? Am I willing to stake my life on it?

I'm no better than a starved animal.

I take another glance around, hoping to see something that will give me an out. The forms are unmoving but for the even rise and fall of breaths.

A small, overly confident group is probably the best shot I have.

It takes every shred of courage in my body to step forward evenly, quietly. The chirping of birds covers some sounds, but not enough for comfort.

As I edge out of the treeline my whole body screams with awareness.

I am exposed.

I tiptoe beside two sleeping bodies, only their hair peeking out of their blankets.

That's good; even if they are partially awake they hopefully won't peek out unless they hear something.

I spot a black cloak tossed over a log across the fire from me. I also see the glint of a dagger embedded in the stump beside it. I'm not a fighter, but something is better than nothing.

As I make it to the center circle, beside the smoking embers, I snag some form of smoked meat laying upon the rock beside it and shove it in the damp pockets of my dress.

Someone's breakfast—now my breakfast.

The smoke makes my eyes burn as I move into its path and lean over, grabbing the woollen cloak slowly. The weight of it is promising as I slowly lift it, trying not to let it drag on the ground. A pair of gloves flops onto the dirt.

I freeze.

I stay perfectly still, waiting for one of the bodies to spring up, catching me in the act.

But nothing.

I lean over and grab the gloves, another treat. Made of dark russet brown leather, they'll keep my hands warm, even though they look much too large. Maybe I should have tried my hand at thievery sooner. I could have saved myself a lot of cold, uncomfortable nights.

I grasp the handle of the dagger, trying to work it out of the stump. The leather-bound handle feels soft from years of grip. I pull harder when it does not easily budge.

It suddenly frees itself, forcing me to take a step backward quickly to keep from falling. I step onto something that I immediately recognize as not-ground. Something with some give.

Another foot.

Firm hands roughly grip my arms, fitting perfectly along my bruises. I feel their warmth seep into my frozen bones and frantically swipe backwards with my new knife.

"That is my favorite knife, you know," a low, gritty voice speaks directly behind my ear. I vaguely recognize it.

How did they get so close? They were right fucking behind me.

The swipe is met with nothing, so I stab again and kick back with my foot, hoping to catch a shin.

No such luck.

My arm is roughly twisted behind me and the dagger torn from my hand in one smooth move. My spirit falls to the mossy ground. I can almost see it.

"I was wondering how far you were going to let her go, Fionn," comes a rich female voice from my left.

My feet are kicked out from underneath me and the breath leaves my lungs as my chest slams into the ground.

My eyes are pulled to the side, trying to see at least one of my killers before they finish me. A woman sits up in her blankets, a shadow peering at me with mild disinterest in her dark eyes. Her skin tone is so deep and dark it almost blends into her black clothing, the pink dawn glowing in her cheeks. Her hood is up, obscuring some of her face and hair. Her bored expression tells me she has known I was here this whole time. Embarrassment twines with my fear.

"I wanted to see what she would go for first. The cloak, or the dagger," comes an unruffled voice from above me.

Someone rolls me over onto my back with a grip on the shoulder and my eyes clash with a gaze so honeyed I would know it anywhere. His face is twisted in a wrathful grimace as it was the last time I had seen it. His eyes ensnare me.

"Looks like the mouse came back to scavenge." His voice is as cruel as his face.

"Don't kill me."

A chuckle—warm and languid as honey—comes from him. A sound I think I would like to hear if it were genuine.

"Why shouldn't I?" His head quirks to the side and his eyebrows lower. He looks genuinely confused.

"Because I—I…"

"'I—I—I… What?" He taunts me, quirking his head to the other side.

Nobody that beautiful should be this cruel.

I look around. All of them gaze coldly back at me, except one. The child I saw sleeping between her parents is peering at me curiously, fearlessly. Her almond eyes are hazel and wide, her lips slightly parted in wonder. She looks to be about twelve years of age.

Perhaps she is my saving grace. Would they kill me in front of her?

I look back at the man holding me down, his hand still on my shoulder.

"Where were you?" For some reason, my mind is focused on what it did not see. Where was he hiding?

His eyes finally lift from my face, head moving back to look up in the trees to my left, where a black cloak still hangs from a branch.

"How?" My mind is foggy—this is not what I should be

focusing on—but how did he jump down from there without making noise? How did he get up there to begin with?

I stare at the stubble on his chin. His hair there is slightly darker than the curled golden locks on his head. His jaw is sharp.

"While you figure it out, I have a few questions to ask. Why are you attempting to steal from my camp? Did you decide to snag something for yourself while you drop off my order?" He chats to me like we are having a perfectly normal conversation. If it weren't for the cruel twist of his face, I would think he was only mildly curious, like there's no dagger in his other hand.

"Diana, she's…" *How can I say it?* "I was running, they were going to kill me." I widen my eyes imploringly, trying to strike a chord of empathy in this man. *I didn't have a choice.* "I promise I would have just left; I wouldn't have hurt anyone."

He's watching me struggle for words, boredom on his face.

"Diana—you. You're a rebel. You all are. She tried to help you. The basket—They killed her for it." My words make no sense, but I'm fighting for my life here. And I've never been particularly good at it.

"What?" The taunting tone melts away.

"She's gone. Dead. They hanged her. In the square. On the stage." Saying it feels like a blow to the face.

"So you ran like a coward. Didn't think to help the old woman that gave you work?" His teeth grit a little at the end. His eyes are turning molten. I've never seen eyes so expressive. "Or did you rat on us?"

"No. No, I would never tell. I didn't know. I swear I—" The air thins; I'm panicking. "My friend came and found me before I got into town. Warned me." My head is shaking back and forth as I speak, eyes squeezing closed. "I would have tried… I wouldn't have just left her! Not like that. I didn't…" My words die out in my throat and my eyes slowly open as I run through what-ifs. What if I found out before? Would I have been brave enough to try and get her out? He continues on before I can produce the answer to that question.

"Are they looking for you, then?" A firm, but feminine voice asks from beside the girl. A woman with fair-hair and delicate features.

"I think so." My voice is a whisper this time.

The fair woman and the male on the other side of the child begin to get up and pack their belongings at the answer, leaving the little girl still watching silently.

I can't look at them, can't watch as Fionn decides I'm not worth the hassle. It would be easier for them to kill me now, ensuring I don't speak of their presence. Or to turn me in and earn some coin if they can. I stare at the cracks of light through the leaves above instead. The rare blue sky peeks at me. I try to feel the sunlight on my face one last time. Try to hear what the leaves whisper to one another.

"Where were you going? What was your plan?" His voice is stern, demanding my attention.

"I don't know. Just to go… away before they figure out I'm gone. Before they…" My voice trails off again, damning myself.

"'Before they'?" he persists, applying more pressure to my shoulder with his hand. I still stare at the leaves shifting with the breeze, waving their little green hands at me from above.

My chest is heaving, the air so evasive it never quite satiating my need for breath.

"I don't know," I gasp.

"Yes, you do." His voice is firm.

My body begins to writhe, unable to stay still, black spots popping across my vision.

I give my head a tiny shake and look him in the eyes again. Try to make him believe me.

Why isn't he dying too? How can he breathe?

He just keeps me pinned, like a leaf in the wind.

Something in those honeyed eyes look likes he's reveling in my breathlessness.

"You're a poor thief and an even poorer liar." His voice turns back into a snarl, mouth twisting. The forgotten dagger comes to rest at my throat. "Before they *what*?"

My eyes return to the sky again, the black spots overtaking the hopeful blue. I feel the cold blade against the lump in my throat. He won't believe me even if I say it.

"Before they find the house empty," I lie.

I feel the blade start to draw blood; the trickle runs down the right side of my neck.

"Before they *what*?" he tries, for what I know is the last time.

The girl won't save me. I feel sorry for her, that she has to witness such a thing at such a young age.

"Before they find the bodies of the Crows," I wheeze. "I was saying goodbye, but they came for me. I don't know what happened I just panicked. Ki-killed them." Tears are streaming into my ears. They blur the beautiful sky—I hate that. I hate this. I search for my icy indifference, but I can't find it.

I just need to feel fresh morning air in my chest one last time.

"You expect me to believe that you, the girl who is skin and bones, bad thief, worse liar, killed those Crows? I wouldn't believe you killed even one."

I could not blame him. I'm still not sure I believe it. I lack any other explanation; I lack the breath to defend myself further. So I just give up and shake my head, blinking rapidly to clear my eyes so I can see the clouds.

"I could go check," the male that has now finished packing his bedroll asks.

I slowly rotate my head to look back at them, chest still violently heaving for air that won't come. The girl is giving big eyes to the speaker, who looks gently down at her. He is… a giant. Broad as an ox. I can only assume they are father and daughter. Twin raven hair and sharp eyes. The fair woman's delicate features are in the girl's face too.

Air rushes into my lungs at last. The freshest, most clear breath to ever grace my chest. I close my eyes and revel in the feeling of crisp air filling me. I take huge, gasping breaths.

"A waste of time. If they are looking for her, we need to get going." Fionn's eyes still search my face for answers he will not find. I've told him the truth. No matter how unbelievable it is.

"Then are you going to kill her? Because you better get on with it," the father of the girl challenges.

Fionn seems to have seen what he needed to see. He makes eye contact with his challenger.

"No." Casual as can be.

I must be imagining things. My eyes jerk towards the family of three; then they race back to Fionn. My mind clears a little.

It must have been nerves controlling my breath. Though the thought feels wrong.

"What are we to do with her?" The father gestures at me.

"She might be of some use to us," Fionn says, jerking his head to another figure near the fire, who has remained silent.

The man in the bedroll's eyes are dull, framed by a forehead slick with sweat. His face is thin and angular, free of facial hair, but still clearly adult. His tired brown eyes stare back into mine.

"Surely, since I'm sparing your life you will help us with something?" Fionn talks to me like I'm dull.

I just nod, still unwilling to believe what I'm hearing.

"Great." He gives me a sarcastic smile. "We have one in need of some medical attention with us." He stands, pulling the knife away from my throat. It burns more in the cool blade's absence.

He leaves me, still on the ground, trying to make sense of this turn of events.

Fionn continues his monologue. "Don't bother trying to get out of it. We are better hunters than those parasites." He spits the last word out, turning his back to me and packing his things. I suppose he knows my answer then.

A dark hand pulls me to my feet. The shadowed woman. I didn't even hear her get up from her blankets. She releases me without any unnecessary roughness. I am left wobbling, but alive, miraculously.

I peer around at the others, taking stock of my captors. There is Fionn, in all of his arrogant, golden glory. He is possibly the leader of this little cadre. The family of three, seemingly benevolent, united. The sick one—angular, thin, with brown eyes and walnut-colored curls dripping with sweat. He still has not willed himself up from the ground; he looks to be trying to muster the strength. The lithe, dark one who is floating around camp already, quietly packing everything up, tossing stones over the embers of the fire, ignoring my observation. Another lingers near the edge of camp. His every feature is devoid of color. Hair as fair as snow, skin as pale as death. His eyes, obsidian in color, reflect a type of mania. He had remained silent throughout the entire interaction. He's leaning against the tree now, eyes glued to me.

As my eyes meet his, I see a glint of warning in them. A warning to not make the mistake of getting comfortable here. Once I am of no more use to them, I'm dead. The message is received.

To earn their trust or to make an escape attempt? Weighing my sparse options, I choose the former. I do not know how to survive on my own, exposed to elements. This place is not for a lone female traveler. They have women with them, and a child. Perhaps I can find a crack to wriggle into.

I don't know what to do or say, so I stand still, arms hugging myself as the group picks up the rest of their camp quickly and efficiently. I watch. There are no introductions, just cold distrust in the gazes that flicker my way. There's no use warding them off with threats or ice, trying to make myself seem powerful. I've already shown my hand in that regard. Trustworthy and helpful is what I'm now trying to give off. I have to find a crack to grow in before they decide I'm not either of those things.

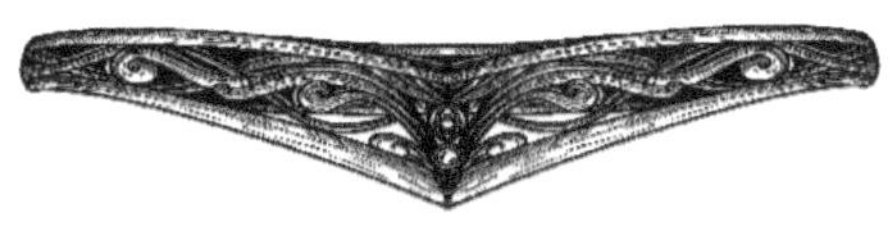

Chapter 6

We walk in single file through the dense brush of the forest. Fionn leads the group, the crazed one directly behind him, keeping close to me. I am trapped between him and the patriarch of the family of three. His wife, presumably, and child trail behind him softly. The sick one takes up the rear of the pack with the shadow, who is utterly silent, floating over the ground, eyes fixed on my back. I have not summoned the courage to look back at her, but I can feel her eyes digging in between my shoulder blades.

As I walk, questions swirl in my mind. Where are we going? How long will they tolerate me with them? What are their plans for me? Are they a part of a larger group, perhaps one organizing against the Crown? Or could they be the Dragon King's raiders, sent across the border to sabotage and unsettle? My position feels so precarious I'm too fearful to ask such questions.

We walk until the sun is directly above us, peeking through the leaves.

The group slows. I stumble, trying not to step on the heel

of the crazed giant in front of me.

Looking up, I peer through the edge of the brush and directly into the southwestern edge of Comraich. My heart drops. I thought we had been moving away from the town, but we have just come at it from another angle.

Have they come back to turn me in? I would run, but I'm trapped between two people who won't let me get far.

"What are we doing back here?" I try to keep my voice calm when I'm fighting the urge to run. The part of me that feels like a trapped animal is willing to take her chances.

Fionn's voice comes from the front, "I just needed one last look at the scenery."

He takes in my fearful state, seeming to enjoy my poorly concealed terror.

"I figured you would need some supplies to help my friend, Armund, here." He jerks his head to the sickly one behind me.

"I don't even know what is wrong with him," I protest in a hushed voice.

Fionn rolls his eyes skyward and the black-eyed one grips my arm, pulling me forward to take his place behind Fionn.

Apparently, big pale man doesn't like to be talked across.

My eyes are locked onto the gray stone buildings, waiting for Crows to descend, flood from between the buildings and kill us all. Even with my gaze drawn elsewhere I can feel the heat of Fionn's hulking form as he steps further into my space and whispers in my ear.

"Here is what is going to happen. You and I are going to take a little jaunt through town into the apothecary to collect supplies needed to heal a wound from a bog creature."

"Bog creature? From the Morrigana bog?" The bog lives northeast of Comraich, just beyond the boundaries of

Wynedd. It's desolate, nobody has reason to travel there, and it spells disaster for anyone bringing through wagons. My mind sifts through the wildlife found within the bogs. Nothing that is poisonous enough to kill with a touch alone resides there. I rip my eyes from the gray stone walls of my death and search Fionn's face for answers instead. "Did he touch some animal?"

Fionn's head bobs side-to-side, deciding what truths I deserve. "Of a sort."

"I can't help you if you don't help me. What did he touch?" I sound like Diana scolding a shameful customer, trying to hide their shameful deeds. Specifically ones that their wives would take issue with, involving the whorehouse on the northwest corner of town. The thought makes a pang move through the newest hole in my heart.

His eyes hold mine and I find myself flustered. His intensity sends thoughts flying from my mind like birds scattering to the wind.

"A Merrow," he states flatly.

I sigh and search the skies for patience, any excuse to break that gilded stare.

"Just tell me, or I am not going into that place to be molested and hung in the square." Perhaps dear Armund had a run-in with some ivy on his favorite part. Perhaps they spin tales of a mythical creature to spare him from the embarrassment of having too much fun and contracting some venereal disease. All men are the same.

"I'm being honest. There is a Merrow living in the bog. We just happened upon it, and it roughed up Armund in a little… skirmish we had." One hand grips his dagger in its hilt, and his other gestures agitatedly.

My silence must be deafening because he finally looks back at me.

"Right. And a troll lives under my footbridge. He gave me this dress. Do you think I am that naive? That I would believe a half-woman-half-fish creature did that to him?" My mind starts to be pulled to other impossible things: claws dragging across the back of my skull where none exist, bodies torn apart by ice and fury. "I would not even know how to heal such a wound."

My mind stutters as I admit my uselessness. *So foolish.*

"Well *you* don't, but maybe Diana did."

"Maybe. But I doubt she believed in bog monsters either."

"She and I have some shared past. I knew she would know how to heal such a wound." He eyes me out of the corner of his gaze, assessing my reaction.

Maybe you don't remember her and our ways, but I do.

Our ways. I never did know where she came from. No one ever spoke about it. It was as if she had just appeared from nowhere, no questions asked. Most people were just grateful to have a healer nearby.

Diana had always rambled on, bumbling about amongst dried herbs and glass vials, and I blocked it out far too often. I wonder how many things she revealed when I was too lost in my own self-obsessed pondering.

My index fingernail has a chipped spot; I scrape at it with my teeth. *I should have asked her about her childhood, about where she learned to be a healer, where she grew up, and why she left. Should have asked her about her favorite book. Should have asked her about her family and if she missed anyone. I should have asked her anything. Everything.*

Remembering my audience, I look back at the others. The manic one is staring at the sky in boredom, fingernails scratching at his arms. The married pair is watching wearily, the father shifting unhappily—his family is too close to the danger that stalks the streets of Comraich. The girl looks at me with owlish eyes—as she has been the whole time. Like she's bursting with questions but has been told to keep quiet. The shadow stares dead-eyed at me, waiting. Fionn waits impatiently for a response. My eyes fall to Armund, the one wrapped in a cloak, the dark circles under his angular face giving him a corpse-like appearance.

"Is this true, Armund?" Something about him feels friendly, even in his weakened state.

Armund shuffles towards me, passing the others in line. He shoves up the sleeve of the cloak covering his arm.

The smell reaches me first. Rotting flesh is, unfortunately, a smell with which I am acquainted. My hand slams over my nose as I peer closer, wishing I had some peppermint oil to rub beneath my nose. The green and yellow ooze is seeping from five lateral slashes across his arm, one on the underside of his forearm, like something tried to grasp him but he slipped out between the claws. The flesh appears swollen twice its normal size and is mottled green, purple, and almost black in some parts. The miscoloration trails all the way up his arm, disappearing into the cloak shoved up to his bicep.

Whatever did this had to be carrying some potent venom. His flesh has become necrotic.

"When did this happen?" I whisper, rotating the arm gently. I take off the rest of the cloak to see how far the trail of redness goes, hoping to see it stop below the shoulder.

"It's only been two days," says a rich feminine voice from behind him. The shadow. Her eyes are almost black, but somehow twinkling, like a night sky. "We rubbed the poultice that Diana gave us on it every few hours and kept it covered, but it only worsened."

I nod slowly, knowing Diana gave them some of our in-house poultice, which usually does the trick for most dirty wounds.

"Just to be clear, you told her a Merrow did this?" I couldn't recall anything like this in any texts she had me study.

"Yes," Fionn answers.

"This… I do not know what she was planning on retrieving for you. I do not know of these wounds." I look back up at Armund, not wanting to say where my train of thought is leading me.

If I can't get the festering under control… the source of the wound must be removed.

It's like he reads my thoughts, because his warm brown eyes widen, and his whole body starts to tremble.

His demeanor before was low, but now his lean form shakes as a bush in the wind, and he finally looks *awake*. He also looks… young. An adult he may be, but his eyes are that of a pup. He is as tall as the others, well above my head, with fair skin and chestnut brown curls. But he is slight of form, better suited to indoor work than to being a mason or farmer like these other oxen of men.

"I—I'm not a fighter." His voice is deep, that of a man, but gentler. He continues, "The others, Fionn, told me to stay back but… I wanted to see something stuck in the silt of the bog. The Merrow just came at me. I didn't see her coming. I tried to get out of the way, but she got me a little…" His voice trails off as my hand reaches out to cover his.

His hand burns with fever.

"Maybe Diana has something in one of her books," I find myself saying, without thought of the consequences. I jerk my hand back from his, turning to Fionn, ignoring the others that had been watching on silently.

Fionn stares, hopelessness written on his face. He cares

for this trembling boy whose fate I seemingly hold in my hands. It takes a second for him to realize I'm looking to him for a plan.

His head whips away from me, back towards the town.

"Okay, so we go to Diana's. It would be more discreet if we went just the two of us. In and out." His voice is firm, commanding.

I nod quietly, eyes locked on the gray wall of a building. My thoughts race, heart pounding.

I look again to Armund, and know what it is to not want to die—to beg for help and receive none. For that, I'll go.

Fionn turns to address his companions.

"I want you all where you were before, formation around the circumference, patrolling your areas. If you notice anything suspicious or hear my signal, amplify it. We meet at the same spot. Any questions, Fianna?"

Silence for a beat.

I turn around to look at them.

Everyone but Fionn is gone. Whispers on the wind.

"Let's go."

I feel eyes on me everywhere. I'm being watched, studied, followed.

Paranoia whispers in my ear, running its fingers down my arms.

But if there was anything there, I would be dead already.

I pull the cloak Fionn had stolen from a cottage at the edge of town closer to my body, tugging the hood further down over my head. It is less conspicuous than my ruined cloak and dress from before—or it would be, if this was not one of the few sunny days we get in a year.

Most people are sunning themselves whenever possible. Sneaking out the back door of work. Hiding in their dying gardens, beside the blighted potato patches. Trying not to look too free, too content. Trying not to draw the eyes of a Crow in need of a meal.

As Fionn and I creep down the side streets of Comraich, ground crunching under boots, I try desperately to push down the fear. The grip on my throat is, this time, definitely all nerves.

Every instinct I have screams at me to get out. Screams at me to get far, far away from this place that begs for my death. But still I walk on, because it is either death at the hands of a Crow, or death at the hands of this evil I don't really know. Could he be more cruel than them? What would he seek to take from me first?

So I walk along this fine line, death awaiting me on either side should a strong wind blow in either direction.

We have stayed clear of the square, giving it, and its reapers, a wide berth.

A familiar thatched roof appears at the end of the road, the front door torn from its hinges, windows shattered. A part of me is surprised to see it still standing.

Once, a family down the hill on this side of town was accused of harboring rebels in their cellars. Their daughter, Caras, would bring by Rhodri's supply of wine casks and she would sing in the tavern whenever she came by. Even I would linger in the doorway when she would sing. The rowdiest of patrons would fall silent to listen as her voice gave the stale air life. The melody told stories of heroes slaying fire-breathing dragons, a king leading his people to freedom, and a love that was worth risking everything for.

Her family's home was found burned to embers after the accusation, and there were no tales of love and heroism floating in the air of Rhodri's tavern from that day on. The bodies of Caras, her parents, and her little brother were charred, nothing but blackened bones when people went to "investigate." They were there to pillage the home, to pick over anything that was worth anything. Nobody was entirely sure who started the rumor. I had always suspected it was Aled, a regular of Rhodri's tavern, who spread the rumor. He had been spurned by her when he drunkenly asked to wed her one night after her song. He glutted himself on booze and herb for weeks after their family burned. He was not a wealthy man before.

I suppose Diana's apothecary was too central, too close to other people's homes and businesses to risk a blaze like that. A blaze hot enough to char human bones and eat away at flesh might catch onto the inn that the Crows had occupied. A nest for a Murder.

As we dash under the doorway, the glass crunches under my feet, breaking the eerie silence.

A few vials of liquid remedy lie broken on the floor, the rest presumably stolen. Remnants of clean cloth are in the hearth, burned beyond use. Only a few corners stick out in the edges of the space. Dried herbs, once lovingly hung, are torn from their hanging string and stomped into the floorboards. Medical instruments are strewn across the floor or tables, bloodied. Perhaps they have a concept of irony, using her healing instruments to injure her own flesh. Any memorabilia from her many years of life are either shattered on the floor or desecrated in some way. This is the entryway that I left through but two evenings ago.

Left, after I had hissed hate at her.

I thought I was familiar with the concept that everything can fall to ash in seconds—that the words you say might be the last that person ever hears. But every time I think I have that reality living in my bones, the world shoves more of it down my throat.

Fionn's eyes on my face. The weight of them. The weight of this scene, the weight of all of the things that are robbed from us for just existing—are heavy on my shoulders.

My eyes stick to one memory, laying amidst the piles of torn books on the floor.

Chapter 7

"I do not have anything to give you." The stubbornness is in my voice, the set of my shoulders, the cross of my arms over my chest. I hope she can see my proverbial heels digging into the ground. See the trails they left as my heart dragged me all the way here.

My father is dying. Slowly. It started with a wet cough and has deteriorated over several seasons. She is the only healer in this godforsaken place. Who really cares if this woman could rob us blind if the alternative for not finding him some help is that he dies?

The woman in front of me simply stares back at me. Her hair is a shade of white so pure, it is hard to believe there was ever any color to it to begin with. Her body, hunched in a chair, may be frail and elderly, but she must have some power to have escaped persecution from the new soldiers lurking around the square lately. A woman with her own business, making her own money, living alone, practicing medicine without the direction of a man. She must be a witch. Hold some sort of leverage over the right people. Instill the right amount of fear.

I keep my back straight, presenting some semblance of togetherness. Do not let her see that she could ask for my right hand and I would sacrifice it for her help. Power is only to be exploited. Everything comes at a cost, but if I play the game correctly, I may be able to get out of here without losing a limb.

She sees through me, the witch.

Her eyes have a twinkle in them, whether from malice or amusement I have not yet decided.

"Nonsense, all people have something." She is playing into my childish fear, just for the fun of seeing me squirm. Like she is going to ask for a lock of my hair to bind my soul into eternal servitude or turn me into a toad.

"I mean it. I don't have two stale pieces of bread to rub together. The crops have turned gray and shriveled. I sold my horse last year to pay for the tariffs. I have nothing to trade." My voice is cold, the comments sound throwaway. I don't care. Perfect. Except that I'm begging for her help. Of course she knows that. I try to stare her down harder.

She chuckles. "Well, do you not have two hands to rub together? Hands that can pick herbs for me. Hands that can mix teas, wrap bandages. Help a poor old woman lift, move, maneuver patients." Her own hands are moving gently, driving her patronizing words into me. "How about a brain? Can you read a recipe? Learn?"

I stare at her deadpan and let her finish her condescending. I hope she sees only the slow freezing of my eyes. I hope she does not see the gross feeling of hope bubbling somewhere deep inside with the other useless things.

"I can't leave him all alone in that house. The farm needs tending to, I need to start new seedlings, I need to try

to fix whatever blight is living in my soil leaching life from all of my damned plants." My hands are tied. There. What are you going to do about that? I don't know either. Please tell me.

"So you would like me to help him in exchange for...." She leaves it hanging for a moment, "... free. Is that what you're suggesting?"

It does sound ridiculous. Nothing in this world is free.

"Why are you trying with that farm, child?" Her expression is pitying. "It does seem that you are no farmer. Let us see if you are a healer, if your black thumb may help preserve human life if it cannot preserve plant life. This way you get to chop up herbs, dry them. They aren't supposed to live through it deary, so you are already half-way there." A twinkle in the eye and a smile follow her words.

She has jokes. Funny.

"If you are done ridiculing my failures, I may point out the small matter of my father and his ailment. I can't just leave him in that house, all by himself. He can hardly even walk from his bed to the hearth. He cannot tend a fire. He can barely feed himself if I bring the food to him." My voice trembles only slightly at the end. I dig my fingers into my thighs to stop it.

Thankfully, she doesn't seem to hear the weakening of my voice. "Well, I had imagined that we could bring him here for a time. See if we can get him spry enough to support himself. See if we can get him toddling about again... I do not think I can reverse the damage already done. But..." She stares at the floor, hands clasped together, thumbs twiddling, and lightly nods her head back and forth. "I do think I can give him some more quality of life for a time. Keep him comfortable. Maybe you'll see a few more good summers together." Her wrinkled eyes return to mine, awaiting my response.

A few more summers, she had said.

"You really can't save him?"

I sound small—like a child. I hate the words as they tumble out. I'm eighteen, not eight. I hate the tears that force their way out of the hole I had them tucked away in. They choke me. Make me weak.

I had not realized that I had hope. That there was any room for "maybe." Some stupid part of me thought she would tell me that she could fix him. Keep him from leaving. But she threw out terms like "keep him comfortable." There is no hope in that.

Her eyes lose any remnants of teasing. "No, deary. But some extra time. Some comfort. That is worth much to a man in his position. It will be better for you as well."

I can't look at her anymore, not while the choking loss rips a tear from my eye. I stare at her drying herbs on the walls.

Her place is cluttered. So full.

My house is empty, only a bed and some near-empty cupboards and the little spot where I sleep on the ground. So empty.

A few more summers is better than what I'm looking at without her. In a few summers maybe I'll be ready. Maybe we can have some good times once he starts feeling better.

I weigh my options. It's easy when this is my only real one. She is the only healer anywhere near here. I could not leave for any considerable length of time to seek out another one. Nor could I afford one should I find one. She doesn't seem to be asking for much. I get to keep my hand. I'm sure she will pile on the conditions once I start.

I whisper my answer.

"Alright." She stays quiet. "I'll work for you. But I don't

have anyone to help me get him here."

She stands from the wooden chair, hobbles over to a shelf full of books, reaches her wrinkled hand up and plucks one from its spot on the top shelf. She turns and holds it out for me. "Rhodri will surely help in exchange for some of Elena's favorite teas." She winks.

So empty. I feel like an empty well.

I take the book slowly.

"You will need to memorize these plants. Their uses, their growing conditions, their names, and appearances. You start tomorrow. So does Gerrick."

My dad's name. I hardly ever hear it anymore.

The faded green cover has an etching of a lily. I skim through the roughened pages, faded with age as the woman who had handed it to me. Every flower, leaf, or root is sketched in ink; directions hand-written in wobbly handwriting. God she has terrible handwriting, like a child. Even I, barely educated in reading and writing, have better script than this.

I stand and make my way to the front door.

Diana speaks again.

"I'm glad we will finally get to know one another. I haven't seen you much since you were a babe. Your hair was almost as white as mine then." She chuckles, lost in a memory. "You used to be so finicky, squealing all hours of the night and day. I'm glad fate gave you to a young couple who had the energy to manage you. That your soul found a world where you can grow into the person you're meant to be."

I stop in my tracks. I never knew she knew my family when I was a babe. Although babies get ill, and it makes sense she would have treated me whenever I did. I have no memories of her from childhood. I wave it off as mere babbling of an old woman. She loves to hear herself talk.

I hum slightly in acknowledgment, unsure what to say to that. I shove the green book under my cloak and step out into the mist.

There weren't a few summers. Things didn't get better. And the way he went wasn't soft or comfortable. But at least for a moment in time, things didn't feel quite as bleak.

A shiver running down my spine tears me from my memory. My eyes trace the etched lily on the cover of a green book. It somehow survived the desecration of the temple around us.

I crouch in front of it, reaching for it hesitantly, like the first time. It still feels the same. It still looks the same. It still carries the touch of her, of me. It was with me in the woods, while I referenced it to find elderberry. I'm sure if I turned to that page it would still be water-stained from when I dropped it onto grass wet with rain. I still cringe when I think of it, the painstakingly drawn diagram blurred with my carelessness. I hope she never saw. She probably did. Somehow, she always knew when I had messed up in some small way. The witch had eyes in the back of her head. The thought makes me smile a tiny bit.

I've memorized the contents front to back, but I cannot bring myself to put it down—to toss it away. I stand with it, eyes still glued to the front cover. I chew on the skin around my last finger, the slight callous that now grows there.

"Are there any other books in the other rooms, or were they all kept in here?" Fionn's voice, low as it may be, echoes in the dark space.

I shake my head. They were all kept here, aside from some romances I know she kept in her bedroom. I teased her about them when I found them, though she bore no shame from it. She must have been lonely.

"Well, we cannot afford to reminisce. Start searching for things that might actually be helpful." His voice is trying to be hard, but fails.

I hear the sounds of him sifting through dried plants, crunching over broken glass.

I force my feet to shuffle forward, pulling my head from the fog it floats in. I search for some stupid mythological remedy for some stupid mythological malady. I'm still unsure if they're lying about the Merrow. They have to be. But what else could have inflicted such a wound? And why would they lie?

I pick up the book with the gray cover. *Animal Bites and Injuries*. Leafing through the pages I only see references to normal things. Real things. Garden snakes, rats, felines, canines. No Merrow.

I grab a book with a maroon cover and gold script. It is high-quality; the stamp on the inside cover reveals it is from the Chof o Byd, said to be the largest library in all of the continents, located in Ashvynd to the west. Diana must have picked this up from a merchant who traveled the channel in between our two countries. A merchant and a thief. Possession of this book alone would get her a trip to the Crow stage.

Few are brave enough or connected enough to get into the Chof o Byd. It is perpetually under guard and very selective about who is permitted entry. Knowledge is power, even to a country that prides itself on freedom. No slaves. Little to no class system. People there can be whoever they want. Except an immigrant. No, immigration from Suri is strictly forbidden. There is no asylum for us there. The Dragon King is fine with letting us be picked off little by little by the birds. There are continents to the south and west, but they are so far, with so few ships going between them that they are hardly viable options. You'd have to sell your soul for a place on one of those ships.

Few people are allowed through the borders or into port due to the ongoing decade-long stalemate between the two countries. The Dragon King put a strict embargo on trade between Ashvynd and Suri. It's all over disputed territory—the Ghaels—the hulking mountains that act as the border between our nations, and the resources they contain. Only kings think those things are worth the lives of so many.

The embargo stops little. Hence the book.

Few people are allowed through the borders, but merchants always find ways. Smuggling through art, spices, alcohol, drugs, anything that has a market., is an art in itself. Anything to grab a coin. Who can really blame them?

I trace the title of another volume with a navy-colored cover, *Poisons and Potions*, and snort. It really is a wonder she wasn't killed sooner. The dark amusement is swallowed quickly by my melancholy. It feels too soon to laugh. I don't know when I'll get it back.

I pick through countless piles of books splayed all over the ground. But my eyes are drawn back again and again to Fionn's ruggedly handsome face. His brow is furrowed, his eyes staring intently at one page of a book. *The Wench and her Wandering Eye*. One of Diana's filthy novels that made its way down the hall into our workspace. I can tell he's not even reading it. Are there drawings in there? Did Diana get to explicit doodling in her spare time?

"Storing material for the lonely nights?" I meant to be teasing but it comes out frustrated. He brought me into a wolves' den so he could read about full bosoms and aching members.

His head whips around like a child caught, golden eyes

wide for a moment before he quickly brings his face back to neutral disinterest.

"Whatever do you mean?" His voice is cool and composed. He snaps the book shut and looks at the front cover, eyes scanning over it quickly before returning to meet mine.

"What does the title say?" I ask scathingly.

He doesn't say anything for a breath and shrugs insolently. "Something about wounds and exudate."

My eyes narrow. Does he not realize I can see it?

"No. It doesn't." I stand from my spot on the ground, storming over to him. He stands his ground. I snatch the book from his hand. "Can you not read?" The question is genuine, not sarcastic.

The grit of his teeth and feathering muscle in his sharp jawline is his giveaway.

Shock and anger battle. Anger wins.

"So you just pretend to be helpful? You don't want to seem dumb, so you say nothing? What if I had thought you already searched that pile and didn't search it myself? What if there was something useful there?" I can feel my lifeless pin-straight hair shifting as I shake my head at him.

He doesn't even have the good grace to apologize.

I huff out a breath and look away as his stare is causing a flush to rise in my cheeks. It's the rage. I'm angry with him. It has nothing to do with his proximity or the sharp edge of his jaw as he grits his teeth, the muscle ticking in the corner.

"I'm not from around here. The continents across the sea write in different languages. I only know how to read in my home language. It is quite different." His excuse is rushed.

I only nod in response and shove past him to look over the pile he was supposedly reading. I knew of the different languages in the lands to the east, they varied greatly.

"Well you could have said so." I could leave it there. I should just leave it there. "Just so you're aware, the book you were reading came from Diana's private library. The book details all of the smutty trysts between a wench and a knight. I thought perhaps you had some trouble bringing your women to completion. Maybe you needed some pointers." I make a show of looking him over from top to bottom and shrug, looking away again. "Just seemed the most likely."

The silence is deafening. I'm pretending to move through the books one by one, but I can feel him approach. Suddenly I remember gasping for breath, the silence with which he sneaked up on me at camp. This man is a predator, and I'm baiting him. I freeze when he gets too close, his heat warming my arm.

"You're certainly brave to say such a thing to me. I remember you at my mercy but a few hours ago. You trembled so pathetically." His words are cruel, as I knew they would be. "I wonder, would you tremble like that if I touched you? Your blush earlier suggests you would. I doubt you would think such a thing about me and my women then."

I glare at him through the heat warming my face.

"I would rather be carrion."

His smirk says he doesn't believe me, and he longs to play the game.

I want to crumble into the floor in embarrassment.

I want to claw the smirk off his face.

I want to say that he's illiterate and insufferable. And that swaggering insolence is usually indicative of a man who feels like a boy and hasn't the first clue how to pleasure a woman.

But I won't. He has not had a problem hurting me. The

scab on my neck where he held his blade only a few hours ago is proof enough. I should not push him. I don't know what he is capable of.

I look away. Letting him win.

I hear his huffed out laugh. Celebrating his win.

I extract myself from the corner I was trapped in, moving into the hall.

I'll check one more place. It's unlikely, and I feel like I'm violating the dead, but I have to check as if my life depends on it. Armund's arm depends on it.

The door creaks as I slide it open.

The bed is mussed; she did not make it after waking. This place waits for her. The clothes hang in the wardrobe. The slippers are messily discarded next to the bed, awaiting her feet. The half-drunk glass of tea on the table beside her bed is over-steeped. This waiting scrapes at fresh wounds.

Diana was a good mentor, an even better person. She would always make extra portion of dinner, early, before I made my way home for the day. She tried to make me eat. She teased me when my eyes were dead. When my silence was loud, she always kept my hands busy. She never minded my sharp tongue when I could do nothing but cut her with it. She kept me with her—kept me from withering away, alone in that house.

How many people does one lose before they have to assume it's them?

Maybe I'm just a poison in the water.

Fionn's obnoxious presence presses against my back.

I sweep around the room, yanking drawers open, looking under the bed frame. Fionn has moved in behind me and is picking his way through the closet. He approaches the bed as I move the pillows, looking under them.

I search and I search and I search.

Every spine on the shelf opposite her bed.

Combing through every dress, searching every pocket.

I'm so lost to the mindless task I don't even notice when Fionn pulls a leather-bound book from underneath her mattress.

"Well, this is promising," he says.

He's scanning the pages from left to right—reading. I move to his side, peeking around his bulk. I behold a foreign language, written in ink. Looping and smooth script scrawls across the parchment. I don't recognize the letters, the words, or the writing. Diana's handwriting was wobbly, written slowly in every piece of parchment she's ever handed to me. She didn't write this. Unless… unless her handwriting was like that because she had just learned to write in that language. She and Fionn have a shared past. She said she knew Fionn's mother. Perhaps her first language is the same as Fionn's.

Fionn turns page after page, seeking.

"Where did you say you were from?" I ask.

"I didn't. These seem to be more medicinal journals…" He trails off, a grin smoothing his handsome face. It's a look I've never seen him wear. Not a mocking smile nor a smirk. This one makes him look boyish, hopeful.

The page shows the naked top of a woman, her breasts and face covered by long inky black hair. A scaled tail starts just below the navel, fading into the skin. It is lean and muscled, contoured for speed and force. A larger diagram shows razor sharp fangs. Canines longer than her pointed incisors are framed by beautifully curved lips. Another diagram of her five-fingered claw is in the bottom right corner. Long talons, drawn black, drip with some sort of fluid at the tip of one claw as long as her finger. Translucent webbing stretches between each digit. The Merrow, I can only assume.

"Where did she get this?" I demand. "Does it say anywhere?" Is this another Chof O Byd find?

"She wrote it. I knew she would have had to write it somewhere." He points to the drawing of a plant on the next page. "It says this plant carries a sort of remedy for the venom of a Merrow."

The plant is drawn in great detail. The white petals have streaks of fading scarlet as they move from the inside to the ends of the petals, like blood streaks on clean linen. Its small round leaves and short stems both have pale striations against a dark green pigment. She uses her usual symbols to depict the method of extracting the active component.

He snaps the book closed. The book is as long as his palm, which is almost half again the length of my own.

"Let's go." He sweeps out of the room.

"Wait! Are you sure that has everything we need? Does it say where that plant is found?" I shout after him. He is already into the front room when I look out into the hallway after him.

"Yes. In the bog. Under the water. Let's go." He looks back at me impatiently. His arms jerk out to his side, lifting a bit in a "what else" motion. "Let's go. This place makes my skin itch."

Hesitantly, I step out of the room and follow him, through the hall and into the front room. He cracks the front door open, peeking through the sliver of space in between it and the wall. Checking for Crows.

I glance around the room and land on the little green book with the lily on it. I don't need it. It lives in my mind as sure as any memory. I could name all of the herbs in that book, their names, their growing conditions, their medicinal uses. But I want it. Want to hoard it like my own treasure. I know I can't. Just as I couldn't take my bracelet. Things like this are just things, they don't keep them with me. They don't keep the memories any fresher, don't keep them from dulling with time.

I turn to see Fionn staring at me silently. Measuring me. Debating if he still needs me now, with the clear instructions, written in his odd language. I would have left me if I were him. I need him more than he needs me.

The silence stretches between us.

Taking one more glance, he opens the door and waves me forward. I slip out right after him, drawing up my hood, feeling like my time with him is measured.

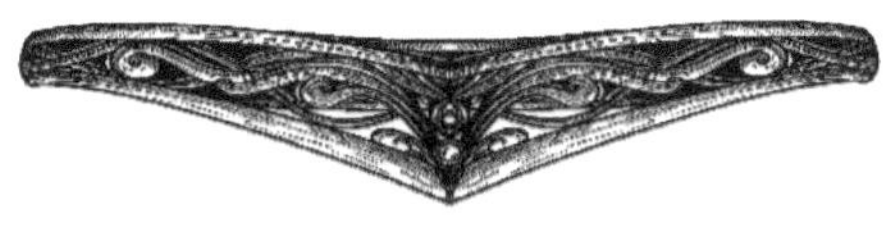

Chapter 8

The sound of my steps are unhurried as they scrape across rough, hardened ground, even though my legs twitch to break into a sprint. I cannot wait to get out of this town. Armund needs to be tended to—soon. I'm glad that we found what we needed so quickly.

The mud that usually cakes the streets is now dry, cracking under the sun's rays. I study my feet moving over it, trying not to cringe into Fionn's side. There are two stationed on the corner as we round another alley. Their dark forms are under a mighty oak, shading them from the day's heat. Their eyes elsewhere, for now.

I wonder what they would make of their brethren, lying in pieces over the herb garden my mother once tended. Did they smell the charred flesh and retch? Does the death of their own kind abhor them? They've never shown any signs of being anything but human, but what person could delight in the death and torture of other people in the way they do?

Fionn is the picture of calm in my periphery. His steps are swaggering and loud.

It is a mistake. Even the men too drunk to be afraid have a mousiness to their steps around here. We scuttle around corners, stay silent, stay unremarkable.

I do not see, but feel, the Crows as they move their gazes over to us. Dark, coaxing claws trailing over the back of my neck.

"You there! Come over here," a dark voice, tinged with authority, barks at us.

Dead. I'll be dead if they see my face.

I try not to let my indecision show—whether to sprint away or pretend to be someone else. To freeze or to fight.

Fionn takes the decision from my hands.

He throws an arm over my shoulders, the weight of it causing me to stumble as he tugs me against him, a seemingly protective gesture. When he begins pushing us forward, towards the Crows, I realize it is controlling. He's making sure I don't run, blow whatever plan he has in mind.

"Whatever seems to be the problem, gentlemen?" Fionn's tone is cocky, taunting.

Idiot.

I look up at the two Crows from under my hood, hoping my features are still hidden. They both size Fionn up, looking directly at him. Usually, they have to look down. The Pretty King has a penchant for large soldiers. Their features are gaunt but filled with malicious excitement. Fionn is a fly in their web. Just being near them gives me the feeling of bugs crawling over my skin. Like trailing claws.

"You're not from here. State your name and business." The look on their faces says it does not matter.

I sink back as far as I can in Fionn's restraining hold, hedging towards running if only I can break his grip.

As I lean back, I smell Fionn's fresh scent, like cold mountain air running through a pine forest.

"Ahh, just two lonesome travelers seeking a place to call home for the night." Fionn's eyes are twinkling, excited. Like he is baiting them, rather than the other way around. "Looking for some privacy. If you know what I mean." He winks.

Winks.

Their faces twist into matching sneers, attention shifting.

The one across from me reaches across and gruffly jerks my hood from my head. I have no time, no courage, to stop them.

It takes them all of one second to recognize me from town. To recognize a traitor.

Swords scrape against scabbards.

Fionn—in a blur too fast for me to track—slams one of them against the wall, grappling with him.

The second comes to grab me.

I duck under a grasping hand.

The hand grips my hair all the way to the base of my skull.

My scalp screams. I grab at the source of the pain.

He was five feet away just a moment ago.

He hauls me against his clinking armor and then slams me—face first—into the wall. I release my hair just in time for my hands to scrape against stone, saving me from having my skull completely bashed in.

Beside us I can hear the clashing of plated armor against the ground, the sounds of Fionn and the Crow.

The Crow holding me jerks me around to face him.

Lascivious eyes look into mine as he has me pinned to the wall. For good measure he pulls me forward and slams me back against the hard rock, bashing the back of my head once more. My vision blurs, ears ringing. I gulp in a breath and try to clear my eyes, my hands desperate to find purchase.

I push at his face, his throat, trying to choke him. He gets rougher.

My eyes clear; his black eyes stare into mine. He is not even trying—not even winded.

My panic intensifies—I think I'm sobbing.

Someone has gripped my heart and lungs in an iron fist. Like my very being is being pulled from my body. The corners of my vision begin to blur. I lose sensation in my toes, in my fingers that are now gripping his braces on his forearms. The ringing in my ears gets louder, drowning out the sounds of Fionn's wondrous plan going to shit.

At least the people of Comraich won't have to see the life leave my eyes.

At least I won't have to look in their eyes as they decide my life isn't worth the risk of speaking up. It would be good penance. I've done the same to others.

Heat blazes in front of my face. The sound of flesh sizzling breaks past the ringing in my ears.

I fall to my hands and knees, gasping, desperately trying to get my brain to reorient. The fog begins to clear and the frantic urge to run returns.

I stumble to my feet, intending to do just that, but am frozen in my tracks at what I see; A vortex of shadow and rippling wind, debris and dirt whirling within it. Two elemental wolves locked in a fight to the death.

The Crow holds his palms out before him in a dark force of manipulation. Shadows grow, licking up the Crow's arms and legs. They seem to swallow the light surrounding him, blending into the black leather under his dark metal armor. The Crow pushes back with brute force. Dark swords jab, meeting broiling air, dissipating the ripples. They reach out as a cloud of darkness to surround Fionn, obscuring him from sight.

The air surrounding Fionn is waving, like ripples in a pond. Like the ground on a hot day. Fionn is graceful, his movements fluid as he manipulates the air with long, sweeping movements, almost too quick to track. Too quick for those shadows to touch his lithe body. The ripples rush outward in precise strikes. Some are enveloped in shadow and darkness, some lick at the armor of the Crow.

Red welts pop up along the Crow's exposed face and neck. He claws at it. The skin on his face begins broiling, bubbling, burning. His hair ignites and shrivels away.

It looks like vengeance.

He *screams.*

Screams.

Screams.

It sounds like penance.

I smell his flesh melting and it smells like vindication.

I want more.

I look for the other.

Fionn's Crow is lying, purple-faced and dead, on the ground. Asphyxiated.

Whispers of silver essence seep from the suffocated Crow in death, proof that even monsters have souls. My jaw slackens and I want to touch it—touch this alluring thing that souls are made of. I want to remember what it feels like.

"Alyx. Alyx, get up." Fionn yanks me to my feet and out of my trance.

My thoughts jumble, fighting for dominance at what just happened as we break into a run. Several townspeople throw themselves out of our paths as we flee through the town.

Did I just hallucinate that? Does Fionn have some special power? Do the Crows?

Where am I?

The answer plows into me as I round the corner.

I'm in the square.

At the Crow Stage.

I can see her stocking poke through the hole in the left boot.

It sways. Drifting calmly in the early summer breeze.

Diana's hands—nails jagged, bloody, and torn.

Diana's neck—tilted to the side, wrapped in a thick, rough noose.

Diana's purple face—flies already covering her eyes and mouth. Eyes glazed, bloodshot, unseeing forever.

Chapter **9**

I become aware of the sharp gravel digging into my knees at the same time I realize the muffled keening sounds are torn from my own throat.

Clamping my palm over the source doesn't help.

They just keep coming.

How many times did I hear a family wail at the sight of a loved one swinging? How many times did I feel nothing as I walked by somebody's child, murdered to prove a point? How many times did I glance up apathetically?

I'm paying for it now.

The price is too high.

I think I've gone mad.

Nothing. I have nothing left.

I left her.

Nobody was there to stop them. I slept through the night and when morning came, I thought of staying on the ground instead of going to her.

Images flash in my mind of her frail body fighting against those Crows. The Crows that do what they want, take what they want, regardless of the consequences. I try not to think about her bloodied hands clawing at the floors as they drag her by her feet out of her home.

I need it to stop.

The sound of footsteps sprinting at me, rapidly crunching the gravel jerks me out of my daze.

Fionn, who had momentarily halted beside me, stunned at the same sight, leaves my side to engage with a pair of Crows advancing towards us.

Some justice-driven part of me hopes he doesn't turn back. Hopes that he leaves me to my fate.

More Crows bleed out from side streets, the sound of their armor clinking through the panicked gasps of the people milling about the square as they take-in this escalating battle.

Having taken out the pair of adversaries, Fionn sprints at the Crow Stage. His tanned fingertips brush along one of the beams for a second. A spark bursts forth and hot purple flame lick up the wooden beams, rapidly consuming the frame, the rope, the body—fanned by some invisible power. Violet hands destroy this unholy stage.

As the flames obscure the final view of her body, Fionn lopes back over to me and throws me over his shoulder; it bites into my abdomen. He begins running out of the square and down the nearest road, heading south.

The jostling and the smell of burning flesh battle to make me vomit. I choke down the acid burning my throat.

Even with the tossing of my vision, I see the square disappearing from sight. Crows lie dead, scattered along the ground in the square, arrows protruding from eyes, heads, chests. There are at least twenty of them. People are watching from windows, peering out from businesses, from behind curtains. None of them has been brave enough to venture out and witness the scene first-hand. Their alliances lie firmly within the walls of their homes.

I see a shadow on the roof of a building overlooking the square. Not a shadow grown and manipulated by an evil being, but a living shadow.

The woman from Fionn's group.

She shot down all of those Crows. The speed with which she sprints across and leaps between rooftops, sloped and uneven, hints at more than archery training.

The shadow leaps down from the rooftops, meeting us on the dirt road, matching our pace. Even her feet pounding the ground is quiet.

I think if Fionn lets me down, I may crumble to the dirt and never get up again. So I let him carry me out. He doesn't try to put me down, not until we have made it deep into the forest on the southern edge of Comraich.

I vomit all over the ferns when he does.

I can feel the eyes of the group on me as the shaking begins. I wipe my mouth with the sleeve of my cloak.

I usually feel better after purging what little food I consume, though this time it was just yellow bile, and I feel far from alright.

"We need to head west, for the bog again," Fionn's firm voice whispers from my right.

The group shifts on their feet restlessly. I pant through my mouth, hands on knees.

"Should we expect them to trail us?" The father gruffly breaks the uneasy silence.

"Yes, but I would say we took out a generous portion of their group this afternoon. It felt good," Fionn's voice holds a hint of a grin, his knuckles cracking. "It might take them a bit to gather themselves."

The words make the light roaring in my ears grow to a deafening cry.

He did it on purpose. He never intended to get in and out peacefully.

A menacing laugh comes from the man beside Fionn, the pale one with the crazed eyes.

"What is wrong with you?" I croak. I'm still panting, staring at a fern leaf, its little red dots coming into focus. We use it for stings, from other plants, from insects. You rub the red pollen on the affected area.

The laughter stops.

I tear my eyes away.

Fionn's fisting his dagger—the one I had tried to steal—as he meets my eyes. His thumb starts lightly running over the bottom part of the blade as he fists the handle.

"We just… those Crows will be chasing us across all of Suri for the rest of our lives. Diana…" I point in the direction of town. "She's dead! Did you see what they did to her?"

"You!" My pointing turns accusatory as it turns to aim in Fionn's apathetic face. "You just—you just… What did you do? Their skin was burning from the air! You lit the stage on fire. You burned her."

His face reveals nothing. The others shift restlessly, unwilling to step in.

He's not going to tell me anything. I see it on his stupid, stoic face.

Helplessness is far from unfamiliar to me. But I've grown tired of its company. Tired of its relentless chains.

My field of view is lost in a cloud of cold rage as I lunge for him, my balled fists pounding wherever I can reach: his chest, his dumb arrogant face. He pins my arms to my sides with ease, but I just start kicking—my fight or flight has not left my body yet, and it wants to fight for once.

"Alyxara, stop," the voice of the shadow says, exasperated.

I'm not sure I could if I wanted to. And I don't want to, I want him to bleed.

Fionn takes me to the hard dirt, pinning my legs out of reach of him. I turn to bite and gnaw, wild in my need to take. I want to take a piece of his vile, smirking arrogance out of his flesh. Payment for disrupting my entire worthless life out of his own carelessness.

He shoves my face into the dirt, laughing at my feeble wrath. As if he is forged in cruelty and vengeance—created from it. Mine is just a cloak I wear, hiding the anguish that is the beginning and end to all I am. And he can tell. It amuses him.

"Let her up Fionn—" Armund says, stepping up beside us.

Fionn's mirth and Armund's presence distracts Fionn just long enough. I wiggle one arm out of his clutches and tear the page from Diana's book from his pocket. He reacts too late, secure in his superiority. I yank away from him just enough, one of my hands still firmly within his grasp, and begin tearing it up between my hand and my teeth.

The page is in shreds before he tears me back by the shoulder, gets me in a chokehold and tries to wrench the scraps from my claws and gnashing teeth, even as they bite at his own hand. I toss the pieces to the wind, and they scatter, fluttering their escape, carried away by the taunting breeze.

The breeze dies mid-flight, a breath halted within lungs. The remnants of Armund's hope drop to the ground. Fionn launches himself off of me, scrambling to pick them up. Many pieces are carried away in the stream beside us, boats on the sea of water trickling, slipping over the river stones, rounding bends, off to the merciless seas leagues away. Multiple days of trudging through the forest will bring you to the cliffs off the coast of Suri.

Armund scuffles after them immediately, even without knowing what they contain. It almost lessens the high from my victory.

Fionn frantically searches the torn bits of parchment, trying to make sense of them. "You spiteful bitch! What about Armund?" The air around him begins to shimmer; the others behind him edge backwards. He snarls as he goes on, "I should have left you to your fate with the Crows. It might have provided some entertainment from this droll country to see you try and fail to survive with nothing but your stupidity and hatefulness. It still could."

He's right. But his words do not incite fear or shame. I survey my audience. They all look at me in varying states of outrage.

"What ever will you do now?" I can feel the deadness in my eyes as I cock my head at him. "What will all of your blistering air and sneaking about do to save your friend?" The silence hangs off the end of my sentence as my nature is revealed to all of them. What does life grow into without light? Without proper care and nourishment? Something brutal and wild, something selfish and ruthless in its quest for survival.

"I could help you," I offer, my voice chilling, even to my own ears. Do you remember the diagram? The picture of that little bog plant? I do. Do you know what ways to use the plant? Do you have an idea? Are you willing to bet Armund's life on your guess? I could tell you everything about that plant on the page. Not just it, but all of the herbs and nettles that cover this forest floor. From this sea to the

Cliffs of Marwholl. All of the lichens and mushrooms that feed from the decay. This will not be the last time Suri bites you or your kin. So let's start answering my questions."

The family is eyeing me with new wariness. The crazy black-eyed one is fighting the urge to throttle me, in good company with Fionn. I swear the shadow is fighting a hint of a smile, just a flicker at the edge of her full mouth. Maybe she thinks Fionn deserves it too. Armund, his damned pitiful expression, is full of betrayal. That he had trust in me at all was astounding. He must have a knack for picking the wrong sides.

"You would let an innocent die to spite us for keeping things from you? Truths you have no right to?" His voice is low, like thunder in the distance, eyes narrowed.

No.

But I don't let it show.

Fionn lets out a growl of frustration as he looks away from me and meets the eyes of every person in his cadre. Taking their measure. Armund turns betrayed eyes to Fionn. Fionn is considering. Considering if Armund's life is worth their secrets. It almost makes me give up my bluff.

Armund's warm brown eyes drop to the ground, looks at his arm, and then back at me with an expression of misery.

He's not a fighter, not even for his own life. I tear my eyes from him before I can change my mind.

"For every question I answer, you answer one about the plant. That is how this is going to work." Fionn sneers as he bends down to pick up the knife that fell to the forest floor in the skirmish. He should have just stabbed me in the gut. He's probably thinking the same thing.

He begins running his thumb over the edge of the blade again.

I struggle to my feet, feeling the weight of the past two

days like an iron weight on my shoulders.

I think through the wording of the question very carefully before I continue.

"What did you do to those Crows?"

He stares at me for a few moments, the eyes of the others darting between us.

"I've always been able to do it. It's like having another sense, like smelling or seeing. I can feel the energy in things. I can will it to move, to change, bend it to my will. Become hot, maybe leave someone's lungs, if I'm feeling prickly." His answer leaves so much unanswered. Leaves me with even more questions.

His thumb whispers over the steel of his dagger while he considers his question.

Where did he get this sense? Can everyone in this cadre do it? Where did he learn it? I don't think that those questions are the top priority at this moment.

A quick glance to the rest of the group shows them giving nothing away either.

He quirks his head to the side, eyes still narrowed. "What part of the plant should we use?"

I run my thumb over the jagged edge of my middle fingernail. I want to bite it off so badly.

"The roots, the leaves, the petals, all of them." No telling him about my treatment plan. "If you have that power, what are you?"

"Human," he states blandly.

"Strange type of humans you are," I say suspiciously, peering around at the group. The girl stares at the ground, as opposed to her usual shameless gawking at me.

I turn back to him.

"More strange that you wouldn't just say Surin, or Ashvian, or anything else, really."

He moves on. "What do we do with the plant to make this medicine? Brew them in a tea? Make a paste?"

"It's so strange it is almost surely a lie."

"So do I need to make a tea with the plant?"

I resolve to play the game he wants to play.

"You toss them over your shoulder," I say, my jaw set.

"What?" His face blanks in confusion.

"The parts of the plant. You toss them over your shoulder and sing a merry tune and then the wound heals itself."

He kicks the ground, the thumb running over the blade more roughly. I'm surprised he does not scrape the skin off.

"Funny. I thought this was now a game of lies."

Armund lets out a soft noise, almost a whimper, eyes cast pleadingly to the sky. The fair-haired woman rests a hand on his shoulder. "Fionn. Just answer her questions so we can go. She is no threat to us."

I bite off the jagged edge, still waiting while he looks at his group, deciding.

Finally, it breaks Armund.

"We are not from here," his words rush out. The others look at him wide-eyed. "We are trapped here. We are Fae, from another realm." He pushes back the deep brown curls around his ear with his good hand, revealing a fine point at the tip of it. "We fled our homes, forced out by the Crows, through some sort of rift in between worlds. They eventually showed up here. We aren't even sure exactly how they got here, nor how we could get back. Or even if we could or should." He gulps down some more breaths as he fights to make me understand, empathize enough to help him.

Fae? Is that supposed to mean something to me? The ears are interesting. I've never seen such a thing.

I look around at the others, all of whom have their ears covered by long hair, or a hood in the shadow's case.

Armund pleads with me with his eyes but I only hold my chin higher. But I want to see how much he will say. How much they'll let him say.

"What Fionn did in town… We all have the ability to feel energy and we all can do things to manipulate it. He just forced energy into the air, warmed it, made the air shift and become wild, destructive—"

"Perhaps that's enough." Fionn claps his hand on Armund's shoulder, making him wince.

He speaks of power from folklore. Like stories of witches and their spells that parents spin up to keep their children in line. No such power exists here. No such creatures exist here. It's all stories from drunken sailors and bored wives.

Armund shoves it off, turning on Fionn. "What is the problem? Are you afraid she is going to turn on us? Run back to her best friends in the empire? Seems like without us, she's dead. I doubt she will pose much of a problem."

I could actually. I could bargain for my freedom with this.

Fionn seems to know this by the look on his face, but he doesn't want to point it out to me in case I haven't yet figured it out. "She doesn't need to know."

"She should know. I wish someone would have warned us," Armund states boldly before turning to me. "Those Crows are beasts of a different kind. We don't even know what they are fully, only that they are greed and destruction. They came from our realm, somewhere across the sea. They call themselves Fomorians. They said they lived in tribes in a land far away, in our home, Danu. But none of us had ever heard of such a place." He's taller than me, but about as thin, his cheekbones sharp and jawline defined. The dark circles under his eyes make him look pitiful. He might be cute otherwise with his brown curls and warm eyes. "They are monsters, Alyx, and you should be afraid of them. And you do want to stay with us, because they will find and kill you, without mercy. It will be worse than any death you could ever imagine. It wasn't until we had watched them here that we realized what their favorite meal is—souls. They feed on the souls of humans, along with all the energy their bodies contain."

The silence hangs between us as I try to process this—try to find some way to believe him, reconcile it with the reality I know. They speak of other worlds, of a race of people called Fae, and powers far beyond whispered lore of witches and flying fire-breathing beasts, but of manipulating the very makeup of the world, of the ground beneath my feet. He spoke of soul-eaters. Even though I had referred to them as monsters in my own thoughts, before today, I thought them monsters of the human kind. I've been held in their grip, walked beside them on my way to work each morning. I cannot deny the truth now that it stares right back at me. Those things are not human, these people are not like me.

If what Armund says is true, there is too much I don't know. I can't even take a human male in a fight. I couldn't even go one day without getting caught by a band of "raiders," although I'm still not sure who these people are. I do know there are raiders out there. Warriors from Ashvynd. There are other Crows out there and they are going to be looking for me once they see what I've done, and after the incident in the square. My best shot is still to be with these… people. Fae.

My options are slim.

I pat Armund's good arm, silently apologizing for forcing his hand, but thanking him for telling me.

I address them all.

"I want to help you. But only if I am one of you. Not an outsider. I want to be a part of your group. I can go with someone to the bog. I can make the medicine. I can heal Armund. We can both benefit from this."

They all look unconvinced, aside from Armund.

"I won't be any trouble. I'll pitch in. I won't betray you." My pride is somewhere dead and buried. My eyes meet the gaze of everyone in the group. They still look the same as when I tore up Diana's page, like they see through me—right to the feral animal that will do anything to protect itself.

Fionn takes the measure of the group silently. I don't watch. I can't watch.

"Fine. But just know, there will be no going back. You cannot be allowed to leave the group once you're in it. Too much risk for us."

I am already in too deep.

I would have nowhere to go regardless.

There is nowhere safe for me to run. Nobody to run to.

I nod.

Chapter 10

We spend the rest of the day trudging through Wynedd at a breakneck pace. *I* spend the rest of the day trying to think of anything but empty eyes and whirling shadows. Fionn leads again, never once looking back at me. Armund gets more pallid and slow with every step.

His condition is rapidly deteriorating. He drank some poppy milk before we set out, but it mostly just made him delirious, and it faded more quickly than it should have.

As I walk behind him silently, I feel the menacing presence of Konan, the one with half-crazed eyes of obsidian, at my back. They gave me the rest of their names as we traveled.

Elva, the shadow, walks just in front of Armund. Her eyes flicker to him occasionally, checking to ensure he remains upright.

The family sticks together. Dealla, the fair-haired mother, seems to take in every branch breaking, every bird call, and every shift in the wind. She walks a few feet behind Fionn, her daughter, Aine, at her back.

Dealla has yet to speak, but Aine… well, she trudges along, boredom causing her to chirp out questions occasionally. How far have we gone? What do we think we will find in the tide pools this time? Do we think there will be crabs? How long will we be able to stay there? Are the trees on the coast really as old as the dirt like Konan said?

The father, Deri, stalks behind her with his protective bulk, patiently listening to every question and answering with genuine responses. Occasionally, he yanks at a tiny strand of her hair, making her twirl around, glaring at him adorably.

I am silent aside from my squeaking boots. Can I trust them? Will Armund make it the day-and-a-half it will take to reach the bog-lands?

He stumbles over a tree root. Elva, moving quicker than I could even react, catches his good arm, keeping him from falling on his face. Her eyes search his face for a moment. She slowly releases his arm, and he smiles weakly at her in thanks. What a poor reassurance it is.

I come up to walk beside him, as much as the narrow animal trails will allow. My shoulder brushes his arm as we walk.

I gesture to his hands in his pockets. "You walk really confidently for a man who can barely stand." It comes out awkwardly.

I want to show him that my threats this morning were what I had to do, not what I wanted to do. I can be a friend. Sometimes people shed layers of humanity to survive. Even though I would do it again, I still feel bad about using him as leverage.

He cracks a slight smile. Generous of him. "What do you mean? I'm as steady as a rock."

I smile back, relieved.

I wrack my brain for something else to say, feeling along the edges of my fingernails, searching for a topic to distract him from trembling of his hands, the wince with every step.

"What was it like?" I blurt out.

Armund glances up at me, brow furrowed.

"The Merrow, what was it like?" Making him think of the monster who mortally wounded him, how comforting. Diana always says my bedside manner needs work. My heart clenches.

It takes a moment for him to respond, and a moment for my heart to beat right again. He looks up and to the side, searching around in his memory.

"Horrible. It was horrible." He sighs, closing his eyes. "I was being foolish. I saw something that made me think…" he grimaces. "Elva had warned me not to disrupt the bog too much." He glances back at Elva, who narrows her eyes in consternation. "But I just wasn't thinking." He moves his eyes back, steadily on the ground. "I just saw something in the silt… It was incredibly foolish of me. Elva had told me that there was evidence that…" He looks at the others. When nobody stops him, he goes on in a lowered voice, like the wind might carry his words. "Other beings, other than us, have slipped through the passages between realms before. We had heard tall-tales of such a thing living in the bog and thought that maybe there was some credibility to the claims."

His warm brown eyes meet mine.

The implications of such a truth goes beyond this one mission—goes beyond this continent, or this world.

The shadow cuts in, "We try to avoid them at all costs. You never know what such things will do to stay safe. To keep their secrets hidden," Elva speaks in that even, low tone of hers, ominous with her ever-raised hood. "Humans are notoriously cruel to those that aren't like them. We have had some unfortunate run-ins before, haven't we, Konan?"

A rough grunt comes from the giant behind me. "How was I supposed to know that was a wood-faerie den? They build them like squirrels, the blasted things, in the most asinine places. At least I didn't almost die for a rock like this prick."

Armund turns slightly to snarl at Konan in all his near-death fury. "I thought it would be like one of the Danaan Merrow." He turns back, pretending Konan isn't chuckling behind us. "As a child, my mother had told me the Merrow were a social people. They would lure in people to the shores to sing to them, see if they could get jewels and trinkets as payment for their songs. They weren't aggressive. They were happy with their lives in seas, ponds, rivers, wherever their schools resided. I guess that's why I didn't take the warning seriously." He shrugs, tone turning wistful.

"This one was different. She looked similar, but when she came at me, she was… accusing. I don't know how to describe it. She was angry at me. She had gone mad." He shakes his head, confusion lining his thin face. "Probably for interrupting her space, her isolation. They usually stay in groups, but this one… there was not another with her. None ever came to her aid. Their communities are tight knit, we are almost certain she's alone in there. Maybe being in a different world warped her brain. I know things are different here… Power is different here," he trails off, glancing at Aine for a second before looking away again. "We aren't sure how she even got here; we didn't get here through any rift. She must have come through the same rift as the Fomorians, though we haven't ever been able to find it. Or maybe someone brought her here from somewhere else."

I don't know if I ever want to see such a thing, yet I get closer to her with every step forward. A monster.

We are not meant to be so alone, Alyx.

When I was left alone in a place that was cold and no longer familiar to me, I turned into a monster too. Maybe it was not the strangeness of a new world, but the strangeness of having nobody to talk to that drives us mad.

I have heard of such a creature—tales of beautiful women who live in the sea, the rivers, those who lure sailors to their deaths to feed on their souls. I thought such things were the product of bored housewives, drunken merchants, anyone seeking adventure or intrigue in our world of monotony. I had never truly believed such a thing could exist, but after this morning, seeing Fionn broil the skin off a Crow, I have no choice but to believe what they say.

"Did you get what was in the silt? The rock?" I'm beginning to tire of discoveries. I hope Armund just found something shiny and that's it.

He sighs again, almost tripping on a stone embedded in the ground. I catch him this time. He is so lanky and narrow, with long limbs. It makes it hard to steady him. He's like an over-sized foal.

"It wasn't just a rock, and yes." He shoots a seething glance back at Konan, who grins back. "Although it certainly was not worth it." He shoves his good hand in the pocket of the cloak. He pulls out... a rock. Gray and irregularly shaped, like it had been recently broken off of a larger piece. It has distinct bands around the sides; some orange, some black, some different shades of gray. Not worth it indeed. "It's just that it holds onto things. When you turn it this way"—he flips it over in his hand, revealing a spiralled imprint of a... shell?—"it holds a memory of something that has since turned to something else. For some reason it just... I could not leave it. It sparked thought in me, so I wanted to hold onto it."

His eyes are so warm when they meet mine. He looks embarrassed by his sentimentality. He really is so cute, in a boyish way. Even if he is on the brink of death.

I give him what I hope is a warm smile, thinking about how Diana shows her compassion, trying to mimic it. He gives me one back, looking relieved at the lack of condemnation from at least one person.

"This one fancies himself a scholar. Thinks that he can think us out of this forsaken realm," the voice from behind me rasps.

I look over my shoulder at Konan, his taunt glittering in his eyes. Armund just shakes his head, agitated.

"As opposed to what? Exactly what do you do?" I snap back. Something about Armund feels delicate, and it goes beyond his wounded condition. It makes me want to protect him.

Konan makes no move to throttle me as I feared he might. He doesn't think the question warrants a response. Or he has no ability to defend himself, either is fine with me.

Armund smiles softly at me, gratitude mixed with something else. Something that makes his eyes linger just a bit too long.

The sky turns into a bruised purple, washed with the gray of clouds between the leaves of the forest canopy. We stop for the evening. The air has the crispness of night, and I can feel the hum of life settle, the forest coming to rest all around us.

The group begins setting up a camp off to the side of the animal trail we had been following. They trample the ferns and plants of the underbrush, making a place to bed down. Packs are slung to the ground, stones are placed, and a fire started so rapidly I can hardly make sense of it. I just stand there. No bedroll, no food, no clothes but the ones on my back. I find a downed tree running along the campsite and sit on it. The dampness that clings to it seeps into my cloak under my bottom. I hunch over, ready to settle in for a long, cold night.

They all find their seats, most choosing spots nearest the fire.

Even Armund lets Fionn drag him over to his side, the two jostling each other, laughing at something asinine, I'm sure. Fionn cuffs Armund's shoulder in fraternal affection, though I see him watching every line on Armund's face, worrying over his friend.

Aine makes her way over to me. She hasn't spoken a word to me yet, a fact I'm glad of; I never know what to say to children.

A cloak is bundled in her arms, a bit of it dragging over the trampled brush.

Every member of the group keeps a watchful eye on the girl. And on me.

Fionn's eyes burn the brightest, and they never leave me.

Her warmth reaches me, radiating out from where she stands, about a foot from me.

Aine, ever-so slowly, lays the sturdy wool cloak on my lap, as if I'm an alley cat, ready to dart any moment.

"My mom had an extra. I asked if you could have it for tonight," her voice is twinkling, like bells.

She stands just around chin-height to me, not close to the end of her growth if her tall companions are any indication. Her littleness extends to her slight form. A little wren with a sing-song voice and curious eyes. Her raven-colored hair, twin to her father's, falls to her waist in gentle waves. The only giveaways of her mother's fairness are her pale complexion and the green shards in her eyes. She screams youthful femininity and loveliness; it makes me scared for her.

I nod in thanks, offering a sheepish smile.

Fionn is still staring when I dare let my eyes wander back to his. He doesn't look away.

"You don't have anything. But I'm sure we can get some things for you. A real bedroll, a change of clothes. When we pass through villages sometimes we barter for supplies or…" Aine looks back at the group. She whispers the next sentence, grinning conspiratorially. "Sometimes we steal it." She shuffles closer. "Konan has the best snacks. He says he just finds them, but I know he goes to the markets." She looks back to make sure he isn't listening. He is, narrow-eyed. But she goes on anyways, just quieter. "He looks really scary, but he sneaks me some of my favorite jerky when he thinks nobody is looking. Anyways, you can come sit by me if you want. The fire is warmer over there." She shifts her weight, rocking back and forth on her feet, waiting, looking suddenly insecure in her bid for friendship.

I cannot bear to turn away Aine's outreached hand.

I follow her, plopping down near her, close to the flames. The warmth of the cloak and the heat emanating from the roaring fire sends my chill skittering away.

Fionn still stares across the blaze. I can't make out his intention. I can't bring myself to stare back.

If he has something to say, he better just say it.

Aine chatters away beside me, needing little to no input of mine into the conversation. She offers me a bit of dried meat. I take it because I know I won't make it through tomorrow without it.

Nobody else says anything to me. The crackle and pops of the fire cover the murmurs between friends.

I wrap the borrowed cloak around my shoulders, and murmur an excuse to Aine, who takes it gracefully. I draw up the hood and lay back, letting the numbness spread to my fingers and tongue, falling into a deep sleep.

I hope the memories don't follow me there.

Such a familiar, inescapable feeling.

That if I ever wake up again, it will be too soon.

Chapter 11

Morning comes too soon.

I awaken covered in dew and dreams of endings.

Ugly ones.

And we walk.

And walk.

And walk.

Until the sun falls.

And I, encumbered with a new life painted in all the same colors, fall straight into another slumber just the same, like leaves to the ground, trusting in the promise that I will rise once more, no matter my wishes.

And I do.

And we walk more.

And I worry more.

About Armund, who, in spite of every fever-calming plant I can harvest along the way, refuses to level out in temperature.

Being a Fae is likely the only reason he still walks and breathes.

My nailbeds are bloody and raw, and I worry because I have nothing left to tear at.

As we get closer to the Morrigana bog, the ground becomes softer and softer, my steps sinking further into the ground.

The dampness is normal for Suri, the near-constant cover of rainclouds is familiar, and it feels like a blanket to my soul. It makes everything green, lush, and alive. I can feel it in the moss beneath my feet, the ferns that caress my shins as I pass by, the trees that whisper to each other. It grows in the air the further we go, its heaviness settling in my lungs with every weary breath.

That lushness reaches throughout the forest, to the best of my knowledge. Everywhere, except for that hopeless patch of ground where Comraich sits, suffering a blight that leaves the crops small and sparse. "Something in the soil must have turned," the people of the town said as year after year the crops dwindled to husks and people began paying the price for outsourced food from Farus. The city and its large sprawling countryside is farmed by indentured servants who were spared, by some fortune, from the mining camps situated in the shadow of the Ghaels. The food is pricey, but once the merchants determined there was a market for it, they made the trip, and people paid.

Some survived on alcohol, tobacco, and the occasional poppy milk if they're lucky. What else are you to do when you're too cowardly to die and too smart to think things will get better?

My introspection turns outward, peering into the gloom as the group begins to slow.

A thick rolling fog creeps along the ground, its tendrils reaching for us, fingers pulling us into its depths, towards the Morrigana bog and her lonely ghost.

Ahead I see Fionn, glowing with the condensation of moisture on his tan skin, mingling with sweat.

The mud sticks to my boots, pulling the ill-fitting things almost off. The ground beneath our feet has become clay-like, water filling the imprints of our footsteps.

As Fionn comes to a halt and peers through the brush, the group is completely silent, the distant calls of ravens the only vibrations in the air.

Fionn's golden eyes shift to me, holding for a moment before meeting the waiting eyes of the rest of the group. He firmly whispers his commands, shoulders shifting to fully face each member as he addresses them. First Elva, then Konan, slither off to their positions as soon as he finishes.

He addresses Dealla, stunning in her fairness, even with the gray noontime light, "I need you to circle to the north. One call periodically to continue on, two calls in warning, three to abort." He turns to Deri. "I need you to the east. Armund will stay with Aine..." Deri scoffs, crossing massive arms. "I know, I know you want to stay with her." Deri advances on Fionn, making him seem smaller than usual. Fionn raises his hands, holding him off.

"No," Deri says.

"Yes. Brother, you know they will be safe here. Armund won't let her get hurt."

"You want me to entrust the safety of my daughter to the one who almost got his arm torn off for a rock?" Deri's voice is menacing, predatory. His normally unshakable demeanor has evaporated.

Nobody has shown a hint of insubordination the whole journey thus far. It seems Deri's fatherly protective instincts overpower his sense of obedience. If he were an animal, his hackles would be raised.

Fionn's voice is calm as he attempts to placate the man

before him.

"Deri, you paint my brother in a bad light. You know him to be generally wise. Wise enough not to put Aine in any undue danger or let her come to any harm. He had one slight"—Fionn pinches his fingers together—"lapse in judgment over a rock, yes." Armund fidgets, apparently dreading a lifetime of embarrassment over his actions. "But he has seen the error of his ways and would never repeat said mistake again. Right, Armund?" Fionn doesn't take his eyes off the predator before him. "Right. So Armund and Aine, you will stay right up there." He points one finger up at the sky, the other hand still out in front of his chest, warding off the snarling father in front of him.

Deri is not soothed.

Dealla has crept back from her position, somehow knowing something was going on, and is assessing the situation.

Aine steps up behind her father, touching his arm gently.

"I'll stay with Armund. I promise. I won't come down the whole time. You know I can scout, even if I can't wield. I can tell if something is coming. I'm old enough."

Can't wield?

She pulls harder at her father's arm, which dwarfs her small delicate fingers.

"Deri, she is right." Dealla's voice is twinkling bells, just like her daughter's, though it's more forceful than I can ever imagine from Aine. She seems to be a silent pillar of stone within her family. Aine and Deri both turn to look at her. After a moment of silent communication, Deri releases Fionn, shoving him really, and begrudgingly waits for the rest of his orders.

Aine gives me a triumphant smile as she walks to stand between Armund and me, unruffled by the confrontation.

She gives Armund's good arm a squeeze. Warmth infuses his expression, crowding out the chagrin. He ruffles her raven black hair, and she giggles and knocks his hand away.

Fionn finishes giving Deri his orders, to report to the east side of the bog and if three calls are sounded, to pull the Merrow's attention elsewhere.

Fionn turns his attention towards me. I had almost forgotten what the full force of his attention feels like—like a burning enchantment. He steps towards me, graceful as a stalking cat despite the sucking mud.

"And you will stay silent. You will come with me. You will be helpful. And you will resist the urge to ruin my glorious plans. Do you understand your orders?" He ends his words glaring down at me, a hairsbreadth from my face, as if he expects me to back away from him.

I would rather die than give him the satisfaction.

"Understood." I try my best to look completely unaffected.

His smirk says he sees through it.

Turning, Fionn tosses his pack at the base of a tree. I lay my cloak atop it, my most prized possession.

He grabs my hand and pulls me through the brush, not slowing even as I stumble.

A faint rustling of leaves behind us is the only sound of Aine and Armund following their own orders.

The bog-lands await on the other side. The water forms a silver mirror to the gray skies and mist that hover just over the top of it, snaking through the interspersed patches of grass and brush. The tree line we broke through fades to nothing but fog in every direction.

The land begins sinking into the water, slowly seeping over my shoes, and filling them. Tearing my hand from Fionn's grip, I lift my feet from the spongy ground, remove my boots, and toss them back in the direction we came from. My feet are bare, pale and wrinkled from days slugging through the ever-dampening ground with leaking boots. The ground squishes beneath my bare feet. If they weren't already numb from cold, the icy water would be painful.

I glance up at Fionn, waiting for further direction. He's staring at me, amusement dancing in his eyes.

"Well, that's one way to do this," he says quietly, keeping his deep voice from vibrating into the water into unwanted ears. He swiftly follows my movements, placing his leather boots, sturdy and whole, on a piece of high ground at our side. Is it possible for feet to be both manly and graceful?

Figures.

These people from another place, another world entirely, are gifted with strength, power, and beauty. What is it about their world that makes them so?

"What?" he asks quietly.

"Nothing," I reply in a whisper.

"Stop looking at my feet."

"Man feet are gross. That's all."

"My feet aren't gross."

"Yes, they are."

"Your feet are small and pale."

"We need to be quiet."

"You need to be quiet," he quips.

I shove back the urge to push him into the water. Arrogant prick. Instead, I brace myself with a deep breath and look at the still water before me.

From this vantage, I can see nothing past my own reflection. I look wild, terrified as I try to see my foot under the water. The days have not been kind to me. My mousy dark blonde hair is knotted and mussed from sleeping on the ground. The circles under my eyes are eyes dark and deep. It has been some time since I have seen my reflection, seen the dead woman in a mirrored realm. She looks like how I feel.

I try not to look at her as I take the first step; the task at hand is more important than my vanity or my fear that I have become something hopeless. Armund is not without hope, and that is what matters.

Fionn and I gently place our feet with every step, careful to avoid disturbing the surface of the water too much. Every ripple across its reflective surface feels like a call to the monster that lurks in its depths. All of our hissed conversation feels like a giant mistake.

After two steps, my feet begin to sink farther, the hem of my wool dress soaking up farther than the dirt had splashed.

Fionn leads me down the edge of the waterline, still gripping my hand steadily. His hand is warm around mine, huge and tan where mine looks veined and pale. His grip is as unyielding as him, palm roughened from the years wielding weapons. I try not to shudder at the warm contact. The feeling of someone's heat seeping into my skin is as unfamiliar as the language across the seas. I fight the pathetic urge to grasp on with my other hand. To extend the feeling. To leech off his warmth.

The bog is much deeper than it appears, sucking me down into its murky depths past my waist. As we make our way, two trilling birds call every minute or so, back and forth. Not ravens, some sort of warbler. Not a native sound. Dealla and Elva signaling the way is clear.

We search for red and white flowers in the siding of the peat moss under the water. We make it about a quarter of the circumference of the silver expanse of water before I spot them, their scarlet teardrop petals a beacon several steps away.

I tug Fionn to a stop and point silently, my body bushing against his warm arm.

A trill from the south sounds.

"Perfect," he whispers, starting for them abruptly.

He knocks into me in his haste, causing me to have to catch my balance.

My hand smacks the surface of the water as I try to keep myself from falling into it completely.

Two trills sound far to the north.

My heart stops.

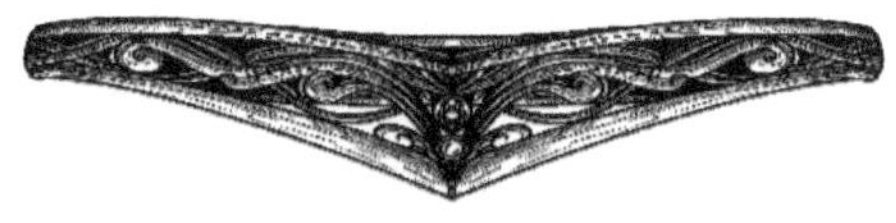

Chapter 12

Fionn doesn't pause, but becomes a pillar of calm and determination for my panic. He slowly, methodically trudges forward.

A single chirp from the south: Elva. Nothing from her end, then. A relief, as we are far closer to her.

The plant we came to retrieve stands proud in its home of monsters. The four tear-shaped petals are scarlet, a splash of color in this place of gray and brown hues.

I take a breath, preparing myself to go under the water to retrieve it; the water whirls around my chest and the flower lies somewhere around my ankles. Fionn nods at me in encouragement.

Icy water shocks my body when I go under.

I carefully grip the base of the plant and gently work the fingers of roots out of the ground, keeping the tearing minimal. We need every tendril of medicine the plant contains. The roots cling to the moss and mud, entwined intimately with its life source, unwilling to leave it. The lack of air burns in my lungs and I'm forced to leave the plant half-hanging from its home.

My head breaks through the surface and I gasp for breath, trying to be as quiet as possible.

Three quick trills break through the silence and echo off of the water behind us.

Abandon mission.

But I think of Armund and push myself back under, grasping for the plant once more.

Fionn, having followed me into the frigid murk, grips my hand where it holds the base of the plant and tears it the rest of the way from the ground.

We both gasp as we re-emerge. I peer back through the surface to look for more.

Roots stick out from where they broke from the plant. Like fingers grasping up from the earth, reaching for sunlight.

A disturbance sounds from far to the west—splashing. Crashing waves in the water.

Deri and Konan.

I lunge to grip whatever is left sticking out.

I get a bit more.

Three more trills sound from behind us.

Fionn has forgotten all pretense of being quiet and gentle. He is fighting to get to the edge of the bog, the gleaming prize gripped in his fist.

I fight to follow, the mud sticking to my bare feet, water pushing against my body, roots clenched in hand.

Fionn heaves himself onto a patch of brush and grass; it sinks under his weight, causing him to struggle to get out.

I am a few arms-lengths behind him when I feel something.

Not a physical touch, but a presence.

Creeping up on me in menacing curiosity.

A shadow in the murk.

I push harder, legs fighting to cut through the deep water.

"Fionn, please!" I reach desperately for him.

His eyes become frantic as he glances behind my right shoulder. It is all the warning I get.

He reaches for me wide-eyed, gripping my slippery arm.

A slick, clawed hand grips my shoulder, tearing me backwards into the water.

Under the water has always been a peaceful place for me. A weightless place of calm power that would block out the constant drone of life. Even after my near-drowning as a child, I still feel safest there.

But now it is a hissing, inescapable cacophony in my ears as I fight for my life. But it is not loud enough to block out the voice of darkness and murk that meets me there.

"You smell of him," it hisses in a voice of endless agony, its rasping voice obscured by the water.

I thrash, panic in my bones, trying to pry free of its slimy grip. Claws dig in but do not pierce my flesh.

The Merrow drags me along the bog floor. The silt and roots grasp for me, some force trying to keep me with Fionn.

"You smell of souls and death," she muses. The voice is now lilting and eager.

I open my eyes despite the water that burns them, so I might see death's face.

She is a thing of nightmares—a creature of vengeance and murk. He is no alluring siren, but a phantom of gray skin, black hair whirling, like ink in water, and webbed fingers tipped with claws. Her skin blends into the clay. Black, beady eyes stare so intently as she pulls me further. That snarling face is twisted in vengeful excitement, gleeful at her prize.

I fight harder, digging my fingers harder into the silt,

panic making me gasp and choke on sharp-tasting bog water.

Something pelts us from above, narrowly missing the Merrow as she moves backwards. Arrows, slicing through the water, stirring up muck with every impact.

"You smell of him. I will have you. I will torment you as I have been tormented. Soul-eater. Kin-killer." The Merrow croons her mantra as she pulls me further.

The thrashing is only serving to exhaust me further, allowing her to drag me to her lair more quickly.

The pelting arrows come less and less frequently, as if the archer above is afraid of hitting me.

I wish they would. Better that than this.

The bog has depth and darkness. Places to hide. It is a place for things that people have forgotten—for those that have no kin but the dirt and the darkness. It *does* feel like it has memory—like if I died right here it would hold me and remember me until the world turned to ash.

The surface gets further and further away, the light dimming, unable to pierce the darkness. As it goes, so does my hope for being saved.

A feeling swells in my chest, more than panic, more than doom. Icy power, wrathful, and intent on saving me.

My frantic search for something, anything, to grab onto is fruitless. No matter what I grip, she is stronger.

That power surges, taking hold of all that I am.

It grips my hand. Makes me tilt it towards her, instead of trailing behind me, grasping at moss.

The water around begins to swirl and take shape, breaking and bending the light. Fracturing and piercing the gloom.

She releases my arm with a hiss, jerking it back, whirling to look back at me again.

Black blood, like ink in water, swims from a long slice

on her arm.

Shards of ice, longer than my arm, whirl like blades through the bog.

Black spots pop across my vision.

I keep fighting, held in the hands of dark power. Even in my darkening view, I can see the murk fracturing and twisting in the sunlight, twisting my reality.

She shrieks and flees in a slash of movement. Her dark scaled tail swishes, propelling her away from this power that feels like a part of both me and something grossly other.

With the dregs of my energy, I push for the surface, that blissful light. Shards of ice caress my skin as I rise, feeling like icy fingers tickling over my face and arms.

My entire being is suffering, drowning slowly, and every second is a lifetime.

And then it's gone.

The air on my face cues me to hack the water from my lungs, begging to get it out so I can get air in. Nothing matters but the air.

Warm hands grip under my arms and yank me out of the water. My water-logged clothes weigh on me, my limbs heavier than stone. As I'm pulled against a heaving chest, I revel in the warmth, eyes closed.

My thoughts are water slipping through the fingers of my mind. All I know is a yawning chasm before me, waiting to envelop me into an endless void.

All I know is I never want to leave this warmth.

"Alyx!" Fionn's firm voice pulls me from the void.

Fingers grip my face, shaking me lightly.

I open my eyes begrudgingly, narrowing them to slits.

Fionn's golden eyes are wide with questions and shock, inches from my own as he leans over me.

"What did you do, Alyx? How did—Are you alright?"

he questions me in loud, panting bursts.

I have no answers for him—for this shaking, scared version of the golden man.

I don't know. I don't know. I don't know.

My mind is but a ship sinking into the waters of unconsciousness. It's inevitable.

I'm only vaguely aware of him calling my name, demanding that I stay awake, before I let the darkness take me.

Chapter 13

Light dances behind my eyelids, singing the song of crackles and pops, whispering in my dreams that were memories. Shards of desperation, webbed fingers, and black eyes; they blend and fade in my mind's eye. They become so abhorrent that my eyes jerk open.

The others are sitting around the fire, the rest of the world gone dark. Dealla and Aine whisper affectionately to one another, warmth on their faces. Deri watches, his entire world in the air between their breaths. Fionn is hovering between Armund and me. Armund is unconscious, his skin clammy and gray.

"Finally." The voice is like smoke itself. The voice of the shadow, who sits across the flame. Elva stares intently at me as the firelight reflects off her dark skin, absorbing none of it, making it glow with a radiance.

I sit up, my every movement stiff, limbs heavy. The others have gone quiet at my awakening.

"You've been out for hours," Fionn says tightly, searching my face. Gone is the contempt that used to live in his eyes when he looked at me, replaced with distrustful curiosity. "We need to get started with Armund, he's… not doing well." He looks to be torn on whether to satiate his curiosity or heal his friend right this moment.

Memories float back. I can't make sense of them anymore than I can the morning I awoke to Crows turned to shattered stone. One thing is clear, however—it's me. I did those things. Somehow, I rendered those Crows into nothing more than chunks of flesh. I turned the water to blades of ice and wielded them against the Merrow. I would have no doubt about it if not for the fact that humans do not have these fae-like powers. And I am undoubtedly human.

My parents could have somehow hidden their own, similar powers from me. But why? And why wouldn't they have used them to save us from poverty and themselves from death? None of it connects.

My hands look ordinary—dirty and rough, with nails bitten down to their quicks. Many ordinary hands like mine kill, but very few in such a terrifying way. Shouldn't there be some tell? Shouldn't you be able to see the difference in the hands of a killer?

I have no answers, and nowhere to search for them. Anyone who would know anything about my past is gone.

My dwelling upon this is useless. Fruitless. The only thing to be done is to move forward, even if I have to do it blind.

Fionn has the Merrow flower neatly bunched in front of him, the roots I had so foolishly risked my life for, lost in the skirmish.

The others sit around the fire, keeping to themselves, continuing their nighttime routines.

Methodically, I separate the roots from the plant, the leaves from the stem, the petals and head of the flower from the stem. I take Fionn's waterskin from beside him and begin boiling water in the small traveling pot he had set out by the plant.

"Care to comment on what happened back there?" Fionn whispers, hands clasped tightly before him.

I don't look at him. I clean the roots from dirt and bog water.

"You. You fought that Merrow. You froze the bog. You… wielded."

I have nothing to offer. It makes as little sense to me as to him.

The water boils. I remove it from the heat and place all of the components into the pot, steeping them.

"Have you ever done such things before?" he pesters.

Only the sounds of fire crackling fill the air. I watch the wisps of color effuse from the bright red petals, tinting the water pink in the firelight. It looks like blood.

"I think so…" I finally reply, unsure of where to start or what to say.

"What did you do before?" Fionn asks.

"I think I killed the Crows. The ones that showed up looking for me."

"What happened to them?" Elva cuts in.

Her words conjure roaming hands, unwanted. Flesh, broken like shards of ice, blend in with the pink tea in front of me.

"They were trying to hurt me."

Silence.

"More than kill me… They wanted to hurt me. Make it drawn out, painful. Take everything they could get before they ended it. I didn't know… I still don't know what happened—with any of it. What I did. I just woke up and they were in pieces. All over the garden."

A muscle in Fionn's jaw flickers. His eyes harden.

I can feel myself retreating in my mind. Seeing everything in front of me from a far-off distance, like watching through a window. I pick at the jagged edge of my thumbnail.

I sniff at the weak tea. It smells sour. "I don't suppose anyone has any peppermint or honey?"

Nothing but stony eyes reply.

"This is going to taste gross." I shrug.

Poor Armund.

"And that was the first time anything like that has happened?" Fionn asks.

I think of the burn scar on the floor of my house. The one that always catches my eye in the morning.

"Yeah," I say.

I move over to Armund, my whole body one gigantic ache. I pat his cheek gently.

He looks so like that child lying in bed, taken by a fever only days ago. Part of me is glad I didn't have to see that end. Chestnut curls stuck to foreheads in sweat.

I urge Armund to sit up slightly. Fionn comes over to his other side, helping. I decant the cooling tea gently into his mouth. He does not seem to see me, or to understand what is going on past the instinct to drink.

"Do you know how this could possibly be?" Fionn questions again.

I scoff, still feeding Armund the acidic tea. "No. My parents are human. I am human. I grew up here. I was born here. I don't know how I possibly could be able to do these things. I am the least special human to ever exist." My head is shaking by the time I'm finished, taking the pot, now drained, from Armund's mouth.

"Some of those things cannot possibly be true," Elva

says gently. "We have roamed these lands for near on thirty years. Not once has a human ever shown to be anything but powerless. Frail. Helpless against the Fomorians. You… may not be."

Thirty years. They have been here longer than I've been alive. They look to be in their mid-twenties, early thirties at the latest. Could they have been wandering as babes?

Fionn sees me running numbers in my head and explains, "We don't exactly age the way you do. We are… older than we look." The corner of his mouth edges up.

What the hell is that supposed to mean?

I hold my hand out for Fionn's favorite knife. He's running it along his hand again. His jaw clenches but he hands the hilt to me.

I remove the petals and the leaves from the pot, now drained of liquid, reserving them. I begin grinding what little we have of the softened roots into paste with the blunt hilt of Fionn's knife.

"What did it feel like? When you used your power?" he pries more.

What does it feel like? It feels like there are two monsters coiled around one another inside me. One that wants to be left to die in some deep dark hole, hissing and spitting at anyone who comes close. And one that roars and fights with everything against the very thought of all of it ending, clawing at any chance at more. And when I wield, if that is what I did, the latter monster triumphs.

"It felt like… like not me. It felt like something just took over. Like I was going to die, and the… power didn't want me to. And I feel terrible when I wake up. Like I've been thrown from a horse into a rock. I am so tired." Yawning at the reminder but satisfied with the consistency of my paste, I unwrap Armund's arm.

His wound looks horrid, the flesh melting off in great green and yellow sheets. The necrosis has spread. I use the knife to scrape the dead flesh from the top of the wound, searching for fresh skin under the rot. He groans but is too weak to pull his arm from my grasp. I wish I had some more milk of the poppy to give him for the pain, but that resource is scarce. The poppies are only farmed in Farus and are tightly controlled by the Crown and traded in Rheol, the river city.

Fionn watches my debriding of the wound with a grimace.

"Regardless of where you got it from or what is the truth, you need to learn how to wield it," Fionn says, seeming to need to focus on anything but the scraping of Armund's wound. "This actually makes my life much easier. Now maybe you can actually be useful to the Fianna." He stands, shaking his arms out when he sees me dig-in a little harder on a stubborn bit of dead skin. "We don't often need a healer. But this wound, could not be healed by our power alone. In Danu it would have been taken to one of the high healers. Thankfully, Diana has… had a similar skill-set."

The change in tense slices through me. But I smother the feeling, shove it down with the rest. It will be in good company there, another wound to add to my collection of them that never quite seem to heal.

I apply a thin layer of paste along the wound, wishing I had held onto the rest of the roots. If for no other reason than to have something to show for my idiocy. Maybe then someone could say it was bravery.

I cannot think of the future. I cannot even force myself to be happy that this will make fitting in easier and solidify my position amongst them.

"Did you really name the Fianna after yourself?" I

scrunch my own nose in distaste.

Konan barks a laugh from his place on the other side of Armund.

Fionn shoots him a deadly look before turning to me and snatching his knife back. "More like I was named after it. My mother was a bit… preoccupied by her duty. She led the Fianna back in Danu. It is what we called our legions. We are all that is left of it now." His jaw clenches.

I nod in response, gently laying the leaves over the paste, letting them stick to the wound in a rudimentary dressing. Part of me would have found it amusing to have the confirmation that Fionn is self-absorbed enough to name the group after himself. The other part of me is relieved that he didn't. I'm not sure I could have ever taken him seriously again if he had.

"Thank you," Fionn says, watching me ensure the wrap on Armund's arm is tight, yet loose enough.

Armund is still out of it, not having stirred much during my ministrations.

"He's kind," I say by way of explanation.

Fionn suddenly stands and grabs his bedroll, unrolling it in sure movements.

I stay fidgeting with Armund, fussing a little, making sure he's comfortable and drying his forehead with my cloak.

I wonder when I'll get a bedroll, how many nights I'll spend on the ground before we go to the next town. The cold seeps so far into my bones in the night I'm surprised I even woke up this morning. At least my bed in my house had walls surrounding it and the floor made of level planks of wood.

Fionn gives me a feral grin that sets me on edge as he comes to stand over me. "You will begin training with me tomorrow. And I promise to only make it..." He tosses his head back and forth, considering. "… extremely difficult. And given your sunny, hopeful disposition I bet you will be an extremely teachable pupil. But I suppose I owe it to the goddess who brought you here, to try and train you." He squats down, pushing into my space. "I cannot wait." He is so close his breath curls against my cheeks, and I fight not to back away from his imposing presence, remembering the heat and roughness of his palms on mine.

He runs so hot and cold. I never know if he hates me or simply enjoys making me feel bad.

Before either one of us can look away he leans in and hefts me into the air, tossing me over his shoulder. For a moment I think it's starting, this torturous training he speaks of. But he only moves over a couple of steps, and unceremoniously lays me down on his bedroll. My head spins but he has already started walking away.

"Sleep here, I'll take first watch." He leaps with feline grace, in only a few bounds, up into the high branches of a great alder tree, settling in a thick branch.

The others flicker their eyes between us, obviously trying not to be too conspicuous about it. Aine is already passed out, drooling on her mom's lap.

My pride might ordinarily cause me to move out of his bedroll. Tell him to shove this gesture up his ass. Just because I now may be able to wield, that means I'm worthy. That means he'll finally treat me better than the dirt on his shoe. Now I'm worth seeing.

I've never worn righteous anger well. Never been able to keep it on for long enough to make a difference. And so I allow the exhaustion that lingers in my bones, muscles, and marrow to pull me down. I roll my face into the slight cushion—it smells like pine trees and snow-capped mountains—and my leaden eyes shut without a fight.

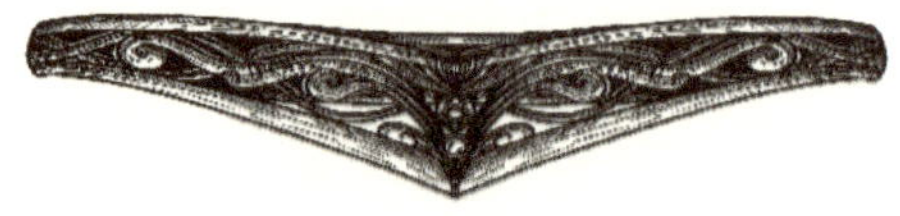

Chapter 14

The morning passes in dawn's freshest rain and relieved sighs as Armund wakes, fever broken, and completely lucid. The Fianna fussed around Armund over breakfast, clapping him gently on the shoulder and hugging him carefully. I asked him how he was feeling, to which he responded he felt much better. I didn't dare break the seal on his wound dressings to check the state of it, the Merrow flower having been completely used up and none of us eager to wander back to a watery grave.

The final bits of our camp are being packed away into packs as I don my cloak. Aine is balancing with her hands out as she walks across a narrow log. Konan tosses small rocks at her feet, trying to get her to lose her balance. He shoots me a glare when he sees me watching.

I hide my smile by pretending to search for something on the ground. Konan isn't fooling anyone. He's not as scary as he seems if he has a gigantic soft spot shaped like a twelve-year-old girl.

"Alyx," Armund greets with a shy smile. His color is much better, his slight tan returned to his skin. "I wanted to thank you. For everything." His face turns serious, his warm eyes boring into mine.

I nod and fidget with my sleeve. "I—yeah, I'm just glad you're better." I give him a sheepish smile. "Are you feeling any pain?" I ask, more comfortable assessing than accepting gratitude.

He looks at his arm. "Not much. It mostly feels numb, maybe slightly tingly." His dimple flashes when he says with a smile, "I'm glad you're here. For more than just this." he lifts his wrapped arm. "It was getting a bit stale around here. Haven't had a change in company much in the past thirty years."

"I'm sure." He's staring into my face too intently for my comfort. Part of me likes it and wants to keep talking to him because he's so friendly and warm. Sweet. I wish I could reciprocate in kind, but I'm just so awkward and socially stunted, I don't know how he does it. "Have you ever had others in your group?"

Immediately, I think of all the ways in which that is the wrong thing to ask. What if someone has died and I just brought it up?

He shakes his head, looking at the others as they gather with their packs slung. We move up behind them, filing out of our camp, starting our day's journey. There has been some talk of where we head next. It sounds like we head west, towards the capitol. There have been murmurs of leaving the continent. I'm too new and my position too precarious to offer any input. I'll go wherever they go.

"We've never had anyone else in the Fianna. We have some allies across the country, and in others, but none that have ever traveled with us. Diana was one," Armund says.

I swallow hard.

His hand settles on my upper back, giving it a slight rub.

"I'm sorry. I shouldn't have brought that up."

I blow it off. "It's fine." Even if it hurts, I don't want people tiptoeing around my feelings.

He nods, pulling his hand back. "She was a great healer." When I do nothing but nod, he goes on. "An even better person. She always gave Fionn a hard time, which he needs." He nudges me with an elbow when I smile and nod. "See, you've already caught on and you've only been with us a couple of days. You're going to fit in just fine."

The comment makes me feel better. "How did you meet Diana? Was she… like you?" I ask.

"We met her about fifteen years ago, while we were traveling through Rheol. She was there, buying some herbs and whatever else she needed. She saw us and just knew. She had come from Danu, too."

The statement baffles me. Never once did Diana seem as though she was anything but ordinary. She was a great healer, yes, but nothing she did was beyond human abilities. The first and only thing I ever saw of her that would have had me asking questions was her journal that Fionn and I found. "I don't understand that. She didn't… look like you. She looked human. Her ears were normal. She never wielded."

"Well, she was different. She was one of the folk—what we call non-wielders. She didn't have the ability to wield as we do, but she was from Danu. It's very rare. But sometimes, children are born and they just… never change. They never develop the power. It's the power that does it, changes us." He blushes a bit and gestures to his ears, "The ears become pointed, and we can then hear better. We can see better. It… grows us. We grow tall, and strong. But for a few, it just never happens, and we don't know why. She was one of those. She said she had worked with the healers of the Tira

Slania. She never told us how she escaped Danu."

His words wash over me. I never knew her at all. She had an entire existence that I never knew a thing about. It feels like betrayal, but I know it's an unjustified feeling. How could she have told me? Did she know that I would eventually be able to wield? What are the odds that it was all coincidence that she settled in my village?

"Alyx! Walk with me," Fionn calls from the front.

He's observing the two of us from his place at the head, gold eyes flickering between us.

I move to take up the space directly behind Fionn. There is some time in which he says nothing. Part of me thinks he doesn't trust me to befriend his friend, who is clearly the most trusting of the group.

We travel animal paths in the crowded undergrowth of the magnificent forest. She towers above our heads, a behemoth of sound and life, from the canopy, to ferns and berry bushes, to the insects crawling along the dirt. Birds call across miles of uninhabited wild, singing songs of birth, life, and death.

Occasionally, large drops of water pour down from leaves, creating waterfalls from the pooling rain.

Behind me, I hear Aine playing a game with Konan, her endless chatter and his occasional grunt. She describes some infinitesimal bit of the verdant forest and makes him guess what she's seeing. It usually starts out with *I see something greeeen.*

Cold water slaps me in the face, jarring me from my listening. The branch Fionn had walked through, and did not bother holding for me, sent droplets spraying into my face and hands, rolling down my nose. The corner of his mouth turns upward in a sly glance back.

I go to kick his feet together as he takes a step, but he

quickly dodges it, not even looking back. I grit my teeth as his chuckling whets my ire.

He clucks his tongue in consternation, teasingly shaking a finger. "Now now, you know better than that. You think you can trip me? I haven't survived this long by allowing drowned rats to get the best of me." He pointedly looks at my sodden appearance.

"And how long is that exactly?" I grit out.

"Longer than you, shorter than Elva." He glances back at her, grinning fiendishly. He's way too cheery this morning. "She's ancient. Isn't that right, Elva?"

"Ancient is a strong word. You're but a babe, and it shows, Fionn." Her tone is bored.

"I was hoping I wasn't the only one who noticed his immaturity," I concur, still glaring ahead at the back of his curly honey hair.

"Immature? Me? Because I let a branch hit you when you weren't paying attention? Let this serve as your first lesson. If you want to survive you have to pay attention. Don't get lost in your thoughts. Especially as I'm sure they're as droll and depressing as you. I could almost feel the angst rolling off you."

"You didn't answer my question," I ask angrily.

"How old are you? What is your favorite color? Could this be a more boring line of questioning?" He looks back at me. "Fine. I'm around seventy of your human years. I've been here in this lovely realm for nigh on thirty of them. I am considered young amongst Fae. Really, we all are. We were in training to be in the Fianna when we… left. Well, all of us except Elva, she just happened to be in the right place at the right time, right, Elva?" He grins at her, but there are shadows in his eyes.

I want to ask what he means. How did they leave? What

happened to all of them?

Elva replies only with, "I would say that you were in the right place at the right time, Fionn."

"Ah, but just think how lonely you would be without all of us in this beautiful realm with you."

"Aine is alright, the rest of you I could do without."

A girlish giggle comes from the far back.

"Maybe if she didn't steal my snacks all the time I would agree," Konan's rough voice sounds.

"Hey!" Aine's voice of twinkling bells is indignant. "It's not my fault you leave them in such close reach. It's almost like you want me to take them."

Indeed, I doubt anyone could take anything from the hulking man without his knowing and allowing such a thing.

Another branch smacks me in the face and the shaking in my limbs is suddenly from more than the cold.

"You're a slow learner, I see."

I master my temper and gently hold the offending branch and pass it off to Elva, who is directly behind me.

"What are we doing here?" I ask instead of launching myself at Fionn like a wildcat. Like the ice in my bones begs for.

"What do you mean?" Fionn asks. His voice has an edge to it.

"I mean what are we doing here? What have you been doing all this time? Where are we headed from here?"

"What? You mean you don't wander aimlessly for years at a time?" His stupid grin is back. He sighs at my unamused face. "You're really no fun. Well, for a long time we were… searching, for anyone else who perhaps had wandered into this same realm. We found none but Diana after all these years. Though she would never tell us how or why she came here. Then, we were searching for a way out. A way back, or to somewhere else once we found the Fomorians had found their way here too. We only ever found one rift… One tear in the fabric of this realm that held…" Fionn falters, looking green. "Well, it was not a place that would have been better than here, even with the Fomorians. I don't know who made it, or why it is there, but it is best that it be left alone."

"Where?" I can't help but ask.

What type of place could make this fearless warrior green with terror? Who could shake the unshakable? I'm not sure I want to find out.

I catch the branch he sends flinging back at me this time. Though, it still gets my cloak and face wet.

"Not far from here, actually. Don't go wandering the mounds if you can help it." He smirks at me. "And as for the rest of your question, we are going to first find you some supplies, while we train. There is a village due south of this forest, by the sea. We will try to snag some supplies up from a leech or two. Maybe some wealthy townspeople, they always have the best stuff, and guard it with the least ferocity. And in the meantime, we will keep looking for a way back. If we find one, it will be your choice whether to follow us or stay here."

I wonder if I will ever have to make the choice. What kinds of horrors will I face between now and then? What else lurks in the mist and shadow of this realm that we excuse as folklore and delusion?

"Have you ever found any other… creatures here? Like the Merrow. Has anything else slipped through?" I think of the rumors of the raider groups that terrorize villages. What does the Pretty King know of this? Could the ruler of our country possibly know that the people in his employ are soul-sucking demons? How could he not know? And what does that make him?

Elva responds, "There are all manner of things that slip through the cracks, girl. You can feel them though. Their otherness. Some wear the skin of familiar beings. Some do not, but when you learn to feel them… it cannot be ignored."

Otherness.

"You made it sound like you saved the rest of them… Did you?"

A long stretch of silence. Even Aine discontinues her game with Konan in the tense silence.

"I was never Fianna. I was an emissary for my own people—a people much older and more advanced than the Danaans. We, who had traveled through realms for generations, had found a world much like our own—one of life and balance. One where the people were different, but similar. I was sent to establish relations with them—the fae. With the Queen of Danu herself. I was in the palace grounds while they celebrated their day of Aberth de Dana. A few young guards were stationed with me—the young Fianna legion who volunteered to stay behind for Queen Maica." She gestures around.

"By the time we discovered what was going on, the Fomorians had overpowered everyone—the Queen herself. Even the healers of the Tira Slania, the most sacred and powerful beings of the Danaans. There was nowhere to go, we were surrounded, outnumbered, overpowered—so I walked through the worlds, as my people had before me and brought those that were with me at the time. My home world… was so far, and I would have needed someone else, one of my kin, to help get us all the way there. So I just walked to the closest world I could find, hoping we would find a way back to the rest of my people, an ocean away—to at least warn them what lurked across the sea. But as I stepped a foot on this ground it was like a blanket had fallen over my power, suffocating it. Power here is dampened." She glances at Aine, who is hardly paying attention. "What you saw of Fionn in the square… those are a shadow of his abilities in another world. We think that's why Aine hasn't developed any wielding ability yet, despite the fact that she has two very powerful parents. It happens that Fae cannot wield, but not often. I cannot… I cannot walk as I once did. I cannot get back by making my own tears. So we are trapped, searching for rifts that already exist. Hopefully one that will take us to a realm where I can reach my full power once more."

I hadn't realized until this moment that I'd never seen Aine wield, but I do recall her mentioning it back at the bog.

I glance at the rest of the Fianna in the silence that follows. The anguish on their faces tells another story. One of loss—a greater loss than my own. I wonder if maybe Elva told this story because she is the only one able to force the words out.

I shouldn't prod at open wounds, so I don't ask any more questions.

Elva's face says she is willing to give nothing more.

And so I keep placing one foot in front of the other.

Branches to the face seem to be the mildest form of training Fionn has planned. It starts with self-defense, reflex testing, and conditioning. No mention of wielding at all. I'm eager to learn to wield, to be more than helpless for once. Maybe then I'll feel like I have my feet on solid ground.

Fionn made a point to slyly attack me as we walked—Konan too—but once I grew wise and quit allowing my guard to drop, he taught me basic escape techniques and evasive maneuvers. He runs over the soft spots on a person to strike—swiftly and brutally—to disarm and escape. When

I had grumbled about this not being the kind of training I had agreed to, he spat back that it would, "be a waste of my time to train you to wield if you would only walk straight off a cliff or be detained as easily as an infant," and proceeded to put me on my ass once more.

I have a feeling that even if he teaches me everything he knows, I won't ever be able to take him on. Diana used to say I have the endurance of a mule. And she wasn't wrong. I've always been naturally fit. Able to run faster and farther than Mariana when we were girls. Able to lift heavy bales of hay that even my dad sometimes struggled with. I just think I've always been highly motivated to get the hard part done and over with.

Even so, Fionn is quicker and stronger than any living being has a right to be—they all are. They slink around like the mountain cats of the Ghaels a merchant once told me about. The merchant was trying to sell a pelt to the poor, the great fool. He explained how they moved around unheard, unseen unless they wish to be. When I tried to knock Fionn down, it was like trying to topple a tree.

These people. They were bested by the Fomorians. A whole society of them, gone. Wiped out by a shipload of Crows. The sheer impossibility of things getting better, of ever getting rid of them, is enough to make me consider laying down on the forest floor and letting the moss grow over me.

We are to reach the town of Tristram tomorrow. I can feel the leagues traveled in every step of my foot. I can feel every time Fionn tripped me in my scraped knees and skinned palms.

I plop down beside Fionn as the sun falls, craving some hot tea and food. Specifically, the tea that Dealla keeps, rationing carefully to last between towns, and any scraps of meat they throw my way from the rabbits Armund and Deri hunted as we traveled today. Perhaps that's what thirty years in the wilderness buys you—the ability to take down belts full of small game before noon. I beg with my eyes like a hound at a table but say nothing. I much prefer the type of hunger that I can easily ignore, letting the silence take me into a deep sleep to the sounds of my howling stomach and atrophying muscles. But with training and walking, my hunger is ravenous, the likes of which I haven't felt in the most sleepless of nights.

"Don't get too settled, I have more tasks for you." Fionn's grin is smug.

A sadist. I made a bargain with a damned sadist.

He grabs my hand and my skin prickles where he touches it. He lays it flat to the frigid ground, the moss soft under the pads of my fingers.

"I want you to tell me what you feel." His gaze is piercing—my brain stops short.

It takes me a moment to realize he is referring to the ground under my hand as opposed to the feel of his callused hand on mine.

I focus on the place where my fingers met the moss.

"It feels… soft, cold." I rub my fingers lightly over the tops of it. Like green fur.

"Deeper. Can you feel who it is? Become it. When you can accomplish this, I will give you some food. When you earn it."

Traveling leagues and leagues only to be attacked by him intermittently does not "earn" me a bit of rabbit, apparently.

I look up at the others who watch me. "Come on Fionn. Let her have some dinner first," Armund sighs, shaking his head at Fionn. The others nod their agreement, Dealla and Elva both verbally agreeing.

"No. She can do this. Hunger is good motivation," Fionn states firmly, watching me with burning eyes. Konan agrees with a nod.

Armund presses his lips together, looking at me apologetically. Elva stalks off. Deri rubs Dealla's back as she watches angrily.

I close my eyes. I want to learn. I want to get better and this is the closest thing to wielding as we have worked on all day. I make sure to keep some measure of awareness on him, not trusting him not to shove me into the fire to prove a point about my "awareness." The move would be crueller than anything he has done before, but I can never be sure.

I try to do what he said, I swear I do. I think about thoughtlessness, simply existing to sprawl on the forest floor and be trodden on. Think about being soft and moist and drinking from the floor of the world. I feel its little fuzzy fingers beneath every nerve in my own fingertips. I repeat that to Fionn.

He shifts slightly. "More. Get closer."

I scrunch up my face, closing my eyes and try harder.

Roasted rabbit and hot tea—stop.

I try to remove myself from my own consciousness, place myself within the tendrils that breathe life into the world.

It's... so otherworldly, yet so intrinsically a part of everything around us.

"It... sparkles. It feels like tiny pricks of light. It... breathes, inhaling and exhaling. Growing and shrinking. It moves and feels, not like us but... I don't know how to describe it." I exhale, keeping my eyes shut, waiting to be scolded—told to dig deeper. My stomach is eating me alive and my fingers tremble where they touch the shaggy moss.

I smell the roasted meat and my eyes fling open. Fionn

dangles a rabbit leg just under my nose.

I barely hold myself back from tearing it from his hands with my teeth. I pluck it quickly from his grasp, lest he decide to take it away again, and tear into it.

He chuckles, saying, "Very good, Alyx. We will continue to train this way as we travel tomorrow. Practice that other sense you have."

A part of me appreciates the slight praise, glad to have done something right—glad to feel like I've made some modicum of progress at my one and only purpose. The other part of me wants to get back at him for treating me like a dog, wants to hate him for his methods.

We eat in silence for a long time, each of us weary and travel worn.

Aine comes to sit beside me and bumps my leg with hers, smiling shyly.

"Did you see the Merrow?" she whispers.

Beady black eyes stare back at me in my mind's eye.

"I did." I lick my fingers clean of rabbit grease, probably licking some dirt off with it.

"What was she like?" Aine's eyes are wide, leaning slightly closer. Armund watches with interest across the fire.

I can see her mother debating whether or not to tell her daughter to stop being nosy in my peripheral vision.

"She was terrible. Utterly wretched, and you would do well to keep far, far away from her."

Aine considers that for a moment before she says, "What do you think she does all day? All alone there."

I stop my finger-licking to consider her question.

Eating unsuspecting humans, taming the fish and frogs, plotting revenge against those who have wronged her. She had claimed I smelled like them. Smelled like him. I have no clue what she was referring to. Madness probably.

"I think she spends a lot of time... biding her time. I think she lies in wait for something. She said I smelled like him. So maybe she wants vengeance against someone for something. But then again, maybe she just blows bubbles at the newts and dreams about her next meal."

"What do you mean she said that you smell like him?" Armund asks, eyes wide.

"Did she tell you who?" Aine continues, ignoring him.

Nobody pretends to be doing anything but listening. Armund's reaction suggests that she didn't whisper anything to him.

"She said that... She said that I smelled of him. That she would torment me as she had been tormented. She called me a Soul-eater. A Kin-killer." Soul-eater she had called me. Only one being had that power, that we know of. A Fomorian. For what if I am... like them somehow? I think of the moment in the square. The dead Crow and his silver essence and my sick urge to feel it. If I don't know where my power came from how can I deny it?

Fionn reads the worry in my eyes.

"She could have just smelled them on you. From when they held you, dragged you through the square. From before... When they tried to—" A deep inhale. "Hurt you." He finishes. He meets my eyes and holds them in his gilded thrall. "I wouldn't be surprised to see the Fomorians seeking out other creatures to torment. To taste. Maybe she had a bad run-in with one of them." He sounds almost soft. Trying to calm me. It's a new look on him. It doesn't fit in with the image of him I have created. The one he has created.

Yes. Yes, they had been all over me, could probably be scented all over my skin. The thought is as disturbing as it is relieving.

I nod in thanks, accepting the explanation as truth.

"Good thing we never have to go back," Armund says, giving a reassuring smile. I'm sure he's just as glad of it as I am.

"Do you miss anyone? From your village, I mean. Did you have friends?" Aine goes on, as if the topic of the Merrow is over. Boring. Apparently, my miserable life is more interesting to her.

Do you miss anyone?

Such a simple question brings such depth of agony.

Yes.

Yes.

Yes.

The feeling of something being missing from me, like a missing lung, has torn me apart for years. Made a ghost of living flesh.

I miss having someone try to take care of me, even though I fought it. I miss my one friend who had given a shit, that I had lost due to my own self-imposed exile. I miss having herbs in the garden and being able to light a fire in the hearth. I miss fruit pies and a mother who would go to the ends of the realm for me. I miss having someone to rely on. I miss having someone. Miss having anyone. There was no one.

"I didn't have any friends. The only reason anyone would realize my absence is because we made such a scene in the square." What could a child know of loss?

"I doubt that's true. If I had a village, I would notice all of them. Everyone. I would notice you. Even if you didn't talk to me," she says, matter-of-fact. She seems to realize I'm being evasive and narrows her already slanted eyes. "You didn't have any parents? Any family?"

"No." My tone is hard, ending this topic of discussion. Nosy pre-teens.

Aine's lower lip compresses a little in disappointment when she reads the solid iron in my eyes. She looks away.

I look up and see Deri, warning blaring in his narrowed eyes. Tread carefully around his precious daughter, it says.

Got it. Don't be a cold, bitter bitch towards this soft-hearted girl.

What it must be like. To have a father who cares.

That small resentful voice, jealous of a twelve-year old—of a child who had lost everything before she ever even existed. I don't need more proof that I don't deserve to be her friend.

The crackling fire fills the night with pops and sizzles.

The silence of that extended hand lowering, withdrawing.

For some reason, I can't take the disappointment wafting from her. Even if I don't deserve to be her friend, she deserves kindness.

"Have you ever seen the sea?" I ask Aine.

She side-eyes me, still frowning, "Yes."

"Tomorrow will be the first time for me. But I love the water… I love the creek that flows beside my house." I flinch. Loved. I loved the creek. And that's not my house anymore.

She nods, still not looking at me fully.

My next words are a whisper, just for her, though I'm certain the rest of them can hear as well. "I'm sorry for snapping at you." I chip at the sharp edge of my middle fingernail. "Talking about my family hurts… I don't like doing it. So if we could just talk about something else…"

I can't look away as I wait—wait for her to dismiss me completely, as she should.

She looks over empathetically, before nodding emphatically. Such an endlessly forgiving heart kids have. I wonder when it goes. I wonder if I ever really had that.

"I'll show you the tide-pools. They're little pools in the boulders that dot the beaches, they have little creatures in them when the seas fall." She moves onto the next topic without hesitation.

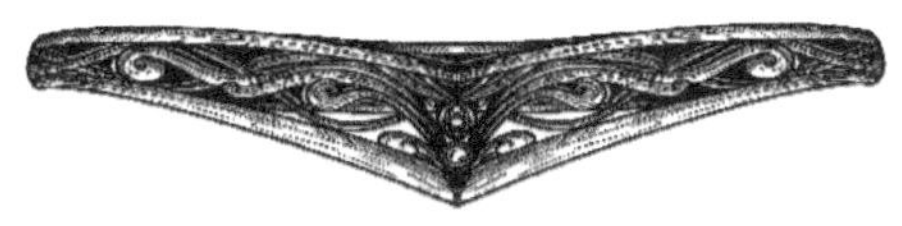

Chapter 15

As the forest meets the coastal cliffs, the trees grow taller and more powerful like their lover, the sea. The morning brings the same torturous training as the day prior, except now Fionn has added sprints. At least with the punishment, I get to practice something exciting with it. Mind reaching; this is what I call what I did with the moss the night before. The rest of the group walks to catch up to us between sets of sprinting. Fionn has me reaching for the plants, the trees, the squirrels in the trees.

My favorite are the trees, so mighty as they tower above us. So silent but thrumming with life. When I trail the tips of my fingers over the stringy red bark of a cedar tree it whispers to me its power in an ancient pulse. Its vibration is low, but rich and warm, so alive. I've had a vague feeling of this before when walking through woods, but I never realized before that trees have a soul. I've never felt it so deeply.

I assumed everyone else could feel the gentle hum of life too, so I never dwelt upon it.

There is so much that I've dismissed that now makes sense, and yet so much more that now doesn't.

As the days wear on, I've begun to realize that Diana was many things to me. And I was grateful for so many of them, but she was also a liar. She had come from another world, and she had kept it from me—kept from me the fact that I am something else entirely. How could she not have known? Could it be mere coincidence that we would meet and work together? That she would make working for her a part of the bargain for my father's life?

She had to have known. And chosen to keep me in the dark.

"Here I thought you were getting over these morose moods of yours," drawls Fionn, stepping out from behind a shadowed tree.

His words don't warrant a response from me. Closing my eyes, I resume reaching out my mind, far up into the canopy, reaching for those flitting sparks of energy in the birds that soar—

"How about we try something." His words tickle the back of my neck.

I keep my eyes closed against the torrent of gooseflesh that springs up along my body. "What do you want, Fionn?" I do my best to sound bored.

He circles me like prey. Lithe and feline in his steps. No doubt delighting in his new favorite pastime of torturing me.

"How about you reach out to me? You haven't been brave enough to try yet. It's been… disappointing me." His voice is smooth, low and reverberating in the damp forest air. His golden eyes twinkle even in the shadows.

"I didn't know if I could. If that would be… rude."

"Oh, it would be. More than rude, it would've been incredibly stupid. Which is why I thought you might try it."

"You are so charming, Fionn, I do wonder why you're single."

He stops right in front of me. I crane my head back to glare at him, gritting my teeth that I have to do so.

"Oh, I have no shortage of female attention, believe me. You would be surprised at how little care for the bounds of society you human women have when a handsome"—I snort—"young man throws them a little attention. It's almost like these human men lack any skill or care for the pleasure of their women. They are so easily charmed, so eager with a few soft touches, a few not-so-soft touches too." He smirks and reaches up to caress my glaring face with callused fingertips. "Do you find this to be true about the human men? Do you find yourself… unsatisfied often?"

I slap his hateful hand away and reach for him with my mind, eager to be done with this gross baiting. Not gently, but aiming to punch through his ego and dig my claws directly into his essence.

My mind slams into a brick wall and my whole body winces, jarred from the inside out.

My brain explodes in pain as Fionn attacks back. His whole being surrounds mine, plundering through energy and feeling. I can do nothing against it but try to keep my body from collapsing. I don't know what he is picking at, draining energy, pouring from the tankard of my body. The echoes of days gone by: numbness, despair, rage, desire, disappointment, jealousy.

It stops so suddenly my vision blurs and knees wobble. I hate that he baited me so easily.

"See now, Alyx, this is why it is foolish to pick a fight with someone much more powerful than you," he purrs. "This is another thing we will be working on from this moment until I am satisfied." My stomach rolls from fatigue.

"You will work on putting up a shield; it will stop others from draining you. It can be anything—picture whatever barrier you can—but make it strong. Make it an extension of yourself. Another limb that serves as a shield, with everything you are behind it. Your energy, your soul, your thoughts, your feelings. And keep it up, always. If I am to trust you to take care of yourself, you will have to master this. All of us do this. Well, aside from the mated ones occasionally, but only when they know it's safe."

"Why would they drop their shields with each other?" I ask, shaking off the lingering feeling of his being surrounding mine. Trying to place a shield around myself as he had described.

"Are you sure you're old enough for this conversation? What are you? Seventeen?" he laughs.

"Twenty," I say stubbornly, feeling like a child.

"Right. Twenty. Plenty old enough. Ancient, for a mortal. Well, let's just say there is some fun to be had when you can drop your shield with a mate. Much like dropping one's clothes, I imagine. You can… consume one another in a different way, I suppose. Very scandalous subject to be talking about in broad daylight, I'm afraid. Little ears are around." He winks.

My cheeks heat.

Girlish shrieks sound behind me. I look back to see Aine being carried over Konan's shoulder, upside down, his arm clamped down on the back of her knees. My eyes dart to Dealla and Deri but they only watch on in amusement, confident in their daughter's safety in the hands of Konan.

"What do you mean by mates? Is that just what Fae call their spouse?"

Fionn considers me for a moment. "No. You humans have quite fickle relationships in comparison with the Fae.

Mates are a far deeper, more intrinsic part of who we are. Some say the Mother chooses, some say that your soul does. But they are matched in every way. They wield better together, play better together, sleep better together, live and die together. Deri would tear himself limb from limb before he ever hurt Dealla. Her heart beats inside his chest. He feels what she feels. It is just a part of our culture, who we are. It is undeniable. It is more than a marriage."

"You seem to have a deep understanding of this." It's a question, but not.

"Wouldn't you like to know," Fionn whispers in my ear with a wink.

"You are truly insufferable. Do you know this, or do you think it's charming?"

He seems amused by the question as he considers it. As he settles on a response his expression falls into seriousness. "I'm trying to help you, you know."

"It feels like you take pleasure in hurting me. And helping me is just a front."

His face falls further as he takes in the seriousness of my expression. "This world is a dangerous place. It's miraculous you're even still alive. You wouldn't be if it weren't for your power's intervention. You need to become competent. Quickly. So yes, my methods are harsh. But you're learning. Quickly. That is what is important to me. Because what I do seems cruel, but it is nothing compared to what they'll do if they get their hands on you."

He's moved closer in his explanation, standing so close I can feel his warmth. He watches me closely.

Somehow the tone has shifted in our closeness. His assessing gaze no longer feels predatory, it feels concerned. It feels like he cares.

"I understand. But I want to learn, quickly. You don't

need to motivate me this way. I am motivated already. You think I'm unaware of the dangers? You think I haven't lived them every single day since the Crows came?" He doesn't respond, letting me continue. "So stop. Stop baiting me. Stop hurting me to prove a point. It doesn't help." I want to say more but I can't find the words.

His eyes run over my face, something in it causing him to smile slightly.

God, I wish his face wasn't so beautiful. Or I wish he wasn't so awful most of the time.

"Fine. But I won't take it easy on you," he says, pushing a bit of my hair behind my shoulder casually before turning and rejoining the rest of the Fianna.

As he walks away, the trail his fingers left along my neck when he pushed my hair back tingles.

Armund, who has been watching our interaction from a distance—pretending not to be, by tossing a stone between his hands—makes his way over to my side. His stride is sure and steady. He's healed remarkably fast.

"Hey. Fionn driven you completely mad yet?" he asks with a friendly smile.

"He's well on his way to it," I say, unwilling to discuss the conversation between Fionn and I. "How is your arm?" I gesture to it, still covered in my rudimentary dressings.

"Take a look for yourself." He holds it out for me.

The rest of them are walking ahead and I see Fionn look back at us, half expecting him to shout at me to start my sprints. I quickly undo Armund's dressings.

I'm astounded. I've never seen a wound that severe heal so quickly. There are thin scars, pink in their newness where the deep wounds used to be. "Armund, that is… incredible."

He shrugs. "What takes humans weeks only takes us days." He grasps my hand, his is so warm and soft, far larger than mine, and looks me deep in the eyes. I'm afraid of what he might find with those warm eyes, so sweet and thankful. "Thank you, Alyx. You saved my life, and almost lost yours in the process. I could never thank you enough. I owe you."

Warmth suffuses my chest. I wonder if this is why Diana chose to be a healer. I was always just the assistant. Perhaps it kept me from feeling this, the full impact of healing. This feeling, if fleeting and fickle, that my existence might not be a complete waste.

Flashes of Armund's face as I threatened to let him die appear before my eyes. How he can thank me after I did such a thing…

I squeeze his hand back and give him a wry grin. "You don't need to keep thanking me. Just… be my friend. I could use a friend. Debt settled."

He looks elated. Like I just told him he would live forever. "I would like that." His thumb runs over the back of my hand.

Fionn shouts back at us.

"You're going to have to start running any moment now. Enjoy Armund's flirting while you can!"

My face warms as I roll my eyes.

Armund scoffs, releasing his hold on my hand.

Why does he have to ruin everything?

"I—I'm not flirting. Fionn is delusional and believes the worst in everyone. He can't believe I would be kind to anyone without wanting to get my di—" He cuts his eyes to me and looks quickly away. "Without trying to flirt with you. But I think that is more reflective of him than me. Trust me. I've known Fionn for almost all of his seventy years." His sentence is hurried and his chiseled cheeks flush. He eyes me from the corner of his vision. Checking to see if I believe him.

"And he's always been this… unbearable?" That's the only word I can think of. That's how he feels. Along with other things.

Armund laughs. "I suppose so. Crossing the rift only… strengthened some of his less desirable attributes but… he's always used anger as a mask. Always embraced that over everything else. I think… I'm not entirely sure he can process other emotions very well. So it's all arrogance and rage, all the time. But he's a good leader despite it. He takes care of us, keeps us all moving forward. He listens to me when others don't." He gestures towards Konan.

"So he's the lesser of evils?"

"I suppose. Dealla and Elva would have been the better leaders, technically. But we did not trust Elva enough in the beginning. She wasn't one of us. And she brought us into this world… It was tense for a long while. And Dealla, well she had a mate, and she would never be impartial enough to lead us as a group. Same reason with Deri, as he is more powerful than all of us except his mate and Elva. After she got pregnant and had Aine, I thought Deri would drag her off to some cave somewhere, live out the rest of their days away from the rest of us who were constantly moving, putting them in danger. But Dealla's word always rules, and she wanted to stay with us. Konan and I are just…not fit. I am more of a historian, not a leader. Konan spent so many years away from people that he is barely social, what you see with Aine is pretty much the extent of it. He and Fionn bond over their penchant for violence. He and I tolerate each other. And that's the quick rundown." He gives me a charming grin.

I can't help but lift the corners of my lips a little at him. His eyes melt a little at the sight and I have to look away.

"Sprints start now!" Fionn is staring back at us, walking backward, face hard. I swear his eyes are simmering as he looks from me to Armund. I guess he doesn't like me getting too close to his friend. I hold back my smirk.

I lean over and give Armund a platonic kiss on the cheek before I take off in a sad jog, toes dragging across the ground.

"Faster!" Fionn barks.

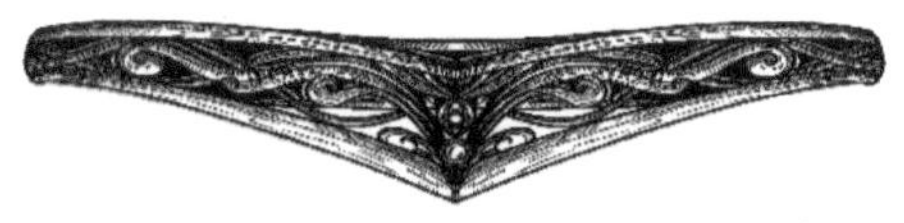

Chapter 16

Tristram, a bustling coastal city, seemingly grows from the rocky cliffs, shrouded in sea mist and clouds. The smell of shellfish entwines with brine of the raging sea as it blows through the streets. Fishermen wheel their carts up the ramps from the dock, shouting and cursing at their shipmates as they go. I've never seen a more brash collection of people. A testament to what happens when the noose around their necks is only slightly looser.

Few Crows pace the stone streets, the shadows of an omnipotent king across the land. A similar number of them as reside in Comraich, however this city dwarfs my small village. Despite the high taxes and exports of fish, stone, and salt, citizens of Tristram seem not to be worried about starving. There aren't beggars in the streets. People appear to be at healthy body conditions. Children seem happy and fed as they run, shrieking through the streets. Precious few in Suri have such freedoms.

The fishermen park their overflowing carts outside businesses, eyeing the Fianna as potential customers as we trudge through the stone streets, our boots splashing in brackish puddles. I'm the only one not feigning the slouch of my shoulders, the stiffness in my walk. The rest of them dutifully play the part of weary travelers.

Comraich had been like this before the Crows brought their blight onto our farmlands, the fruits from the trees rotting as they passed through. We knew only how to survive from there on out. Sometimes I think that's all there is, survival. Who can play this game the longest? I see no proof to the contrary.

The Crows still patrol Tristram's streets, stalking along alleyways and perched near the busy intersections of main streets. I keep my eyes on the ground in front of my boots, certain that the missive with my description made its way here days ago. I'm a wanted woman. I almost snort at the idea of it all. My life is unrecognizable from a week ago.

The city has an artist's soul trapped between two wild forces: shadows and monsters of the forest of Wynedd, and the Great Salt Sea bashing against the edge of the continent. The sea must whisper stories to the people who dwell near her; it's in every mosaic of shell and seaglass that lives along the walls of buildings, every twinkle of wind-chimes, every driftwood statue.

We rent four rooms from an inn above a tavern. Shivers run down my spine when I behold a siren carved from a pale drift-log draped over the front stoop: a more beautiful sister to the monster of the bog.

Aine and her family stay together in one room, Elva and I are in another, and the men draw sticks for who gets the remaining one to themselves. Appearances must be upheld, so we purchased the extra to give the impression of married couples traveling together with an extra male.

Elva is draped in exotic clothing of the continent to the

west. Her rich skin tone is uncommon here in Suri. The vibrant orange headscarf and cotton dress is a drastic change from the black leather and hood that allows her to melt into shadows. My eyes had grown wide at the sight of her flowing into the group from off the trail this morning, having donned her new clothes.

I spend the day hiding in our room, uncaring what the rest of them are up to. Staring at the ceiling, hearing the moaning of the building around me, not daring to mind-reach towards the denizens below. I need space from Fionn and his relentless training.

Elva had closed the blinds, inspected any cracks in the wood, seemed satisfied, and then disappeared. We aren't close enough for me to ask what she's doing or if I can come with her. So I just pretended to sleep until she left.

If I close my eyes for long enough, I can pretend I'm in a miserable shack on the outside of Comraich.

Armund pokes his head in once the light from between the curtains has faded to a dim gray. He bids me to come eat dinner with the group. "Fionn's wife should be present for dinner. We have a narrative to uphold," he cites as his reason with a slight smile. I sigh deeply and rise from my place on the bed.

The dimly lit tavern is filled with bellowing laughter and sloshing drinks. My steps stick slightly to the wooden floor. The air smells of stale alcohol and stew. I keep my eyes on the ground as I approach the table with Fionn, Konan, and Elva already present. Unsurprisingly, the trio decides to stay away from this pit.

My teeth grit as I begrudgingly sit, straight-backed, beside Fionn. Judging by the slumped posture and annoying chuckling, he's already drunk. Konan with him, judging by his crazed laughter and six empties on his side of the table.

They must have spent the entire afternoon here, letting loose in a strange place with strange people while we are all being hunted by the king's lackeys.

Idiots.

My back collapses somewhat as Fionn slings his arm over my shoulders, pressing me against him from shoulder to knee, warming my chilled bones.

"There's my beautiful wife. You look ravishing, darling." The ale-drenched scent of his breath curls against my ear as I lean my face away from his. "You could try harder to blow our cover," he whispers in my ear, no more than a drunk, handsy husband trying and failing to seduce his wife who is tired of finding him falling-down drunk in taverns.

I turn my face to his, forcing a meek smile to my face and looking into his surprisingly clear eyes, eyelids slouched to appear inebriated.

I feel every inch of contact in that gaze. Every space where the warmth of him presses against my chilled skin, separated only by pieces of fabric.

I look away.

I make myself settle into Fionn's side.

I pick up the spoon. The soup is some sort of fish in a broth with coarsely chopped root vegetables. The taste is bland, but it warms me all the way down, from the inside out. I eat more, drowning out the sound of Fionn telling some fantastic tale of a hero waltzing to a fiery death, Konan and the men at surrounding tables are his rapt audience.

"Nobody could have known that all the tales were real. That something far more sinister lurked under the Mounds of Dun. Something with a horde to protect and no fear of man." I could have sworn the noise in the room settled on that note. A charge goes through the crowd.

Those grass-covered mounds, north of the bog, in northeastern Suri. They roll all the way to the sea cliffs of the north, each one larger than any castle of this country. Holding all manner of creatures and inviting bad luck to any that near them. Some say that the entrance to Hell lay there, under the mounds.

Given Fionn's mention of them, I know where the lore comes from.

"MacCumhail cared not for the warnings, nor the scent of fear that wafted from lesser warriors." Fionn basks in the attention of revellers beside me, letting them watch with bated breath. I'm certain he's making it all up. "He drew his sword, Mac un Luin, determined he would slay the beast that tormented Dun. Alone, but for his great storm shield and blade as mighty as the waves of the Great Salt Sea, MacCumhail found a crack in the worlds. Saw the home of his mighty opponent. Saw the smoke of endless flame slither through the sky, mountains spitting flame in the distance. Nothing could have prepared him for the creature who made such a place its home. Scales, black as night, slithering against stone. Wings, casting shadows bigger than whole towns. He saw how it clawed over its rocky home, talons on all four legs larger than MacCumhail himself. How it bathed in the rivers of fire and the charred corpses of other beasts, predators in their own right, that dared stumble fearlessly into its path."

Dragon.

The whispers proclaim it. The sigil of the Dragon King has always been thought to be an exaggerated tale. A once-great king who ruled Ashvynd upon the back of a great red dragon.

Flashes of a dream from a lifetime ago appear in my mind's eye. From that Deathless death. *A river of fire, black iridescent scales against a smoke-filled sky.*

The tavern has grown quiet, and suddenly I find Fionn more interesting than my half-finished stew.

Fionn looks over at me before he goes on. The molten gold of his eyes melts through me, holding me.

"He knew he must bring this creature out of its lair. Draw it towards the surface. Bring it to the rift in the worlds. So he did exactly that." Fionn finally looks back at the room. The absence of his gaze leaves me cold in a new way, despite the heat from his body pressed against the side of mine.

"The beast scented the warrior quickly. Snapped its head towards him, and despite years of war under his belt, he knew he had never raised his blade to an opponent such as this. Never met someone who matched his lethality in such a way. Perhaps surpassed it. Some say his self-confidence even wavered for a moment." Fionn smirks.

"MacCumhail barely made it beyond the rift, could smell the burning of the cloak at his back as he scrambled through the stone of the world. Could hear the wing beats like the earth itself had rumbled until he heard the talons scrape against shale as it clambered after him. He barely made it through. Barely threw himself to the side just as a violet flame seared the place he had just stood. Its roar could have ended worlds. They met in a flash of wits and their own sharp blades. For this beast, it was smarter than most men, its sinister thoughts were present in every attack, every malicious swipe of its claw. Toying with him, he realized. Playing with its prey. Letting him give it all he had before it finally ended their dance."

Fionn almost looks green. Like he's remembering something he can hardly bear.

It could pass for alcohol dizziness if I didn't know his look so well.

He takes a restorative breath, pastes that smirk to his face, and continues, "But MacCumhail was not legendary for nothing. He had crossed worlds, fought winless wars and spent every day of his life with purpose. One purpose. To find his way back. To return to his home the hero that his people needed. To be the male that would defeat enemies so large they crowded out all hope with their shadows. He knew that if he could not defeat this adversary, he was worthless to his people, to the ones that needed it most. So he drew up his own power, his last stand, a hand he kept secret until he had no other choice. Unleashing the might of his power, he pinned the mighty beast to the earth, drew Mac an Luin, and sliced straight through that violet eye, right to the hilt. Slaying it where it lay, its shrieks ringing through the world, declaring him ready. Declaring him the warrior he needed to be."

Roars of triumph echo through the tavern. The loudest by Konan, who has not sobered any through the tale. Thumping tankards on the wood tables, they cheer for MacCumhail's victory. His bravery and grit. Even I can't help a small upturn of one side of my mouth as I gaze upon him. As he looks back at me, there is something somber in his eyes. They lack his usual swaggering arrogance, malice, or spite.

It feels as though he told the story for me.

Never one to allow a good moment to linger, he reaches over to my half-eaten bowl of stew and proceeds to finish it while the patrons ply him with more ale. He accepts, downing it to the sounds of fists pounding on tables. The Fianna, Konan aside, are all watching with begrudging smiles and shaking heads.

I haven't seen such life in a room in many years. Even Rhodri's tavern, murky in my memory, never was as lively as this, even before the Crows moved in. Maybe these people of the sea have her spirit—have her roaring, forceful presence, untamed by fear or oppressor.

The thought makes me wish to feel it. The brined air on my face, wisps of sea-spray in my hair.

Maybe I can find just a shred of it too.

I get up from the table, mostly unnoticed. Only Elva marks me with a nod of her head and a pointed look, telling me to stay close.

The air outside is exactly as I hoped it would be. It smells of salt, and kelp, sand and stone washed with watery fury. I walk alone, searching for that elusive feeling. That thing that coils away from my grasping hands.

I keep going, even as I hear footsteps behind me.

I keep going even as he drapes a familiarly heavy arm over my shoulders once again.

"Cannot let my wife walk down the streets alone, can I?" Fionn says from beside me.

"No, but Fionn could let Alyx walk alone," I snip back, though there is no ice behind the words. "Already tired of drunken re-tellings of your glory days?"

Fionn chuckles. "I wish I could get drunk on your human piss-ale. It's probably the thing I miss most, good alcohol."

I huff a laugh. "So you just act drunk for fun? Or did you have an agenda?"

"Of a sort, but what gave me away?" Playfully narrowed golden eyes trace my face. "I didn't even give my first name."

"Something about the way you talked the hero up, it gave you away. You could only think that highly of yourself."

Fionn laughs heartily. "You read me so well."

"So… you really did fight something that looked like that? You really killed it?"

The scuff of our boots on stone mingle on the wind under the drone of the crashing waves.

"Yes. I did fight it." Our steps pause. I look up at him. He's already staring back. "But I don't know if I killed it. It fled, my sword with it, still stuck in its eye. If I had to guess, it's still there. Under the mounds."

A chill sweeps over my whole body.

"Don't look so afraid," he says softly, brushing a lock of sea-swept hair behind my ear.

I can't tell if it's the whooshing in my own head, or the sound of the waves crashing, but it creates a white noise that drowns out all distractions. Our faces are indecently close.

Fionn has always been attractive. But the moonlight washes over him and suddenly it feels like there's a tide pulling me to him. After our conversation yesterday, he doesn't feel so much like a monster, but like a man with a purpose. What I had once thought was malice, was actually fear: fear for the Fianna, fear for me.

It's as if he grasped at everything I am and holds it still for him to look at.

Golden eyes run all over my face, catching on my mouth. My lips part.

He walks me back until my back hits the wall of a building, crowding me against the stone. I'm swept away, floating in the sea. Under the might of his body and power.

"You look beautiful like this," he breathes. "You look beautiful always. You're strong. You're fierce. And spiteful. And challenging. I'm tired of you looking at Armund like he will save you from me. I'm not one to pretend I don't want something. I want you."

I only have time to pull in one swift breath, one of shock and relief. Relief that, at least in this feeling, I'm not alone.

His lips are on mine.

On mine. Consuming me.

I had been dead before. Recently. My body a cage to a ghost. Floating in a sea of numb and choice-less apathy.

But his lips on mine make me burn.

Burn with want and feeling.

Pressing all of me against all of him. Trapped between the stone wall and every hard line of his body.

Every stubborn, arrogant, infuriatingly handsome, hot line of him.

I breathe him in.

Smoke. Inebriating me. Setting me ablaze and adrift.

My hands dive into his golden curls, so soft and silky beneath my fingers.

I feel the lightly pointed tips of his ears beneath my palms and feel him shiver.

The warmth from his hands spans my waist as they roam desperately, down over my behind, back up and along the sides of my ribs and breasts.

I live and die in this kiss.

I find life in his breaths, the feeling of his chest panting against mine.

The burn spreads, spreads, spreads.

Making me lift my leg and hitch it around his hip. He pushes me more firmly against the wall, groaning, pressing his hardness where I desperately need him.

And then it's gone, gone, gone.

His lips tear from mine and he drops my leg with a snarl. Jolting me from that place where I am passion and wildfire. Leaving me in free-fall.

Opening my eyes in confusion, I see the broad expanse of his back, caging me in against the wall. Breaths tear from him in big heaving movements.

"Just thought we would come check on you. Didn't

realize what we would be interrupting. Sorry, brother," Konan's voice is a smirk-laced grumble. Peeking around Fionn, I see the rest of the Fianna.

Fionn heaves a sigh, visibly pulling himself together.

My face is the only thing on fire now. How it must look for the weak human to be seen with Fionn, leader of the Fianna and immortal asshole. How foolish I am to allow such a thing to jeopardize my place here, to make me look like some preening harlot, willing to do anything for protection.

Shoving Fionn's arm out of the way, I come out from behind him.

"I'm going to bed." My voice is as wobbly as my knees. I hate it.

I run like a coward.

Elva watches Fionn with pressed lips. Konan fights a laugh as he meets my eyes. And Armund… disgust and betrayal lines his face.

My eyes drop, guilt blooming in my chest. Placeless shame, for what right does he have to feel betrayed? We are friends.

I can't bear to look back at Fionn and see what's left after we crossed that line. So I keep my eyes forward and my pace slow back into the inn. I can feel, more than hear, Elva following in my steps.

Elva forces me to take the bed for the night, stating she will be taking the first watch tonight, and will hardly be sleeping anyways.

As I lie in this straw bed, only one thought drags me the rest of the way back into that gray room of numbness.

I've never slept in a bed before.

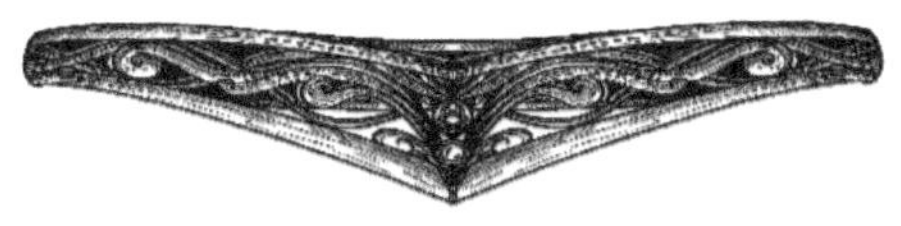

Chapter 17

The next day passes in pointed silences. Fionn seems as content as I to ignore what happened. It confirms my suspicions that Fionn was picking the low-hanging fruit. He wouldn't be the first man to say what a woman wants to hear to get what he wants. What could someone like him possibly want with someone like me? He could find a more beautiful woman in any town in Suri. Not to mention my droll and depressing personality. How did he go from that to *I want you*?

It's irreconcilable.

So I put one foot in front of the other as we walk through the bustling streets of Tristram. I pretend that I was the one picking the low-hanging fruit. I have nothing to be ashamed of, I was just a person seeking some human touch. *You're fierce. And spiteful. And challenging.* Echoes of his beautiful lies reverberate in my ears. They felt so sweet when they brushed over my cheeks, yet so bitter as they ring in my memory. I keep my face forward and pretend that I'm not drowning in self-hatred and embarrassment.

Now, as the sun is dipping below the horizon somewhere far beyond the clouds and seas, I sit in the sand above the lowering tide, where the sand is soft and dry. My bare feet burrow under it, marvelling at its softness. The grains run through my fingers like the days I spent too sad to remember. The only proof of its existence is the grit on my skin, on my soul.

The rest of the group pairs off, aside from Elva, who disappears giving no explanation. Konan and Aine are splashing in the tide pools. Deri and Dealla are off doing…whatever mated couples do best, I presume. Armund and Fionn have wandered into the woods, jostling and laughing with one another, brothers in all but name. I guess Fionn's crimes are easily forgiven, more palatable when they come from one with so much charm and influence. He is forgivable, but Armund wouldn't even look at me today.

As the waves break over and kiss the sand, earth in its finest form and water at its wildest, I feel small. So infinitesimal that nothing matters. I don't matter. My life is a waste, and every breath in my lungs is too. No wonder god is so apathetic towards our suffering, if he too can see the might of his creation in every wave and gusting wind, every wildfire and towering oak. I am beginning to understand how he could think so little of me as I reach for the great trees and feel their ancient hum of life. I would care more for them too. They are not petty or spiteful. They do not kill mercilessly nor take for the sake of taking. They don't get stuck on a beach, immovable in their sadness. They don't—

Flickers of movement flash in the corner of my eye.

I barely have enough time to spy the shrouded group of people as they make their way single-file along the beach. Someone grabs me under the armpits and drags me backwards into the trees. A hand is slammed over my mouth.

My feet peddle wildly underneath me, trying to gain solid ground. I fly around the second I am released within the cover of the tree line, meeting the warning glare of Fionn. Armund is beside him.

Fionn presses his fingers to his lips.

His proximity disarms me for a second, flashes of shared breaths and want play in my mind. From the way his eyes flicker to my parted mouth, he remembers it too. I shuffle over to Armund, warmth emanating from where our shoulders brush, and peer through the spaces between the leaves, begging myself to become shadow, as Elva does.

Where are the others? I whip around to ask Fionn, but he just shakes his head. Armund places a hand on my shoulder, to soothe my still-wild breathing. Fionn marks it. I look away.

The group of strangers is picking their way along the rocks. They move with a human clumsiness, garbed in all black.

My curiosity becomes an extension of me, a limb on the wind.

I find myself reaching for one of them.

It feels like slipping into a haze of malice, oil running over my skin as I pass through the aura of him. This night-shrouded man. I feel the core of him, the hum of his vile existence.

Adrenaline and excitement still thrum in my veins, in time with my heartbeat.

Shivers run up my spine in a slick, oily anticipation.

Vile hunger saps at my energy, feeling like a pot over-boiling—

It's like falling in a dream and jerking awake.

Finding myself back in my own body, but feeling the remnants of that other soul still coating my skin, in my chest...

Armund is lightly shaking my shoulders, warm brown eyes running over my face in concern, whispering my name. I must have been looking at him for some time, but I only now begin to see him—

I sigh in relief, at being away from that man; his soul makes me want to retch. His existence feels like a stain on everything. How I slipped straight into his mind without trying much is concerning.

Armund looks relieved too as he runs his hand over the back of my head, stroking my hair. It feels nice. His eyes flicker over my shoulder. I can hear the group walking quietly right in front of where we hide in the shadows.

He tenses, and I follow his gaze.

The strange group has stopped, looking at the sand. My footprints. The place where I sat and dragged my feet all the way into the tree line. Their gazes track it all the way to where we stand in the dark.

They can't see us. I know they can't. But they are looking right at us, and the man whose energy I just felt is smiling, eyes alight with excitement. His face is ordinary, just like any other man I would pass in town, but he is a monster, and I don't need to know exactly what he was thinking about to know that.

We cannot move, the ground is too covered in twigs, rocks, and brush that makes sound.

Fionn seems to know something I don't, as he takes a step forward into the light, casual and unhurried.

Armund hesitates, but takes a step forward with him, hand extended back at me telling me to stay.

Fionn's voice is full of bravado as he says, "What do we have here? A group of snivelling marauders I would bet, judging by the reek of you."

The sneer on the monster's face does not waver as he sees Armund come to stand shoulder-to-shoulder with Fionn. The two Fae are still outnumbered by eight.

"Feeling brave?" the monster asks. "Looks to me like you should keep your heads down and pray to god we are merciful."

"You aren't merciful," Fionn states blandly. "Something tells me you make a habit of destroying family homes for fun. Killing children for sport. All in the name of your Dragon King."

The monster chuckles. "You Surins are so self-righteous. So it's okay to let the children die in the streets of Raith, when there is plenty of food for the Pretty King and the wealthy, but you draw the line at us ending them now. Action versus inaction, the ends are the same. I find it more virtuous to stop the scourge on the land now, while they're young. Those little shits would grow up to be the Pretty King's army, would see my own home burn."

"How very selfless of you. A true patriot," Armund sneers.

"If anyone's a scourge on the land it's you. Maybe I'll exercise the same mentality. I could use a good bonfire on the beach." Fionn unsheathes the knife at his side as he says it, surely running it over the palm of his other hand as he always does.

"Where's the little woman you have with you?" another raider asks, clearly impatient. I can see the gleam in his eyes from back in the shadows, hopeful for more spoils.

"Woman?" Armund asks, cocking his head to the side. The lie is so convincing, I would believe him if I didn't know.

The man gestures to the sand between them. "You didn't make an imprint that small. Are you trying to keep her to yourselves?" His eyes somehow become more wicked in the silence. "We don't blame you for sharing her. We share too, sometimes."

Fionn chuckles, the sound wrathful. "You just keep making this better. This is my favorite game."

The raiders chuckle with him, feeling comfortable in the majority.

The laughs break off with a flash of motion. One moment Fionn is there, the next he's gone.

Armund pulls his own knife and attacks the one monster, who has escaped the doom that awaits his comrades.

A whirlwind of sand, rising from the ground by a phantom wind, surrounds and obscures. The wrath of its master makes it thrash and slice through the marauders as they panic, shrieks of surprise and agony tearing from their throats. Flashes of Fionn's blade, his lithe powerful body, peek through. Blood paints the sand beneath their feet the darkest of maroon as their screams paint the air around us.

Armund is more evenly matched with the marauder he has taken on. The two grapple, knives flashing between them as they both twist and contort to dodge attacks, teeth bared. Armund uses no power. He is half a head taller than the man he fights, and seems to be far faster and more graceful, but the monster has quite a bit of strength and weight on him and seemingly more experience fighting.

I'm not a fighter.

His first words to me.

They send a shiver of fear down my spine, and I take a step towards them.

I fight within myself, tearing through everything in my body, searching for a kernel of power. The pathway to that thing inside me that turns Crows to icy bits of flesh and bone. I grasp at something within me, but it is like grasping at sunlight. Feeling its warmth but not able to hold it. I push at it, make it tangible in my muscles, the feeling in my fingers. I breathe through it, willing it to obey, to suffuse my marrow with power.

Something surges, like a breaking of some barrier.

I am it and nothing.

All within myself, this body.

I am a raging force with a singular purpose.

To eradicate this thing. This monster who takes and takes. Who plays god with any shred of power he finds himself wielding.

Armund is thrown from the monster, propelled by some merciful force away from the destruction I wreak.

The oil of his soul, his very existence is within my fingertips as I destroy it. It freezes and screams as I crush it with everything I have.

The power ebbs and eddies in my veins, but I cannot stop it. It just drains and drains.

I see people running towards us with inhuman speed—allies.

My vision blurs but I have a singular focus on that thing now lying in the sand, its grip on my subconscious is unyielding.

Somewhere in the haze, I process that the monster is dead. They're all dead. The monster is nothing but shards of frozen flesh chilling the ground beneath it. It is nothing now. Anything remaining has left, abandoning the flesh that held it. It is nothing.

"Easy. You're good. Armund is good." A honeyed voice says in my ear.

The power is searching, fury and fear holding its reins. Everything is so far away. I am so far away.

"Come on Alyx, just let it go. Let it go." That voice.

Somewhere, in a different plane, I can feel that warmth surrounding me, holding me.

Somewhere so close, I could swear it was right next to me, I can feel something soft press against my pulse. Something softly rocks me back and forth and I tear my eyes away from the destruction I created.

I jerk back into my body and turn my head, making Fionn move his face from my neck.

He surrounds me, holding me in his arms from behind, arms pinned to my sides, soothingly rocking me back and forth. Both a restraint and a comfort. My breaths are coming out in huge bellowing pants.

I am raw. Every nerve exposed. My arms are so heavy I could not tear myself from his arms if I tried.

"You're fine. Keep breathing."

I do. I still feel adrift, but I can feel my toes and hands again, can feel his heat at my back.

My voice is a rasp as I say, "That was an interesting trick you did out there."

He barks a laugh. "Right back at you, frosty. I've uh… I've never seen someone do such a thing. Creative."

The comment sends me back into that dark place, far away.

"I didn't mean to."

"I know," he says gently.

"I was scared."

"I know."

"I hated it." Am I a monster too?

"I know. It'll get better."

"I don't want to do this anymore." Overgrown herb gardens, scraggly and unkempt. Falling asleep on cold flooring. Flame-less hearths. Nameless hurt.

"You'll learn to control it. It only feels like this for now.

We will help you." His voice is smooth and gentle for once. He squeezes me a little tighter.

I stay silent at that.

He doesn't understand.

Armund's voice is the thing that makes me tear my eyes from Fionn's.

"Alyx, you didn't have to do that. I was fine." Resentment twists his face as he pushes into the tree line, the rest of the Fianna with him.

Konan scoffs. "From where we were standing it looked like the girl saved your hide."

Armund turns to fully face Konan, scowling. "And where were you? You were just going to leave us to our fate, then? What good is a half-feral brute from the Scar if he doesn't come to be the muscle when he's needed?"

The words find their mark.

Konan moves to tower over Armund, who, to his credit, does not cower, "And what good is an idiot scholar who cannot wield his brain nor a blade to get us off this goddess-forsaken realm? Fionn took on nine men to your one. One human, who was too much for you to handle on your own. What a waste of resources you are, Armund. If you were born in the Scar we would have dropped you directly into the Wastes."

"Stop it. Both of you." Fionn's command rumbles against my back. The two males quiet but make no move away from one another. He addresses the others, "The rest of you did good. We were fine, thanks to Alyx. We didn't need anyone else getting in the crossfire. Staying back and waiting was the right call."

The rest of the group is watching wearily, Aine tucked behind Deri and Dealla, looking between the two quarreling males with disappointment and apprehension. Elva is watching only me, as if I'm a riddle to solve.

Her stare reminds me of my position in Fionn's lap and forces me to slide off of it. Limbs the weight of boulders barely hold me up. Fionn keeps an arm around my waist, steadying me. I clamber to my feet.

"So the raiders aren't a lie?" I ask, wrestling my face into neutrality against the black splotches floating through my vision.

Fionn replies, "No, though the Pretty King certainly does nothing to stop it."

"Well that's…" I stop myself from saying 'good.' Good that not every single thing in my world is a lie. "Better than the alternative, I suppose."

Elva chimes in, "We run into them on occasion. The ones with enough hatred in their hearts to venture all the way here are usually vile creatures."

Nausea churns my stomach as I say, "I know, that one in front was horrible." I close my eyes against the memory.

"You reached for him?" Dealla asks.

I nod.

Concern flares in Dealla's eyes, but it's Elva that addresses me.

"You need to be careful with that. Some beings here do not take kindly to lurkers. Most humans don't know. But there are others here." Other than human.

"I know." I shoot Fionn a narrowed glare at the reminder of his lesson on this issue the other day. "I just… I was clueless, and they couldn't tell me who those men were. So I… looked."

Silence follows my excuse for a beat. Fionn breaks it.

"It's impressive. That you can do such a thing so soon. That you can discern what you're seeing, target someone already. You're doing well. But I think you've had enough for today. We need to deal with the bodies and find a new spot to rest for the night."

I try not to care that Fionn is coddling me. That he normally would have been my harshest corrector. Would have normally taught me a hard-learned lesson. Perhaps I look as fragile as I feel.

I don't care that it's impressive. I don't want this. But we rarely get what we want

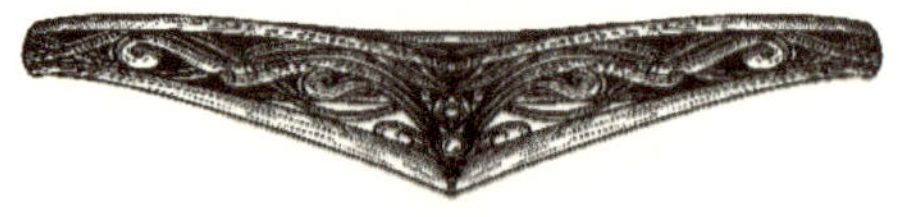

Chapter 18

"Your hair is turning white," Fionn's teases.

Treating me as though I was fragile had lasted all of one night.

"I may be aging faster. You do bring me closer to death with every asinine task you assign," I respond, grinding my teeth in concentration.

The white-petaled flower, barely the length of one finger, flutters delicately in the sea breeze.

I want to crush the damned thing in my fist.

Fine trickles of power live deep inside it, running up its stem and webbing through its petals. They're so small I can barely sense them. They flow and surge, the tiniest of flames. But I can't grasp them; it's like trying to grab onto the air.

"I'm not joking. Your roots are coming in white." His breath rustles the hair on top of my head. He picks up a strand and tickles my cheek with it. "Or maybe extremely light blonde."

I try to smack away his hand, but he just yanks on the strand.

I can feel the warmth of his body, his chest, brushing

against my shoulder. I refocus on that trickle of power and try to touch it in my mind. Coax it to follow me.

Like a moth to a flame, I feel my shoulder lean slightly against his chest. His face leans into the side of mine, where I steadfastly furrow my brow and try to pull the power into me.

"Isn't it so frustrating?" he asks, his breath sweet like the berries he was eating earlier. "Don't you just want to hit me right now?"

I do.

Desperately.

But I close my eyes and block out everything else. The sounds of the others making camp a few paces away. Fionn's antagonizing presence at my side.

I try again.

"You know, I like blondes. They've always been a favorite of mine. If your hair does keep growing in this color, maybe you'll have a chance at sharing a room with me next time we stop at an inn."

I hit him. Just once, in the stomach. Just to get him to stop.

All the force in my body goes into it. Somehow, he braces his abdominals and absorbs it completely, and the force shoots back up my wrist and shoulder. I grimace and shake out my arm.

For a second I think the shock has stunned him into silence, miraculously.

But when I look up at him, he's staring at the ground, at my feet.

Frost covers the grass, creating a circle around us as wide as I am tall. The blades are brown and dead, husks clinging to the ground, and when I look back at the flower, it is the same. The light extinguished.

It reminds me of the first year my father was too weak to tend the farm. How I would spend entire mornings tending to crops only to come back and find them shrivelled and dying the next morning. No matter how diligently I tended to them, how carefully I followed my father's directions, they always ended in that same state. Now I know it was me. Not just my terrible farming abilities, but my very being, actually sucking the life from them.

"You hold onto that anger. That's how you can wield," Fionn says. "However, I think I'll stop making myself the bait before I end up like that flower. Or living in a block of ice."

He's smirking now, golden triumph.

I gingerly step outside the circle, disconcerted at the destruction I caused.

"I don't see you killing every living thing around you when you channel your power," I murmur, kicking the deadened ground. I already know it's me. I do this. Death follows me.

He cocks his head at me, the movement lupine. "You're just taking energy from where it exists around you. Plant and animal life is easiest, hence the flower. When you get better, like me"—he smiles and points to himself, not a shred of humility—"you'll stop being a power leech and choose to use other sources. But seeing as you couldn't even pull from a flower, I'm not going to have you move onto more slippery forms of energy."

Elva walks into the conversation, face blank as ever, addressing me, "And if you're not careful, you'll turn out like the grass." She stares pointedly at the graveyard of brown blades. "Be glad your luck did not run out before we found you, otherwise you would have found your death beside those Crows. Sometimes your power will isolate.

Instead of reaching for other energy, it will drain your own. That's why you feel so drained after those episodes. You also don't eat enough, and you don't rest enough. You need to change that. We have plenty of available food between the rations we buy and the food on the land. Putting muscle on should be one of your top priorities. Muscle will store extra energy; physical strength will help with your power stores." She hesitates for a moment as she looks me up and down. "You're skin and bone. I don't know how long you were starving or why, but you're done with it."

My cheeks flush at her bluntness.

I'm aware of how I look. The sharpness to my cheekbones, how my ribs protrude and my stomach caves. I didn't mean to get this way. There were just too many days when I could not get off the floor—when Diana's stew tasted like I didn't deserve it—the kindness and concern. Some days, I still feel that way.

"I'll eat more," I say, shrugging off the concern. Anything to stop them from looking at me like that.

"Good," Elva says, with firm approval.

I meet Fionn's burning gaze.

I look away. The three of us start walking back to the rest of the group.

"So why does my power always come out as ice?" I ask, attempting to distract them from thinking too deeply about my past.

Fionn responds, "I'm not sure. I've rarely seen this. Most Danaans have an aptitude for one or two elements. They may be able to do some basic manipulation of others, but they have a clear preference for one. Usually, that preference is evident from the beginning of ability. It seems like yours is water, though it is strange for it to come out so violently and so… particularly, with ice." We come to stand amongst the others near the beginnings of a fire that Dealla is still adding to, building and coercing the licking flames.

"Are there any who can manipulate all things equally well?" I ask, staring into the fire.

Silence follows for a moment. One tinged with grief for those lost.

Deri, surprisingly, is the one to break it. "Very few. I only know of our Queen and her son. Even her mate couldn't wield as well as her. Though Elva's people did not seem to be afflicted with the same limitations."

"My people were from a different world, and wield many things differently than even your cousin, Deri," Elva responds vaguely.

"Your cousin?" I ask.

"My mother was the Queen's sister. The prince, you would say, is my cousin, Erron," Deri says as he strokes his daughter's raven hair. She stares up at him with unadulterated admiration.

"So you're… Fae royalty," I say in awe.

Everyone chuckles slightly at that.

Deri slightly rolls his eyes. "We do not view royals in the terms of humans. Queen Maica is queen not just because of her power, but because she has earned the hearts of the Danaans and the heart of the very earth we tread. Erron succeeding her is—was—not a sure thing. Even with him being an only child. He would need to prove himself fair and just, would need to earn the approval of Danu herself… I have no doubt he would have." Deri looks away, gritting his teeth. "He was the best of her and his father. He was my best friend." A hard swallow. Dealla leaves the fire, and drapes herself around her mate, running her thin fingers through his raven hair. It gives him strength to finish his thought. "I was no more royalty than Konan of the Scar over there. I had to earn my place like everyone else."

"So did… did any of them get out? The Queen?" I ask hesitantly.

Tension reigns.

Fionn speaks next, "We have looked for evidence everywhere for them here. There was…" He shifts restlessly. "Right before we left there was a mighty wave of power; at first, I thought it was Danu herself, raging against the atrocities that were taking place. Elva said it was a tear forming somewhere. But if someone left, they did not come here. And if it was more of the parasites coming… There are surely none of our people left."

My mom used to say the world rages. That Suri would make us feel her anguish, her loss. She would say that the seasons turn more punishing with each year as we grow more disconnected as a people, as we take and burn and destroy our world with no regard for the blessings given to us. We would watch through the glass windowpane, dappled with violent rains, as wind whipped through the Wynedd forest, branches tearing from their mother tree, as the torrents wash the sins of man to the sea in great violent currents. At some point my young mind would grow bored of watching. I would turn away from the window and walk away from her side, so certain we would see it again, so certain I would hear more of her stories of how things used to be, so certain I would feel the warmth of her at my back again. One day I left the window, and we never stood there together again. I used to think that the windowpane missed the two of us looking through it too.

It's all I can think of as I plop my weather-worn body onto the hard bench in the ill-lit tavern somewhere along the southwestern coast of Suri. My cloak is sopping wet against my body. Rainwater from the midsummer storm drips along the bridge of my nose, from the long ends of my hair, off my pruned fingertips. The storm raging against the coastline drove us indoors, along with everyone else. We sit huddled together at the table, a matching group of rain-soaked travelers seated across from us, warming themselves over tankards of ale and bowls of soup.

Days have passed since Fionn told me to hold onto my anger to help channel my power. As we pick our way across the coastline, my days are ravaged with practice of drawing out power and reaching with the limbs of my mind. I become a psychic hand, reaching to touch and understand the world around me. I think of all the things that make my hands shake and teeth grit. Through my efforts, I can now grasp and hold, coax and move forms of energy from sources such as flowers and plants. It hurts to watch them whither under my influence, so I move quickly on to trees and heartier sources. Dispelling and manipulating the energy is a harder feat.

I keep to myself and try not to look at Fionn. At his broad shoulders and arrogance. His callused hands as they run a finger over his favored blades. His soft-looking curls against the tan skin of his forehead. I try not to notice the way the muscles in his back shift under the thin fabric of his shirt. And try to ignore the way he stares. How his eyes shimmer with gold and want when they run down my face. How he uses any excuse to resurrect the memory of his hands on my body: casual touches to my hand, my shoulders, my hair, the small of my back.

Yet he hasn't mentioned what happened between us in Tristram. Neither will I. But the silence can't stop the burning.

"If you're trying to bore a hole into the table with your mind, you had better do it discreetly." The feel of Fionn's breath caressing my ear makes my eyes close and head tilt away.

Turning with narrowed eyes, I ignore his comment and swipe the ale sitting in front of him.

I've been doing my best to stop my wallowing. Eating things, at the very least, to dispel the assessing looks. I lift the cup to my lips as I hold eye contact. A slight tilt to his lips and the flicker of his golden eyes to my own are his only responses before he turns back to face the men in front of him.

The group of male travelers looks as rough as I do. The days without bathing have taken their toll. Dirt climbs my legs and is spattered across our faces. The group looks to be gossiping; one man's northern accent twists his words, nodding to an ill-educated upbringing. Lack of schooling is common in the north, amongst the scant villages around Dun to the slave mines in the northwest, along the Ghael mountains.

I was lucky, being so far from wealth, that I received the extent of education that I did from my mother. I can read and write, and I know my numbers. It's sufficient. I also hide the poverty from my diction. Firstly, I use words like diction. I use proper grammar and don't "speak lazy" as my father had called it, referring to the dropping of letters from words. I always refrained from pointing out that he spoke "lazy" and that really, he should have said "lazily," but that was an argument that would have taken too many words between us.

"What incident out east?" Fionn butts into the whispered conversation between the men sitting across from us. His arm curls around my shoulder, playing the part of concerned, protective husband. I try not to lean away from his warmth and the feelings it brings with it, to play my own part.

"'Dere 'ave been whispers from outta da' forest." The

filth from the road looks as if it lives beneath the man's aged skin as he dramatically looks side-to-side, assessing his audience before he finishes, "Whispers in da' form o' smoke."

"What do these whispers say?" Konan asks impatiently from down the table, his arm slung around a stiff and uncomfortable Elva. Her face is stony, hardness around her eyes. You would think she would get used to her companions' proximity, but Elva tends to stay to the shadows—hiding in darkened alleys and rooftops as opposed to walking brazenly through streets with the rest of us. Like she can't seem to stand the brushing of our shoulders.

My interest is piqued. I'm certain the Crows didn't take kindly to what occurred that day Fionn and I went to get Diana's journal. I've pleaded to distant stars that the iron fist they brought down on the town wasn't too brutal. Hopefully this man speaks of another place. I hope he hasn't already spread whispers of the Fianna's presence along the coast.

"Wha's it to ya'?" the man asks, blearily belligerent.

"Just need to know what we are headed for." Fionn's voice lowers. "Can't be taking my wife and our family straight to a place on fire, can I?"

Good of him to blur the path, mislead any questions about where our group is headed.

"You lot would do well t' stay away."

Suddenly I have to know. Have to know what became of the village that grew me. A series of faces flash in my mind. The butcher and his wife, who used to throw in free portions when my father fell ill. The seamstress, whose daughter lived in Diana's infirmary one cold weekend. Her terrified face turning to relief as I told her the fever had broken overnight and the bone-crushing hug she had bestowed on me directly after. She didn't know, but that was the first motherly embrace I had felt in years, and the last one I'll probably ever have. The baker, on the edge of town, her withered hands kneading bread day and night. She was one of three visitors after my mother "left." She brought me some sweet cookies and sat in front of the fire with me, telling countless stories to the fire in the hearth, until my father came home from the bar. I pretended to be asleep on the floor, but I could hear her fury as she told my father what would happen if she saw him sitting at that bar one more night while I stayed home alone. I see Mariana, and her little seven-year-old face cheering for her slug as we race them down an old moss-covered log behind her father's tavern. Her face as she shoved me off the road and into the woods, all terror and fiery determination. A debt to her inner child.

By the time my father died, there were no more outreached hands. The Crows had descended, spreading fear and driving people far into their homes. People do not know kinship when their every thought is consumed with survival. But despite their absence in my most lonely hours, it is their faces I see as I interrupt.

"What of the village of Comraich?" I try to keep my voice casual, staring at the wet ends of my hair.

"Aye, thas where te' smoke was born. Dey say te' whole place went up in a blaze big enough only te' sea can stop it."

All I can see is the water dripping from the end of my hair between my fingers. I cannot move, I cannot blink, I cannot breathe.

I thought that somewhere along the way, loss stops being so all-consuming. Stops feasting on your flesh in a room full of people. Is that not what all of this solitude was for? What was the point in becoming nothing and no one if I can still feel this way?

Somewhere in the background I feel Fionn take my hand, lowering it into my lap while he keeps the conversation going.

I've already gone somewhere deep inside, somewhere far, far away from that shrieking raging part of me that still lives, still wanting to maim and freeze and end life. My body has a will of its own as it stands from the table, shoving Fionn's arm off my shoulders. It isn't until I'm in the room I share with Elva, pack slung over a shoulder, that the door opens behind me.

"You could not have drawn more attention if you tried," Fionn says. "I don't know if I was able to dispel the questions well enough. So thanks for that."

I don't bother responding. I don't know if I can. I just shoulder past him and reach for the door handle. It only opens a fraction before a hand slams it shut.

"Let me the fuck out." I don't turn around. I sound different than I have these past weeks. I sound like I used to.

When did I start sounding like a real person again? Where had the wraith that spoke through my mouth gone?

How close had she lurked under the surface?

Fionn doesn't seem to notice. He's mad. Not more than I am though.

"No. I don't think I will. What the hell was that, Alyx? I had to cover up every single track that you left on the way here. The fucking ale was frozen in its glass. The place where you sat had a frozen puddle under it," Fionn hisses, getting in my face. "You're reckless." A slam of his fist against the wall beside my head. "You're out of control. You will get us all killed. And you don't even care."

I don't care? I don't care. I wish he could see it. How much I don't care.

They're dead. All of them. All of it.

Whirling around, I grab onto whatever I can, grasping for every single scrap of energy in the room and shove it at him. I find it in the air, the candlelight, the blazing well of energy coming from him.

I can feel the energy I harness taking shape and unfurling in a wave of frost, spreading along the cage of this room, Fionn the jailer. It freezes and hardens, a blunt force lashing out in a lethal, bitter cold—anything to get him out of my way.

Fionn is flung across the room, falling onto hands and knees, heaving visible breaths. He looks up at me with burning golden eyes, glancing around at the ice-scape I have created. Candlelight dies, casting the room into darkness. Only the moonlight filtering through the frosted window illuminates us.

"Let me up," he demands.

"No, I don't think I will," I parrot his words back to him. I have no clue what I've done. His rain-wet pants are frozen to the wood floor. "I have to go. To find whoever…" My voice trails off as I wonder who is left. If any of them are. If they've all fallen to the Crows' fury and fun. "I have to go."

He's shaking with anger, or is it exhaustion? Glaring up at me.

"For what, Alyx? Huh? For the people that would just as soon leave you to die? For those selfish, pathetic people that let the Fomorians prey on the old, the children, the sick? Are those the people you're willing to risk it all for? And who would do the same for you? You have no family there. You have no friends. They're probably all ash in the wind anyways. Give it up."

His words hit every single mark.

"Some might have survived. I cannot just leave them."

"You already did. You left. Knowing that the Fomorians

would not just let this slide. You left and now what? You feel bad? You feel like a coward now, Alyx? Too bad. It's done."

Am I bleeding? I feel like I'm bleeding.

Drip, drip, drip.

All over the floor.

He doesn't stop.

"I know what you're feeling. I've felt it, I still feel it. Every time I think of them. Of my mother. Of my father. My neighbors and everyone I've ever known. They were stuck there, I could have stayed and fought for them. But I ran. I took the out I was given, not realizing that I would never be able to take it back, never be able to go back. And I will spend every second for the rest of my long existence looking for a way to make those reeking parasites pay. Taking every single opportunity to make those bastards suffer for their crimes against them. I have failed my people in every conceivable way, but I will not fail them in this. I will allow no one to get in the way of this Alyx, no one. Not even you."

Not even you.

The silence stretches and I begin to understand.

"I won't get in the way." I turn to go once more.

But Fionn has had time to gather himself, un-stick himself from the floor. He has me pinned against the wall beside the door before I can open it. His warm body an even tighter cage than the room.

"I meant what I said, Alyx. This would be a mistake. One that would endanger everyone I have left. You could be caught and tortured. You could tell them about us. I couldn't even blame you. The Fomorians, you have no idea what they would do to you..." I swear I feel him shudder against me. His next words are gentle but firm. "You can't go. I mean it."

"Then come with me." My voice is small. So is the hope. But as I say it, I realize how much I want it. How much I don't want to be on my own again.

He would keep me here, against my will. Logically, I've known this. That I could not leave knowing what I know, but I thought things might have changed somewhere along the way. Somewhere between him and a wall, somewhere between longing glances.

"We would be headed straight to a trap. They want us to come scurrying back. Plus, the word of what we've done, our faces, have reached the capital by now. We need to be focused on laying low, getting out of here, that's why we head to Raith. I have a way out, to Ashvynd."

I can't stay. I can't go with him. Not yet.

I shake my head. "Please don't make me stay."

Mariana, she could be out there. The need to help her is a song in my blood.

Fionn ducks his head, squeezing his eyes shut, pain etched into the lines around his eyes and mouth. When his eyes open again, they look as raw and vulnerable as I feel. Looking straight into my soul. His voice drops to a trembling whisper, so at odds with this self-assured, vengeful man I have come to know. "Alyx. I cannot. I cannot. You need to stay with us. I need you… I need you to stay with us."

"Because of my power? Because of what I know? I swear I won't let myself get caught. I swear." It's a pleading whisper. I will die first.

He moves a tendril of hair behind my ear. "You know why, Alyx." The words are so soft, it's as if he is afraid the fates will hear it.

All that can be heard is our heartbeats, echoing in the frozen room.

Oh. *Oh.*

I can't bring myself to break this holy silence. He looks like he doesn't want to say it, like some part of him rages against the want in his eyes.

I'm so utterly taken by surprise, that the look he gives me sends every other thought flying from my mind. Somewhere in the shocked haze, my hands rise up to his face, feeling the rough stubble on his sharp jaw.

His stunning eyes flutter closed.

His head falls closer, pulled by some force beyond the two of us. His nose runs along the side of mine, breaths curling between us.

My fingers shift to his hair. So unimaginably soft are the curls, a million shades of fair and honey. They settle at his nape, where they curl more tightly.

Our lips meet. The first kiss we shared was burning, this one is soft; exploring and languid. His hands aren't urgent, now that they've left my wrists. They are soft and sweet, caressing barely over my cheeks, brushing away the tears I only now feel.

I'll never know how long we live in this moment. How long we bask in the feeling.

The look in his eyes says he feels it too.

"I was a fool to leave so much unsaid between us after Tristram. I was a fool not to claim you then—to let the days go by and say nothing when all I wanted was for you to look at me like you did that night. I won't be a fool again. You're mine. I want you to know it. I want the others to know it." His heated gaze runs over my face, proprietorial and masculine.

I'm spinning and I don't know how to make it stop.

"I didn't know you were serious. I wasn't sure if… if you were just, taking what you could get." I sound so young and insecure. I twirl one of the curls at the nape of his neck around my finger. He shivers.

His face takes on a cocky smirk that I don't miss. Never one to leave a moment unsullied.

"So you're saying… I could get you?"

I roll my eyes and shove him away lightly, not really budging him. "You're what? Seventy years old? You're just like every teenage boy I've ever met."

He gathers me up again, accepting not a breath's space between us. He whispers in my ear, "I'm not sure if I can let you go. I want you to stay with me tonight. We don't have to do anything, not if you're not comfortable. But I just don't… I want you with me, always."

For the first time he looks vulnerable and embarrassed for asking. He shifts slightly, the only sign of human restlessness I've seen from him.

My heart stutters, then bursts, then dies and comes alive again.

I'm so distracted by the feel of him, by the feeling of being held that I think I may just stay here for the rest of my life. But even with the sheer perfection of being in his arms, I begin to remember. To feel that tiny niggling thought that grows with every heartbeat.

I shove it away, for just one more moment.

"Does this mean Elva has to bunk with the boys now? Because that makes me feel guilty." I grimace.

Fionn tosses his head back, laughing.

"She's done it before. And I think she's unaffected. Does this mean…yes?"

I memorize that hopeful look, draw it over and over again in my mind. Take in the exact tilt of his lips and the slightest crinkle around his eyes, take the scent of him deep into my lungs. I carefully put it into a place where it will never get lost. Where nobody can ever touch it or take it away from me.

Dread and sorrow twine at the edges of this memory as I preserve it, at what I know I have to do.

"Yes, it means yes." I do my best to look happy about it. I let my eyes make promises my body and my soul cannot keep.

The silence is as golden as his beaming smile, full of promise and prose.

He places a kiss on my lips and lets me go.

It's sweet and quick, like we will do it many more times.

"I'll go tell her. We will take this room, it's smaller." He closes the door behind him as he leaves.

I'm so cold now.

I only have a few minutes.

I dart to the door, the pack still slung over my shoulder.

Mariana might be out there. And as much as I meant everything with Fionn, I have to go find her and whomever else may be left. Because maybe, just this once, I'm better than nobody.

I shove open the window, the frost having dissipated in the time we stood clasped together in passion. I look down. Why did we have to be on the top floor? I drop my pack to the ground, holding it as far down as I can. It makes a hard sound as it hits the ground below. I wince.

I take a deep breath and sling one leg out the window.

I take another deep breath. I can do this. I can try to heal myself if I break something. I turn to throw my second leg out, the move turning me to face the door on the other side of the room.

Where a shadow now stands.

Chapter 19

I don't stay long enough to see who it is.

I jump.

The fall is simultaneously quicker than breath and longer than life.

In my frantic escape I'm ill prepared for the brutal hardness of earth as it meets me. I collapse onto my front, something in my left ankle popping. My pack breaks my fall on my front, saving my face from the impact.

Run.

I see them all, like I see the world before me: Mariana, her frantic eyes and fluttering movements saving me, hands kneading bread, too-full sacks of meat, and that flaming hearth with a wizened old woman sitting beside it, saving me. They all saved me.

I grab my pack and stumble to my feet, my ankle giving out a bit under any pressure.

Gritting my teeth, I hobble forward—faster and faster with every step. Muffled cries leave my mouth with every shooting pain.

The lightest of thumps breaks the sounds of my flight as my pursuer lands on the ground behind me.

"Alyxara, stop," her rich voice says. I should have known—nobody else is made of shadow in the way Elva is.

My footsteps come faster, every step punctuating the chant in my mind of unpayable debts, of inescapable responsibility.

A gentle but firm hand grasps my arm. I whip around to the side, landing hard on my bad ankle. I gasp in pain and try to jerk my arm from her unyielding grasp.

I try to reach for any power left. There are no candles, no trees or plants. Elva's energy is firmly behind a wall. I reach for my own energy, hoping it's enough.

All I get are frosted puffs of breath and less energy than I started with.

I continue my struggle, pleading, "You have to let me go. You have to let me do this. I promise, Elva, I won't put you at risk. You of all people have to understand, these are my people."

"I'm sorry. I was given an order." Elva's voice is as steady as the earth. Effortlessly subduing me, clasping my arms to my sides from behind and holding me in place.

All fight flees my bones. I can never win a battle against this woman, this ageless warrior who walks between worlds. She only has one soft spot.

"You could help me. There must be some left, they have to be wandering Wynedd. We—we would just help them find somewhere safe. We could be back here or in Raith in a matter of weeks. It'll just be a detour. These people have worth. They have lives to live, however brief in the scope of yours."

There's a moment of silence before she rebuts.

"Do you think there is any corner of this realm that is

safe?" Her voice is cold stone. "I would help you, girl, but what you ask is impossible. Whoever made it out of that blaze will have enough grit and cunning to save themselves. There is no amount of putting yourself in harm's way that will sooth this ache. None. You just learn to live with it."

A laugh so cold comes in the sound of my voice. I sound like a Crow, a Fomorian.

"Is that what you're doing? Living with it? It seems to me that you have all the power and ability to help people, yet you do nothing. You wander these lands, searching for what? A way back to your doomed homeland? What are you living for? There are people right here who are living under the thumb of the same people who tore your word apart and you do nothing to stop them from doing the same to my people. You're all cowards." It ends on a sob and a weak thrash of my shoulders. Hopeless fury. Fury at them, fury at the Crows. Fury at myself for not being strong enough to save them yet.

Another voice, seeped in a coldness I had hoped never to hear again, comes from behind us, "We do what we can, Alyx."

Fionn, bathed in moonlight, steps into my field of view. In this moment, I hate him.

Why do I want so desperately for him to hold me?

Through the haze I recall what Elva had said first.

"You were given an order?" I look at her over my shoulder.

I meet her midnight eyes. She nods once, then turns a cold look to Fionn, releasing her grip on me.

"Do you think I don't know you, Alyx? Did you think that you could fool me so completely with pretty words that I would think you had just dropped it?" Flat apathy is all he is made of as he runs his blade over the palm of his other hand. "I meant what I said earlier. I meant all of it. But it seems you did not hear me when I said that I would not allow anyone to get in my way."

"I told you; I would die before I said anything to anyone about you!"

Pointless—it's pointless to keep trying. I've lost my opportunity.

"I cannot allow that either." He's just the leader of the Fianna now. Not Fionn, the man who kissed me sweetly only minutes ago.

"Why? *Why!* It's my choice." I'm sobbing, unable to maintain chilled anger.

"I mean what I say, Alyx. Always. Even when you have no qualms about lying." He doesn't look at me anymore.

I don't have any room to think about that. It's all taken up by screaming, helpless fury. I feel like a caged animal.

"So what, we just keep training? Keep wandering? Get on a ship to fucking Ashvynd and leave everyone here for dead until they inevitably reach there, too?" I ask, throwing my arms to the sky.

"We will reassess your training, considering your willingness to use it against us."

"What?" I ask, aghast.

"We don't even know what you are. Much less what you're capable of."

That blow hits harder than anything he's said up to this point. I suspect he wanted it to. That perhaps I had hit him just as hard with my escape attempt after his declarations.

I just nod and look back at the sky. Cruel stars on an early summer night. How they watch me make a fool of myself over and over. Watch me fail over and over.

I give one succinct nod, unable to form words. I've lost this battle—completely and utterly.

I walk back to the inn.

When Fionn shows up in my room after a while, I don't speak to him.

Words don't exist to me anymore. They're all gone. Used up.

"You won't be leaving my sight anytime soon," he says as he settles into the bed.

I lay down on the floor, its familiar hard boards giving some pathetic comfort.

He snorts, thinking I'm being petty, making a point. I wish it was that. But the thought of feeling his heat at my back, accidentally brushing his skin in sleep... It's suffocating.

So I sleep on the ground.

Chapter 20

Mariana - Comraich, four days prior

I'm not sure who is more surprised when the blow claps across my face.

Myself, from the shock of having such an obvious, simple strike land on me for the first time in years.

Or my mother, from having actually landed a direct, obvious hit for the first time in years.

Which is exactly the response I'm hoping for.

She doesn't see the distraction for what it is, brilliant as she is. My beautiful mother—unruly red hairs at her temples escaping their restraints, her brown eyes blown wide with surprise—is not expecting me to strike abruptly afterward. I grip her still partially extended arm, bringing it behind her more swiftly than an adder. A shove brings her to the ground, and I spring over her fallen form, lifting my dagger under her throat, the blade not touching her fair skin. She tries to gather herself and fight it, she really does, but the damage has already been done, solidified in one second of hesitation.

Our panting fills the silence before a booming laugh

comes from across the room where my father leans against a cask of ale, our only audience.

I try so hard to keep the taunting look from my face. I really do. But a triumphant smile breaks through as I lift the dagger from her neck and whoop in victory. The sound breaks off when my mother knocks me off her back, springing to her feet.

It's not often I'm able to best my highly trained, highly competitive, mother.

She pretends for a moment to be upset, narrowing her warm eyes, but the smile pulls at the edges of her lips, her expression giving way to the lines of age that reveal her as my mother and not sister.

"She got you with that one, Elena. Fair and square." My father's smiling blue eyes dance from across the cellar, which lives under our family's tavern—doubling as our training area. He savors this win as much as I do. He gave up sparring with her some time ago, favoring only to spar with me. Though he would never admit that she was better hand-to-hand than him. Their competitive streak goes back farther than my life. It spans across seas and kingdoms. Twines intimately with the love they have for each other.

"She gets that cunning underhandedness from you, Rhodri. Insufferable, both of you," Mom says, dusting off her skirts.

The conspiratorial look my father and I share confirms her statement. My father may have the look of a brute—tall and muscled from years of training to maintain his physique as an assassin before I was born—but his form contradicts his favored function: poisons and politics. My mother is the more direct type; fighting hand-to-hand with her assignments was her favored tactic back in the days as the Dragon King's personal assassin in our neighboring country of Ashvynd. She and my father met on a distant battlefield—one of ballrooms and rooftops—two unstoppable forces pitted against one another for opposing causes. A story I have heard too many times to count. One they love telling. It always turns into them sharing longing glances and me feigning nausea.

My father sweeps Mom into his arms. She lets him, but pretends to be holding a grudge, looking down her nose at him. It only makes him smile harder.

"Come now, don't be cross with me for giving our daughter the best parts of me, Dove. You should be glad for her victory," he laughs. My mother is nothing if not a sore loser. While she may be playing up the bitterness, its foundations are real. She'll lure him to spar with her before long. So predictable, yet he's falling right into her trap. Her ego is bruised, and my father is about to pay the price for it.

Above us, I hear the creak of floorboards, indicating the arrival of a patron. It's early. Too early for our regulars to peel themselves out of their beds in search of hair of the dog.

My father makes to go upstairs, but I stop him. "I'll get it. Don't be too upset, Mom. At your age it's a wonder you can still walk up the stairs." I blow her a taunting kiss. I'm as much of a sore winner as she is a loser.

I quickly skip upstairs, escaping her wrath. I hear a deep chuckle, broken off by an "oomph," then a scuffle—he always takes the bait.

Gross.

My skipping stumbles to a stop once I see who stands drenched in self-importance and the scent of many vices.

"What do you want, Aled?" I don't bother making my voice friendly. I'm not worried about losing his business; there are no other taverns in Comraich that he hasn't been barred from.

Everything about him is greasy, from his stubbled face to his shoulder-length unkempt hair. If only he knew to whom he speaks, what I could do to him.

"Message from the Crows. Be at the square by high noon today. They have an announcement to make." His chest swells with self-importance. The Crows' bitch his highest title.

I lean against the bar and make a point to look at my nails, see the perfect ovals, long enough to make deep gouges in an attacker, but not long enough to break under pressure.

"I suppose you're their little rat now. With your new position you could at least make it a point to bathe occasionally," I say blandly, inspecting the ends of my deep red hair. They could use a trim.

"Watch how you speak to me, bitch. To speak so disrespectfully to me is to speak disrespectfully to the Crows," he spits back.

I can't help but huff out a laugh at that. "Is it too much to ask you to come up with a more creative insult? That one is getting a little tired." I lay my hand down flat on the polished wooden bar top and level him with a stare, let him see the hint of predator in my blue eyes. "Would the Crows protect you from me, Aled? Would you like to find out?"

Just a spark of fear flares in his eyes, just underneath the haze of whatever is dulling his senses. It's thrilling.

"It's you who would need protecting from me, bitch." The threat lingers between us.

But I fear no man.

I sigh, despairing over his limited vocabulary.

He continues. "Just be at the stage, all of you. The sun is already half-way up." His sneer says he wishes I wouldn't.

I don't even bother to acknowledge his departure.

This month they sent the newsprint with Alyx's portrait. It was alongside a fair-haired male, 'nameless' over his portrait. The propaganda comes in every month from the capital. Usually detailing the ongoing struggle with Ashvynd; which towns have been struck by raiders this month, who is wanted by the Pretty King—names and descriptions beside their drawn portraits. They're always littered with justifications for increased troops, increased control, stories of rebels and their brutal endings.

The artist's rendition looked like Alyx—sort of. The artist missed one of her most defining characteristics. The sad sort of strength that lives deep in the shadows of one's eyes, the kind of strength that looks like loneliness from a certain angle. To me, it looks like someone who went through hell alone, and still keeps getting up in the morning. She looks like the paintings of the great salt sea from the coastal artists. Her eyes are as deep as the ocean. I remember the last time I saw her, felt her bony body under my hands. Even in her terror—she seemed lost at sea. Her portrait only captures her straight nose, eyes down-turned at the sides, the whites showing underneath the irises, straight, dirty-blonde hair.

I hope she ran somewhere far away. I hope she disappears like a shadow under the water.

That day… I couldn't leave her. Couldn't leave the little girl who raced slugs with me and gave me her coat when I was cold, who half-carried me all the way back to town when I twisted my ankle at her house one day. I've always regretted letting her freeze me out so fiercely. She deserved someone to keep trying for her.

A rough hand grips my shoulder. Taken by surprise I shove an elbow back, turning to grab the wrist and bend it behind their back, but I'm thwarted with every move.

I stop my struggling and sigh deeply. He tugs me into a comforting hug, chuckling. His warmth is always my favorite respite.

"Any thoughts too heavy for you to carry, Mary?" he whispers into my hair. Our words. A promise. Some thoughts are so big that you need someone to carry some of them for you. He also always calls me Mary when he wants to take my mind off things. He knows that I am my mother's daughter, and the best way to take my mind off things is to get under my skin.

"Don't call me that." I shove his chest and ignore his question, having already talked this issue out with him too many times to count. "Did Mom win?"

He turns me around. Twin laughing blue eyes meet. "I thought we were supposed to be allies against the brown-eyed one. You sound like you were hoping I would lose."

"I just want to sleep peacefully and not with one eye open tonight. You know how she gets when she loses twice."

He sighs deeply, looking skyward. "Fine. She won. But I let her."

"You. Did. Not."

I jump. Mom stands, scowling at the other end of the bar. Sneaky witch.

Nobody in this damned house makes a noise as they move.

Their bickering begins. An endless drone in my ears.

"We are to be at the stage today by noon," I interrupt.

"What for?" Mom asks.

"Some sort of message." I gulp. "Probably the usual." I kick at the ground. I need to sweep in here before patrons come flooding in. They always want to flush out the taste of boot in the mouth. Drown the fear, anger, and helplessness with alcohol.

"Probably," sighs Dad, face turned skyward. He's never found answers in between the cracks of ceiling boards, but he always tries.

"This cannot go on, Rhodri," Mom murmurs.

They share a look. One that speaks of winless arguments and nights spent going in circles.

"What are we to do?" I ask. Who are we to stand against an empire?

"Your mother thinks we should… rally," Dad says, jaw feathering. The scar going through his brow looks menacing when his eyes are laugh-less.

I wait for more, looking to Mom.

"We cannot run again. We can run to the ends of the world, but it seems that the problem of greed and evil has legs too." Mom stands in her iron will. Ready to battle it out.

"Look around, Elena, do any of these people look to be in any shape to help anyone? Allies." He scoffs. "These things take time. It takes planning, infrastructure, resources. We cannot simply rise up." Dad seems like he's said this endless times before.

"Then we make them. We cannot just sit here and hope someone else steps up. It's not happening. We've been waiting, and the water just keeps getting hotter," Mom says evenly.

She's not wrong. Since Alyx's escape and the show she made of it at the stage, things have gotten even worse. Curfew is enforced strictly at sundown. Any private gatherings larger than four to a party are forbidden. The nights in the tavern are monitored by the Crows. They station themselves at the edges of the room and watch, listen, and find prey. Comraich has grown numb. Alcohol is one of the few things that allow the people to cope with our circumstances; they're not about to take it away. Hangings are frequent and an audience is required. Some of them aren't even given justification anymore. They will kill us all off. Soon.

"Tonight, Rhodri," Mom says, her voice stern, but her eyes pleading.

She needs his support in this. Strong as she is, he is her partner, in everything. Every choice they make, they make together.

I've long since given up hope of finding what they have. There is no way such a love could exist twice in such close quarters, in such a close timeline. It is unfathomable. And if I cannot have what they have, then I will have nothing.

Dad moves into her space, her will crumbling slightly at his closeness. He captures her face in his broad hands. "Tonight."

She isn't happy. It's a bittersweet resolution. To know that the one you love will follow you into Hell.

Melting into each other, my mother holds out her hand to me. A gesture and a question. They would never force me into such a thing.

I could no sooner abandon them than I could cut off a limb.

I step in.

So we stand there, basking in one another. In the charged choice we have made. I know we are all wondering what the consequences will be, for wanting more.

When I was a kid, I used to run wild in the square on summer market days. Dad would chase me from the baker to the stonemason, from the apothecary to the seamstress, making me shriek and giggle the whole way. He could have caught my little legs, could have stopped me. But he let me run. Let me hide and sneak around corners and between farm stands.

The sun basks these memories in love and warmth.

Now its rays warm the sun-drying bodies of the stonemason and the baker where they hang like chimes in the wind from the stage. Eyes that once watched my little legs run are now picked clean by vultures—empty of sight and life, skin splitting and rotting from days in the sun. Their legs are now just bones from where the feral dogs, rats, and cats have stripped flesh from bone.

Where laughter once rang through the air, now flies buzz and vultures caw. No voices, whispers, nor shrieks of joy pierce the droning of flies. No matter how much I bat the incessant buzzing insects away, off my arms, off my hair, they just keep landing. Like they know I'll be their next meal, and they cannot wait to have a taste. I'll never understand how some people just let them crawl over their skin, tickle their scalps, and buzz in their ear.

The sun bakes my fair skin, the early summer heat near unbearable when all that's left of the town stand shoulder to shoulder in front of the stage.

The clouds in the distance are a dark gray, sweeping in a summer storm.

Four Crows look out onto us from between the hanging bodies. The others, numbering thirty or so, surround us.

There's a new one today. His armor is newly polished, obsidian shining even in the shadows. His gaunt skin matches that of the others, like they haven't seen the daylight all their lives. Deep circles are under deep-set coal-black eyes. His bald head still has the imprint of his helmet that sat upon it. He has it placed in front of him on the ground. The helmet depicts a red-eyed hellhound, snarling at the crowd from its metallic prison.

It's terribly beautiful.

This one. He smiles. It twists one side of his mouth,

beautifully white, straight teeth bared. His nose lifts slightly on one side, a gleeful snarl more than a true smile. It matches the art on his helmet.

He speaks.

"What a pitiful showing. Is this everyone?" He turns only slightly to the Crow beside him for confirmation. The Crow gives a slight jerk of the chin, looking bored. The newcomer shakes his head disapprovingly. "What a disappointment."

He doesn't sound disappointed. He sounds excited; his eyes almost twinkle in anticipation.

"I've been sent here personally, by the king." His lip lifts slightly in distaste when he says it. Interesting that one of the king's more trusted men would sneer his name in such a way. "To oversee a transitional period here. He states this sorry place has been a hotbed of rebellion. Frankly, I don't see a spark of any of it in you pathetic bastards. But the reports have been numerous. Reports of escapes that should not be possible. Such a thing must have been aided." He searches every face. We all stare at the dirt. The stranger begins to speak more quickly, whatever blackened spirit he has alight with sick anticipation.

"He states that such traitors put our nation at risk. Such a place poses a danger to the Crown. To the peace we have fought so hard for. I suggested he kill you all." He waits, smiling down at us. "Luckily for you miscreants, the king is more than just pretty," he spits the word out in mockery. "He is also a fair and just king." He chuckles. "And he stated that there may be some loyal amongst you, some that are worthy of the life of peace and prosperity we have made possible." He looks to Aled in the front row, who stands there, chin high with sickening pride. The speaker cocks his head, considering him for a moment before going on, "And while I have my doubts, I am nothing if not a humble servant to our lord king. So, beginning tomorrow at first light, we will begin a pilgrimage to lands unsoiled by the stain of rebellion. You are to gather whatever"—he gestures an armored hand weakly—"measly belongings you may have that are of importance to you. You are to meet us here. You are to walk with us to a land where you may be monitored under the watchful eye of the king. To a place where you may be of some value to the Crown. Those who are worthy shall make it there, by the will of god and king." He looks out on us at the end. Begging for some whisper of discontent, eager to dish out a messy end. I fear he is disappointed. "You are dismissed."

The first strike of thunder sounds in the distance.

A storm is coming.

None of us move. None of us speak. Some are in shock. But I am in awe. Awe at the blessed timing. In awe at the gift we've been given.

Rebellion is a flame. Every fire starts from a spark. This Crow has given us the gift of one.

Chapter 21

Daylight comes and with every step, that chasm between me and the rest of them grows wider.

The pain from my injured ankle is searing penance with every pace forward.

Fionn had said it. From the beginning. That I could not be allowed to leave once I became a part of the group. I knew that and agreed, but they should understand this need. They have to know that I would never give them up. If this were a group of their people, they would have dropped everything to go save them.

I trail at the back of the pack. The rest of them are giving me space. I cannot tell which of them agree with Fionn. Most, probably. It doesn't matter really, because even if they thought I should be able to go, none of them spoke up.

Armund sneaks glances at me from his place near Konan and Fionn, but is ultimately too much of a coward to come talk to my wall of anger.

Aine, who seems to be too sensitive to the tension to play her usual games, keeps sneaking concerned glances back at me.

I avoid her eyes.

She may be the one person I'm not angry with, but she is also the one person who might make me break. To see compassion in her eyes, to see the good in this group. The good that extends to one another, but not to me—it's too much. So I watch the ground, and feel her eyes run over me instead.

It's been days on the road. Days of silence.

They speak, they play. Almost every single one of them tries to talk to me at one point or another. They seem to have forgiven my transgression, citing that they understand why I tried to run, and they don't hold it against me. Great for them.

But I don't forgive them.

So I fill my water-skin. I think about them, those who made it out of the fire. I eat berries. I bite my nails until they bleed. I sit on the outskirts of the fire at night, on my own bedroll, far, far away from Fionn. I wonder where they all went, if they're scared. I don't practice wielding or reaching. My ankle was so swollen from re-rolling it that I fashioned a brace for it. It's getting better now.

And so the days pass by, and I stay deep in a dark room in my mind, staring out the windows at people who think I'm a wild animal, in need of chains.

Elva has taken up Alyx duty. She walks beside me, a silent sentry.

Sweat drips down the side of my face. My hair is lightening from the roots down, just like it used to in the summer when I would work in the fields under endless sunshine. It is more dramatic this time, almost a white-blonde, and I wonder if it is from stress.

We make it to the western coast, the city of Farus is only

a few days walk away. The blisters on my feet remember every step, every league across Suri, and I wonder if any step will ever hold any answers. What city could I travel to, trail could I follow, that will tell me why? Why can I do these things? Where am I headed? What am I still walking for?

I don't have answers, and I suspect I never will.

"This is getting ridiculous. It's foolish to stop training," Elva's voice breaks through my thoughts.

It isn't.

"You could at least continue to practice." If I did not know any better, I would say there was a flicker of irritation on her face, in her voice.

I can't.

"We could have let you go. It's not as if you knew where we were going specifically. The Crown already knows we exist somewhere. You wouldn't be able to tell them anything very useful. Some of us realize this. We agree with you," she says.

The scathing look I shoot her says: *Then why did you stop me?*

"I allowed Fionn to lead. I saw who he was, his motives, his character, and I chose to follow him. He may not always do what I would, but I had made my choice many years ago. This is honor and duty. It is the choice I made. Just as you have made a choice to come with us, knowing he would not allow you to leave."

I have nothing to say to that.

Konan chuckles darkly at something said ahead, drawing my attention. All of his laughs sound dark.

Fionn shoves him with all of his strength, sending Konan stumbling sideways, but still chuckling.

Elva looks me over with her expressionless face before turning back to the front. "Fionn was teaching you poorly anyways, too distracted by your form and availability." A tiny smirk pulls at the corner of her mouth. "And while you're obviously attractive, I'm typically not into the moody, sullen women. So we shouldn't have a problem there."

I trip over a pebble, and almost go careening to the ground.

Not into moody, sullen women. But she's into some women? I've heard of such things, but they aren't widely accepted in Suri. Something about nature and it being an affront to the order of things. However, I've never thought nature would really care that much what our romantic dalliances are like.

Elva doesn't seem to care about what she just revealed to me, for she just moves on. I stumble to keep up with her brisk pace.

"If you train with me, we will make sure you see your people again. We will find them. Or you will find them. It's not over. It's not over until you decide to give up on them."

Have I given up on them? No. But I didn't know where to go from here. If I tried to run, they would drag me back.

But perhaps not anymore.

Her words give me a spark of hope, and my mind starts running again.

Breathe in, pull yourself in, breathe out, extend.

My essence moves with the breath, just as Elva showed me. I can feel it reaching and unfurling. Caressing the energy that lives in the ether. It tangles with the air, tingling sparks of energy, like when your hand falls asleep, and it feels like hundreds of tiny pinpricks. As I breathe in, I pull myself back, though I can still feel the prickles of consciousness in my surroundings, the bright lights of souls eating their meals in peace. I'm used to their presence and can easily ignore them. I count the souls that stand watch over my exercises.

One, two, three.

One is welcome, the other two males, not so much.

Armund and Fionn watch me from the campsite.

Elva supervises my breaths with an assessing gaze.

"Next time, I need you to push it on your exhale. See if you can move the wind. Create space between the points of energy. If you need to move with your breath, do so." With Elva's terse command, she demonstrates, pulling in a deep breath all the way down to her belly, hands holding the breath in for a moment. On her exhale, her hands move with her breath, outward in an airy motion. A cloud of dust and wind blows from where she stands, all the way to the creek down the hill, where Deri is teaching Aine how to fish.

Elva makes it look effortless.

I concentrate on each point of energy. Feel them wanting to stick to my essence, wanting to be absorbed by it. I push it but it sticks. Like thorns to fabric.

I scowl in frustration and try again. More sticking this time.

"Good," Elva says.

I furrow my brow in question. "I did it?"

She nods.

"But I wasn't really pushing it. It was...sticking to me," I sigh. Elva is easy to be honest with, and she expects nothing less.

She cocks her head. "It's not the way my power works but, perhaps..."

"Her wielding could be different," says Fionn, lurking several paces away.

I cannot look at him.

I go back to my breaths and extensions.

In the silence I can feel his attention along my profile. My extension stutters and fails.

He interprets my silence as challenge and moves to loom over me.

Elva interjects, "Alyxara doesn't have anything to say to you. Nor does she need your input. Go be a domineering prick somewhere else."

"I think I prefer to be a domineering prick right here. Come take a walk with me," he commands me.

We don't even know what you are. Much less what you're capable of.

Breathe in-

He's crouched at my level now, breathing in my space.

"When, oh when, will I hear your voice speaking to me again?" he asks. I can hear the smile in his voice.

He thinks I'm funny.

Funny, petty little toy.

Breathe out, exten—

"Leave her alone, Fionn. I won't ask nicely again," Elva says, her voice more threatening than I have ever heard it.

The tension pries my eyes open. Fionn is considering her, crouched at my seated level. Considering whose power is greater. I know who my coin is on—a woman of shadows who walks between the stars.

But I won't drive a wedge between them. They had a dynamic before I came along. Before I created sides and pulled it apart.

"It's fine," I say to Elva as I stand, the three of us so close we practically share breath. Armund watches us all from the sidelines, having taken to watching my lessons the last few days. "I'll hear what horse-shit orders he has."

Fionn's brows flick up in surprise at my venom but Elva smirks slightly, still looking unsure.

I leave the circle before Fionn, leading us into the woods around the clearing.

His tread is utterly silent, but I feel him. I always feel him. I push a branch out of my way, letting it snap back in his face. A memory resurfaces of him doing the same. I think he catches it though. Shame.

"Looks like you picked out the most powerful guard dog. I would applaud you, but it's kind of a pain in my ass." His tone is trying to be casual, but irritation seeps through. "Look. I'm sorry if you feel like I'm domineering. If you feel I was being unfair the other day. I don't intend to be high-handed, but I cannot allow you to go traipsing off to save people that are probably already dead. I'm sorry if that reality hurts, I wish I could save you from that, but it's the truth. Those humans stood no chance." He dodges another one of my branches. His voice finally turns slightly rushed, earnest. "I'm sorry Alyx, I really am. I never meant for this to happen. I never meant to hurt you. I never meant to control you. But I have to. You don't know what it's like. To feel like everything rests on my shoulders. To have lost so much and feel like I'm about to lose more. You just don't understand—" He jerks me to a stop.

I thrash, forcing him to either hurt me or release me. He releases for once.

As we stand and finally look at one another, I let him see my anger, not my hurt. The hurt that is alive and writhing in my chest. It's like he's digging at an open wound, scraping dead flesh with a blade.

It all comes out in a trembling mess of words, quiet but fierce.

"You know nothing. *Nothing*." A gasping breath. "Nothing of my life, of my loss. I know. *I know,* Fionn. You do not." I point my finger at him.

None of it is coming out right.

There are no words left in me. They are lost to the wind. Lost in some endless sea of grief.

His brow furrows, eyes shining in genuine confusion but compassion. Hands up, surrendering if only for now. "Okay. Okay. I don't know. But you also never said."

Incommunicable anguish stands between us. It always has.

He comes forward, closer and closer, as if approaching a feral animal.

He's not wrong, I didn't say. I never say it. I can't.

It lurks in the corner of every happy moment. It taints brightness and makes everything feel like an inevitable ending. And if I say it, they'll know it.

Somehow it makes all of this feel like my fault. Because how could he know the depths of this need? How could he have known that I understand his need to protect me, as it is the same as mine to save the people I grew up with? But the fact that I understand doesn't change that I need to do this. That he is forcing me to give up on people I'm not ready to give up on yet.

He's all the way in front of me now, invading my space as he so likes to do. He looks to be bracing himself for battle.

"Look, I just want you to try to understand where I'm coming from. To know that it's my job to make sure nobody else gets hurt. To make sure that you don't get hurt. And then to have you so selfishly throw all caution to the wind. I was angry, Alyx. So impossibly, inescapably angry at you. First, for saying everything I had been wanting to hear, and then for tossing it straight out the window. But I'm ready to move forward, and I hope you can too."

How do I suddenly feel like the worst sort of person?

"Can we start this over? Go back to the beginning?

Because I feel like we keep fucking this up, and I don't want that. I don't want to hurt you. I want us. I want to touch you and feel like I have a right to. I want you to talk to me and want to. I want you, even when you're acting droll." His mouth turns up, unable to help but tease me.

Can we start over? Can I pretend that he could love me? Can I live in a dream and ignore everything else? Can I live with myself, knowing all that I abandon, just for a chance at *this*? Can I pretend that I don't see the end before it even starts, if only for a little while?

Not to mention the mates issue. I'm pretty sure one of us would know by now if I were his and he were mine.

But even so, I crave him. I want to curl up in his arms every night and just stay there. It's so cold being so alone.

I don't have the strength to say no. I don't have the strength to explain that our end is inevitable. One day, when I do something terrible and ruin it all. One day when my moroseness isn't something he feels like joking about anymore.   One day when we go to Raith and he's reminded of all of the women who smile and laugh easy.

Despite the thought of the agony that will follow, I nod my head.

"Yeah?" His face lights up, like a child given a new toy. "No more running?"

I nod again.

His hands come up to frame my face, thumbs moving over my cheeks. They are so warm, so comforting. His eyes are my favorite color right now, like honey in the sunlight, sweet and warm.

I feel like a coward. Accepting some bit of good while those that need me are possibly suffering.

"You can trust me," He says, softly.

It's too bright; the future he promises, his eyes. I turn my head to the side and lay my head on his broad chest. Feeling his muscles bunch as he wraps his arms around me.

He still isn't going to come with me to find my people. He still won't let me leave.

Maybe Elva was right the other night. The people who made it out will have to be made of iron and grit, and I just have to pray to whatever god that we meet again one day. The thought is a blade to the gut, but maybe the only way forward for me.

Maybe I just have to make the best of this. Train. Go along with their plans of running and searching. Become the most powerful version of myself. Ensure that next time, nobody could stop me. Not even him.

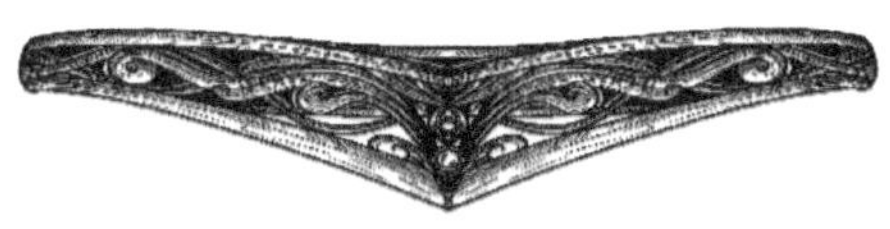

Chapter 22

"Remember your rage, Alyx," Fionn whispers encouragingly as he stands beside Elva, watching me practice.

He's casually wielding, flames dancing at his fingertips, weaving them between his fingers as if it's a thoughtless dance.

Show-off.

Remember your rage. As if I could ever forget it.

The water in the pot dances and bubbles, like it wants to play with me, but I just can't quite get it.

Water is heavy. It feels like one massive body of energy, and moving it is like moving a mountain. So it dances like it wants to boil, when I'm trying to move it in one long limb.

Elva did it so easily, moving a long rope of water through the air like a dancing ribbon, flowing with her movements. So did Konan, Deri, and Dealla. They all have some aptitude for water. Fionn, as it goes, does not. Finally, something he can't do better than me.

It's been a few weeks since we became "us." Since we

returned from the woods, hand in hand. Since we began sleeping beside one another. Since my silence was exchanged for kisses in the shadows and affectionate touches.

Elva and the girls seemed wary of the change at first. Unconvinced that Fionn deserves forgiveness, deserves to be holding my hand; or perhaps they're unconvinced that I deserve to be holding *his*.

Dealla still shoots us wary glances occasionally, from her place under the weight of her mate's arm. Then she smiles at me, as if trying to be happy for us. It's easy to judge another when your relationship is as unwavering as stone.

I finally get a fine rope of water to pull apart from the rest of the pot. It wobbles as I pull up with my hand, as if strained. Keeping my concentration, I hold it in place, a fine bead of sweat on my forehead, then clench my hand into a fist, freezing it with a series of pops and cracks.

I look at the little stick of ice protruding from the pool of water in the pot and smile, satisfied.

"Good. Very good Alyxara," Elva states. Armund nods beside her.

I smile timidly at her praise, casting Armund a small smile.

I'm trying to be better. Wield, smile, mind-reach, all in the name of becoming an actual asset. In the name of moving forward, because I'm pounding it in my head that Fionn is right, the people of Comraich are, in all likelihood, dead. Pounding into my head that the best course of action now is to get on the first ship away from Suri before the Crows find and kill all of us. We manage to dodge them, staying away from towns and cities, weather allowing. And when we cannot, we keep to crowded spaces, out of their faces.

"It seems as though I have another water wielder here.

Armund, she'll have you beat by the time we leave Suri." Fionn smacks Armund's arm. His joke is in poor taste. It's not hard to be better than Armund at wielding.

"Maybe, but she'll never be able to tell you more about rocks than Armund." Konan smacks Armund's other arm.

I walk up to Armund and place my hand on his shoulder, shooting Fionn an exasperated look. "Don't listen to them, Armund. I like how brilliant you are. Fionn and Konan are just jealous because they have to share two halves of one brain."

Armund chuckles and pulls me into him, slinging an arm over my shoulder, tucking me into his side. "That's why I let them have their fun. Don't pity me, pity the stupid." He leans down to whisper in my ear, "You really are doing amazing, Alyx."

"Thank you," I say, grateful.

"Alright, get your scent off my female." Fionn shoves Armund's arm off my shoulder and pulls me to him. He's grinning lightheartedly, but there's a slight warning in it. Armund just rolls his eyes and shakes his head.

I've learned recently that the Fae males are protective and possessive by nature.

Fionn explained it to me the other night when we laid down together, my head resting on his chest. I kept prying more and more about the mate bond, trying not to look too much like I'm collecting a list of symptoms to look out for.

"Dealla and Deri, they have been together since before we arrived. They trained together, they used to be insufferable." He chuckled. "I could barely stand to be near them at first, right after everything... happened. Traveling with them, seeing them have someone. They never had to feel alone. Not like the rest of us. And then came Aine, the truest blessing, but at the most terrifying time. And Deri, you think

he's protective now, but he's so much better. At first, he wouldn't even let anyone near Aine, much less hold her. Wouldn't let anyone near Dealla as her power recovered after birth. It was... a trying time for all of us, to say the least. There was nothing I could do. Mates are the bane of every leader's existence. There is no challenging them. There is nothing I could do to force them against their instincts; you saw at the bog when I tried to get Aine to stay with Armund." He shook his head. "But that is the way of our people. There are fierce feelings when it comes to mates and offspring, more so for the males. It's one of the main reasons we have females vastly outnumber males in leadership positions; they at least, can keep a level head."

Remembering him say that still makes me shake my head in bewilderment. Kings rule here. Women try to keep a low profile, hope for a husband that doesn't beat them, and try to find scraps of happiness in the midst of a power struggle between men that never ends. How did we get here, yet the Fae went to entirely different rationale?

Coming back to the present moment, I shoot Fionn an exasperated look.

Fionn just cocks an eyebrow, but his gaze quickly narrows, and he grabs my face. I push him away, not in the mood for his sweet kisses.

"Stop," he says firmly, giving me pause. He looks more closely, pulling my right eyelid up a tiny bit.

I pull my face away, uncomfortable with his inspection. "What?"

He doesn't grab for me again, only looks on, concerned. "Your eye. Does it hurt at all. Are you seeing alright?"

I scoff. "It's fine. Nothing feels wrong with it. Why? Is it red?"

Could I have got some dirt in it? Infection can happen

easily. I've seen people lose an eye because of it. I try to find anything reflective, a pond, a puddle, but Fionn grabs me and takes another look.

"No, it doesn't look hurt, it's just… you have purple in it. In your iris. A slice of violet where there used to be gray. But it doesn't extend past the iris." His concern furrows his brow and makes his jaw feather.

My face scrunches up, mind running through various ailments and cases I've seen. None concerning violet irises come to mind.

The others in the Fianna approach and assess me. I sink a little further into Fionn's grip.

Aine comes and grips my hand and smiles at me like nothing is wrong.

Dealla looks at me with motherly concern. "Do you think it could be related to your hair?"

"It has always turned blonde in the summers. Whenever I spend time under the sun. I've never seen my eyes change with it."

Dealla nods, unconvinced.

Konan breaks in next. I once thought his eyes black, but in the sunshine I see a gleam of rich dark brown. "I've seen eyes like that before."

The statement makes everyone shift in discomfort. Except Deri the unshakable, who says, "In the Scar?"

Konan nods, looking nonchalant. "Yes. Some babes would come out with violet eyes, but only ever if their mothers were pregnant while they worked in the stone. Not common, but it happens."

"It's nothing. I'm obviously not from 'the Scar' or whatever you call it." I wave the notion away. "I don't know… why I'm like this. Why I can do these… things. And it doesn't matter. I'm not hurt, I won't hurt anyone else. So can we just forget this?" I gesture to my eye, staring at the ground. The implications are that my parents, so normal in every way, had led some secret life. That perhaps they were from some far away realm and never bothered to tell me. That my father may have had power and yet he let us starve and wilt with every passing year. That could not be it.

They all look wary. Elva looks like she is desperately biting something back.

"Fine," Fionn says, grinding his jaw. "But you're starting to look… a bit too distinctive for my comfort, Alyx. We reach Raith in a handful of days. And we are looking to be as inconspicuous as possible. You'll need to… keep your hood up, at the very least. Try not to speak to people. Maybe it's best you stick to our rooms."

The thought of sitting alone in my room for several days sounds miserable. I've never been to Raith, but I've always been curious about it. It might as well have been a foreign nation. But I can understand his reasoning. The last thing we need is people asking questions about the strange-haired, purple-eyed girl, so I grit my teeth and nod.

Chapter 23

The sight of rotting bodies became commonplace to me after the Crows came. However, as we approach the gates of Raith and see uncountable numbers of them strung up along the eastern wall, like a macabre garland, I realized that the numbness I had clung to does not come so easily anymore. What a sick re-acquaintance. The smell of baking human flesh on a hot summer day. The sight of birds tearing skin from muscle, muscle from bone. A warning, to those that would search for another way. A warning, to those that would look at their lives and ask for more.

Fionn tucks me further under his arm, that pulls with his swaggering gait. He plays well any part the world asks of him. I school my face, trying to match him.

We move amongst a large group of people traveling along the worn road that approaches the capital. We're approaching the seat of the Pretty King. The city swarms with Crows on every street corner, lurking in every tavern, "protecting the peace."

Whose peace is it? The king's peace? Certainly not the

people's. Certainly not the mothers, fathers, children, sisters, brothers swinging in a dry summer breeze.

The walls tower over the city, only the highest of noon-sun shining into the walls as they stretch leagues to the salt sea in the west. The sea under the scorching heat of the sun smells different than the sea under endless clouds and storm. Like baked sand and warm salt underneath the waste and rot of the bustling city before us.

Ahead, the rest of the Fianna pass under the shadow of the gate. The Crows look for Fionn's face and mine, so we stay away from the others. Fionn feigns poor posture, avoiding notice from his height. He still stands a head higher than me and at least a half-head above the rest of the men. In the end, we pass by unnoticed, a drop in a river of travelers that flood the city of great riches and even greater poverty.

As we are swallowed by the city, cast into the shadows of the wall, Raith Castle looms far to the west, the road we tread a direct route to the seat of the king. Its spindling towers of forest green stone are a blot on the otherwise airy, sand-colored style of Raith. Darkly beautiful, the whispers do it a disservice, for none could have prepared me for the draw it has on my gaze. From leagues away, I can still see the giant gilded rivulets that run through the rock, sparkling like the tendrils of energy I grasp for. The seat of the king was long ago constructed from the living stone mined from the Ghael mountains that form our only border between Suri and Ashvynd. The mines ran dry of that stone at the construction of such a monument; however, the slaves still mine for other things of value in the Ghaels. Such things that cause the Dragon King in Ashvynd to wage petty war on Suri.

Merchants selling wares line the street: oddities brought across seas, spices from exotic lands conquered by ambitious royals, swaths of silks fit for kings right at the gates. Performers toss flaming torches, palm readers look coyly from their rickety tables, trying to entice with the promise of foresight. Musicians play their fiddles and lutes, painters spattered in oils and pastels brush stories of war and glory on canvas.

The entrance to Raith is both a welcome and a promise, that the city holds any and everything one could seek. But a few streets in, the light and color washes out to gray and waste; homes of the most unfortunate who perform for the wealthy that flood through the gates. They crawl out of their decaying forts to put on a show for those that were born of bigger purses and privilege, then slink back in the night to their outer-edges homes. They delight and entertain for scraps of nothing—generosities that are tossed with an upturned nose wrapped in silken robes worth the cost of a whole life in Raith.

Walking down the streets, hood drawn against the blazing sun, I see them. Planted on the shaded corners, lurking down alleys, just inside doorways to the taverns lining the road. They fly in the places where the river of people narrows. Down a side-road, harassing a filthy street urchin, picking at his pockets, gaunt smirking faces satisfied with their afternoon entertainment.

Each step brings us closer to the castle and further away from poverty, further away from artists, and closer to middle class workers. The smiths, the bakers, the stone masons. Smells of exotic spices burn my nose as I pass what I can only assume is a restaurant, tables packed together in the space, all patrons delicately picking into their plates. Such luxury, to have someone cook for you, use such spices, and wait on your needs. My stomach, caved inwards, is practically yowling in desire, but I turn my face away and keep walking.

We turn down a side street in the middle-class district. Expansive properties can be seen ahead, lining the walkways and gates of the king's keep. The wealthiest of merchant's estates. Ragged servants unload carriages, moving along animals I have never seen, striped horses, large baskets covered with blankets. A scaled tail, the color of butter, hangs over the edge of one. The servant seems to hold the basket as far away from his body as possible.

"Looks as though someone is having a party tonight." Fionn's mouth lifts slightly, but his eyes burn as they watch. "I've had the pleasure of attending one such festivity. Disgusting wretches are the elite of humans. The embodiment of greed and excess. No wonder they care not if they live amongst parasites, for they are the same."

The words coming from his mouth are those of disgust, but his face is pleasant, as if remarking on the sunny afternoon.

He leans down to whisper in my ear, "There are eyes Alyx, eyes everywhere." His face says he just whispered some sweet nothing to a lover.

Fionn is not much for sweet nothings. The past week has shown him to be much for touch and kisses and endless nettling and challenging. Much for sneaking off into the woods for stolen kisses and wandering hands. Much for teasing me about my hair, about my skinny arms, and about my stance.

I nod and smile sweetly up at him, nestling deeper into his side despite the unendurable heat.

That night, we find ourselves meeting under the candlelight, crowded into one of our rooms, having arrived at the inn separately and unable to debrief until this moment. And by debrief, I mean argue about what we will do to pass the time in the coming days.

"I'm not going to some ridiculous theater so I can watch a bunch of powder-faced boys prance around a stage. I don't care how pretty the actresses are," Konan gruffly states. "I've got my own entertainment in mind." He smirks, a manic twinkle in his eyes.

I have no desire to know what his preferred form of entertainment is.

"You cannot be serious," Dealla says, looking back at him from her place perched on her mate's lap, who is sitting on the bed, mindlessly caressing her sides.

"Oh fair one, I am," Konan teases with an excited grin.

"What exactly is the point in fighting these humans if they don't even stand a chance? It's cowardly," Dealla huffs.

"I'm not your mate to drag around, Dealla. Deri would join me if he weren't so wrapped around your finger." Konan looks nettled. "The point is that it keeps me from needing to beat the shit out of your mate for being so boring. Besides, it only makes them stronger."

Dealla is glowing, even in her ferocity. Deri doesn't even bother to look back at Konan as he strokes a hand down Dealla's hair and says, "Your adoption of human slang lacks, brother. When you say, 'beat the shit out of someone,' it implies you would win. Last time we sparred I believe you came away with a few fractured ribs. At least in the human fighting pits, you pick fights you won't lose."

Konan's biceps bunch and flex under his tunic. I've seen little of Deri's fighting abilities, but if he can beat Konan... He must be powerful indeed. He is related to the most powerful of his race; maybe he nears that level of power as well.

Fionn steps in, commanding, "It also draws eyes, Konan. So if you're going to risk it, at least ensure you bring home coin." His seriousness melts into a male smirk. Elva rolls her eyes from the corner.

"Perhaps you could allow one of them to break your nose. Really sell the whole human thing," Armund drawls from beside me.

"Nobody wants to go to the master's library. Get over it or go by yourself," Konan snarls.

Armund crosses his arms in front of his chest, seemingly put-out by Konan's answer. It's true though, nobody can agree on where to go.

Aine chirps in from where she leans into my other side, "Can we go to the docks? I remember a few years ago when we landed back here, there were those giant seals! Can we please, please, please go tomorrow?" She is practically vibrating in her seat.

"Well, we have to go tomorrow anyways, to meet up with our contact. I don't see why we cannot spare a few minutes to go look for them on the rocks," Fionn says, with a grin at her.

Aine squeals and the sound makes me smile at the ground.

"But absolutely no feeding them, Aine. I mean it," Dealla speaks sternly.

Aine's excitement dies instantly as her squeals turn into a whine only a child can release. "Mom, but Konan did it last time!"

Dealla shoots Konan a glare. "I know. But he isn't going to do it this time either." She speaks firmly, but his answering grin is a baring of teeth, and something tells me he will be feeding those seals.

"Fine," Aine says, mischief flinting in her green eyes. She is already plotting what type of food to bring. She turns to me. "They are bigger than even Konan, and they just flop

around on the sand because they don't have any real legs!"
She giggles.

Fionn leans across me to say, "Aine, Alyx won't be going tomorrow. With her eye and the hair, she draws too much attention. Her posters are already plastered all over the city. She will be staying here." He eyes me briefly, assessing my reaction. I smother my disappointment for Aine as she begins whining anew.

I place my hand on her leg as I grit out my agreement with Fionn, though it chokes me as it comes out. In a city full of thousands, what attention does one stranger with a hood up warrant? And if someone does talk to me, it's not as if I'm incapable of acting inconspicuous. People have strange eye colors sometimes. Fionn is just being overly cautious.

Is it born from lack of trust in me? Is he just that protective? Of me? Of the Fianna? Does he just want time away from me?

That last thought pangs through my chest. We have been spending much time together. Our nights spent sharing breath under the stars, our days spent training on the road. Endless companionship that, to me, feels like eating hot soup after a cold day outside, but probably not to Fionn. After all, he's always had people. He's had romance and connection. The endless contact with someone he willingly described as "dull" and "morose" not long ago must get old after some time.

I eye him a little, watching his gorgeous profile as he continues planning with the Fianna. He is so handsome it makes my heart flutter, with his tan skin and sparkling gold eyes, ever-glinting with humor. His beautiful lips pull up at the side as he smiles at something Konan says. I see him now... I see him laugh, and redirect tension, and read every single room. I see him be the leader worth following, and I know why the rest of us do. He is the reason nothing has dissolved completely between this group, why they are unfractured. And he… likes me—well enough, even if he might need space from me. That is normal, right? And I will let him have it. Far be it from me to cling when I'm not wanted somewhere.

My resolve hardens and I force a slight smile to my lips as he looks at me for one warm moment, and gives me a soft, sweet smile. One that he reserves for me, for our times alone in the woods—for the heartbeats between kisses.

Will someone be waiting outside my window if I try to go spend time on my own? Am I but an errant child to control?

As he looks back at the rest of the Fianna, Fionn rubs my knee in consolation. He's grateful for my acceptance without a fight.

Chapter 24

Mariana

Lightning glints off my blade a second before thunder hides the sound of it decapitating the Crow where he stands watch on the wall between turrets. The feeling of the heavy blade slicing through flesh and bone feels far more jarring than I ever imagined. The sound of it is slick and popping—the sounds of retribution.

The endless dark of night stretches out in all directions, the summer sun having set on the town of Comraich an hour ago. Ominous clouds obscure the moon. Bolts of lightning flash across the night sky.

As his body hits the stone at my feet, I lower back into a low crouch, running along at wall-height. The weight of the blade in my hand, taken from a Crow in the first tower—the first life I took—is heavier than any sword I've ever trained with. My left arm strains to keep it in position as I run. I should feel more about it, but all I can think about is bodies hanging, flesh pulled from bone, and eyes picked clean. I wish I could have given him that death.

My bones vibrate with the energy of battle. I've already cleared two turrets and this stretch of wall.

I run over my parents' lessons in my mind. Never let them see you coming. These soldiers have been trained well. They are stronger, faster, more brutal than anyone raised in Comraich. There is no way to drive them out head-on. Not with the few trained fighters amongst us.

Thankfully, a storm is raging. The wind whips through the trees of the forest. The trees hide both foe and friend on either side of the wall, so I stay low. I make it to the other turret, the shadows swallowing me, but if I had to guess, I would say my flaming hair catches any flicker of light in the darkness. I should have covered it with a hood.

My mother fights to clear the other two walls that surround Comraich. Dad is in the town, gathering all who will join us. They can help us fight or they can part ways with our group on the other side of the wall.

Needless to say, he won't be asking Aled to come.

The tap of metal on stone clinks through me. On instinct, I raise my sword to the noise, ready to volley, and come face-to-face with my mother. I sigh in relief as I lower my sword, not letting it drag on the ground.

"If I were a Crow, you would not have gotten the warning, and you would already be dead," her voice is harsh but spoken quietly. She looks sleek and vicious in her black leathers, hair tied back in a tight plait. She advances on me with every statement. "Sharpen your mind, Mariana. I need you to be everything we've trained you to be. You do not soften. You do not show mercy. You do not let yourself be caught unawares. You are our daughter." I look slightly down at her. Her voice loses the edge, warmth returning to her eyes, even as they tighten in worry. "I love you, Mar. Please." She chokes on her words for a second, "Please, be careful. Like my life depends on it, alright? Not yours, mine."

I nod, face warming.

There is no room for carelessness in a game played with lives.

"Is it clear?" I ask, driving out all whispers of consequence that haunt the edges of my thoughts.

Sharpen.

She nods, an emotionless mask slipping over her usually playful features.

"Onto the next?"

She nods again.

She begins securing a rope to the scuppers that are used for drainage on the outside of the turrets. She doesn't even look at the ground as she gracefully hops over the wall, lands on the scupper, takes the rope and uses it to rappel down the side of the wall quickly, as though she has done it hundreds of times before. Hell, she probably has.

She hits the ground in a graceful leap. Thunder drowns out the sound of her blade being unsheathed as she slinks into Wynedd. As much as my ears strain, I cannot hear any sounds over the drone of the storm. No sounds of the flaming assassin of Ashvynd unleashing herself on the Crows that dwell in the darkness, awaiting anyone fleeing the persecution of the Crown.

I turn away, faith in her abilities the only thing that allows my eyes to turn away from the spot where she was swallowed by the gloom. I let the raging storm suffuse my bones with its essence, let it drive out fear. *Sharpen your mind, Mariana.* I do. I am the blade that cuts the air, severs the mind from body. I am the flame of this rebellion, and I will not falter or dim.

When the first of our members meet me at the turret,

there is no fear left. There is no room for doubt, as I bring them to the rope hanging down the walls of our home. As I direct the last of the fifty or so rebels to my mother who awaits in the forest, I can feel the tides of the universe, shifting. Some scale in the universe, tipping. No amount of pleading can bring us back.

Not a single step wavers on the way down the stone steps. My father waits at the bottom. The flame of the sconce by the doorway illuminates the ruthless gleam in his eyes that I know is mirrored in my own.

Together we are twin pillars of righteous flame as we swiftly and silently make our way home. I thought it would be difficult, leaving. That saying goodbye to the only house I have ever lived in would drag up fond memories. But I'm bringing my home with me; it's made of two heartbeats and more memories than the four walls of a house could ever hold. It gives me the strength to grab those few remaining wooden boxes of hard liquor, to slosh a few over the wooden bar, the wooden floors, the beams of polished strength that hold everything together.

The flames devour the thatched roof, roaring over the storm, snapping and consuming every bit of history that wooden house carries when we make the leap to the next rooftop over. The flames follow us as we pick our way from rooftop to rooftop, all the way to the entrance to town. It feeds on the liquor my father sprinkled all over the siding, the rooftops of almost every building in town as he gathered the people of Comraich.

We hear Crows flocking to the source of the fire, running from their posts, from their houses that they commandeered from families that had "turned from the Crown." Commanding snarls pierce the buffeting noise of flame and storm: "Get to the wells! Fucking drag them from their beds to help. I don't give a fuck! Where are the fucking humans?"

It's a spur to our flanks. The entrance to town—a wooden lift-gate—is shut, guarded by two restlessly shifting Crows.

Dad takes a steadying breath, the only sign of nerves in his body.

"I engage. You finish, Mar. They'll have most of their focus on me, but you take advantage of that," his voice is a rumble, barely audible over the noise.

I can only nod. The part of me that speaks is somewhere far away, buried under hot vengeance.

Every move we make is tandem, silent, up until the point we drop from the rooftop beside the doorway.

My father is quick, his bulk no hindrance. His movements have always been beautiful, quick as an asp, brutal as a bear, sheer expertise and strength. I've always been in awe of him.

Even so, the Crows are faster, more savage, stronger. The clash of weapons rings out even in the massive cacophony made by the fire screaming its destructive mirth.

We have to end this quickly, or more will come. And we will not walk away from it.

I follow the plan.

As my father fights off two at once, his years of experience the only thing keeping him alive, I use their single-minded focus to take one off-guard.

I kick the back of the knee of the closest and duck out of the way as he lashes backwards, blade slicing the air where I once stood.

His focus switches to me, the fierce blows raining down on me harder than any storm.

The blows are so much harder than any I've

encountered—any my parents have thrown at me, even in the most serious of sparring. They jar through my blade and up my arm, into my shoulder, even when I try to keep my movements sweeping, redirecting the momentum. I meet every one with singular focus and a blazing heart.

He has me on my back foot so quickly my parents would be ashamed.

And the anticipation that sparkles in the black chasm of his eyes says he knows it—is reveling in it.

I cannot spare a glance at my father.

Sharpen your mind, Mariana.

I try. I do.

The breath I heave into my lungs is stuttering and shattering in my chest.

His blade slices just under my cheekbone as I lean back to avoid it.

Better than going through my neck.

My warm blood is running down my cheek, my neck, burning in the cold wind.

I breathe in and sharpen.

Sharpen my mind. Sharpen my eyes, my perception, sharpen my movements. Sharpen everything that makes up my body.

The dead body in the corner of my vision gives me hope.

And the flurry of blows I give back are enough. Enough to give me a modicum of confidence.

Enough to give my father an opening.

His longsword pierces through the front obsidian armor just as the Crow has his blade up to block my own.

The battle ends with a choke and gurgle, shocked black eyes meeting my triumphant ones.

There is heat at our backs and rage-filled cries coming towards us from afar—the heat of flame driving Crows towards the exit—the only exit—slowly but surely.

There are no words said as we work in tandem to open the gate.

There is only years of sparring, laughter, and love to guide every mirrored movement. Four blue eyes that dance at a plan well-executed.

We slip through the slight opening and grab the flaming torch from the sconce beside the gate.

Liquor bottles are sitting there, awaiting us. We go back in and douse the inside with as much as we can before setting it alight from the other side.

The gate becomes a flaming pyre, a closed door to this room of desecrated lives and hope.

It will take a while for all of this to burn to the ground. I look back at the flames licking up the sides, moving to the top of the carved gate. I can feel the heat emanating from the town, even as my father and I run to our meet-up point.

I hope their blood boils in their veins.

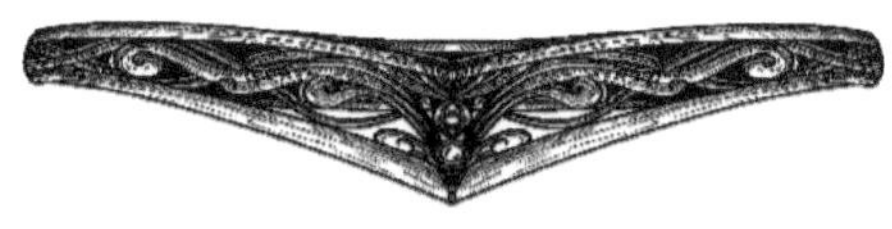

Chapter 25

All I know is desire and flame. The burning of that night in Tristram was but a taste of what rides me every time Fionn and I spend time wrapped in one another. His hand tangles in my hair, pulling my head back, allowing him access to my neck. Every line of him presses against me, but it isn't close enough. No matter how hard I press against him through our clothes, it leaves me wanting. Even as I straddle his lap and try desperately for what my body is begging of me.

It wrings a groan from him as his broad hand slides to the crease where my thigh meets groin over my skirt.

"I have to go," he gasps out. But he rains kisses on my face, and moves once more to my mouth, devouring and tasting, like it is never enough for him either.

"Okay," I say, pulling myself a little closer.

His groan is more of exasperation now, annoyed at his own desire, annoyed at his past self for making a commitment to leave our room this morning.

The night before was uneventful, both of us too tired to take advantage of our shared private chambers, though I saw the thought flit over his face. I all but fainted into bed, its soft sheets a luxury I don't think I will ever get used to.

He pulls back and looks at me, his eyes falling like rain over my hair, surely tousled and strange in color, my eyes, surely wanton and glazed. He draws his finger lightly down my nose and lips in tandem with his eyes. That contented honey-glazed look of his turns my bones soft and heavy, makes me caress his tanned skin back. He chuckles, warm and rich at the move.

"You have to go," I whisper, teasing. Daring him to want his space now. "I could go with you," I offer one last time.

He sighs, the happiness melting slightly. He softly moves my hair from my face, tucking it behind my ears. "Alyx, you know I want you to come, right?"

Lies. If he wanted me to come, he would let me come.

"I know." I don't let my smile budge.

"But you... are so beautiful. But so memorable." He winces. "So memorable that if anything at all happens, you will stand out. We are stuck here for a few more days. And you know you don't even have to be doing anything for a Crow to decide to harass you. You're noticeable. And if one of those parasites sets his sights on you... I'll have to stop it. You don't know what they're like... what they could do to people."

I'm afraid my soft smile wavers, a ripple in the water. I do know.

He sees it. "I mean—I know you know—sort of. But they hold themselves back in front of humans. There are still pretenses to keep up here. They weren't holding back when they destroyed my whole world. They weren't holding back when they killed my Queen. They weren't holding back when they leeched every bit of life from the ground beneath my feet and rendered hundred-year-old warriors helpless babes. If Elva hadn't been there, we all would have been dead. The influx of all of that energy they wielded… none of us stood a chance." Torment fills his eyes—something like bitter fear and hatred. "Which is why, we are going far away from here, for as long as we can. I have searched every corner of this realm for the rest of our people. They are nowhere. They are gone. We all know it. So now, we have each other." He swallows hard. And his eyes turn possessive as they run over me, hands grasping a little harder. "And they will not lay a finger on you again. So, I need you to stay here. I'm just trying to make sure things go smoothly."

I don't argue with him. I know him enough to know he won't listen to what I have to say when I really don't need to go out—I just want to.

"Okay," I say, softly.

And when we pry ourselves apart and Fionn takes one last look at me sitting on the bed, pulling at the water in the glass on the table, making it into wobbly shapes and trying to freeze them, I try to look understanding. I try not to look like a child put in the corner. I keep trying after the door clicks shut and I hear his swift footsteps recede.

I stay there for hours. For as long as it takes for the air to feel stale and stifling. The small window is the only source of light in the small room. I move to sit on the floor, hoping it will be cooler on my skin.

Even as my breathing slows and sweat beads on my forehead, I fight the feelings that pull me down, down, down. I lose any strength to move the water—to move the air. I lose the ability to be anything.

I just sit there where he left me. He will be back, I remind myself.

Even when I can feel the melodrama of my emotions annoy some small self-condemning part of me, I can't stop them.

I pick at my nails, and the woodgrains on the floor. I try to reason with myself. *He has his reasons; he just wants to be able to focus on the task at hand. He cannot do that if he's always worried about you. He will come back.*

Does he really feel that way? Or are his reasons just convenient?

I chew on the skin around my nails, my lungs tightening. I watch the dust float through the air in rays of sunlight.

It all reminds me of so many days spent sitting in nothingness. Being stuck.

God, I couldn't leave, for so long.

Does it matter? If I just spend a little bit of time outside today. He won't even notice I left. I can keep my head low. I just need to get out. I just need a distraction.

The salty streams run from my eyes to the bottom of my jaw. I can feel them drip off my chin. I don't know how long I've been crying.

What if he finds me like this?

That thought make me wipe my tears away violently, breathing deeply. I may have always been some weeping creature, rotting on some floor in a past life. But I won't let anyone see that from me again.

I stand up.

My cloak is on, hood up, before I can think. I quietly open my door and slink into the hallway. Doors line the entire length of it, a window at the end of the hallway the only lighting.

What if he has someone waiting for me to sneak out?

Do you think I don't know you, Alyx? A ghost of a memory echoes in my lover's voice.

Wanting to avoid angering Fionn wars with this driving urge to run—to get as far away from this place as possible.

They don't play fair, but in the end, I slip out the back door.

The sunlight outside is blinding. The heat is less stale than the room, the breeze warm and briny.

I secure my hood around my face, cursing its heavy woollen fabric, and merge with the crowd. The others wear hoods of linen and fine, summer fabrics that merely provide shade. My damned hair bleeding white from my scalp prevents me from shedding mine.

The tightness in my chest fades, burning away with the sun and the sea air. Too much stimulus drags me from the recesses of my brain.

I move through the middle-class district, small as it may be, as it bleeds to ruin and gray, the outermost district.

The minstrel's songs ring in the background as I wander, seeking something unknown even to me. Seeing, but not touching the softest blankets from the eastern continents, the spun glass vases from the glass roads in Ashvynd. They're illegal, but tolerated for the most part as the wealthy buy them as status symbols.

I've heard of the wonders of the capital my entire life. How the company of many wanderers all meld together in this place, a seamless immersion. I see skins of many shades and clothes of many fashions. The spices are warm, sharp, and tingling in my nostrils. They carry stories of meals shared across hearths all around the world, served from a loving mother, a servant to a king, wives to husbands after long working days in sun or snow. Songs in languages unknown to me float throughout the crowd, but the heart of it is familiar. Awe crawls up my throat at the sound of heartbreak known through tone if not by diction.

If this is the only time I ever have here, I'm glad to have gotten to have it.

I'm so lost in my pondering, I don't feel them. The gleaming obsidian of armor in my down-turned vision sends alarm skittering over every inch of my body.

They are depravity in a sea of culture and communion, tainting it with every breath and leer. As they trample their way through the crowd, treading upon instruments, paints, fabrics that were abandoned in the fray in the name of self-preservation, I wonder if this is what happened to the villages overrun by the Crows. Our culture stolen from us years ago from those that only know greed. Those that know nothing of art, of love and creation—that know only greed and taking. And all that is left is this little district on the outskirts of Raith. These people who still create and hold onto culture because they have no choice. For what do we have if not those things?

I keep my eyes to the ground as I jerk out of their way. They force their way through the crowd, parting the sea of people without a single touch. Though they look hungry for it—for an adversary. They will find none in me, for now.

I slip down an alleyway, slinking into back-streets sullied by waste and drug-addled denizens of the king's road that seek a moment's solace. The streets this way are lined with slums and seedy taverns, unfit for the wealth that walks the road that leads to the king's seat.

A blood-red door sits on the corner, its color stark in the otherwise drab street. My steps slow as I look up at its many stories, the windows faded and obscuring its contents, though I see the glow of candlelight through them.

"Something tells me you're lost, girl," a husky feminine voice says from the dark alleyway beside the building.

A black-heeled boot emerges first, and a blood-red silk robe follows, draped over a lithe body. The woman that emerges is long and graceful, every movement fluid and sensual. Her arm crosses over her chest, smoking a roll of some smelly herb from a long, golden holder with the other. Her face is sharp and angular—perfect. Her skin as fair as moonlight and her hair darker than night, cut to her chin in a blunt line. She has narrow, sharp eyes, similar to those of Deri and Aine, that peer at me curiously. A mountain cat surveying a fawn.

I suck in a breath, lifting my chin only slightly. "I'm right where I want to be."

She looks at me a bit closer. "I think you are exactly where you shouldn't be. In more ways than one. Were you planning to enter my employ? I could use a tall girl. You could step on a few throats for me, there's a market for that."

I keep my face free of the confusion that swarms me. Free of the embarrassment that comes when it dawns on me—a pleasure house—that's what the red door contains. And this must be the Madame. I've heard of such women. Owning their own business, even a distasteful one, is a marked accomplishment in such a place as Suri.

I pretend to look at my nails, bitten to the quick and bloody. I hope she can't see them. "I'm not seeking such employment, thank you. And I won't be stepping on any throats, no matter how many people want to pay you for it."

"Something tells me you'll be stepping on throats, healer. You just need to find ones that deserve it," she purrs.

Every bit of me turns to ice at the word healer. I abandon my survey of my fingers and look up at this terrifyingly beautiful stranger where she grins at me. Her white teeth are slightly too sharp. Without thought, I reach for her in my mind. I meet a wall of sound.

Sharp, screeching sound.

I drop to my knees and cover my ears at the ungodly screech rings in my ears, echoing down every pathway in my mind. The pitch is maddening and relentless.

She clucks disapprovingly. "That was very rude." She moves to stand over me, the scent of burning lavender wafting from her. "You are but a babe. How did you get here, healer? And why are you in the king's city? The very city where your name and likeness are plastered over every news-board."

The ringing. The screaming. I can feel myself drop further to the ground, curling around myself, trying to do anything to muffle the sound that comes from nowhere.

"Why don't you step into my office. We can have some girl-talk."

The ringing stops, the agony replaced by the sounds of my gasping breaths. The bustling street noises sound like whispers in comparison. I look up at her where she waits expectantly, all dark feline amusement.

I clamber to my feet and wonder how quickly my lifeless body would hit the stone if I ran.

She must see the thought as it flits across my face. "None of that. Come along now." She tilts her head this way and that, seeing down to the marrow of my bones. "I promise, you won't make it far. If you come with me, we may trade secrets. I find them to be far more useful than money. I won't tell anyone, not even your beautiful companion. What's his name? Fionn? I remember seeing him around, years ago. How finely his immortality suits him. Unchanging, so glaringly recognizable because of it."

I know my eyes are blown wide. How does this stranger know these things? And what is she? Her build and mental power says Danaan. But there is something else that lurks under her skin and I'm reminded of when Elva spoke of others that walk through rifts and glide between worlds.

She turns and begins walking back to the shadows of the

alley, each step loud on the stone streets.

As she knows I will, I follow. I look each way, seeking a rescuer. A pair of Crows wander into the road a few cross-streets down, seeking out prey. I cannot help but think I stand a greater chance getting away from them than getting away from her.

But years of conditioning keep me from engaging with them.

As the shadow of the pleasure-house swallows me, I pray to whatever apathetic god that I see sunlight again.

She stands in front of the brick wall and, after a moment, the sound of stone grating against stone grits against my ears. A glance reveals a segment of brick shifting back to reveal a hidden alcove with steps leading underneath the building.

As I follow her through, flame bursts to life. Sconces running along the stone tunnel illuminate the way, which is seemingly endless. I follow her down a short stretch of it and through a wooden door, into what must be her office.

The walls are swathed in green velvet drapes decorated with silver beads. Red wood furniture fills the space. Tchotchkes clutter every surface. Heavy golden statues depict all manner of beings, from nude goddesses to three-headed serpents stare at me. A diadem of heavy silver and ruby hangs from a curvy feminine statue's hand. A heavy bookshelf is on the opposite side of the room, containing tomes older than the ground beneath my feet. It's a hoard of treasure.

"Why am I here?" I gather the courage to ask, standing awkwardly in the center of the room, blatantly out of place.

She ignores me, sinking down into a plush chair at a desk, and pours herself a crystal tumbler of amber liquid. Lighting another rolled smoke, she takes a long drag. I smell something more warmly spiced this time. "Can I not just be curious about you? So rare to see, your kind."

"My kind?"

"Fae, I suppose. You don't look odd enough to be any other mind-reaching kind. I've never seen humans mind-reach, have you?" She looks at me expectantly. "Even though you clearly need practice."

"I'm human," I say.

She narrows her eyes at me, assessing. "Is that so? What an interesting new development for your kind, then." She sounds placating though as she runs her eyes over my body.

"What are you?"

She chuckles. "What do you think I am, healer?" She looks to be playing her favorite game, leaning back in her chair, taking another pull, then another sip from her drink.

"Well you say, 'your kind' a lot for a Fae," I surmise. "So you're something other. Not of this world."

She smirks. "That leaves an indefinite number of other species, if I'm counting right."

"You're Fomorian." I feel the walls closing in on me even as I guess it.

She laughs deeply at that. The sound is loud and jarring, out-of-place from her lips. "That's too rich, actually. The way you're so clueless is almost… charming. No, healer, I'm not one of those. How about this: I'll tell you one secret for another, and it has to be one I don't already know, and your answer has to be the truth. I'll know if it is not." She smiles coyly.

"Why do you keep calling me that?" I ask, agitated. I was never a healer, not truly. A healer's apprentice at best.

"I'll ask questions first, I think." She twirls the tumbler in her clawed hands, painted blood-red to match the door of her business. "Who are you?"

"I thought you already knew that." It takes everything in

me to keep my voice strong. She still awaits my answer, as if I had said nothing. What a loaded question. How does one summarize the entirety of their being? I can think of no other way than to begin listing the things I know with unequivocal certainty. "My name is Alyxara vch Seren, daughter of Garrick Erisson. I used to be a healer's apprentice. I'm a human with powers that came from somewhere... I don't know. I can mind-reach, I can wield..." I trail off as she looks at me in boredom.

"How droll. You really know nothing." She sighs and leans back again. She waves her hand dismissively. "You may go."

I blink stupidly. "What? I did what you said! You owe me a secret."

Her lip curls as she gets to her feet and hisses, "You speak lies."

I shake my head in denial. "I spoke truth. What do you want to hear?"

She comes to stand directly in front of me. Her eyes narrow and go distant for only a moment, before she hisses, "I thought to speak to someone who might have something interesting to say. You think that you're just a special human? Like you don't follow the rules of nature? I'll tell you this for free. You aren't special. Rare, yes. But not something that lives outside of the natural order of the goddess that created you. Rack your brain, healer. And take care in this city—better yet, run from it as fast as you can, or you'll learn things you would rather stay blind to." She lifts her chin elegantly, gesturing to the door, waiting for me to leave. "Go. I have an appointment shortly."

Mind spinning at the interaction, I turn on my heel to leave.

"Feel free to return when you have a real answer to my

question, Alyxara."

Chapter 26

Mariana

Inhuman roars echo across planes of green and farmland, shrouded in the dark of night. So faint, they fly underneath the wind. I almost feel them across the hair on my arms. They ring and grate across every nerve—nerves that already sit on high ledges.

Rebels. Traitors to the Crown.

The title feels like an honor and a noose.

That's what we all are now.

Last year, our town was nearly six hundred. The Crow's sadistic hunting of us and the many that have peeled off in the night, searching for a safer place to live out their life has thinned the herd. A hundred or so of us remain. A hundred and Eldrick's dog. The wiry-haired hound weaves through the company at knee-height, tongue flopping about in ignorant glee. He periodically comes to walk with his master, shoving his head beneath Eldrick's hand which swings tiredly at his side. The sight begrudgingly pulls the corner of my lip upward.

We've traveled across Surin soil these past several weeks, picking our way in the dead of night slowly. Now I know what it is to be mourning while also feeling hopeful.

"The Banshee," Mom leans over to whisper in my ear, our red hair tangling slightly in the wind. "Her cries supposedly ring in the silence before death, that's what the locals claim at least. Let's hope they're wrong." She wiggles her eyebrows at me.

I smile placatingly and shake my head.

The Mounds. Leagues away they loom, the cries echoing from them. They are gargantuan shadows, even in the night, obscuring the starlit sky. Treeless specters, coated in smooth lush grass, they protrude without reason from the flatlands near Dun.

"The entrance to Hell, they claim. Fitting that the banshee would be calling souls to the underworld from such a place," She goes on, boredom forcing the whispered chatter. She never could stand a quiet moment.

"Maybe Hell would welcome us. Maybe they could be our allies," I whisper back sardonically.

My mother shakes her head in amusement, but defeated worry flickers across her fair features.

We have no allies. We have nothing but our fire, a tiny flickering flame of rebellion, hoping the winds of oppression don't snuff it out.

While we believe we burned all of the Crows of Comraich to the ground, there is bound to be word reaching the king soon. Bound to be whispers in taverns and gossip returning to nearby posts. Enough gossip to warrant a nearby troop to wander through Wynedd to confirm or deny.

So we keep a low profile, seeking a stronghold. Seeking a hearth in which to build a true fire. People argue for fleeing to Ashvynd for sanctuary or to join their raiders—try to channel their energy into something more productive. Some say we should flee to the eastern continents, seeking asylum. Some say we should go straight to Raith and start a war— rally the people and rise up.

Some people are fools.

Grasping at shadows, betting on poor odds—we all know it. It makes the days long and tense at camp, and the travels at night full of whispered arguments. It makes our numbers dwindle with every coward that flees.

Fleeing to where?

There is no safe place in Suri.

No relief comes with the dawning of the light. Lilac skies only make the mounds to the northeast feel larger, darker through the large barn window. The cries have gone silent with the growing sunlight, allowing some semblance of peace to fall over camp. We found the barn on the edge of a farmer's land, no livestock currently occupying the stalls, so we all huddle in, lying down on bales of straw, finding rest where we can.

It's nice. Aside from the smell of shit.

My father sits with his circle, the carrier of our little flame, my mother at his side, tucked into his broad shoulder. I sit to his left, maintaining a united front—something solid in the ever-changing tides of our reality.

I stare at the golden sun as we have a variation of the same argument we have every night. I listen to the birds sing their morning songs.

"Those men are savages. We should surpass them and fall in with the Dragon King's cause," Eldrick argues. He's speaking of the 'savage men' of the Ghael mountains, the Reaper their savage leader.

"And trade one tyrant for another?" My father is as tired of the argument as I. "We stick to the plan. The Dragon King has his own agenda. He knows no morals. He will not be fighting our war. He will be fighting his own."

"How could you possibly know that? Besides, does it matter? If we have a common enemy, it makes us allies," Eldrick keeps hammering, running his hand over his furry companion's head. The dog sleeps—blissfully unaware, last I checked.

"Because I know." My father's voice is firm. Hard, because, while people noticed our fighting in the escape, none have received answers as to how we can do such things with such skill. Nobody needs to know right now—better to play our cards close. "And we are allies until we find ourselves under another regime of terror and control. We are allies until he places himself as the Pretty King's successor before his body is cold. I don't know about you, Eldrick, but that is not the future I am fighting for."

The silence is pointed.

"What are you fighting for?" Sara asks from her spot beside her neighbor. Her curly-haired child sleeps tucked into her side. We had thought him a goner after everything with Alyx and Diana. Without a healer, his mother was sure he would die, but the strong boy pulled through and is now healthy as can be.

My father's eyes soften slightly before he says, "Safety, freedom. I fight for my daughter to live however she wants, without fear. I fight because I want to wake up and not be crippled with fear that today is the day they'll make an example of me, my wife, my child. I fight against the dying of hope. We will not find that in the Dragon King's war."

I fight the urge to pinch his side when he calls me *his child*. As if I'm not twenty.

The words are my mother's, I hear her in them. I've heard her whisper them to him when they thought I was asleep. But people will only listen to them in the tenor of a man's voice. So we follow suit. Maybe this new world would be different, but until then, we pick our battles.

Maybe that's what all new empires say. "Don't try to force too much change, it will make you fail." "Don't take a stance too radical, it will lose you support. It will lose you allies." And now here we still are, no progress having been made. My mother, who is every bit as capable and strong and smart as my father, is silent at his side, relying on him to say what she wants to say. Thankfully he does, because what would she do if he didn't?

Suddenly it all feels like an excuse—a pile of shit.

I drown out the sounds of more discussion. Who else will ally with us? Where will we strike first? With what? We seem to be getting a little ahead of ourselves.

Through it all, I watch the long wheat sway in the breeze, and let it begin to lull me into dreams of more than this— more than hiding in barns and whispered hopes.

Shadows lurk in between the stocks of wheat. They move with the wind. Rhythmic and worldly. Ominous.

They shift, grow and shrink. That's when I notice them truly. They have their own movements. And the violent orange of dawn has nothing to reflect on, so why is there something of glittering red moving through the grass?

I jolt to my feet and walk slowly to the doorway.

Silence falls behind me, except the quiet sounds of my people rising to their feet.

The birdsong has quieted.

They are perhaps three quarters of the way through the field, the wheat parting with their smooth advancement.

"There is something out there," I whisper. "They're

stalking towards us."

Hunted. We are being hunted.

Swords scrape against sheaths as we prepare to defend ourselves against…something.

I quickly wake our people, quieting all of their rumblings with a look.

We shuffle out a stall opening in the back, nothing but an open field and the light of day awaiting us.

My father forces us all to take the lead, him falling to the rear, ready to defend against whatever pursues us. My mother and I are at the head, swiftly jogging towards a small wood far off the edge of the field. The wheat whips against my arms, the ground beneath my feet uneven from the bunches that grow together.

We crest the top of a hill and stop dead in our tracks.

Crows. Tens of them advancing up the hill, waiting for us. Their mounts wait at the bottom in armor fit for a king's steed.

They were herding us.

The bald Crow, unburnt, is leading the troop up the hill, his smile twisted in malicious anticipation.

Commotion from behind forces me against my mother, brushing my arm along hers, sliding together, back-to-back. I see them.

Monsters of the darkest kind. Snarling, red-eyed hounds, their jet-black coats consuming the light. The eyes I saw glittering in the wheat.

Dad, sword drawn, engages with one on swift feet. It morphs before my eyes, shifting and twisting onto two feet, front legs elongating into spindling long-fingered claws. Maintaining nothing but its night black coat and red eyes. It swipes, moving with inhuman speed and strength, slashing right through my father's leather vest, gouging long scratches that pour scarlet.

I try not to let my mom feel my jagged breathing as Dad, battling his own terror strikes swift as a serpent. His movements are well-honed and decisive.

Four more of those things slink towards us in the long wheat.

I look back at the Crows, who stare at their hounds in glee. Several of them watch in concentration, muttering to themselves.

My mother moves against my back, the sound of blades clashing rings out.

I turn against all instinct, giving the monsters my back. The men are closer threats.

Taking a centering breath, I unleash myself upon them.

These opponents seem to ooze brute strength and power.

Every slash of mine is met with greater strength and swiftness than should be possible. I push myself to the edge, battling with every thought, every movement driven by instinct.

The few people behind me draw their own blades and give it everything they have. Their lives depend upon it. The blade is metaphorically and physically at their throats, and they resist it.

The little training we have done in daylight hours these past few weeks is not enough. They begin to fall—quickly.

My ire blazes, providing much-needed strength to my blows.

A distracted Crow, one without a blade drawn, watches the hounds decimate our group from behind.

I take the killing blow.

His life ends with a blade through the heart and a wet fluid-filled breath, the sounds slating my thirst. I hear a yelp behind me and chance a look back. A hound stumbles around, running from an injury that doesn't exist. Bits of it peel away; flecks of black, like ash from a fire, float away on the dawn breeze until it is nothing but a memory of horror.

I look back at the Crow I just ended, a theory forming. A quick glance around tells me more. Another Crow lies dead, no wound on him. One of the ones that muttered. One of the ones whose hound my father killed.

"Where are the fucking humans?" they had said as *Comraich burned.*

"…Humans."

"The fucking humans… "

I had thought about it many times. Finding the wording odd.

But now I don't.

These things, these Crows and hounds live by rules outside of humanity.

My new targets are the other two that stand behind the other battling Crows, my theory giving me a renewed vigor.

I have no time to search for Mom and Dad. They can handle themselves.

A shadow falls over me. The bald Crow, the leader, steps into my path of destruction. My head meets his pectorals and he is easily three times my weight.

I lunge without hesitation.

There is no humanity in what meets me.

He battles lazily, as if toying with me.

He rushes forward, swinging wide to keep me from escaping, from rolling out of reach. Clearly hoping to scare me with his size and strength.

I duck towards the blow, just under it. His broadsword catches only the ends of my flying hair, trimming it slightly.

The slight tug of my hair happens at the same time I slice through the tendons at his heels.

They give out in a powerful snap just as his hand comes back to tangle in my flowing hair, jerking my head back and down to the ground as he falls forward.

The world spins from the impact, I try to roll away despite the daze, but his hand is fisted in my hair. I aim to slice it off. Either my hair or his hand, I have no preference, but he yanks me up and I cry out, my blade missing either target.

His sword comes to my neck as I settle against his broad chest, somehow cold against my back. We are both sprawled in the wheat.

"You flaming bitch!" he grits out, yanking my hair in rage.

His blade presses so hard, quaking with rage, that blood begins spilling down my neck, wetting the tunic around my collar bones.

Something claws in the back of my mind, making the air freeze in my chest. He has a grip on something inside of me. It feels like freezing pressure, pulling on my chest. The edges of my vision blur.

A cry of rage so fierce rings through the air just enough to pull his blade from my neck.

A cry I recognize as well as my own.

That internal hold releases with his physical one. I gasp for precious air, rolling away from him.

He gets up just in time to meet my father as he descends upon him.

My father is everything I've ever striven to be, as he not just handles the attacks, but puts the leader on his back foot. Driving him far from me, down the hill. He stumbles over his bad leg, severed tendons rendering it unusable.

I don't squander the opportunity he has given me, dispatching the few Crows linked to the hounds, proving my theory as the hounds dissolve in the wind.

Dad and the leader still battle at the bottom of the hill. Blow for blow, neither giving nor wavering. It's an impressive feat, that the leader can even fight back with one leg.

I stalk down the hill towards them.

A pool of shadow grows from nothing behind the bald Crow. Eating and consuming all that lies underneath it.

And from it a hound claws its way out.

I start running down the hill.

It is no use. The hound leaps on my father's back, clamping its jaws around the back of his neck.

I've never heard my dad scream before.

Shrieks tear from him, born from more than just pain, but terror.

I'm sprinting, then tripping, then rolling down the hill. Springing to my feet and sprinting harder.

Through whatever terror my father is living through, he pulls a dagger from his belt and slides it between the beast's ribs. Over, and over, and over again.

The bald Crow, having stood back to watch, slices through something inked in the skin at his forearm, somehow releasing the hound that has only just released my dad. It's too wounded to continue. It dissipates like the others, floating away in flecks of nightmare.

I won't ever remember the last steps I stumble down the hillside, the bald Crow kneeling in front of his conquest locked in my gaze. Pleasure suffusing his expression as he does... something to him. My father's corpse desiccates in a blink.

There are no thoughts as I reach him, nothing but purpose as I pull his own dagger from his waist.

There is nothing.

Nothing.

Nothing.

Except fire in my veins.

As I leap up his body, wrapping my legs around him from behind, and plunge the dagger straight into his eye, carving it from his skull.

He throws me off him as one would fling a cat, but I keep my hold on his dagger. His eye, torn from its socket, is nothing but a round bit of blood, flesh, and jelly in the dirt.

Satisfaction and disappointment leave a taste so disgusting in one's mouth.

He stumbles back to his mount, blood pouring from his face, and takes off.

There are no Crows left to follow him. No hounds left to terrorize.

It's so heavy. So, so heavy now. And he's not here to help me carry it anymore.

I don't know how long I stare at his figure disappearing over the horizon.

I don't know how long until my mother finds us, falling to her knees before Dad.

I don't know how long she screams or how long I stand there, a ghostly specter clutching the dagger of my enemy.

I don't know how long it takes us to burn the corpses of battle, my father's amongst them on that field.

I know the sound the Crow's eye makes sizzling in the flames.

I know that dusk's sun melts into the horizon when I finally get up from where I kneel.

I know that there is no beauty in this ending.

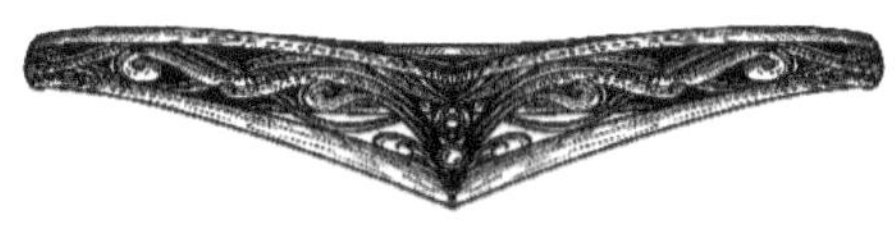

Chapter 27

When I make it to the middle-class district, the sun has fallen far behind the walls surrounding Raith, casting the city into shadow. My pace is quick as I move through the crowded king's road and come upon the theater, the stage uplifted so the majority can see over the crowd. I shoulder my way through the swarm of bodies, the heat still unbearable even in the late afternoon.

On stage, the play is running, the actors shouting their lines across the space. I gather it is the story of the Pretty King's ascension to the throne of Suri. The prior king is draped weakly across his deathbed giving his monologue.

"Son of no blood. I lie in my deathbed, no heir to my name nor seat. I have not one person I trust to carry on my legacy, but you. From the moment you stepped foot on Surin soil, I knew you to be a patriot. I knew you to be the embodiment of the hopes and dreams of my people. Finish what I have started. Rid us of the scourge of the Dragon King."

A painted wooden dragon of flaming cobalt carried by

two stagehands bolts across the stage, their human roars echoing in the silence after the king's speech. It runs off the other side of the stage, disappearing behind curtains.

"With this mission I bestow you, and the power to do so."

The actor playing the Pretty King sits at the king's bedside, the rouge on his cheeks bright even from here. He's a tanned, sharp-jawed male, his hair painted a dark brown. A crown of gold and emerald already sits at his brow, a green and black cloak drapes around his broad shoulders. Surin colors, with the white fox sigil emblazoned at his breast. He sits there in regal solemnity, accepting his crown earned from no blood but from sheer fondness from the heir-less once-king.

The actor, beautiful in his own right, continues on in newly crowned splendor. His voice, rich and beautiful, sings about the beginning of the king's reign. His passion for the people and hunger for the end of the Dragon King. The actor has such heart, such ferocity underlining every movement and word, that I actually believe it for a moment.

It truly is something special. I wonder what he could make me feel if he had a subject he actually believed in to perform.

The Crows line the crowd, watching intently for any slight, any lewd joke, any hint of impropriety attached to the Pretty King's name.

In the beginning, there was much dissent. Many claimed he obtained his crown through deceit, that he was a snake in the grass sent from the Dragon King himself. Shortly after his coronation, the Crows flooded cities and countryside. Those dissenters found themselves strung up along the walls, and any art condemning the Pretty King's reign was replaced with odes to his glory.

Keeping my head low, I duck down an alleyway, fleeing the crowd. I take a side-street to the back end of the inn, hoping to sneak back in. I almost sob in relief when I reach the back door.

A hand from behind slams against the door as I go to open it. I know his hands immediately—their every vein and callous. Know them from when they've run over my body, memorizing me, holding me. The sight of them freezes the air in my lungs.

I've never heard Fionn's voice tremble with restraint before, but it does now as he says, "Did you enjoy yourself?"

I turn slowly, my shoulder brushing his heaving chest. To say his eyes are burning is an understatement.

"I'm sorry. I needed to get out. I just needed… some air." My voice sounds pathetic even to me. It sounds like carelessness. It sounds like I'm a self-centered fool.

"Did you try opening the window?" His voice is caustic grit.

My throat is held in the vice grip of his anger as his body keeps me pinned to the door.

I shake my head, unable to meet the venom in his eyes anymore. The words choke me as I force them out. "I just… I was getting so upset. I don't like being left alone, in that room. I'm sorry for worrying you. But I kept my hood up the entire time. You had to know that the risk was minimal." I try to reason with him. I reach to put my hand on his chest but think better of it, and let it fall.

"You don't like it?" he spits back. "You know what I don't like, Alyx? I don't like thinking you are safe in our room, only to come back and feel like a fool when you aren't there. Feeling like a fool for believing the words that come out of your mouth. I thought what we had warranted truth from you. I thought I could trust you."

The guilt shakes more words from my mouth. "I didn't mean to. I wasn't planning on leaving, alright? I just couldn't breathe in there, I felt like I was dying." I'm aware that I sound ridiculous and that the truth is pathetic. And to make matters worse, I'm now crying big manipulative tears that I cannot stop. Wiping them away as fast as they fall, as if I could keep him from seeing them. Disappointing him feels like falling down an endless hole. And I'm scared. Scared that this moment came so soon and I'm not ready. "I'm sorry, I'm sorry. I didn't mean to go so far and to be gone so long."

He pushes off the wall, pacing the alley.

I can finally take a deep breath in the space.

I don't want this to be the reason he decides I'm not worth it.

I just went for a walk. But I don't know how to fix it.

He's wild-eyed when he turns back around, pulling at his hair.

"I looked for you. I searched everywhere. The others are risking themselves, searching for you. That is why! That is why, Alyx. It's selfish. After I tried to explain it to you. I try to make you understand and you just don't. To put everyone at risk because you went a little stir-crazy. Do you know what it does to me? I could not breathe. You know I care about you. You know I am responsible for you. To have spent the last hour searching the city for you, knowing that you could already be in a dungeon. Or a corpse?" He heaves a big trembling sigh, staring at the brick wall above my head.

He won't hear me. Maybe if I just stop talking, I won't feed his ire. Maybe I can let him talk it out—rage if he needs to. I'll just take it, whatever it is. I knew the consequences and now I have to face them.

I just stare at the filthy street and wait for him to

continue.

"Where did you go?" he finally asks, turning to me.

I just shake my head; the truth won't make him calm down.

"Tell me."

I finally look up at him. He only seems to be getting more self-righteous.

"Nowhere important," I say, looking back to the ground.

He's right back there, in my face, taking it between his rough hands. Hands that usually feel so good against my skin, warm, gentle caresses. Now they feel too rough on the skin of my face. They squeeze just slightly too hard. "Tell. Me."

"I just went to the end of the king's road, to see the performers," I say, looking him in the eyes, trying to be convincing. I'll tell him the rest when we are on the boat to Ashvynd tomorrow. When he isn't steeped in rage and paranoia.

"I checked there." He nods, cocking his head to the side, muscle in his jaw feathering underneath his golden skin. "Where else?"

His consciousness brushes against the outside of mine. Gauging me. I make sure my shields are strong.

My hands start to shake. I shrug and say, "Just down a couple of side streets. The Crows were heavy on the main road, so I dipped off to the sides. I stopped at the play a couple of blocks away. Watched a couple of scenes." I account for the extra time with that little lie.

His eyes narrow. "Is that it?"

"Yes. Then I came back here." My eyes flicker between his.

It feels as if giant hands are painfully pulling my walls apart in my mind. I whimper as I fight it. If he feels my emotions he will feel that I'm keeping things from him.

"You're lying to me."

I'm building my walls again, part by part, as he tears them down. His mental strength is too much to combat.

"It was nothing," I whisper. "I promise, I'm sorry, it was nothing."

My hands clasp over the sides of my head, like that can stop the unravelling. The painful tearing. Like he's in my house, kicking around all the furniture and breaking the windows.

"Tell me, then. You know I have to know. For everyone's safety."

He's right. I've put them in danger. That woman certainly didn't seem harmless. But the thought of telling him how I've messed up, when he's like this, feels dangerous.

"When I went down the alley there was a woman—"a heaving breath—"she called me a healer. She knew us—you—she said she remembered you. I don't know how. She made me come with her to her office—"

He withdraws quickly, and the pressure collapses.

Every line of him trembles now as he stumbles back.

I only have time to take a step back before it becomes too much.

The power he wields is always so tightly leashed. I don't anticipate the sheer force of it as he bursts into flame.

Every bit of me deserves it as I lift my arm over my face, an errant limb singeing through cloth and skin.

It's hot, so hot for a few seconds, as my skin sizzles and so does my heart.

The moment is so painfully slow as I experience it.

We never got much snow in Comraich, but one winter we did. One winter the whole world was covered in white, and I remember thinking that everything was so quiet. Like the entire universe stopped singing. The trickling of the creak, the song of birds paused. Frozen under a blanket of snow.

As the dust clears and I fall to my knees, it is that silence.

I take a shuddering breath as my head raises to the threat where he stands panting, looking at the wreckage with abject horror.

I've pushed him so far. Too far.

"I'm sorry. I'm sorry. I'm sorry," I whisper, desperately trying to placate him.

He's slowly approaching me, as if I'm an injured animal, hands up.

I wait for further condemnation. To pay penance for my selfishness and lies, but none of that comes.

I try not to flinch as he kneels before me and wipes at my cheek.

The tear is gray with soot, and I wonder what my face must look like.

"Alyx…I'm so sorry. So, so sorry—"

Boot-steps, light and swift sound down the alley. A small group of them.

Fionn covers me from view, as if hiding his crimes. I peak behind him anyways, needing to see who approaches.

"Fionn, what did you do?" Deri snarls when he beholds us, kneeling in the rubble. He sees the wall, painted with soot behind us.

Dealla gasps, sidling up to her mate. Horror melts from her face and turns to stark feminine rage, cold as stone and pointed directly at Fionn. She advances on him in a blink, and he is thrown from his place at my knees down the alley, rolling from the force of it, kicking up dust and dirt. He coughs.

Armund stares in shocked horror, seemingly torn between running to me and going to help Fionn. He chooses nobody, forever the victim of indecision and inaction.

Dealla is pure righteous fury as she stalks Fionn down the alley. "What kind of male are you? Using your power to hurt people weaker than you. Pick on someone your own strength for once." Every sentence is punctuated by another blow of power, some solid wind knocking Fionn back several paces with every strike.

Deri appears at my side, one eye on his mate. Fionn has finally begun defending himself, deflecting the blows only. Behind him Konan watches, hand on Aine's shoulder, holding her back, looking disapprovingly at me. Elva is nowhere to be found.

Deri picks me up from where I kneel, surprisingly gentle for his hulking size. He peers into my eyes, taking in the mess my face must be. I don't try to hide anything. I don't feel anything. It's all ringing in my ears—all white snow covering the whole world.

"I would sooner carve my heart from my chest before raising a hand to Dealla or Aine. You should have faith that Fionn would do the same." Deri's words are hard. He's not much for words, except when he feels they're needed. There is regret lining his eyes, strange on his normally gruff exterior. He strokes a hand down the back of my head, and it fractures the snow-covered peace. I can feel my hands shake now.

I nod, but I don't believe him. Dealla and Aine are his mate and child. Fionn doesn't even know what I am. Fionn does not know me… not really. All I to do is drag him and his Fianna into trouble. All I am is a burden.

All I've ever been able to do, is bring ruin. It can't be a coincidence.

How can I keep pretending it isn't me?

When everything around me wilts, how can I pretend I'm not poison in the water?

I don't know why. All I know is that it is real.

I wonder if Deri's words would hold if he knew that I have endangered all of us. Endangered his mate and child.

"Well, this day just keeps getting sweeter," a dark voice sounds from behind Konan and Aine.

My blood runs cold.

I turn to see a group of fifteen Crows advancing on us, painting the world in darkness as their shadows crowd out the world behind them. The one at the front's eyes glitter with hunger, even in the blackness. A twisted smile mars his gaunt face.

"I knew I felt Fae."

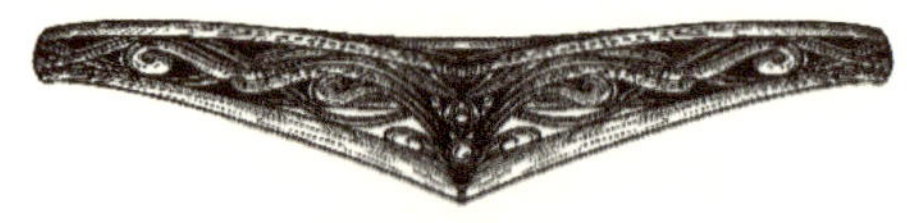

Chapter 28

Konan is the first to spring to action as the Crows descend. Grabbing Aine from her stunned silence, he sprints to the rest of us. Armund follows just as fast.

A whip of shadow and menace shoots out at their retreating backs.

One makes contact, Konan's grunt of agony the only indication of his pain. His hold on Aine doesn't waver.

Half the group of Crows pursue the pair, their inhuman speed reaching the rest of us before I can blink.

Deri meets the group in pursuit of his child head on—an unstoppable force of will in a dark alley.

The ground trembles as a wave of stone rushes to meet them, flowing like water over the earth.

Arms of ivy snake out to wrap around throats and whip across faces, barely slowing a descent of shadow and wrath. Dealla leaps over Deri's wall of stone to better wield them, an extension of her own fear and fury.

I soak in the energy from the ether, begging my mind and

body to recall, to center, to be able to wield—to be of use. To be anything but sitting prey.

Konan has gotten his ward to safety and has turned around, shooting vengeance for the strike at his back. Flame bursts past my ear, consuming shadow and choking the air with smoke and power. He leans his whole being into the hit, punching flame down the whole stretch between buildings, teeth gritted. It twists in a dance with the shadows that consume and become consumed by it.

I can feel frost gathering beneath my feet.

Fionn's wind pulls at shadows from all directions, manipulating flame and feeding it. He's bleeding from his own cuts and bruises as he passes me, and I worry he is already weakened. He moves to the front regardless.

I step forward, ready to defend. I will not cower in the corner and wait for death.

The Crows keep coming, seemingly unaffected, waving away power with their combined might. Almost dismissive of the display as their shadows choke and blur the whole world.

The shadows—they whisper.

Shivers raise over every morsel of my skin.

They were nothing.

They were the absence of everything.

Sucking in a breath, I almost feel them crawl down my throat.

I raise my hands.

They lick at my face.

I see a group surround Dealla as she twists with hundreds of vines.

Fear rises up, and with it, power.

She gives up on the vines and they fall limply back against their stone home.

She punches spears of earth through their chests.

I can't see through the shadows behind the group, but I know there will be blood splattered on the stone wall behind them.

I pick my target—the one at the back, the one who spoke. The one who commands.

I reach for him, for the flesh he is made of.

My hand claws as I turn it to ice.

As I picture every drop of blood solidifying in his veins.

The pull on my energy is horrifying; I drop to a knee.

He grasps at his chest. His lips, once a pale shade, turn blue.

I clench my hand to a fist, feeling his heart, sluggishly pumping in his chest. I feel the strands of every muscle and synapse that keep it pumping.

Even these monsters are made of flesh.

And flesh is power. Flesh is energy.

I try not to let the flame still shooting past my face distract me.

I don't let my eyes wander to Fionn, locked in battle with a group of his own, receding by small steps.

I don't see anything as the Crow's eyes snap to me, widening with awe and horror as I pull.

He falls to his knees, and I feel a tiny smile lift the corner of my lips.

I push.

He shatters.

Pieces of him fly to the winds. Wisps of silver—a mist of life—float up from his remnants.

I fall down to all fours with every shred of strength fleeing my bones.

"Mom!" Aine's scream curdles my blood.

I whip my head back at the purest of us, dreading what

I'll see.

But she's not fighting a foe. She fights her friend. Konan barely keeps his grip on her.

I had not noticed the flame's absence. I see the wielder holding Aine back as she thrashes—wildly striking out at him, flinging every limb and fist as she screams.

And screams.

And screams.

"Mom!"

The forest across the creek only holds shadows, and no answers. The tears streaming from my eyes freeze on my little chubby cheeks.

I call again, begging, hiccupping sobs. I sit there and listen for her response, eyes darting, looking for every moving shadow. I wait for her to walk through the branches. Any second.

"Mom!" I sob.

She just went to gather more wood. She said she would be right back. She left me in front of the fire, eating my breakfast, alone. But that was so, so long ago.

The fire went out, and Daddy won't be back from town until after dark. It's so cold. So cold and she isn't here.

I wonder if this is punishment for throwing a fit when she said I couldn't go play with Mar today. She said the snow was too high to trudge all the way over there on my "little legs." I cried a lot and called her mean. I'm sorry. She's not mean, she's nice most of the time. I'll tell her. As soon as she comes back.

I stand there and call for her.

My pleas turn to accusation after my voice turns hoarse. I'm sorry, I'm sorry, I'm sorry. I would tell her that if she would just come back. I fist my hands in my dress, pulling it tight, trying to make it warm again. It's all hard and cold now.

I sit down, the snow crunching under me as I tuck my knees into my chest and wait. And watch the woods. And wait, until the water stops coming out of my eyes, and I can't really breathe, just hiccup. My cries are nothing but tiny little croaks. I wait until I can't feel my face, my hands, or my bare feet in the snow.

The glow of sun behind clouds has faded into darkness and my father races down the path, having heard my cries, now weak and husky.

She left me here.

I still stare into the shadows over his shoulder as he lifts me and carries me inside.

Why did she leave me here?

I watch Aine as she lives my nightmares.

I look back at her mom fight.

But she's no longer fighting.

She's kneeling on the ground, a Fomorian's fist around her throat. She stares up at him in agony, face purple and veined as he just… stares at her.

Deri has lost all sense of tactics. He's screaming too. Fighting, clawing his way across the ground to his mate. But the Fomorians are on top of him, barely containing him as his power slashes around him, too.

Fionn is similarly beaten back by his foes. Barely holding his ground.

I try to get off the ground, lifting one feeble hand. My weight too much for one arm, I fall to my chest and face. Standing might as well be climbing a mountain.

The ones holding Deri burst into flame, bodies like the driest tinder. Too late.

I see the moment all life fades from Dealla. I hear the moment she dies in Deri's screams.

She looks like a corpse already weeks gone as she slumps to the ground.

The Fomorian stands back to his full height. He looks like a man who just got a hit of the most potent drug.

Deri chokes and sobs, holding one hand to his chest, dragging himself to her body with his other hand.

He strokes her hair, sobbing endless apologies and pleas. He still grasps at his chest, as though he is hemorrhaging blood.

The Fomorian, still stumbling as if drunk, looks down at him, evil incarnate.

He unsheathes the blade at his waist, its blackened blade glinting as he twirls it once, casually.

Deri's face does not even waver from soul-crushed despair, despite knowing his death awaits him.

The Fomorian does not even give him the honor of last words before he lops off his head.

It makes such a horrid noise as it rolls across the stone.

Aine's screams, a constant horrific drone in the background, begin to get farther away.

Konan's back is a blur as he takes Aine and flees.

Armund follows them.

Fionn falls as I look back to my last ally.

He looks back at me, all-consuming fear in his golden eyes as he sees me, prone. The Fomorian above him raises his shadows, preparing a death blow.

I lift my hand, but not my head. Reaching not for the man that somehow still holds my heart, but his attacker.

I don't care if I die. I never have. I just wish my life could have been more useful than a shot in the dark.

Pulling from every dreg of strength in my pitiful

muscles, my heart, the marrow in my bones, I take aim and channel—flinging the small stone, the size of a berry, straight through the head of the male about to kill Fionn.

It crunches going through his skull.

My vision goes dark as the rest of the remaining Fomorians pick over corpses of friend and foe, making their way towards me. One already replaces the one I killed, incapacitating Fionn with a single blow.

Chapter 29

Mariana

The world is on fire.

I scan the horizon, invisible smoke in every mountain in the midnight skyline.

It's there. I can't see it, I just know.

Whispers at my back. Traitorous murmurs of replacement. Snakes in the grass grasping at my father's seat that he left to no heir. A kingdom of dreams with no castle, no power, nor money, only a dying flame.

Their whispers mean nothing. My solemn silence at the front burns a trail through the grasslands of Suri.

The only thing that means anything to me is this task. Justice.

Reach the mountains, establish a place to put these hopes, some place that may hold them.

Then what?

I used to dream of traveling across the Great Salt Seas. I used to dream that my family would wander, unbroken, seeing everything. I wanted to see every bit of water that ever fell over a cliff-side. I wanted to see every animal that ever lived its quiet life of survival. I wanted. I wanted everything all the time. I wanted to know what it was to live and experience. I had so many dreams I never thought one single life could contain them all, but I would have tried.

Whatever demon holds my leash now wants nothing but justice.

"We need someone with strength." "Someone wise; you barely know how to read." "Someone with vision, Rhodri's shared vision." Their words ring in my ears. Three men vie for the opportunity to lead this mewling rebellion, squabbling amongst themselves.

Eldrick may be the obvious choice. He made a good showing of himself in the battle with the hounds and Crows. He knows it too. His arrogance grates at my raw nerves.

Osian is cunning. Exactly the kind that would have drawn my father's eye to mentor and made my mother wary. His family always had new leather shoes and food that went to spoil. He is educated, far more than the others in town. Fair-haired but slender in build. He has been to the capital, felt its riches, fit right in with his soft hands. But he's not cunning enough to defend his position from men that would take it.

Men like Tarrant. The smith's son has dark features, large stature, and hands roughened by years learning to craft iron, making him a formidable opponent. Ruthless enough to challenge Osian and take his place like taking a toy from a child.

Their endless debate hammers at my walls of apathy long enough.

"None of you deserve to stand where he stood," I rasp, stopping in my tracks and turning to face the men that follow behind me.

They stop, shocked at my input.

"Who would you back then, princess?" Osian sneers.

None of them can hold my stare as I go down the line. Every one of them is a weak man, desperate to be corrupted by power. They pretend to share looks with one another to avoid my bleak assessment.

"I would back someone with a brain and body to hold power. I would back someone who has even a shred of honor that my father had." I hold the silence in my fist. "I see none of those things in you lot."

Tarrant rolls his dark eyes and looks at me as one would look at a child. "This cause needs a head."

"Obviously," I reply dryly.

Eldrick speaks it to life, though his voice is full of doubt. "Are you suggesting you lead, Mariana?"

My mother, dead-eyed, shifts on her feet beside me. She has not uttered a word. She only walks silently beside me, occasionally brushing our shoulders. A reminder to both of us that we didn't lose everything, it just feels like it.

I assess the rest of my audience. Our numbers are at half that of yesterday. Sara, her hand on her son's head, looks at me with a speck of encouragement. Does she know the consequences? Does she know the price of choosing a woman as the leader of a movement so important?

"Only if people are willing to follow me." My sentence hangs in the air, coloring it with disbelief. Sara nods at me though, and it feels like a maternal hand on my shoulder.

"Exactly why a woman cannot be allowed to lead. Do you wish to quash this movement before it even really begins?" Osian states, jaw fluttering in dislike.

"What is it? About me. What makes you think I would be a poor leader? And do try to come up with a better reason than what's between my legs." I look at my fingernails. They have blood under the whites. I haven't cleaned them after the battle.

I hear scoffs from a few, far less than I had anticipated.

"Well for one, what would you do if someone tried to take it from you? Tried to kill you dead, just like your father?" Tarrant spits.

His words roar in my ears.

I look from my nails to him, cocking my head. I know he's baiting me. He's not the clever one.

"Would you like to try?" I whisper.

They all saw me fight. Saw the Crows that fell under my blade. None have had the guts to question my mother and I about it. I think most are just grateful to have people who know how to wield a blade, regardless of their gender. Tarrant's arrogance gets the best of him in the best of times though, much more quickly when there is power on the line.

His smirk spells his confidence and his death. "Certainly, princess."

The smile that crawls across my face is fueled by nothing but violent anticipation.

"Draw your blade. I'll wait." I look back at my nails.

It scrapes against its sheath.

I hear steps shuffle back in the grass from the spectators. My mother caresses one hand across my cheek as she turns to join the others. She's not worried.

I don't draw a weapon. I don't need one.

His sword whistles through the air as I dance a step over, ducking under his slashing blow, landing behind him while he desperately whirls around to see where I went.

"It's alright. You didn't get a chance to warm up. Try again, princess," I mock.

He might be decent with a blade against an ordinary

opponent. He even held his own with the Crows. His every slash and thrust is swift and smooth, the blade an extension of himself. But he was not trained by the best assassins of an age. There is no comparison.

I lead the dance, blade never making a single moment's contact.

I'm waiting for him to tire, performing to make a point.

His frustration makes him careless. So pitifully careless.

Using his own movement to trip him, I grab his arm, wrenching it behind his back, disarming and pinning him. I force him to his knees as he cries out in pain.

"Have I addressed the claims you've laid against me?" My voice is as dead as my heart.

"You fucking bitch! I'll kill you." He spits the words between pants.

I let the weak threat pass, unaffected. "An example needed to be made. Thank you for volunteering." My voice, sweet as honey, sings to his cries.

I wrench his arm until I feel and hear the crack of his shoulder tearing from his socket. I kick him to the ground. Ignoring his screams, I pin him with my boot.

"Have you any other concerns?" I ask, benevolently.

He's crying like a child now, gasping through tears.

Men. So unable to push through pain the way a woman can. However did we all become so deluded into believing women the weaker sex? Was it the muscles?

I leave him there, whimpering in pain, and turn to the rest of the group.

"Is anyone else wanting to test their hand against me? Or are you satisfied that issue is laid to rest?"

No one steps up, they only stare in wary admiration. I nod, satisfied.

"What else?" I ask Osian, cocking my head.

"It's not just about what we think. What of the other leaders? The other kings, landowners, people with money—how will we ever gain allies when nobody could ever take you seriously?"

I look around, noting the nods. I nod with them.

Mom isn't nodding. Sara isn't nodding. Most women aren't. They look disappointed. Pinned in a corner of societal expectation and narrative. They've taken the advice of the men and stopped asking for more. Look where their leadership has gotten us.

"Yes, that is a problem," I state, looking back at Osian's smug face. Sara stares at the ground, no doubt bracing herself to be disappointed. "I fear my father may not have been clear about what we are fighting for. Not clear enough. It needs to be known that we aren't fighting to simply usurp a ruler. We are fighting for something more. We aren't meant to simply survive—to scrape through each day and call that life. No man, nor woman, nor child, should be brought to that. If you don't believe woman are worthy of representation, aren't worthy to lead, perhaps we aren't fighting for the same thing. Perhaps you would never ally with this movement to begin with. Perhaps they don't belong here." I look at Osian and Tarrant, looking down their noses at me. "Perhaps you don't belong here. For what is freedom if it only extends to the few? What do you believe in, Osian? Should only the wealthy have this new world? People like your family. Only the men then? Where are your lines that you would draw? Who do they leave to rot? Would you have us all serve at your table? Would you have us at your feet?"

With that maneuver the tides change.

My mom even has the tiniest spark in her eye.

"Of course not," he says, glaring back at me.

Eldrick pipes in, dog panting at his feet. "Your vision

and approach, while admirable, may leave us destitute. May doom us all. May doom a revolution that has promise. Is it worth the risk?

"I think you'll find that we are not alone in our ideals. I think we will find that the masses probably have similar thoughts. Our circumstances were not wholly unique. We have lived under the same tyranny as many. We have seen the same injustices. Endured the same atrocities. It would be irrational to believe these same circumstances have not birthed a similar thought. I believe many outside of our party will want to fight this fight," I assert, looking around at the rest of my people, seeing approval in the eyes of most. "I will not force anyone to follow me, just as my father wouldn't. You may leave. Find another movement, push your own vision of a better world. But if you believe in mine, in my father's, I would be most grateful to serve you as your leader." I only wish my voice could sound more than bleak as I say the words that rally a revolution.

It's Sara who speaks first, my speech seeming to have given her a leg-up as I elevated myself. "Everyone in favor?" She looks down at them all, finding her power in mine.

Suri is diseased. Something rotten spreads. Something greedy takes.

I ask myself what coin, unjustly taken, will be the last.

What gust of wind will be the one that topples a precariously perched empire?

As I look out at my people, I think it will be me.

My lips curl into a tiny smile, my first since my father fell.

And with their acknowledgment, even Osian, Tarrant, and Eldrick, we walk into the new dawn, a burgeoning flame, and I, their leader.

My mother says her first words since he died, "You're

just like your father."

Chapter 30

All I know is stone ground under my skin, ringing silence, and endless night without a star in sight. Sometimes I wonder if it's me. Have I gone blind and I just don't know it?

Days must have passed since that fateful fight—since the world crumbled beneath my feet and I woke up here in this purgatory of nothingness. It's a guess. There have been no signs of guards coming in or out, aside from the scent of stale bread beside my face, metal cups of water beside it. They seem to always wait until I slip into unconsciousness before leaving my food. By my hunger I assume it comes less than once per day. Pride eludes me in the moments where I consume it like a rabid beast.

The air feels… empty. Like there is nothing here for me to wield, even when I know this to be impossible. When I reach out my mind, seeking anything, it is as if someone is talking to me, but I've lost my hearing. I can tell there is communication happening, energy sparking, but I can't hear it, can't feel it.

The torment is question-less. Without interrogation from my captors. Purposeless.

Why am I alive?

A head rolling on cobbled stones.

Fionn's head slamming into the ground as he looks back at me. Gold eyes meeting mine across a battlefield, wide in fear for me, for us.

Blood spraying, a rock crunching through bone.

I tried to save him.

I hope he's dead.

At least then he wouldn't be subjected to this imprisonment and the guilt that salts my wounds.

Even if the thought of never again seeing his molten eyes soften with want for me makes the air scald my lungs. The thought that I'll never again feel his rough hands softly wander over my skin pangs through my emptiness.

My tears have dried up. I've received too little water to form them. So I sit in the ache they make in my eyes.

What is there to rage at but my own failures that led us all here? What do these feelings do but become acid eating at my soul? Who is there to destroy but myself?

I've crawled every speck of ground in this cell. Felt the crack where the doorway is, felt its solid stone, tore every fingernail in my desperation to open it.

My foot touches the door even now, hoping to be awakened by a guard coming in.

I should stop eating. Let myself waste away until I truly am nothing but a husk. End my own torment.

My instincts are becoming my enemy. They are unwilling to let me die. If I had only been strong enough to fight them all those other times. When I stared at that lump in the ground as the sun rose and fell. When I first felt those claws in my mind, grabbing, taking. I should have let them.

My toes smash into the stone wall behind the door. Someone's coming in. Sharp light assaults my eyes.

I would fight the large figure who yanks me to my feet, but my joints are frozen in their bent position. I've barely moved in what feels like an eternity.

When the guard throws me out the door, there is no choice but to stumble on blind feet and blind eyes until I collapse once more. The stone beneath my knees is rough, but blessedly less cold—downright warm. I press every inch of my skin to it, still squeezing my eyes shut. Practically prostrating myself to whatever fate awaits me in this bright room just to end the agony of freezing.

I can feel the dark presence when he stands in front of my prone form.

My eyes still cannot bear the flaming light of the torches. I curl in on myself, protecting my organs.

His voice is deep and rumbling when he says, "Another poor showing from the Fae. What a pathetic excuse for life you are." His steel-toed boot pushes me over.

I squint up at my tormentor.

Gaunt skin is cloaked in black-as-night armor from neck to toe.

There's a raw wound where his eye should be. Even with my limited vision I note the swelling, the crusted blood around the jagged cuts that are evidence to the method of removal. There is deep purple and red bruising all around the flesh. His other black iris watches me as I take him in. The torchlight flickers in the reflections off his bald head.

He's waiting for me to say something.

There is a panting in the silence, somewhere behind the guard. Deep, like a giant dog after a sprint. The light illuminates the green stone walls, polished and smooth, so deep in shade it nears black, with gold veins glimmering throughout.

The castle.

The only place made of this stone.

That is who holds me.

The Pretty King.

I look to the Fomorian who stares down at me hungrily.

There is nothing left for me, even as I feel distant sparks of energy now that I've left my cell. I can't wield such power; I cannot even wield my own limbs.

What can I say to change an inescapable fate?

He squats down slowly, meeting my eyes with his one remaining, unashamed of his wound.

His nose scrunches up, such a human movement of disgust. "You reek."

Surely I do. The skirt from the day I readied myself to go see Raith is stuck to my skin with my own piss. I haven't had the awareness to notice it until this moment, as it melts in the warmth of the room outside my cell. "No matter, I can always get you cleaned." He tilts his head, the move all lupine predator. "The king—he says if I can get you to break, I can have you." He bares his white teeth in a smile, looking over my emaciated body before meeting my dead eyes again. "What a treat that would be."

Something in his tone is sarcastic, the most personality I've ever known a Fomorian to show.

He moves his leather-gloved hand over my raw and scraped jaw, the move burning. "Now that I have you warmed up, you can tell me what I want to know."

I just stare and listen to the deep panting in the corner.

What he wants to know? What could he possibly want to know?

"How many were traveling with you?" His eyes gleam,

excited.

I have nothing if not my allegiance to the people who helped when they had every reason not to. And I will not fail them now.

He tilts his head the other way. "We have your friend. What's his name? The one with the gold eyes? What pretty eyes the Fae always have. What pretty eyes you have. Two different colors." He shakes his head and looks closer; I can feel his breath on my face. "Fascinating."

I hope he sees hatred burning in my "fascinating" eyes.

The corner of his mouth quirks up again as he takes my hand and places it, palm down, on the stone floor. "It's just been so long. So long since I've seen one of you. Since I've tasted one of you. Such boring morsels, humans are. They taste so bland. They fight so poorly, there's no enjoyment in it. They have so little to offer."

"Then why bother with them?" I rasp, sounding as if I've been screaming for days. Perhaps I have.

He smashes the metal hilt of his blade down on the knuckle of my pinkie finger, shattering it.

I scream in agony.

He moves to whisper in my ear, "Because they have something that belongs to us."

My hand is on fire as I meet his glittering onyx eyes again, gasping as my whole body begins to shake at what I know I must endure before the end.

"How many were in your group?" he asks again.

"Just us. Just him and the other two your men killed," I sob. I will not crack.

He strikes again, shattering the knuckle of my ring finger.

I wonder if Fionn is here. If he hears my screams and thinks I deserve it for landing us here.

In my bleariness that rings with pain, I note windowless doors lining the room. More cells.

"Please lie to me again. You scream so prettily." He laughs, maniacally. "Where did the others go? The three that ran off." He lifts his eyebrows.

Mad. He's insane. And suddenly I know.

I know none of this will end quickly.

He will keep me here, breaking every bone in my body with joy in his heart. He will peel the skin from my bones and flay me alive. When he's done, he will rape what is left of me. I see it in the run of his eyes over my breasts, my legs. He's making plans. How best to take what he wants.

He sees my realization and nods with a smile.

The hardest thing I have ever done is keep the sobs from ripping free from my chest. The tears are already running from the pain, my body already trembling from shock.

I try to let the fear filter through my eyes though, play off the reactions my body is too far gone to hide.

My lies come out in big blubbers. "They are going to the southern continent. There is a ship that was supposed to take them, it has probably already left." I look in his depth-less eyes, begging him to believe me.

He cocks his head again. Giving nothing away.

Death cannot come soon enough.

My plan has been unfurling in the back of my shielded mind.

I jab my finger in his injured eye, feeling it tear through the still-healing wound. Flying into the attack as abruptly as my broken body will allow.

Blood spurts from his eye as he chokes out a low shout.

I kick, scratch, and punch any weak point I can find through his armor, hoping to send him into a blind rage.

My torturer shoves me to the ground, half-blind by pain,

grasping at my flailing limbs.

My claws on my good hand rake down his face, talons of vengeance and desperation. Blood wells in their wake as he grips my wrists and smashes them to the stone by my head.

I scream too, my newly broken bones crunching against the stone.

I kick out at his abdomen with every bit of energy I have, earning a grunt.

He works his way between my thighs and my bare feet hammer desperately at his lower back, aiming for kidneys.

He grips my shoulders, picking my torso up and slamming me into the ground again and again.

I let my neck go limp against every instinct, feeling the back of my head cracking on the stone again and again.

The sound of it echoes in my head and the room around me.

Torchlight blinks out of existence—once—twice—but they come back as I struggle for breath against all effort.

The wrath twisting his face, blood-streaked from his re-opened wound, tells me it is not enough. Close, but not enough.

He doesn't break another finger.

He rips me to my feet by my arm and begins dragging me as I stumble behind him.

He brings my back to his chest, face to face with a nightmare.

He brings me to face the source of the panting from the corner—no Surin beast.

Built of shadow and ether, a hound-like projection stands, twisting and writhing as if in pain. Elongating limbs crack into spindling claws. Teeth snap at the air as they grow upward, towering over even the Fomorian who holds me.

The metamorphosis settles as a hunched beast on two

legs of glowing red eyes and blade-like teeth.

My torturer whispers in my ear as I face the most horrific creature I've ever encountered, "Look at him. Look how he looks at you. You thought I would kill you?" I feel his panting breaths on my neck as he shakes his head. "Usually it takes years to break you Fae. Looks like the time in the human realm has caused you to weaken as they do. What a shame. I do wonder which you will taste like though, but I'll hold off until I get my king's permission." He spits the word out like a curse. "The Pooka made no such promise—has no such loyalty. Things get out of hand at times, it's unavoidable." He lurches me towards the beast—the Pooka—laughing as I press back into him, somehow the lesser of two evils.

The beast drops slightly, one of his fists curling and meeting the ground as he leans forward to smell me. I can feel flaming hot fluttering breaths on my arm.

The Pooka growls low.

The Fomorian's hand caresses my filthy hair as a lover would, right over the part of my head that's cracked and bleeding from being smashed into the floor. I grit my teeth. He whispers in my ear, "I think… that I'm done for today. I think I'll let my beast have his reward."

He throws me at its feet, backing away with a releasing whistle.

I look up into the red glowing eyes of a nightmare as paralysis creeps over me.

The Pooka grips my arm in its claws, blood rolling from the places it pierces. His breath is hot on my neck, fluttering in moist exhales before he bites down, tearing at the place where my neck meets my shoulder.

The pain is drowned out by a sea of nightmares—so many bloody visions of a life lived alone that feel as fresh as the first day.

Visions of rattling, bloody coughs, lumps in the ground that have no reason, freezing toes in the snow, screeching beasts of a silver fogged bog, and screaming. It's amazing I recognize them all. Horrible that I recognize them all. Fionn's, Aine's, Elva's, Mariana's, my mother's, my father's.

It goes on forever.

It goes on forever.

Chapter 31

Mariana

My muscles burn with purpose, yet are lax with exhaustion as I join the group in the cave. Mist clings to my skin, forming little drops on my flaming hair as I pass beneath the roaring falls.

We will rest here for the night, having spent the past two days traversing the Ghael mountains, overlooking Slaver's Canyon. Far beneath us, in the roots of the mountain, corpses litter the mines. Slaves clamber over skeletons of their fallen comrades, fallen family, just to make it through one more day in hell. I can see them, like ants scurrying about. Dark figures observe, herding, whipping, keeping the peace.

Some sick humor remains, tearing a macabre laugh from my chest at the thought. Peace.

The Ghaels are brutal, stone mountains, jutting from the earth like vicious teeth. Titans lording over the pass between nations, waiting for you to die at their feet. Every step feels like a defiance of some greater god. A few of our group has already fallen halfway down cliff-sides due to the rock peeling away beneath their feet. They're hurt and chastened, but alive.

We are scraped and starved, exhausted and losing purpose. My fragile leadership weighs heavy, bringing me to the verge of collapse.

Whispers of the Wildes, the group of raiders said to haunt these mountains, flit through the camp like embers, sparking fear. The Reaper who leads them is legendary. He has eradicated entire towns in his quest to be a thorn in the side of the Crown. A worthy cause, I almost think, but his method leaves something to be desired. Is there a way to wage a war without the deaths of bystanders and innocents? That thought haunts my every waking moment. It seems the Reaper has rid himself of such a heavy debate.

The days have been long and the nights longer, growling stomachs roaring through the night. My family and I have our portraits on newsstands by now. We've sent a few less-recognizable rebels into the villages and towns along the way. They purchase rations, supplies, and anything we can get away with. They try to spark discussion in taverns of fairness and justice. Perhaps a rallying cry always begins as a whisper.

We hunt and forage along the way to fill the gaps in sustenance. It slows us in our trek, but dead men need not worry about pace. The groundhogs and rodents that burrow within the stone have been tricky. Way too intelligent and keen-eyed to be overgrown rats, as they appear. Our funds have dwindled to almost nothing. A painful precipice, a gust of wind may topple an entire rebellion. The thought runs in circles through my mind from moonrise to sunset.

My people pass around their meager dinners, sucking the marrow from bones, licking filthy fingers clean of whatever fats melt onto them. Someone offers me a bit of leg of some poor mountain goat as I stand over the group, ensuring everyone has something to eat. I accept, gratefully. It is gone quickly, but I needed to silence the sound of my organs devouring themselves. Mom says I'm a stress-eater. Unfortunately, we haven't had the resources these days to cope in such a way, so I'm a ball of restless energy.

As people mill about, their murmurs and community echoing through the cave, I grasp my arms, holding myself back to keep from pacing, despite barely having the energy to keep standing. I see the vultures, though. I see Tarrant, arm in a sling but with a full belly, staring up at me like he waits for the moment I pass out so he can kill me.

He doesn't realize that I fear no man. I could kill him in my sleep. I could kill him as a corpse.

His eyes make the dagger at my hip feel heavier. Veins of cobalt run through its blade. It is formed from a strange metal—a rare type of ore, one might think—so rare I've never seen it before. One that could fund a rebellion, or at least stave off hunger for another fortnight.

My voice is authoritative as I shoulder my pack and declare, "We will stay here for the next couple of nights. Or until I return. I will be going to town briefly to see if I can upturn our position. I think I can get us some coin, some more rations. I will return by tomorrow night. We need rest anyways. A day of hunting for more rations to dry and preserve will serve us well as we ascend further into the Ghaels."

I look to my people, hollow-eyed, but looking up at me with trust. Trust that I will prove myself worthy of. That trust burns something in my chest.

"You need rest too, Mariana," Sara says, from her place in the corner. Her son, Henry is asleep under her arm. "Rest a night and then go down." She gestures at the fire.

The thought of spending another sleepless night in these caves, with nothing but my thoughts and hunger chasing me in circles is unbearable.

"I must go now. I can move quickly alone. I'll see you again tomorrow." I force something like confidence into my shoulders, my face. "Keep out of trouble. Especially Henry." I smirk lightly, forcing energy into my steps as I depart.

"I'll go with you," my mom says, appearing by my side suddenly.

I flinch. God, will she ever stop moving as quiet as a ghost? "No, Mom. I'll go alone, and you'll stay here and make sure Osian doesn't convince everyone to leave me."

"Sara is right. You have to slow down. Sleep through the night."

"I don't want to. There is too much that needs doing."

She grips my arm, pulling me to a stop just outside the entrance to the cave. The waterfall roars in our ears.

"You have to stop feeling guilty. He would have wanted you to take care of yourself. You can't keep on like this. You'll fall asleep on your feet and tumble over a cliff. You have to slow down." She's practically yelling to be heard over the cacophony. The mist collects in water droplets that run over her freckled face. They look like tears.

"You too," I say simply. I see her bloodshot eyes. I know she doesn't sleep. She barely eats, she sneaks it to Henry whenever she thinks I'm not looking. She's trying to be strong for me, but I know better. I'm trying to be strong for her too—for everyone. And it makes me feel like I'm going insane. Maybe I am. Maybe we both are. "I'll be back tomorrow. Stay here. Do all those things you told me to do, and I'll do the same when I get back if you do. Keep them safe. Keep them smart. I need you here. There is no one that I trust more. Please."

She starts to shake her head in denial, water flicking everywhere. She must see the look on my face though, for she just sighs deeply, puts her palm to my cheek—scarred from the slice across it the night we set Comraich ablaze—and says, "Like my life depends on it, Mar."

One nod. Then I'm off.

I make good time on my journey down, but my muscles are weak. Even so, I only slip on the rolling pebbles a few times.

My ass is going to be bruised in the morning.

As I revel at the silence of the night, I'm already beginning to dread my trek back up tomorrow.

The night melts into lavender dawn as I take my first step on level ground. I skirt around the canyon, crossing back over the roaring river at its lowest point. Back on the merchant-worn road, I keep my hood over my flaming hair as I traipse into town, keeping an eye out for the Crows and their otherworldly hounds. Keeping an eye out for a particular, single-eyed monster.

The town of Gormes, nestled at the foot of the mountains, is filthy busy. Everything is covered in a layer of grime born of dirty deeds. Earning coin off the back of slaves—poor souls who did not pay their taxes pay now with flesh, sweat, and blood, until the Crown deems their debts repaid. The mine owners are some of the wealthiest people in Suri, combating even those of the rolling green estates of Farus. The slave owners facilitate the repayment of debt to the Crown, taking a huge cut. They uphold a bustling economy for the merchants that pass through, always willing to throw their coin at a trader for a rare artifact, if only to display that they can.

I amble past a newsstand, running my eyes over it as I walk. Nothing specific of our rebellion in the postings. Only the normal propaganda. News of the raiders, fearmongering, justifying the oppressive presence of the Crows. The Dragon King's threats of war loom over the country.

As I slide my eyes over the ransom posters, I spy one of the Reaper. His face is frightening. Some say his flesh was melted off by the Pretty King himself, punishment for some offense before he turned enemy to the Crown. Whatever the reason, his skin is scarred, melted together in twisted masses. Ordinary blue eyes stare out of scarred skin. The man that haunts my people's nightmares.

I'll kiss the dirt of the Ghaels if my group never runs into his.

A poster of my father stops my heart in my chest. My eyes in another face. What a cruel twist of fate for the artists to capture the likeness of this one face so startlingly true. The scar through his eyebrow makes him look positively criminal. My mother's portrait is beside his, looking so like me that I tuck my hood closer.

I shouldn't stare at the posters; I'll draw attention. I barely keep my trembling knees locked in place, keeping me from falling to them.

Will I ever get another chance to simply look into his face?

I cried for others. When the Crows came and laid waste to entire families and displayed their cruel trophies for all to see, I cried for their families—for their loss. I don't know if it is a strength or a weakness, to feel the loss of another.

I have not cried for this loss though. It feels like too small a gesture—too little to pay tribute. This burning emptiness feels like a more apt offering. To live with a gaping wound in the center of one's chest forever, silently and stoically. Is it enough?

Never.

Like my life depends on it.

I walk away.

My steps are forceful, splashing mud up my pants as I storm further into town, seeking a merchant with whom to bargain.

I wonder if this is what drove Alyx away—this rage. Living with injustice pressing on your chest every waking moment, having to pretend it's not. Masquerading for others' sake.

The collectors ride past, hauling a cart full of freshly enslaved men, women, and children. The last one draws a second glance from me. I had heard of forcing children to pay the debts of their non-able bodied parents, but the sheer number of them makes my steps falter. Unseeing eyes, hopeless.

The kind of anger it incites is of another kind.

Burning resentment feeds into burning injustice—something I can hold and use.

The crowds around me mill about, unaffected. Trading, bartering, funnelling through the streets in apathetic greed.

I come upon a building crowded with an eclectic mix of tools and statues. The door creaks as I push it open, finding an even more overwhelming number of trinkets and oddities crowding the small shop. It smells of must and dirt. My footsteps thump against hollow wood in the silence.

"Hellooooo," a croaking female voice calls out. I square my shoulders and harden my eyes as I round a tower of eccentric baubles. A veritable maze of maces, cheese knifes, saddles, stone carvings of some voluptuous goddess, snowshoes, and hats.

The hunched figure stands at a counter polished from use, various blades and weapons hanging from the wall behind her. Wiry white hair is messily pulled back, revealing a wrinkled face, tanned and spotted by the sun.

"What have ye' lass?" a toothless mouth lisps.

I don't put my hood down, keeping my hair tucked back and face lowered.

"Something that requires a bit of discretion. Do you have it?" I keep my voice low.

Her eyes take on a greedy gleam through their opaqueness. "Certainly… For a price."

Of course. A creature born of greed would always demand more.

I cock my head at her, contemplating. "Funny thing, discretion. It's only worth anything if we both have it." I cock my head the other way. "So how about this? You see what I have, sell it for what I'm sure is a pretty coin, keep your mouth shut about where it came from, and I won't tip the Crows off about the gigantic cellar you have underneath your floorboards, full of unsavory objects, I'm sure." It's only a hunch, but the tightening of her lips tells me it was a good one. "I know I can uphold my end of discretion, but can you? Or will you have to hope that I don't reach you before the Crows do? It would truly be a fun game for me."

Her lips mash together in annoyance. I wonder how she likes the taste of her own poison.

"I don't take threats kindly, lass." But I see the waver in her brow, the quiver in the corner of her mouth. "And I would na' stay in business so long if I allowed customers to bully me out of a fair price. I believe our transaction to be over. Me son will be back soon, ye' best run along now."

I have to admire the way she straightens and strengthens. But I don't deserve my people if I cannot provide for them— if I cannot win for them every time.

I lean casually on her counter, propping my chin on my palm, my voice lilting and wretched. "You don't have a son.

And nobody is coming to save you from me." I let her see the cruel in me. "But I fear we have gotten a bit out of hand, don't you agree? I simply want to draw on your expertise and perhaps make a trade. A fair trade. Can we not do that?"

It's almost funny, how little pressure it takes to crush a worm. It almost makes me sick. It makes me see how easy it must have been for the Crows. How easily we bend.

Well I am done bending—breaking.

If I am to break, I'll shatter and make them all bleed.

She gives a singular, begrudging nod.

My smile is as fake as fake gets, showing her my teeth just as surely as I showed them to her with my threats.

I pull the dagger from my belt, showing the cobalt streaks running through black steel, glinting under the candlelight. It thumps heavily on the counter as I lay it in front of her.

It may as well be a viper.

She takes a wobbly step back and her eyes widen. "Where did ye' get tha', girl?"

"Not in question," I push back firmly, baffled by her reaction. "How much will you give me for it?"

She shakes her head. "Nothing. But ye' best take it and get going." Her wrinkled hands go to her generous hips. "Go on, girl. I won't say a word, but ye' have to leave."

"Why won't you take it? Clearly it is of impeccable build. And a rarity."

She stares mulishly at me before saying, "Tha' blade is made only for the king's use. For his highest-ranking generals. Mined by the slaves in these very mountains. Coveted by two kings for some reason I'm not privy to. I trade in many things, girl. But I will na' trade in such wickedness. Its mere presence is a death sentence."

So she fears that it's owner will come seeking it. "Surely

you can put it in your floorboards like you do your other less savory trades."

"Girl. The only way ye' got yer hands on that thing is by killing one of those things. Now I don't know how ye' did it, or what game yer playin', but I'll do ye' a favor and tell ye' to get that and get out of town. Throw it in the river if ye' must, but ye' won't find a willin' buyer anywhere here. Don't go wearing it about. It's the mark of a traitor. And more than that, I would also urge you to find sometin' to blacken yer hair. Ye' think I don't recognize ye' from those posters?" She raises her non-existent eyebrows at me. "Go, before ye' get us both killed. I won't utter a word of it, but ye' must leave. Now. I've told ye' everything ye need know."

My face flushes slightly. If she recognizes me because I look so like my mother, who else did?

The look in her opaque eyes tells me that I will not be asked nicely again.

I swipe the dagger from the counter and fasten it back to my belt.

The morning is well under way as I step out, drawing my hood further down my face.

How am I going to feed my people? I have no money, and no means to earn it quickly.

I make it to the river, lost in my thoughts, unable to cross it—unable to return empty-handed.

The mines sit upriver, across the bank from the city. I can see them from here, a giant wound in the root of the mountain. I may as well be one of the ants milling around, toiling away in it. Is this madness? This life we live. Is this all it is? Can fighting every day to merely survive be everything?

I stare at the fast-moving waters, smelling its freshness, its chilled viciousness. I could let it carry me down, winding down through the countryside. I could see all I can survive, be grateful for its thrashing and simplicity in my final moments.

I have no clue how long I stare at it. How long I think about following my fears into the white waters.

But when I come to, I have a plan.

Dusk's valiant light warms me with a promise of more as I dip behind the waterfall, squinting against the mist.

Blades scrape against sheaths at the sound of my steps. I raise my hands and call out, "It's me!"

Sighs of relief fill the deep cave as I come up on them. They all seem more well-rested than when I left, sitting around a blazing fire, chewing on mountain goat. I'm glad their hunts were successful today. My trio of adversaries look disappointed; I suppose they hoped I would be arrested or killed in town. I give them a sardonic smile. I'm certain at least one of them tried to make a play for my seat while I was gone.

Mom looks only slightly better as she walks to my side, rubbing a hand over my shoulder, in thanks for returning, I suppose. I'm not certain she will ever lose that solemnity. How does one go on when they lose a soul-mate? Walking around with only half of a heart for the rest of your days?

Sara gives me a warm smile, running her eyes over me as she looks for anything awry.

"We cannot continue on like this. We need to make a power play. One that will help our cause and our struggles. One that makes a statement," I begin.

The crowd watches with rapt attention, my words apparently resonating with them.

"As I was in Gormes, I found myself pondering our problems. If we continue into the Ghaels, we will probably all meet our ends. And it leaves us with the possibility of meeting the Wildes." People nervously gulp as I give voice to everyone's fears. "We have a mountain full of potential allies beneath our feet. Not only allies, but a mountain full of injustice beneath our feet. A mountain full of mineral that is highly desired by both Ashvynd and Suri. A fort full of supplies and infrastructure, nestled against a mountainside, easily held." Silence rings in the wake of my proposition.

"Yes, Marianna, a mountain easily held." Osian looks at me like I'm daft. "A mountain crawling with Crows who far outnumber us." He shakes his head at me, looking around at all the agreeing faces, gathering power from it.

"They outnumber us, now. But by my count they do not outnumber the slaves. All we need to do is what we've needed to do all along—liberate them. Something tells me they won't need much convincing to join our cause. Or they may flee, seeking asylum in Ashvynd. They will find themselves pondering the same roads we look down. I know what we all have chosen. I want to believe they will feel the same and join us."

"How do you propose we liberate them?" Eldrick asks. "They are within and we are outside."

"I propose that we have forces inside and out. I propose we maintain our position out here, while we send in a few to rally within the camps. Coordinate an attack from both sides."

Apprehension thickens the air. Apprehension mingled with possibility. My people are considering it.

"You'll have a difficult time getting one of us to go into the slave camps," sneers Tarrant.

I nod. "You're right. I wouldn't venture to ask such a thing. I will go."

I snub the largest flame of doubt with those words.

My mother grits her teeth beside me, but she won't oppose me in front of the others.

"Mariana, you are our leader. You will have to learn to delegate such dangerous tasks," Sara speaks out, shaking her head in concern. "What if we fail? Who will lead?"

I consider her for a moment.

"Perhaps… but not now. This rebellion is a fledgling, and we all know it. I would not ask any of you to risk so much, not now. If we are to succeed, we may discuss my delegating such tasks. But for now, I am not so important that I cannot be replaced." I consider her question, who will lead if I die? Can I leave such things up to chance? "As for who will lead… I propose you elect a new leader. The numbers will tell where the people's trust lies." I nod, satisfied with my solution. But I am unwilling to throw my backing behind anyone. Perhaps the offer is enough to prevent betrayal from those who begrudge my being a woman. From those who want my seat for themselves.

There are no more protests, the people uneasy but accepting. I think many of them don't relish the thought of all this uncertainty but understand the need for it. We are weak. We need strength in numbers and resources and have no other way to get it.

Mom pulls me aside as conversation begins to buzz about the cave.

"I will go with you," my mother says firmly.

"You know you can't." I look her in her brown eyes. "I need someone I trust, implicitly, on the outside. I know you won't leave me there. And I won't be able to do my job effectively if you're there with me. People will know you're my mother. We look too alike."

She looks as if I asked her to leap off a cliff. "You want me to let my daughter walk into a slave camp, without me?

That is your play? Do you know what you're asking?"

"If we both go in, where is the promise we will get out? Can you look me in the eye and say that you have enough trust in any one of them to ensure we aren't left behind?" I think of the starving faces of my people. Corpses littering the floor of a mine. There is no other choice to be made.

"Then send me. That is a much safer move. I have more years of experience. I am far less important. Send me." Her eyes narrow, sure of her win.

For a moment I think she has.

"I don't trust you," I whisper.

Her eyebrows raise in surprise. "What do you mean?"

"I don't trust you to come back. To not take unnecessary risks. You've also never been much for politics or diplomacy, which we might need if we are to convince these people to agree to a war. And I won."

She flounders for all of two seconds before saying, "You won?"

"The sparring match. The last one. I won."

She scoffs. "Only by cheating."

"I didn't cheat. I outmaneuvered you. I won," I assert, bristling at her tone.

Her mouth is slightly ajar. "I'm still less important than you."

"Not to me," I say, firmly. "And besides, I don't plan on dying in that place."

She nods, looking irate at having been pinned in a corner. "You won't die in that place." It's more of an assertion but comes out as a question.

"I will not."

She looks around, as if unable to look me in the eyes as she nods her defeat.

"Thanks mama," I say gently.

I haven't called her that in years.

As the dusk fades to night, we plot.

By the time I wake the next morning, sunrise brings with it the hope of justice.

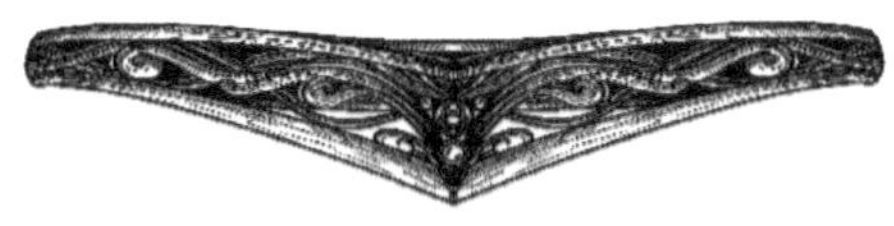

Chapter 32

Even when it ends, it doesn't.

Even when the Pooka's jaws unlock, the teeth slicking from my torn flesh.

Even when my body falls to the ground in a catatonic jumble.

Even when I curl in on myself on that familiar cell floor, the cold chilling me to my core, and hope to meet an icy death.

It does not end.

The nightmares both lived and imagined.

Mariana's ocean blue eyes, wide with fear—Thatched roofs afire, the smoke choking me, everything I had known, every speck of good littered between the bad, burning to embers. I hear them. The sounds of helpless desperation and sizzling flesh.

Endings that come screaming and stained with crimson blood.

Every fleeting moment of happiness tainted with loss.

Fionn's body, the place where his eyes once burned into

mine, sockets picked clean by crows, staring towards a hopeless sky.

It's all happening in my head. Does that mean that it isn't real?

Aine's laughter comes to a shattered halt, morphing to screams of unimaginable agony. Blood spilled on castles of sand. Screaming for me to help, but I am a phantom existing only in shadows. Poison in the water.

I can taste the brine in the air, I can feel the chill of the breeze and the sand between my fingers as I try to crawl to her but move nowhere.

Huge hiccuping sobs, tears freezing on chubby cheeks.

I reach up to my face, wiping them from the sharp-faced stranger I have become.

They run in an endless, cruel cycle in my mind. They curl around one another, blending together until I cannot tell lies from reality.

In all of them, the Pooka's hot breath fans across the back of my neck. The lurking nightmare of it shadows every memory.

Violet horn-tipped wings, huge and membranous, obscure the path of bleeding smoke on an overcast sky. Filtered light trickles through, veins webbing under the skin that catches wind and sweeps their owner upward and onward.

I pry my cheek from the floor for only a moment before it becomes too heavy. Sweat beads on my skin and my clothes cling to my limbs, making me claustrophobic. I let unconsciousness swallow me once more, unsure what torment is worse, that of my body or of my mind.

Warm candlelight casts shadows on a night-darkened room. A muscled arm falls off the side of a bed, the rest of the owner obscured by my mind's limitations. Sweat beads along the strong length of his arm as his fist clenches, tense even in rest. Bold scarlet ink is etched into tan skin—a scaled pattern that sweeps and defines the contoured muscles of his tricep and trails down his forearm, fanning out across the back of his broad hand in even patterns that point to his knuckles. The hand trembles and I watch a drop of sweat fall, glinting in the firelight, to the burnt-orange stone floor.

A hand smacks me across the face, jarring me from the dream, the first that doesn't feel like a nightmare in some time. It feels like a loss, to wake up back in this cell—greater than any I've known.

Peeling my eyes open to the twisted face of my torturer almost makes my tears fall. Almost.

I ask no questions as he pulls me from the room. He takes me from the chamber in which my deepest nightmares resurface and melt to new ones.

I take no note of the path we travel, withdrawing into some familiar dark room, seeing the world around me only distantly. We navigate endless tunnels, and he drags me up stone steps; their coolness feels good on my too-hot feet. They feel good even when I trip, unable to keep up with my captor's pace, and scrape the skin from my feet.

A double-door, larger than any house in Comraich, greets us at the end of a long windowless hallway. It's made from a dark wood, ageless and rich against the dark emerald and gold stone. Gold filigree flows over the wooden surface, carrying the golden veins of stone through the wood. Torches line the way, the only light permeating the space as my captor's footsteps echo in the large empty space.

The door opens seemingly of its own accord, revealing a throne room of dark regalia. A dark stranger sits atop the throne on the dais, his figure striking, elegant, in a way men usually aren't. Dark brown hair, cropped short on the sides, curls slightly around the golden crown, encrusted with emeralds. As my steps lightly pad against the smooth ground towards this man, the Pretty King, I know why they call him so.   His eyes are so blue I can see them from halfway across the room, piercing in their iciness. They almost sparkle, glinting with shared curiosity, while the rest of his face remains stoic.

Kneeling, chained, at the base of the dais, is Fionn.

My knees buckle in both despair and breathtaking relief.

He doesn't look at me, he only trembles, panting, staring at the stone in front of him. Unravelling before my eyes.

Now that they've found him, my eyes see nothing else in the room. I trace over every injury; see the way he holds his torso just so. His breaths are short: anger or pain. One shoulder seems lower than the other, arm hanging limply at his side, the nails on his fingers removed, leaving only swollen, bloody beds. His cheekbone is obviously fractured, its hugeness obscuring his peripheral vision. Beaten and tortured, he is a gilded knight returned from a bloody battle.

I had wished him dead for this reason. I would have taken all of this for myself if I could, while he slept peacefully in whatever afterlife awaits the brave and strong. Only the dead know peace. And while I deserve none for landing us both here, he deserves it all.

Guilt could not drive my gaze from its well-worn path over every line of him. It consumes me, churns my empty stomach, but it hardens my resolve to save him—to fix this. To get him out of this place where no quick death awaits.

For I know what they may not. That their efforts will always be fruitless with him. That he will bite off his own tongue before betraying the Fianna. And they will let him, for their own wicked entertainment.

My torturer forces me to my knees beside Fionn. I am

uncuffed, whereas Fionn has cobalt chains on both ankles and wrists.

A cold voice breaks the tense silence, its tone low and dead.

"I had hoped the Fae that escaped to this realm would have some valor. That you would be daring enough to pose a challenge to my men. How disappointing that you didn't."

"The hundreds of Fomorian corpses that lie rotting in the earth by my hand would say otherwise," Fionn grits out, not looking up from the floor in front of him. Not looking at where I kneel beside him.

I finally look at the king before me.

My eyes clash with his piercing stare.

He wears emerald green from knee to throat, the sleeves coming down to his wrists. His black cloak, gloves and boots almost blend into the dark emerald coloring of the castle. He looks… human. But somehow not. He has that gaunt look about him, almost sickly, but almost stunning. But his gorgeous eyes are distinctly un-Fomorian. They hold so much, but his expression tells so little. Something about his fine features feel so familiar, though I've only seen sketches of him before in the papers that come from Raith. None were a good likeness.

Despite my instincts prickling, begging me to appear small and uninteresting to this new unknown threat, I raise my chin and let him look. Let him see my two-toned eyes, my hair, streaked with white-blonde from the roots. Let him see me for the more interesting oddity than Fionn.

His eyes glint in understanding as he looks his fill, though his gaze is not lecherous, but pondering.

"What is your name?" his voice is languid with authority.

"Alyx." Knowing my name will tell him nothing.

"Alyx." He picks up the golden goblet beside him,

drinking thoroughly. "I understand you injured my captain here, Gyddeon. Or re-injured, I should say." He smirks only slightly, jerking his chin at the torturer behind me, who grunts begrudgingly. "Good. He needs to be humbled occasionally, by someone who isn't me. You may leave us, Gyddeon. Don't you have some rebels to quash?"

Suddenly, I know why Gyddeon spat his title out at me the other day. There seems to be no love lost between these two. I wonder how Gyddeon got in his position if not by the king's favor.

There is a pause before Gyddeon's footsteps recede. As if he took an extra second for defiance alone.

With the absence of Gyddeon, there are two guards by the doors and the king. Fionn still stares silently at the ground.

The king rises, lazily stepping down from the dais. "He tells me that you are somewhat uncooperative. I suppose you won't tell *me* where the rest of your group is."

I reinforce my stubborn gaze. "I did tell him where. He just did not believe me."

"Ah yes, the boat to the southern continents that has already left." He nods, considering, then waves an elegant, dismissive hand. "You're about to make this messy, Alyx. I would ask that you don't."

I harden my features, willing to die a painful death with my secrets.

The Pretty King sighs in annoyance.

Fionn chokes on a gasp, collapsing beside me.

He is purple-faced, clawing at his throat with chained hands, making his dislocated shoulder hang oddly as his working arm tries to save him. His power is surely somewhere with mine, beyond reach.

"Stop! Please. Please stop!" I plead.

I run my hands uselessly over Fionn's arm. His whole body is clenched in agony, rolling over stone to escape an invisible torturer.

"I—I don't know where they went! I don't know! Fionn knows more than me! Don't kill him!" I beg again.

My heart is bleeding. Hemorrhaging in my chest, drowning me in my own helpless blood.

The king continues the torture by some sick power.

The veins in Fionn's eyes are popping, flooding the whites with scarlet.

I go for the king in all of my weakness, desperate to end Fionn's agony. I will leech every trickle of essence from regal bones. Claw my way up the Pretty King's body and scar his body and soul as mine has been.

I hit a wall, real under my hands, but invisible to my eyes. I pound on it, peeling at it with any energy left in my bones. Trying to harness power feels like trying to sip from an empty cup. Regardless, I throw everything from my muscles, from my mind at the unbudging shield before me.

"What *are* you?" I scream.

His face turns hard, meeting my eyes with a bitter smile.

Fionn suddenly gasps, dragging in air through damaged lungs and I sob in relief, able to breathe now that the drowning in my own body ceases. I scramble my way over to him, helping him roll into a sitting position.

"Oh how amusing you are, Alyx," the king says, tapping his pale fingers on his pants. "So clueless." He seems wrathfully amused as he crouches down to my eye level. "The eyes are so telling, are they not? Telling that I do not belong. What do your eyes say, Alyx?"

A sudden secret circles the air between us. I cannot grasp it.

Beside us, Fionn rolls up to his knees again, unable to

stop his choked cries of pain: something is broken inside him. "Leave her alone," he says—the first words of acknowledgment since I entered the throne room. "She knows nothing." The first wavers of fear are on his face, knowing that his words are damning. For what reason do they keep me alive, if I know nothing?

When I look back, the king's eyes are hungry as they look between the two different tones of mine. "Did you know that Fomorians, when first born, have violet eyes? Only once they consume a soul do they darken to the black you so often see."

His words are so unexpected that it takes me a moment before my heart stutters—before my vision tunnels on him.

Clink, clink, clink.

The fragile pieces of my reality shatter and *fall, fall, fall.*

Straight onto unrelenting ground.

I search his face for any hint of a lie, shaking my head until he begins nodding, in amused pity.

"I have my mother's eyes," he whispers.

The implication is enough.

His mother, not a Fomorian, who would have violet or black eyes. His gaunt skin-tone suggests definite Fomorian heritage, though the rest of him is something else. Something more normal.

These things are breeding with us: the humans or the Fae. How?

He turns to Fionn, perhaps satisfied that he left me sufficiently reeling. "Were you there, Fionn? You must have been, the kind of hatred in your face isn't born. Did you see them hack down your people like stalks of wheat? Did you watch them rape your females? And then, did you run?" His face reveals nothing, like he's discussing the weather.

It's the first time Fionn has ever looked defeated. Looked

like just any other man. He stares back at the king with a blend of agony, nausea, and utter hatred.

The king looks back at me, as if he did not just eviscerate Fionn with words alone. Standing back to his full, impressive height, he goes on, confusing me more with every word, "You have your mother's hair, Alyx. The silvery-blonde. She was, truly, very beautiful, though of course, no match for your father."

Somewhere along this conversation my world feels as if it's tilting—like the ground beneath my knees is shifting to one side and I cannot reorient. My understanding of everything left unsaid, of everything that does not align, blurs in my mind.

"Where were you hiding, exactly?" He turns to walk away, back up the steps to his throne. "We looked for you. For twenty years we searched, and you were simply… gone."

Where was I hiding?

He's looking at me expectantly, starry eyes waiting.

"I don't…You weren't looking for me. I am nobody. I am just a daughter of two humans. I—I lived in Comraich." My explanation is lacking. And for a second, I worry for Comraich, before I remember it is a pile of embers now. A pile of embers at his orders. "My mother's hair was brown."

"Comraich." He tosses his head back and forth, seeming stumped for a moment. "That shitty timber town out east?" I say nothing. "Figures. I assume before you discovered your power you looked quite ordinary. Lifeless eyes, dead hair, both without the pigment of power. No wonder nobody thought about you twice."

He's not listening to me. I'm not who he thinks I am, and the thought begins to feel like panic.

"Let me spell it out for you, if I must." He waits for me

to nod. "You are a child of two worlds—and the only one lost. I know it because there are… few of us. The people who raised you, I guess, are not your true mother and father. Your true mother is Irene; she was renowned with the Fae for her healing abilities. It is they who conspired to send you away, before the new king could return from conquering the lands to the west with those filthy world-walkers and see his new child." His resentment is palpable. "Your mother paid for it—for her insolence. For her rebellion. She paid for a long time before he killed her."

Down is up, and up is down. My world tilts on its axis.

I would refuse to believe him if not for my questions. Didn't I blow a group of Fomorians to chunks outside my house? Did I not fight off a Merrow, turning liquid water to blades of ice? Have I not painstakingly trained with Fionn these past few weeks, wielding a power that should not exist in me?

My mother, my mom. They are not one and the same. They exist separate from one another. Does it make sense to feel devastated, if they are both gone now? If it changes nothing?

"With that in mind, Alyx. I offer you something merciful—your life. Come home. Come back to us, and we will teach you how to control it. Your power is different from his." He jerks his chin to where Fionn kneels. "He has nothing to offer you. Isn't that right, Fionn?" The king waits on him, a sneer on his beautiful face.

I can't help but look. Look into those golden eyes that held me so enraptured before I ruined it all. I look to him for answers, look to him as the leader of the Fianna. What do I do? I would not help the king. But should I pretend?

What I see in his eyes is not what I had imagined.

There are no answers there.

Only sheer contempt. Burning disgust.

His face, bloody and swollen, shows no hint of affection. This is the face that the Crows see before he buries a knife in their abdomen.

I should have seen it coming.

I *know* Fionn. I know how he loves to run his thumb over his knife's blade just to reassure himself of its cutting presence. I know how he still wakes in the night, dreams of flame coming to consume him as he battles under the mounds. I know the hatred that burns slowly and then all at once in his chest. Hatred for the Fomorians, for everything they have done and will do. I know that I now represent every one of his worst fears. That I now represent the destruction of his people, the people he swore to go to the ends of every earth to avenge. That I am a direct result of the rape and destruction of his entire race.

I will spend every second for the rest of my long existence looking for a way to make those reeking parasites pay.

He had said it.

The words echo in my mind.

I should have seen it coming.

But that's the thing about betrayal. It requires trust.

"Fucking have her for all I care. Teach her to eat souls and ruin lives," Fionn spits the words at me, disowning me in front of our shared enemy. He turns his broken cheek to me, looking back at the ground before him. Even in his anger I see the devastation on his face. Not devastation for the loss of me. Devastation for my mother. Devastation for his people at having suffered this fate.

I'm grateful he doesn't see how his words hit me. How they suck the air from my lungs and harden my heart. I shut down my expression before the betrayal takes over too much of my face.

"Lovely. See, Alyx. There's nothing for you with him. Come willingly, and it will be easier—less painful—for all of us." He awaits my response, hands clasped behind his back.

I have none.

I have nothing.

"I'll give you some time to think," the king says, gesturing to his guards to escort us out.

Chapter 33

The days following meeting the king are a torment of their own. My mind's questions buzz relentlessly as a swarm of flies to a corpse, inhibiting me from slipping into blissful nothingness.

Thoughts of past crimes and the sentence I now endure pound at me with every heartbeat. Knowledge that my life up to this point has been retribution for my very existence. Dreams of a mother that sacrificed herself for my miserable life float through my subconscious. A healer. A healer who endured unimaginable torment to give me a life. One I have squandered being a selfish, bitter, waste. Who gave me her hair and somehow, her life's purpose.

I wonder if Diana knew with all of her ramblings and nonsense. With her book of otherworldly language and training. Did she look at me and see something familiar? A token from her home that fell short of every expectation?

At last it all finally aligns, like viewing something from a different perspective. Why nobody could survive me. Why the plants wither beneath my touch. Why I feel so disconnected from the people I so desperately want to belong to.

Because I don't belong with anyone. My solitude has always been the only outcome.

Who could love a monster who is predetermined to take and take and take?

What future can I have? Living within this body, this fractured soul torn in every direction, belonging to everyone and no one?

Should I not try? Could I be more than this?

Can I do anything to be worthy of such a sacrifice? Can I mitigate any of my atrocities?

Light from the doorway pierces the darkness and my retinas.

The detached voice that greets me is muffled beneath my pounding thoughts, "Get up, I have need of you."

I cling to the floor, knowing I'll have to face the world if I leave this cell. I'll have to walk and talk. I'll have to pretend to be a life worth words and feeling.

A guard jerks me to my feet, my knees wobbling under the weight of it all, bringing me to face the king outside my cell.

I'm relieved that I didn't have to bring myself to my feet; I don't think I could have.

I meet the king's ice blue eyes as they peer through me. "Come."

No words are exchanged as I am bound by the same cobalt chains Fionn wore in the throne room. They feel like a blanket over my senses. The cuffs are power-dampers. Like an extension of the cells.

The king walks with a smooth, casual gait. Unrushed, almost insolent.

I claw my way up from my mental pit of despair to note the hallways, the guards, the doorways, the windows, the light that trickles through them, how it glints off the golden crown. Mentally, I map out the layout, for Fionn. For him, I scrape my mind together off the floor and I plot.

We arrive in a chamber of lush emerald curtains, floor-to-ceiling shelves lined with books—timeless tomes of war and rule, scattered with tales of heroes of old. Paintings hang in the spaces between. Oil paintings of various landscapes ranging from rolling farmlands to sea cliffs bashed by roaring waves, forests of rowan and pine. Streets I recognize, bustling faceless patrons. The kingdom of Suri, painted. The view from the windows indicate we are several stories above the ground, in what I assume to be a receiving room.

A terribly beautiful ruse the king creates. It's all so human. From the story books to the fine artwork, clearly captured by an artist that sees the soul of something. And such a monster resides here—pretends to belong here.

A light hum of music streams from the seated man strumming some gargantuan instrument. The notes vibrate softly, beautifully. Like every string has a life of loss and love that it sings about. The man doesn't look up from his playing as we enter, humming slightly underneath the chords, as if wanting to sing but knowing better. He's strikingly handsome with his light blonde hair and sharp features. Something about him seems so familiar.

A table at the center of the room is set with fine, golden utensils and bone-white tableware with golden detailing. Succulent meats, prepared with rich sauces, and roasted vegetables sit at the center.

"Sit," says the king, gesturing to the seat across from him.

My mind whirls, contemplating in what ways he will turn

this into a game. Will this be a new method of torture?

I observe him. His delicate features and stoic expression give nothing away.

I sit.

The smell of rich food assaults me, spurring something like revulsion. I don't recall the last piece of stale bread that was thrown at me. Perhaps it was days ago. I clench my fists in my lap and prepare to watch as he consumes his lavish meal, likely the third of the day. Surely, I am not welcome to eat at the king's table.

White-gloved servants move to place food on the empty plate in front of me. One child—perhaps eight years old, pours wine into the two goblets on the table. The king begins to eat, all refined manners and elegance trapped in the beautiful body of greed.

He notices my stare and gestures to the plate in front of me. "Eat, Alyx."

Surely this is a trap. Surely some ghoulish punishment awaits me the moment any of this decadence hits my tongue.

Or perhaps it will be less bluntly painful. Perhaps it is poison to make me delirious. Perhaps something to purge truth from me.

Besides, there are so many *forks*. Which one would I even use?

He sighs deeply across from me. "Poisoning you would be a waste of a good execution, Alyx."

I don't waver in my certainty that my eating will be worse than starving to death.

"Surely you're starving. I know what accommodations we keep down in the cells. Leaves a lot to be desired." He quirks a brow, dead-eyed. He reaches across the space between us, spearing some strange root vegetable on my plate with an elegant, gloved hand and eating it, the muscle in his jaw moving with every bite. "There. See. Not poisoned or tampered with in any way."

I can't even tell if I am hungry, if I am even capable of such a feeling anymore. I pick up a fork, uncaring if it's the correct one, and spear a vegetable, the same type he had eaten, and place it warily in my mouth. It tastes sweet and spicy, glazed in some sort of sauce that coats my mouth as I chew. It tastes like a trap.

I look back at him and he rolls his starry eyes, taking a gulp from the goblet in front of him. "So mistrusting. What have I ever done to you?" He huffs a dry laugh at his own joke.

This is a joke to him. All of it, laughable. All of the death and destruction he wreaks.

I place my fork down on the cloth, uncaring that I soil it with the glaze from the vegetable.

I feel some force caress the ice surface of my mental shield and scramble to freeze any thawing edges.

He smiles at me knowingly. "I had to try."

"What is this?" I ask.

He looks at me like I'm dull. "Well, pain doesn't seem to work very well on you. Pity, it is my favorite method of getting what I want." He quirks a soulless smile at me. I may puke all over his beautifully decorated table. "I figured, why not show you what you're saying no to?" He gestures at the food. "Surely this is preferable to dying a slow, painful death. To sitting in my dungeon. To having dates with Gyddeon and his beasts."

"Perhaps that works on you soulless leeches. You know no loyalty."

Unaffected, he goes on. "Leeches, what a lovely comparison your companion makes. Tell me, what was the nature of the relationship between the two of you? You looked so devastated when he gave you up, it was almost sickening."

I give him dead eyes of my own. He doesn't get to touch any of it. Nothing of Fionn. Nothing of us.

He quirks his head to the side, leaning forward, ruining his impeccable posture to speak lowly to me, as if telling a secret, "You know, he gave you up. He told us that he found you trying to steal from them. He told us how you discovered your powers at your ramshackle little house, killing our kind, avoiding the consequences awaiting you in town. How you two developed a little romance, how you threw yourself at him." He leans back again, assessing me, twirling the fork in his hand. "This is what you are loyal to, Alyx. This male, you mean nothing to him." He straightens, catching me in his ice blue eyes. "But you mean something to me. You have more power here, with me, than you ever will with him. I can teach you. I can make you into someone who inspires fear. Males would crawl for you. We could take you to Danu, make you their queen. You deserve more than what Fionn can give you."

"What is there to rule over, if your people laid it all to ruin?" I ask.

"Much has been laid to ruin, as you say, certainly. But the leaders of the Fomorians did not seek to destroy it all. It is a beautiful place." The king swirls the liquid in his goblet. The look in his eyes says he likes my engagement. Likes that I'm looking at the pieces in his game.

"Aren't there more like us? Why would you need to find me?"

The king chews a bite of his food, giving him time to find the right answer. "No. There aren't more like us."

I blink.

"What do you mean? Surely there are more than two of

us," I say.

His starry eyes bore into mine as he says, "There were."

"What happened to them?"

"Nothing pleasant."

"And won't there be more?" My stomach turns, thinking of those few Fae left. Trapped, and kept like broodmares.

"Probably not."

"Why not?"

He takes another bite, this time of the succulent lamb shank. He fully chews and swallows before he responds, "Such dreary table conversation that is. Suffice it to say that we are special."

"Were the others killed?"

"No." He takes another bite, chewing thoroughly before continuing. "Nobody killed them. At least not purposely. It's probably for the best. You're very powerful, you just don't know the extent of it yet. Let me show you. Take me up on the offer, Alyx."

He's so…normal. So good at playing a part that I could almost forget how lethal he is. How he had Fionn on the brink of death in that throne room. The monster within him is buried so deep, I cannot even see it in his eyes.

"Why not you then? If we are the same, why are you here and not there?" I ask, blowing by the proposition.

The corner of his mouth quirks up. "I am needed here if we are to continue our mission in this realm. If you agree to help me, I will tell you what that is, but as things are now, I cannot divulge that information."

I feign consideration, infusing my expression with stubborn loyalty but letting my eyes flicker in struggle. Laying my own traps.

I let my voice wobble, sticking my chin out. "I want to talk to Fionn."

"Unfortunately, I don't think he wants to talk to you."

That truth pings through me, but I shove it down. I just need to tell Fionn what I learn—need to get him out.

The musician doesn't halt his playing as I look over and make eye-contact with him again.

It hits me where I recognize him—the actor in the square, the one who played the Pretty King and performed so perfectly. This man is in the employ of the king, willingly or unwillingly. Regardless, he's sat in these rooms. Listened in on meetings. Observed the king perhaps more than any other.

A servant comes to the king's side, who glances up at the man in regal question. The servant hands him a note, which he reads, a muscle in his jaw beginning to tick, eyes flickering over the note rapidly. He stands, placing the napkin from his lap onto the table. He seems to search the tablecloth for a path forward, like eyeing a chessboard. "I hate to cut the meal short, but I have some duties to attend to. If you would like some more time to think on it, you may have it. Just know that if you would like to be returned to a more comfortable room, all you must do is tell me about the rest of the party you were traveling with, and if perhaps they are in contact with a much larger group." He cocks an eyebrow at me, eye contact unflinching.

A much larger group?

I keep my face neutral. Would it be too obvious if I were to accept now?

He grinds his teeth.

I've taken too long to respond.

I wait for the other shoe—the demonstration of power. I wait for him to steal the breath from my lungs and force me to the floor.

"Fine. Don't say I never tried to do this together. Enjoy

your cell." He sweeps from the room, presumably onto whatever has his usually stoic demeanor so agitated.

I map the hallways again on my way back, verifying the partial layout I have in mind.

When I'm back in my cell, cuffs removed, I plot. For everyone I owe a life debt. So that I may do something worthy of them, just once.

As I readjust, rolling onto my side facing the door, I see it.

A tiny sliver of light, the most infinitesimal crack where the door is.

I scramble towards it. Using my cracked and bloody fingers to grasp the ledge, I pull the heavy door open.

Chapter 34

My hands tremble as I peer out into the chamber where Gyddeon interrogated me.

Not a soul awaits on the other side, and I wonder how long my door stood cracked like that.

I don't trust it.

Heart pounding, I peer in each direction.

Nothing but cell doors and empty stone.

I crawl out on hands and knees, leaving the door open behind me should I need to dart back in and pretend it's locked.

My every joint and muscle shriek as I stand.

Unbreathing, I tiptoe down the hall, listening for any sign of movement in the connecting halls.

Fionn is in one of these cells. One of these windowless cells that I don't have keys to.

Despair washes over me as I am faced with possibly giving myself away to try to find him, possibly damning us both and ruining any chance of escape. Or leaving him, hoping I'm able to come back with help to get him out.

"Fionn," I whisper into the silence. I run my hands over every door, whispering his name, a prayer. "Fionn, Fionn, Fionn," the name trembles in my mouth.

Nothing.

How can I leave him here?

Do I have a choice?

I reach the end of the hallway where it turns right and left. More doors line each way on the inside. I keep searching, his name a mantra on my lips.

"Please don't tell me you were planning on pacing the halls until you find him," a cold voice shatters my insides. "That's just pathetic."

I turn and look at the king where he waits at the end of the hall, just inside an antechamber presumably leading out of the cells. A circular manhole is open beside him.

He tires of my frozen state, stalking up to me and yanking me back into the antechamber with him. I would scream but some part of me lives in the space where I'm still trying not to draw attention to myself.

He gestures to the hole in the floor. I cannot see what is within it, but the smell is horrid. "Go," he states calmly.

I look at him with wide eyes.

What new game is this? First he wants me to join him, now he's freeing me?

Ire flashes in his icy blue eyes as he grits out, "Go. Before I change my mind." He tries to shove me into the hole. I fall to one knee beside it, hands on either side of the opening.

"Fionn. Let me get him first!" I whisper, pleading with my eyes. "Whatever you want. I'll do anything, let me just have Fionn. Please."

I've never seen a gaze colder as he states, "You would have to pry him from my cold, dead, hands. Now go."

I reach for the dagger at his waist, intending to do just that, but he's much quicker. He grips my wrist with bruising force and twists my arm behind my back. I bite back my cry of pain. He all but spits at me, "Listen here, little brat. I have an agenda, and you are not privy to it. If you want to have a single chance in this world, you will do as I say and get the fuck out of here. Do not stop. Do not play the hero. Get out. And do it before I decide you deserve the fate that you escaped."

He enunciates every word, yanking my arm farther back with every point. I can feel my shoulder about to tear from its socket as my legs dangle over the manhole

I look back up at him, wondering what his angle is, hoping to plead my case once more.

Plead that I have no connections, no knowledge of where to go without him.

But as I look up into the eyes of the king, I see determination that I could never combat. I see wrath and resentment. I see more emotion than that heartless man in the throne room could ever muster.

It's the last thing I see before he shoves me the rest of the way down, stomping on my fingers as I try to grasp onto the ledge to prevent myself from falling.

The fall is brief, but I'll forever remember the sight of that lid shutting out the light. Forcing me to abandon the one person I swore to myself I never would.

Chapter 35

Mariana

Black hair looks ghastly on me. But somehow the darkness feels right as it brushes the skin between my shoulder blades. The cloak to my dagger. Holding onto pride will do me no favors in the mines.

As my cage rattles down the merchant's road, I fold myself into a tighter ball. The scent of human odors fill my nose; it's been days in this cage, toiling away in our own waste. The kids have long since stopped crying every time they cannot hold it in anymore. They now stare blankly at the road behind us, their homes and families getting farther and farther away with every roll of the wheel. I hope the feeling of betrayal gets smaller with every roll of the wheel too. The youngest girl, no older than eight, presses up against an older woman I know to be someone else from her village, but not her mother. No, her mother gave her to the Crows.

Children always inherit the consequences of our parent's choices. For better or worse.

The solitary reprieve from the torment of body and soul

comes at the end of the day when we rise on pained joints, released from our pen, and stumble, chained at our wrists and ankles, to the river. Ravenous thirst forces us to press our faces to the surface, gulping down the cold river water like animals, drinking as much as we can before they drag us away moments later. The tiniest of relief from the soul-leeching thirst.

The slavers are servants to no king. They are monsters of a different sort. Those who find their pleasure in degradation of the powerless. Those that take just to rid themselves of the taste of the Crows' boots in their mouths. Anything to feel power. Anything to feel like someone worth fearing.

With every waking breath, I plot. Whenever my mind strays from my people up in the Ghaels, training, hunting, building, scouting. I think of what I'll do when a slaver tries to take too much. I think of if I'll be able to keep my cover. If I'll take it to avoid the gallows. And I stare and stare and stare at the road as it passes, my dyed black hair hiding my face from curious eyes.

Those scenarios run in my mind until we rattle through the wrought-iron gates in a canyon haunted by the wronged.

Getting here is easy. Though I'm certain leaving may be the greatest challenge yet.

The family thought me an angel. Some black-haired phantom answering every prayer. The proposition was simple: I would take their place in the mines, if they say that I'm their daughter. It took some convincing that I was not here as some sick incriminating torment. A difficult task without divulging many of my intentions.

It took days more for the slavers to show up to collect their payment. And once their debt was paid in my blood and bones, the family of three, a middle-aged couple and the husband's elderly mother, left with Eldrick to join my people in the Ghaels.

I've pondered who they would have sent otherwise. The sole earner of the family, without whom they would surely starve or turn to far more unseemly ways to earn coin? Would the husband send his crippled mother or his wife?

I'm glad none of us had to know the answer.

I look up at the Titans before me, standing indomitable over the mines that we rattle up to—the same mountains that house all I have left. I hope they're alright. I hope they are getting enough to eat. I hope they are training with Tarrant, learning more than the basic grappling and self-defense we were able to teach them these many weeks on the road. Learning archery and swordsmanship. I'm depending on it.

Our rebellion rests on the backs of stonemasons, butchers, and bakers. And our adversaries are trained monsters, wielding dark power, that want us dead or suffering beneath their boots. We know the extent of their depravity. We don't know the extent of their advantage over us.

The exchange of a human being is a disgustingly quick thing. They go through their parchments and inspections, seeing if any of us are dead or mortally wounded, give the slavers their payment, and wrench us from our cage.

Chains cut into ankles and wrists, tight for the sake of pain, as we make our way through the camp, passing guardhouses and whipping posts with fresh puddles beneath them. The hauntingly familiar scent follows us as we move further into the camp. It grows greater with every step. The scent of it brings me back to my worst day. The pile of bodies burning could be anyone; the flesh of the dead slaves or those of my father and fallen people in an open field.

The chill of night is just beginning to creep into the

canyon after the departure of sunlight. Dirt and rocks cut into my bare feet, growing larger and more jagged the closer we get to the caves. I keep my head low in the presence of leering guards. The Crows have roosts, overseeing the everyday atrocities. The rest of the guards are monsters of the human variety. I can see their differences now, even from the corner of my eyes. The tanned skin from days exacting punishment under the harsh sun.

The slaves on either side of me stumble and retch. The days of starvation and bent limbs exact their price. I feel it myself. Lifting my leg to step is a conscious effort, every placement of my foot is an agonizing submission to my oppressors.

In the end, we are thrown in a shack built into the side of the cliff, beside the entrance to the mines. We stumble about in pitch darkness, feeling our way through smooth wooden poles. I lead the small group of eight new slaves inside. The shack is really just a narrow hallway with slots from floor to ceiling. Cabinets in which to rest. As my eyes adjust, I see the whites of at least thirty eyes peering at us in the silence. Tens of their forms, lying in tiny bunks stacked up to the ceiling.

"Hello?" I whisper finally, the hair on my arms standing up at the unknown people observing warily, silently. Nobody answers my greeting. "Are there any free bunks? Is there anywhere for us to sleep?"

A light groaning of wood is the only reply as one shadowed form sits up slowly and hops down from her bunk a few feet from the ground. A figure watches from the bottom bunk, which is essentially floorspace.

A feminine voice finally answers—the figure who rose from her bunk. "There are a few at the end there. I believe after today there should be seven open. Just find any that aren't occupied." A hand gestures to the back of the shack. "If you need to relieve yourselves there is a trench outside, around back. Though I caution against going in the night. The Crows prey on wanderers." With that, she leads us to the back of the shack. I swear I hear her limbs creak.

The Crows prey on wanderers. I picture the desiccated corpse of my father and wonder what happens to those they ensnare. Are they bound by secrecy? Do they try to pass as humans here as they did in Comraich?

While the others scramble to find their bunks, I sit on the ground, leaning my back against the stone wall at the very end. Best not to get into a fight. Best to win their trust with acquiescence. Every move I make will be crucial in winning their favor. And so I spend the night on the ground, allowing myself this night of restoration.

Tomorrow, the war begins.

My hands are shredded, bloody ribbons of a former life. Callouses from wielding blades my entire life are torn to ruin with every swing of a pickaxe—with every shovel full of stone hefted into carts. Tear tracks run through the dust on my face by the end of every day. There is no end. If you stop, you get the whip; a death sentence. Infections kill faster than the mine collapses or the tunnel fever.

The brutality of this place goes beyond what I had imagined.

Whatever spoiled food would be tossed after the Crows and slavers are done is fed to us in troughs—but not before the floggings. While I ate that first night, I could still feel the spray of blood from those who committed the crime of collapsing from lack of sustenance or water during the day's work.

Aled once drunkenly touted from his seat at the bar that

slaves deserve this for being reckless with their coin. That the mines are a productive way to ensure the repayment of debts—to ensure fairness.

I wish more than my own freedom that he was here, that he paid for those words with his own flesh.

As I endure, I plot. I seek allies in every free moment. I seek familiar faces, hoping and not hoping that I see Alyx. I never do. I watch. I watch the guards and their routines. I watch the other slaves.

I watch Dierdre, the woman who spoke to us that first night. She's beautiful, with thick, curly hair braided into many long strands. Her dark skin speaks to a heritage across the sea, with freckles painted across her cheeks. Though I know it isn't her beauty that wins her favor amongst the slaves. I watch the others seek her out, look to her as she laments stories at mealtime. Stories of wicked kings and great flying beasts. Lore of the Reaper, and his ruined face. How he sought great treasures beneath the earth to the east and then fled to the hills to escape what he found. I see her as the pillar that upholds the rest of them. They feed her the best scraps of meat, the softest parts of bread. I realize now how she's survived for so long, for she's been here for years. The concept seems inconceivable to me, how anyone can endure this for so long.

So when I sit beside her on the ground during that third day, purposefully elbowing through the others to position myself, I earn glares. I keep my black hair falling over my face and begin picking out the best bits of food from the handful I was able to grab. I feel her eyes fall on me.

My hunger is fierce enough that I don't look as I shovel my handful into my mouth, chewing and grimacing at the foul texture and flavor.

A chuckle comes from beside me and I turn to Dierdre,

laughing at my expense. She says, "Your sense of taste will die off here soon."

I give her a look of commiseration and say, "I sure hope so."

She chuckles again before asking, "You hope you last long enough for it to happen?" I nod. "Where are you from?" she asks.

"Comraich," I reply through mouthfuls of foul food. Something about her warns against lying. Like she sees right through every word, spoken and unspoken. If I lie, I'll lose her trust, which I so desperately need.

She ponders for a moment. "Wynedd forest? Not a whole lot going on out there from what I hear. Depends on who you ask, I suppose."

I nod, grimacing at the next horrible bite.

"Some folks came through here a few weeks ago. They said Comraich is nothing but embers now." Her eyebrows lift in question.

News travels to the mines too, I see.

I give one more nod, looking her in the eyes, letting my grief shine through.

She places a scarred hand on my shoulder for a light squeeze, then goes back to picking at her food.

"Where are you from? Your name is Dierdre, correct?" I ask, playing it like I haven't had my ears on every word. Her accent gives very little clue as to her home, though I can say she certainly isn't from around the canyon. The slavers all have a distinct drawl; nobody here goes to school other than the owners of the camps.

The twinkle in her eyes says she sees through me, but she doesn't comment. "A little town off the coast." She speaks softly, almost demurely. "I've been here for quite a while. Two winters. Two long winters." She looks into the distance in solemn reminiscence.

"What was your home like?" I ask. People love talking of themselves.

A slow smile spreads across her face. Aglow with memory, even in this hell. "It was… Well how could you not love the place you grew up? I suppose I'm a bit biased." She chuckles, the sound rich and out of place. "There was something about the sea there. It was always so alive. The tide-pools always had treasures, the sands always had stones of every color. The waves always were the right mix of ferocious and fun. And the markets always full of wonders." The smile melts, a slow death. "We all grow up. There is less time for treasures and tide-pools. More responsibility. Bad things happen and suddenly there isn't an adult to run to. My story isn't really all that unique." She looks at me now, shared experiences in our eyes. "I could never tell if I was just seeing things for how they always were, or if things had completely changed. It was like the world was angry, the seas became angry, the soil became angry. And it's been that way ever since."

I remember that first day the Crows showed in the square. It was as if the clouds covered the sun and it never shone fully again. "You should be a bard."

Her laugh is booming now, no longer a small chuckle. It draws the guard's attention. I shrink in on myself, unable to keep the smallest of smirks from my face at her brazen laughter. To hear such a thing in a place like this: it's like having a butterfly land on you, knowing it will soon fly away, but you still try to prolong it by holding still.

Dierdre is unaffected by the stares as she says, "Now that is rich. I'll be lucky to make it out of this place alive, but I'll keep it in mind." She shakes her head.

"You must be close. You've been here longer than

anyone," I point out. I've never heard of a soul leaving the mines, but I always assumed it's because they never lived long enough to see their debts through.

She shakes her head at me with a pitying glance. "Nobody leaves these mines." She lowers her voice. "Nobody ever sees the numbers. It doesn't matter how long you stay. It doesn't matter how minor your debt. Nobody here has a debt that won't be paid with life."

I soak in her statement. I wish I could say I am struck by it, but the truth already sat in my bones, waiting to be acknowledged by someone other than my own suspicion. "That's wrong," I whisper back, steel in my voice.

She huffs a sad laugh this time, looking at me strangely. "What in this world have you seen that is right?"

Some things. Laughing over breakfast with Mom and Dad. Flames being born from injustice.

I weigh my choices in a moment. I weigh it in the days I have left to spark an uprising. I weigh it in the goodness in her eyes. I weigh it in every day that passes where more and more atrocities are committed. More wrongs that can never be set to right.

From my vantage, I spy a particular white cloth fluttering reassurances high above. A reminder that I am not alone down here. There are others, watching over me.

"It doesn't have to be that way," I lower my voice.

She copies my tone. "You speak like that, and you'll be dead by morning."

I was expecting the threat.

"Only if you say anything. I hear whispers, Dierdre. Whispers from the mountains. Of something new."

She doesn't ask with her words, but with her eyes, though there is little hope there.

"There's a new player. And if the whispers are right, she

would not leave us here. She would never stand for it."

Her eyes flicker between mine, serious as death. "There is nobody coming to save you. I'm not being mean, I just think you need to see the reality of it. There is no rebel leader from the mountains who will care for your life. None."

I assess the scales once more.

"You don't believe that. If you did, you would have died a long time ago. You would have accepted your fate a winter ago. You live—you try to stay alive—for a reason. Because somewhere beneath all of the pessimism disguised as realism, there is a glimmer of hope that you'll get out of here one day." I let us both absorb it. "I've felt the same. After it all. After Comraich. Before it was ash on the wind, really. That this is wrong." I gesture to the state of the empire, with a tiny wave of my bloody hand. "And I promised myself I would fight for something more. I was already hanging on for the hope of it. Even after…Even after I knew the cost. And I think you should too, because, if you want the truth of it, I've done more than heard whispers." I implore her to look. "Something is coming. I just need you to hear me and I need you to pay attention. I need you to tell others to pay attention."

She looks at me now, seeing. I let her see not the poor slave girl trapped in a hopeless circumstance, but the woman who plots and rages against the wrongs.

"Just let yourself hope, just a tiny bit." I look back down at my messy hands, licking the remnants of food off them, a predator cleaning her paws, grimacing at the dirt that comes up with the grease. I wipe the rest on my tattered slave clothes that barely qualify as clothes.

"You shouldn't make promises you can't keep." All at once she sounds like a slave. Defeated. "And I'll hate to say I told you so when that day comes."

"Just hold on." I get up and leave her to her people.
They'll be mine one day too, but I'll need her help.

Chapter 36

Sewage soaks the hem of my dress, the same dress that I wore to the markets and wasted away in a cell in. The scent burns my nostrils, my eyes, churning my stomach as I slosh through the tunnels. The underground network of pipes runs through the city, collecting human waste. I assume I've reached the end of the palace's network of pipes, spilling me out into the rest of Raith's underground. Chutes of sunlight peek through the openings above me. The light is blinding, making it impossible to gauge my position under the city, so I keep going.

Indecision and desperation whirl in my mind, clouding every thought but the ones that sing in my blood *do not stop. Do not play the hero. Get out.*

Every instinct I have agrees with this command, even as my heart cries out in betrayal. Every step I make away from Fionn damns me further.

But I will go.

I will go and I will find help and I will bring them back here and get him out.

I will get him out.
I will get him out.
I will get him out.

The thought punctuates every step as I wade through the tunnels until I reach the end—an end. I'm unsure if it is *the* end. Or if I just have to find another route.

My heavy breathing echoes in the endless cavern of possibilities.

One deep breath helps me calm my racing mind and heart. Where am I going? How will I find the others? People will take one look at me, covered in filth and sewage, starved and feral, and report me.

There are no answers to my problem in the wastewater beneath my feet, nor in between the streams of my racing thoughts, only more problems.

Where is Aine? And Elva. And Armund and Konan? They could be across the world by now. Or they could be seeking ways to rescue Fionn and I. They could be dead. I have to find them too.

I shake my head and resolve to keep moving forward. Just keep going.

The door to the world above is rough under my abraded fingertips as I push up, standing on my tiptoes to reach it. My arms quake, every meal-less day trembling in my bicep as I budge it upward with everything left.

I will get him out.

A sob tears from my throat as the door slams back down. I'm too weak. I curse myself up and down—why couldn't I have eaten that meal with the king?

I take another deep breath and reach.

My body and soul are so weak—both muscles themselves, unfed, unrested, and unused for god knows how long we have been held prisoner. But even as I feel my mind quiver in exhaustion, I feel it pull on those little sparks of energy in the air. I feel it reach for the weeds that grow between cobblestones. I feel it consume them, powering itself.

It feels like a breath of crisp morning air after a long night. I'm unsure what those cells were made of, but they kept all of this from me—kept me chained in my own body.

It's strange. I've spent nearly my entire life without having exercised my abilities, yet after just a few months, I have gotten so used to wielding that the absence of it feels like having a hand tied behind my back.

I look back up at the world beyond the sewers and I take another breath.

Pulling everything to one fine point, I direct the air to *push* that door open.

It feels just as heavy in my power's hands as it did in my own, but I have more to give now, if only slightly. The door wobbles as it lifts to reveal more light, scraping the ground as it moves over, revealing blue sky and gray brick.

Do not stop. The king's words resonate.

I pull myself up and out of the tunnels below.

The tunnels stop at the outer edge of the middle-class district, this amenity belonging to only the wealthy. Unfortunately for me that means I need to traverse an entire third of the city before I reach the walls.

Luckily, I'm in a side-street, an empty one, with nobody lingering to see me crawl from the underground.

My hem drips waste, leaving a trail behind me on the dry summer streets. I keep to alleyways, melting into the stone with every step. I pull down a dress hanging from a line, threadbare and fluttering. I know its owner has almost nothing from just the look of it, but somehow I've gotten to the point where I need it more than she. Donning my clean attire feels like a fresh breath, though I fear I may never be clean again beneath the threads. I snag a light headscarf from a different clothesline to cover my damning hair. Not only is it filthy beyond belief, but I can see the white-blonde streaking into the hair by my cheekbones now.

I turn my attention to the next step. Where would the others have gone? I know little of their times here from the past. I doubt they would return to the inn we had stayed at that first night here. Did they take that ship to Ashvynd?

Bringing my hand to my mouth I almost chew on my nail before I see how disgusting my hands are, then I jerk it far away from my face.

Every second I spend breathing free air is another that Fionn sits inside a cell. Seconds that Gyddeon gets to play with him, set his nightmare hound on him. Precious breaths that the Pretty King gets to use Fionn as a pawn to meet whatever sick end he has in mind.

I will get him out.

At any cost.

The thought rumbles underneath my pounding purpose, another slithering along beside it. That I might be leading the king directly to the rest of the Fianna. That perhaps I am the trap.

Who else do I have?

I search the cloudless sky for answers, if only for a moment, as I quickly walk through the streets of Raith.

Maroon.

The color flashes through my mind.

Maroon.

I chase it through my mind until it appears in front of me in the form of a door.

The madame.

The door to the pleasure house feels like the entrance to a tomb now.

Feel free to return when you have a real answer to my question, Alyxara.

I think I have her answer. I just hope she has mine.

The door opens to a room of fine silks and incense. Men drape themselves over couches of velvet, nude women draped over them. Some nude men draped over men. Rooms are created with flowing fabrics and smoky beams of light.

I keep my eyes searching for her—for that being that was something other. Searching through bodies, taking one another carnally in every position. Moans and exaggerated shrieks float through the hallways. One woman holds a leash of a man on hands and knees. They both gaze at me in interest as I bypass them, keeping my eyes sweeping for a woman cloaked in red with the eyes of a snake.

A rough hand grabs me by the upper arm. I immediately try to jerk out of it. "You're disrupting the guests," a voice growls. A brutish man leans into my face. "If you're looking for employment you must ask at the door." He begins to drag me away.

"I'm here to answer to the madame. She has a question for me!" I hiss.

He freezes in his step. "Your name?"

"Alyxara." My full name feels wrong in my mouth. I don't feel like her anymore.

He looks me over, face scrunched in disgust. "You could have at least bathed before seeking out the madame. She does not take kindly to street rats ruining the ambience."

I look down at my skin, covered in filth. I haven't had time to find a mirror, or the care to look into it.

He leads me through a side door despite my foul appearance, which leads straight into a familiar torch-lit hallway. A short jaunt down the hall brings me to her office.

The room looks the same. The madame looks the same, but swathed in emerald green this time, nails still painted that vivid maroon that flashed in my head.

She looks me up and down, scrunching up her face as the man before her did.

The silence hangs between all three of us, the room being completely devoid of ambient noise from the world above.

She dismisses the man who brought me with an elegant nod, maintaining her gaze looking down at me.

"I see you did not heed my advice, healer." Her voice holds an edge. She folds herself into her plush lounge chair.

"And I paid for it." Oh, how I did. How I still am.

She smiles coyly, too-sharp teeth flashing. "And yet, here you stand. Clearly you did not pay for it as I had imagined." She lets the statement hang as she searches my body for answers before she asks, "How?"

I ignore her question. "You knew. Who I was. You called me a healer. You called me a liar. I did not know then that you were right. I just can't work out how."

She looks at me in pointed silence.

"An answer for an answer then?" I propose, unwilling to answer her initial question without a bargain.

How? She had asked. How indeed. I'm still unsure how I get so lucky yet unlucky at the same time. What cruel fate frees the body but leaves the heart locked in a cell?

"Quick learner." She nods bluntly, lighting up another rolled bit of herb, perching it between her two elegant fingers. "You have yet to answer my earlier question."

Who are you?

The truth comes up like shards of glass.

"I am a product of two peoples. Of three really. Child of Irene, healer of the Fae and the king of the Fomorians… My rea—my mother sacrificed herself in some way, to get me here, to get me out of Danu. To save me from them. I… is that the truth you wanted?"

I couldn't say it. *Real.* Could I cheapen my mom's place in my life like that? All the pies and laughs? The endless love and devotion, there one moment, and then inexplicably gone?

She swirls her goblet, maroon liquid whirling within. "I suppose that will do. For now."

"Where are the rest of the Fianna?" I ask, swallowing back the chasm that looms, waiting for me to stop moving.

"Where are they? What a question. Smoke on the wind, I suppose. Once their ride across the sea fell through, they fled to other corners. Fionn, I fear, will never see the skies again." Her tone is almost soft at the end.

What spies does she have? How can she know everything?

She must have seen it all on my face because she gives me a feline smile and taunts, "Ask it."

I narrow my eyes at her. I will not be side-tracked.

"How do I get someone out of those prisons? The cells. The castle. There must be a way to do it quietly. Especially for a wielder."

She takes a long drag before answering.

"Many have asked that question and to them all I have said this: it is impossible to get out once you get in—not without the king knowing. He has power beyond what other Fomorians have. He has it beyond what the Fae have. Something about the mixture of the two… very rarely born, but very powerful beings once created. But to you, I say this: you are the only one in this realm who could be his equal, but you are not yet, clearly." She waves a sardonic hand at me. "If you go in now, it will be a waste of the freedom you were somehow granted. You will not come out twice."

My teeth grit. "Fionn does not have time to wait for me to practice until I am more powerful than the king. This is not an option. You have resources. You have ears inside the castle. There is no other way you could know what you do. Help me. I will give you anything. Anything."

"I would not compromise my position—sacrifice my birds for the life of one measly Fae male. Especially one who has spent so long doing so little, even if he is stunning." She grins knowingly at me. "You will not find that kind of help from me. But perhaps there is another that would find that sort of thing amenable. And I could help in a more discreet way." She looks as though she has backed me into the corner she wanted me in.

"Who?" My nails dig into my palm.

She shakes a condescending finger my way. "I believe you owe me another answer." She takes another drag; clouds of smoke billow out of her red lips before she adds an addendum. "Two actually."

"Ask."

"Who let you out?" Eagerness lightens her feline eyes.

Limits. She has limits to her little birds, and what they know.

"The only one who could." She knows I mean the king. I have no loyalty to him. Fuck the fact that he let me out; he kept Fionn. He kept him in cruelty.

Her eyes widen in amazement and suspicion.

A pounding fist bangs behind the bookshelf in the corner.

"Madame! Madame, the Crows are out. They conduct a search, say they are looking for a certain prisoner. If you wish to gather the ransom or get her out, we must act." The voice of the man from earlier rumbles out through the wood.

Blood drains from my face. Whatever dregs of energy

remain in my muscles and bones rile up. I prepare to wield for my life.

She sighs deeply, as if in aggravation of being interrupted right when we get to the good part. "Well, I suppose you aren't keen on being thrown back into the cobalt cells, are you, Alyx? Would you like my help?"

It feels like a trap. This whole interaction has shown I am already in one.

What choice do I have?

"Yes," I grit the words out. "Yes, I would like your help."

"Perfect. I'll have my men get you out of the city." She rises from her plush seat, looking perfectly bored at the turn in events.

"Who?" I ask one more time, knowing she will catch my meaning.

She rolls her feline eyes. "You are racking up quite the bill."

"Who?"

She glides to the door, all inhuman grace, every inch of her, other. "The mounds of Dun, I suspect might hold some allies. Ones that live under the mounds." She gives me a pointed look, knocking on the door that leads to the hallway. A figure dressed in night-black clothes answers the call. She whispers something to them. Turning back to me, she warns, "I always collect on my debts, daughter of lost worlds, even if I have to cross rifts to find you. Do not forget it."

I don't think I ever could.

Chapter 37

Some twisted, horrible mortal part of me propels me forward. Some cruel, masochistic thing keeps me drinking water and sucking in breaths.

Every step I make, gravel crunching under borrowed boots, feels like a hunt now.

Only I am the prey.

It has been days since I was unceremoniously dumped at a dock fifty leagues down the gulf from Raith after a nauseating day on choppy storm-ridden waters. I still feel nightmares on my heels.

I'm a starving animal picking my way across lowlands and mountains. Hiding in the day, writhing in nightmares by night. Trembling in fear in the moments between.

Gulping down the last dregs of water in my water-skin, I thank the heavens for Rheol only a few leagues away. The heat of the summer boils my once-frozen blood. It makes me feel like a creature, foreign in this body of ice and otherness. It points out the blatant truth that I don't belong.

Looking at the pasture before me I see Rheol in the distance, the snaking river Shana a shimmering taunt on the horizon. Its waters run fast, wide, and vicious—running from the frigid snow-melt off the Ghaels, through the center of Suri, branching off in smaller segments, webbing through the Wynedd forest, one such passing through Comraich itself, curving down to meet a delta near Tristram. Another branch meets a delta in Raith. It is the main vessel of travel and life through the country. The crossing in Comraich is modest and free moving. The crossing is Rheol is large and popular because of its central nature, sure to be bustling with people from all over.

The city is also swarming with Crows. Surely my description and news of my escape has reached the city on horseback. There is no way around it though, not one that I am willing to accept. It would take days to go around it, back through Comraich, going back the same way I came with the Fianna. The logical aversions to that route bring relief; the thought of going back to that place makes me break out in a cold sweat. Especially the thought of seeing a pile of ash where my childhood used to be. I fear one more anguish will make me lie down in them, burrow my useless body beneath what's left of the town and just let myself end there. How fitting it would be.

But I think of Fionn and everything between us I can't begin to name. Elva and her loyalty to me, her steadfastness and strength. Aine, somewhere coping with what she saw; coping with what her life now is. Armund and his sweet smiles and friendship. Even Konan, how he loves Aine. How he protected all of us, but especially her. I could not give up on any of them. I will find the allies they've always sought. I will find them. I will get Fionn out.

The other crossings are just as dangerous. I may have been able to sneak through the lowlands, largely made up of farmlands and large estates owned by the wealthy in Farus—

the city I was dropped closest to a few days prior—but I can wield my way through, unseen. Surely I can.

Instead of eating, I pull energy from the grass, from the trees, their ancient power so large and sustainable I cannot resist the urge to pull from it, to let it power my solemn, purposeful steps. It isn't a lot. I still tremble from hunger. I can still see my skin dulling, my hair beginning to pull out in stringy dual-colored strands—but it has to be enough. I haven't the time to hunt, to steal, not when the energy around me will keep my feet moving forward.

I still haven't derived the Pretty King's motives. I peer behind me every few breaths, certain I'll see a Crow or a hound lurking in the grass to my rear. The paranoia has a hold on me. I feel as close to mad as ever. Waking in the night only to pace around, spending hours peering up into trees and searching the shadows. Nothing is ever there, at least, nothing that makes itself known to me. But can it really all be in my head? And who's to say that means it's nothing? I can't be sure anymore. I can't be sure.

My sleep is haunted too. The Pooka. Fionn's screams and his soft touches that only the two of us knew about. The purple hue of his face as he gasped for breath in the throne room, but in my dreams, he never gasps those life-giving breaths. Haunted by the look in his eyes right before he kissed me that first time. Haunted by the words he spat at me when he saw who I was. Haunted by every moment we probably won't ever get to have.

I can't tell which nightmares I prefer, the ones where I'm awake or sleeping.

Chapter 38

Mariana

She looks just like me.

Some nameless slave, her pale skin, flaming hair, all wild temper. Now, she lies in puddles, her hair in wet tangles where it hangs into scarlet pools—her death painted on the rocks in her own blood.

She was a fool. She fought back for her dignity, fought the soldiers that dragged her to the post and readied themselves to lash her. I cannot decide if it was suicide or bravery. I cannot tell if it was strength. If it would have taken more strength to shut up and take it.

I swipe at my cheeks, smearing the spatters of her blood across my sweat-dampened skin. War paint.

This is what it means to ask for more. This could be the consequence of this choice I'm making. Playing chess with lives.

As they drag her limp body off to the burn piles and the numb drift off to their dinner, I stay there. I watch the trail of blood fade into dried dark smudges on the tan rock.

I look back up at the cliffs above, seeking that cloth, fluttering in the wind far above, peeking out from a cliff.

It's been fourteen days.

Fourteen days of pain and back-breaking work.

I count them on the wall I sleep against. A small rock scratching tallies in the wood of the shack. Every day feels like an eternity.

In those days, fire has spread—flame licking across a dry field.

I can't learn their names. Too many that I break my fast with, don't see the dusk. So I know Dierdre, and two of her most valuable assets to my plan, Emris and Zarah. I try not to get to know the others too well. Knowing their names makes them a full person, not just a slave. Knowing their name reminds me that their mother painstakingly picked it out for them when they were babies. Reminds me they were children once. Reminds me they had lives and loved ones.

The slaves, the ones trusted by Dierdre, know that something is coming. It takes a steady hand to keep them from riling. Few of them have genuine hope, but a few have a spark in their eyes. It's dangerous to my plan, but I need the majority of them to have my back when the time comes.

"You'll miss dinner if you keep standing there," comes a voice from my left.

Dierdre stands there, back ramrod straight, shoulders pulled back, chin lifted. Such perfect posture for a slave. Everything about her screams well-bred—her speech, her countenance, her influence. How she ended up in this hell, I'll never know.

It's interesting how even here, in a place where we know only survival, people still seek community. Still look for hope and reason in each other's eyes. Still look for someone who might be able to make choices for us, give comfort and advice.

I wonder if I will ever be enough of that for my people. And I wonder if I look like that to them—like a pillar. My posture certainly isn't as good as Dierdre's, no matter how much my mother poked and prodded at me about it.

I follow her, tearing my eyes from the waving cloth. As I go, I see them. The markings on the roosts, the guard houses, the back alleyways. Signals marked in my own blood to my outside friends, telling them where to strike first and hardest.

"Dinner is a really generous term, Dierdre," I grumble. "Did you ask them?"

Her bare feet must hurt on the rocks as mine do, but she doesn't show it. Her face is immovable, serene even, as she continues our walk to the troughs. She gives only a shallow nod.

I try not to look too eager, too hopeful. A slave never looks hopeful.

The Crows watch from their roosts, eyes following the two of us—like they hear us. I remember the hounds, the inhuman power they and those that control them possess, and I wonder if they *can* hear us from all the way up there.

"How were your sections today?" Dierdre asks innocently as we find our seats amongst the others. She gracefully accepts the piece of still-good meat from the man that sits beside her. Is everything still on for tomorrow?

One of the guards passes behind my back. I cannot see them, but I feel their vile presence, always lurking.

"As they always have been," I say casually, our code familiar to me. The cloth is still white and waving.

"The birds are awfully restless today," she observes.

She's right. It's like they can feel the hum in the air. The one I try with all my might to keep down. None of us comment further, the apprehension palpable.

The guards here are lazy at best, grossly negligent at worst—assured in their conquest, their control. Today is different. Their armor is polished. They stand at firmer attention. The Crows exert more control over the human guards, shoving and threatening them when they dawdle. Someone is holding them to standard, and I don't know why. It is one factor that I hope my compatriots on the outside will see. Will they change the color of the cloth if necessary? Having to trust the others, sitting in my own ignorance, feels like an itch under my skin.

"We could use some rain. I miss the wildflowers," Dierdre says. The few in our circle know what we are on about. They know not to care for the stupid questions. The slave mines are in a brutally dry area of Suri. Of course we could use some rain, but what she says is *we could use some weapons.*

"You never know, maybe the gods will pull through. Perhaps it will even bring enough flowers for all of us," I reply, nonchalant.

"We will need them. We cannot ward off the hopelessness for long without them." The others in the circle look at me seriously, nodding their agreement.

"They'll come," I assure. "I'll tell you when I see some." I take a big bite of foul-looking sludge, grateful to have abandoned my sense of taste as Dierdre predicted. I must eat something; I feel the lack of food in my bones. Literally. The couple of weeks of going without, of long days wielding the axe, are making themselves known in the jut of my hipbones and caving in of my stomach. The shaking of my arms from simply existing. But I know, as I know the sun will rise, that when the time comes, I will not fail. I will not falter.

I am a flame of this rebellion, and I will not falter or dim.

As the days have turned to weeks, this mission has turned into something more. Freeing these people is more important than my own purposes. Even if it would not serve my cause, this is a worthy cause to fight for.

The only part that gives me pause is this: what life am I freeing them to, if the rebellion dies?

One of endless struggle, living only to survive? That is no life.

And so I will not falter or dim.

I will *burn, and burn, and burn* until there is nothing left of me.

Chapter 39

I made it through Rheol, weaving my way through its sprawling riverside wealth and roosts fit for the murder of Crows that live there. I avoided the newsstands, fearful of being recognized. I'm sure they paint me in shades of wicked rebellion and depravity—I wonder if the colors would help the likeness.

Rheol, the river city, is built on the fork of three great rivers merging, the town is a central hub of trade and port for travelers passing through to the southern ports. Diana used to travel to the market far inland to stock up on supplies.

The people felt familiar as I brushed cloaks through busy roads, like the people of Comraich the last I felt them, firmly under thumb. Existing only to make it through the days, slinking through shadows and keeping heads turned ground-ward.

The ferryman carried me across the river Shana in his humble boat discreetly, though I spent my last coin for his silence, the sum given to me by the madame to aid me in my travels. The ferryman was a rebel at heart; I was nearly certain that he would have kept his tongue for the mere fact that I was clearly going against the Crown for one reason or another, but he took the bribe. He left me at the other side of the river with a parting whisper, tidings from the Ghaels, of safe haven for resisters.

What a pointless risk he took for a stranger. What a reckless whisper for the rebellion, sinking ships and all that.

Whatever rebellion lives there will surely be snuffed out by the time I come back over the river. The Crown suffocates all of us, perhaps because flames need air.

Days have passed in shades of gray and nights have passed in shadow monsters and paranoia since then.

Surely, I have died and am living in hell, a wandering specter.

What else could explain the torture of living in my head unable to retreat in apathy and nothingness? My fear won't allow it. My one pillar of existence that is left, saving Fionn and the others, won't allow it. It drags me, kicking and screaming, into reality, making me feel the unbearable every waking moment.

How could I have forgotten how cruel love is? I knew it before. God, I've known it in my bones. But knowing it apparently was not enough to stop me from grasping for it again. Like some starved street urchin grasping at a fallen crust of bread.

Is this love?

It seems right. What else has ever torn me apart like this? Only love can leave one so bereft but full of purpose. I've never felt so full—near bursting from terror and anguish. Like my guts are being held in by nothing but my own hand of purpose.

None of it matters. None of it. That's what I say to keep my feet moving. What runs circles in my mind as I place one foot going up the mound. It doesn't matter that I hurt, that I bleed, that I long for a wakeless sleep. My agony is inconsequential, because somewhere out there, Aine is parentless, and what's left of the Fianna wanders in a world doomed. It is all moot when Fionn is imprisoned because of me. I wander free, yet he was apparently too valuable to give up. And now his only hope is me. What a sad prospect that must be for him.

He probably thinks I abandoned him or died. I wonder if it makes a difference to him.

Every step I take over days and days towards the towering mounds of Dun is made while swimming in these thoughts. I'll escape them one way or another. I'll either accomplish my mission or take my last breath.

Folks say that you can hear the Banshee's cries from the town of Dun, leagues away from the foot of the first mound, but I hear nothing. Fionn said that no such creature lives here, that the being that dwells here is far more fearsome than a crying vow of death, but I see nothing. The only thing that warns me away is the scent of sulfur. A whisper of something wrong.

And so I wander. I look for my allies between blades of emerald grass, hoping the madame did not lead me across the country for nothing—that this is not some twisted joke. I reach for something, anything with my mind. I comb through the web of life in the grass, the tiny golden tendrils cover the ground as sure as the green strands do. And in my search, I find a lot of nothing. It disturbs me. There is not a hare nor a rodent in sight. The air is quiet of birdsong in the eeriest of ways. Not even the chirp of insects breaks the uncanny stillness. And so I wander, until dusk comes, its pink and orange radiance a taunt.

Such otherworldly beauty in an ending. Every day I have

walked until dusk. And every time I look at it, painting the sky in promises, I wish that it would lie only once. It promises to always come back. That in the most beautiful things there is always more. That perhaps, no matter how hard the day is—at the end of it—you can always look to the sky and know that another day awaits in its twin. It promises that if you hold on one more day, you might get to see beauty and valor again. If the fates have a shred of kindness, maybe, there will be some beauty in your endings.

The sky is bleeding violet when I find it—the smallest of rocky crags in the otherwise rolling green hills, nestled in the foot of a mound, the scent of sulfur wafting from it.

Under the mounds, she said.

I pull from the grass, sipping down the tiniest spark of energy, just enough to suffuse my muscles, preparing for the unknown. I step down into the crag, twisting my way into the darkened tunnel below, feet first.

Up to my torso in the crevice, feeling more space in the cavern below—enough to swing my feet a little—I look to the sky. The stars are beginning to shine in the waxing dark. I remember looking to the sky and begging in another life— peering through cracks of light and begging for my useless life. And now I have a use, a purpose. Maybe this fullness was the cost—this clawing purpose that demands more.

I move further into the dark and find myself in pitch blackness. It must be a cave of sorts.

The rocks roll under my feet, small echoes in the dank space. I feel my way forward, hoping to avoid smashing my face into sharp stone.

Glad to have one version of sight, I reach out my mind, feeling many openings, long tunnels that reach out like fingers in the mound. I cannot keep track of where they go as they drift off beyond my mind's eyes.

I take baby steps forward, kicking rocks and shuffling through narrow crevices, navigating the rocky tunnel until I find myself in a large room. At the end of the room I feel it— like a wall of pure life and energy, flat and powerful.

I move forward, steps echoing loudly, until I meet it with my hand. Solid as a rock but completely smooth, without flaw or blemish—like running your fingers over impenetrable, flowing water.

I reach out with my mind more closely. It twines together, infinite fingers gripping one another, forming a wall of glittering life.

And I have no clue how to get through it.

I place both hands on it, leaning my weight on it, searching for any obvious gives. Feeling foolish, I lean back, pulling my hands from its soft surface. At least nobody witnesses my naivety.

How did Fionn get through? He would have had to, to reach whatever hellish dimension he claimed lives on the other side.

I reach for it again, caressing its glowing surface. I try to weaken it by pulling from it, but I find no purchase, no loose thread to draw from; it is so wound together, so utterly one.

I try everything. I try throwing my body against it. I try begging it. I try waiting for it.

It's impassable… impossible.

So frustratingly ironic. So laughably humorless.

My failure so stupidly predictable.

I'm so tired.

I'm so tired.

It builds in me—all of it. All of the terrible things assault me at once. The salty tears dribble down my face, unfettered, and pathetic, and because there is nobody here to witness it, I let them take me. The rocky ground is not kind to my knees as I fall to them, but I cannot bring myself to care.

"Please," I whisper, pounding one weak fist at the wall where it meets the ground. "Please," I whisper again.

It becomes a mantra, for I have nothing to offer it other than my pleas.

Its solemn silence makes me shrink further, like I can hold myself together only if I am as small as possible.

As I sit there, some crumpled, pathetic piece of life, I leave my hand on it, hoping that if someone ever finds my body, they'll know I tried.

I tried I tried I tried.

I gave everything, *everything*. And it wasn't enough. This was just another instance in a long-lived, cruel pattern—but I had to try, or else I was never worth any of his kisses and caresses, any of Aine's outreached hands, any of Elva's defenses, any of Armund's sweet glances, of Konan's tolerance. Any glances that could have been shared between mates that were spared on me. Otherwise, I was never anything but poison in the water—nothing but a bad omen. A sour girl who should have frozen to death at six, begging for her mom, instead of living long enough to ruin anything that could have been good. I fear that even this final act is not enough to spare me that condemnation, but at least I tried.

As I press my cheek to the rocks, wet with salt streams, I give whatever I have left, tired of taking. Too tired to move, too tired to keep trying. That makes me weak, and a coward, but I'm tired of trying to pretend that I'm better, even to myself.

My tendrils of life curl into the wall, the last dregs of energy that I stole from the grass. Something pulls in my chest as my head spins.

I feel the wall beneath my hand blink out of existence.

As I look where it used to be, I see the softest glow of warm light and with all I have left, I crawl towards it.

I crawl until I fall.

Right into Hell.

I never gave much thought to what waited on the other side of life. Some devote their lives to beliefs surrounding it, but I was always certain that even if I tried, I was always going to be irredeemable. The sight in front of me is enough to tell me I'm right.

The ground is scorched, blackened rock, rough on my face, rolling into rivers of flame that hiss and spit.

Smoke overtakes the scent of sulfur as I roll onto my back, pinpointing my location at the mouth of a cave, a world of fire before me.

Somehow, I still feel held by the needs of a body. Every bit of me feels bruised and bleeding. I lack the energy to lift my limbs or head, so I just lie there, closing my eyes once more, awaiting burning eternity.

My heart beats in my head, whooshing and pounding, louder than I've ever heard it.

A breeze picks up, coming in a rhythmic pulse, picking up my limp hair and throwing it around my face.

A grumble fills the air, vibrating my bones. The sound rattles in the lowest tenor, knocking anything else from it. Chills break out across my entire body as I jolt upwards, scrambling onto my palms. My eyes meet the creature of Fionn's tales.

If there was a drop of liquid in my dehydrated body, I would piss myself.

Slitted yellow eyes observe me, grumbling menacingly, sizing me up to eat in one bite.

A dragon.

I scramble slightly back, every muscle shaking violently.

A green-scaled head the size of my house bobs slightly from side to side. Teeth the size of children fang out, creating rows in a slightly opened mouth. A long, forked tongue darts out to taste my terror. It approaches in a slow, stalking gait on four enormously clawed feet. The ground trembles with every movement. Large membranous wings block out the daylight.

It huffs a breath at me once it is arms-length away. The foul scent of rotting meat and scorching heat blows back my hair as I peer at my death approaching.

I've lost all ability to flee, frozen in its reeking breath as I await its blazing judgment.

I can only watch—watch as violet flame curls in the back of the monster's throat as it grumbles again, rattling my brain in my skull. I close my eyes, not wanting to see my scorching coming anymore.

The flames never come.

Instead a scaled fist clamps around my torso. Claws larger than my limbs crush the air from my lungs.

I kick my legs in a fruitless attempt to wriggle from its grasp.

My stomach drops as it takes a running leap. Its wings— in two booming flaps—lift us into smoke-filled skies.

Chapter 40

The underworld rushes past in whirling black stone and liquid flame. My hair whips with every gust of wing-swept wind. My stomach is about to come out through my mouth.

The black stone turns to a burnt orange as the beast travels across leagues in a seemingly endless flight. Sparse greenery begins to grow larger, the leaves blowing in the wake of the beast.

And suddenly my body is in free-fall. I barely have the thought to roll as I hit the ground. The beast had the foresight to drop me a survivable distance from the ground, possibly unwilling to kill me before playing with me first.

I squint my eyes against orange dust billowing in the wind, choking me, the chalky texture coating my skin and clothes.

And somehow, I gather my thoughts enough to realize that I am not dead. That this is the place under the mounds. With spitting mountains of fire that feed rivers of such. I made it here, to the place where the madame sent me—to the nest of dragons.

Across a rift. For that is what that wall was. A barrier, separating two worlds.

The ground trembles with the force of the beast landing near me, the breaking of its flight tossing more dust into the air.

The faint sound of boots scuffing lightly on grit has me jerking my head up, eyes squinted against the debris.

A figure stalks towards me in the dust, tendrils of long brown hair whipping in the wind, a longsword gripped in hand.

The tip of a blade comes to rest at my throat.

The woman before me is ethereally beautiful, with tan skin and light brown hair, dark features and full lips. A Fae.

Her ears come to gentle points through her wind-blown hair.

"Where did you come from?" she demands.

My voice trembles, "The… the mounds… I—I was sent here to find someone—"

The blade pushes harder into my throat, forcing me back as she comes to stand over me.

The emerald dragon waiting on the other side of the plateau watches us with… curiosity? Is it possible for monsters to feel such things?

"Who?"

"The—the madame—from Raith. She said I could find allies here. I need—" I look desperately around, making sense of nothing. "—I need help. You're Fae! My friends, so are they—"

She digs the tip in harder; I feel the blood pool in the indent. Her head cocks ever-so-slightly to the side.

"I am unfamiliar with such a person. This madame, or this… Raith. What are they? What do you need help for?"

"I promise, I mean no harm. I am nothing. I just need…

My friends are in danger." My thoughts are whirring and I try desperately to gather them. I squeeze my eyes shut, I can't concentrate when she pierces me with her eyes. "Raith. Raith is the capitol of where I come from. The king… He lives there. He captured my… friend." It feels wrong to call Fionn my friend: he is my bleeding heart, locked away in a dungeon.

"And the madame, she is a woman… No, she is a creature. I'm not sure what she is, but she has jet black hair—willowy. Not Fae, nor human or Fomorian—"

The word is a trigger for her. She drops onto her haunches, cutting me off with a fist in my hair, and grits, "Fomorians?"

My scalp burns, but it is the smallest of my hurts. "They took over. They feed on us—on souls. I only learned because my friend, Fionn—he's a Fae too— he told me about what they did in his world, in Danu. I have power… I was, lost—sent away. He taught me how to wield, how to fight them."

Her eyes are blown wide with dismay. I think I have stunned her into silence.

She drops me as if I've burned her, standing up and backing up a step. The dragon growls that buffeting sound, its tail whipping back and forth in agitation, kicking up dust. It's as if he feels her dismay.

I see her about to flee and scramble after her, pleading, "Wait!"

But she is gone in a blurred dash, her moves graceful and fluid as she leaps from the dragon's extended leg, up onto its back, seating herself between unfurling wings.

I'm on my feet, running after her without a thought, but I'm far slower than her as the beast ascends on strong wings. I slow to a stop, watching the magnificence of it all. Craning my head back, I watch the glittering green scales and massive wings lifting high into the sky, blocking out the light.

Then it dives for me.

And as futile as it is, my feet cannot help but scramble backwards, fear taking over.

But as it lifts me in its forest green fore-claw once more, I think that I'm just glad it didn't pick me up in its mouth.

The blur of my surroundings grows greener for some time before I'm dropped once more. My legs are still weak when I hit the ground, so I land hard on my knees. I feel it in my teeth.

I frantically attempt to orient myself, fearful of another dragon making a meal out of me. I'm in the shadow of a red stone cliff-face. Strange windows dot the entire face. I see small people milling about behind them, like ants.

People.

People live here.

In the stone—Fae.

I'm brought to my feet by the same woman's firm hand. In my gawking she must have dismounted, her green mount having taken to the skies once more. Now that I stand beside her I realize that I'm taller than her, only slightly, though she is far curvier and more feminine.

We enter the cliffside through a large, yawning opening, large enough for a dragon to pass through.

Giant flaming chandeliers illuminate the largest entrance room, fueled by nothing; I suspect it is the work of a wielder. Smaller balls of flame dance along narrower hallways, casting flickering shadows on the walls.

Shuffling through the red dirt, extending that psychic hand into my surroundings, I find that the air is utterly full. The ground beneath my feet hums. The flames illuminating the space are veritable bombs of power, it's enough that my muscles twitch. My other sense—battered and exhausted—still pushes out, caressing the power surrounding me.

The Fae milling about, halt me in my tracks.

Hundreds of them—pointed ears and grace, leather-clad and bustling. Some peer at me in curiosity, no doubt taking in my disheveled appearance and odd hair.

Living in the cliffs—under the mounds—the allies the madame promised.

Casual wielding is all around: flame figurines dance, manipulated by a female entertaining the few children settled around the large bonfire in the center—tendrils of water float from a running stream of water into a Fae female's basket. Some males use bursts of wind to buffet around a stone, a game, to keep the stone from their opponent's hoop at the end.

A buzzing whir zips past my ear—a strange blue iridescent bird flying past where I stand. Tracking it's swooping movements, it lands on the shoulder of a Fae female, one swathed in gauzy white linen. It nestles against her neck, its long, lizard-like tail trailing over her shoulder. It huffs and a small tuft of smoke billows out its nostrils.

It's a dragon, one the size of a palm, with feathered wings like a bird.

I look to the hooded woman leading me by the arm.

"So many?" My whispered question is drowned by the cacophony.

Her dark eyes look me up and down sternly before saying, "Yes."

I search for the word for a moment. "Danaan?"

Her eyes flare in sadness for a beat. "Used to be."

"Where are you taking me?" I finally ask, unable to help but meet the many curious eyes that stop to look at me as I pass through the crowd. They are all so stunning, so graceful and wild—more so than the Fianna, like living in this place intensified their traits.

"To the Donn," she says. "He will want to hear your story from you."

"Will he help me?" I picture Fionn's face, etched in agony, filthy from lying unwashed in a cell for weeks.

"I cannot speak for him." She tugs me along once again.

We navigate through seemingly endless hallways and rooms, twisting and curving, carved into the stone, burrowing further underground.

"What is this place?" I whisper in wonder.

She glances back at me. "Annwyn—that is the world. As I'm sure you know you're no longer in your own. More specifically, you're in Tech Duinn, the Stone city."

"How did you get here?" I gnaw at my thumbnail, trying to file down the jagged edge with my teeth, my other hand trapped in the hand of this stranger.

"That's a story for another time, I'm afraid." Her voice is soft. She's reserved, but no longer seems to want to kill me. However, her emotions seem barely caged—on edge.

At least we have one thing in common.

After climbing many sets of stairs and moving through endless long hallways, we find ourselves at an archway. The room beyond is airy and bright, opening into a balcony high above where we entered.

My escort pulls me through, keeping a hand lightly gripping my arm.

The red stone room—a collection of scrolls, an artfully crafted dark-wood desk, and several wooden chairs facing the desk—is occupied by one man, gray-haired and wizened, clad in brown leather. Though he still has a powerful form, standing tall, he is undeniably older. I never thought Fae displayed age in such a way, he must be very old. He stands at a heavy wooden table, leaning over some sketches. As he looks up at us, something about him seems to look through us, like he is hollowed out. His features are masculine and handsome, even if slightly wrinkled.

"Gwen," he states, voice pointed as he looks at me.

The woman, presumably Gwen, nods her head. "Wyll. Where is the Donn? Will he be back soon?" She asks kindly enough, though a bit impatiently, seeming mildly distressed that the Donn is not awaiting us in this chamber.

I swallow relief that this man is not the Donn we sought. He seems blocked off, unreachable.

His gaze doesn't stray from my form, not in a leering way, but as if trying to figure out without having to be told. "He said he wanted to look for something in the ice caves. He's been gone all day, though I expect him back at any moment."

Gwen barely muffles a sigh, releasing my arm to cross hers. "I found this girl wandering the fire fields. Right near the rift…" she trails off pointedly.

Wyll's eyes widen almost imperceptibly.

The conversation discontinues and we all wait with baited breaths.

I have no concept of how long I stand there, swaying on my feet. How long I think about Fionn, trapped in that cell. Hating me. Worrying over Aine—hearing her sobs last I saw her. Any manner of horrid things could befall them all while I stand here and gnaw at my fingernails.

My fingers are all bleeding by the time I hear it.

Heavy steps echo in the impatient silence, from behind.

Wyll's eyes lift slightly to the space beyond the doorway.

Gwen whips around, letting out a relieved breath. As graceful as she is, something about her feels wild and impatient.

I'm far slower to turn, the days weigh me down more with every minute. The space around me blurs as I turn in shuffling steps.

And when my eyes focus on the man filling the archway, I lose my breath.

He is the most disgustingly, ruggedly handsome male I've ever seen—even above Fionn.

He fills the archway, massive in a way that only comes with an eternity of hard work and height that only comes with immortality.

His hair, black as night, is long and straight, falling behind his back but for the sides, which are cropped quite close to the skin. He has scruff on his face, showing a lack of cleanliness unfitting of a ruler.

His eyes pierce mine directly, cutting right through me with clarity.

Black leather melds to his body from neck to toe to fingers.

"Donn." Gwen bends her head slightly, the most casual of bows.

It jerks me from my stupor, I realize I'm standing before another king.

My knee hits the ground—more like slams into it, as I bow. "Your Grace," I say, voice cracking.

Silence reigns.

"You don't have to do that, you know. We don't do… whatever that is," Gwen says, sounding like she may laugh.

I peer up carefully, first at the Donn, who's looking at me with a tight jaw. Then at Wyll, who is watching me with an empty expression. Then at Gwen who is, yes, holding back a smile with one elegant hand.

I take a deep breath and gather what strength I have to

push myself to my feet. I manage without losing whatever scraps of dignity I have left, though the room spins slightly once I lock my knees, standing.

Gwen breaks the silence once more, "I found this one near the rift. Says she's from across it. In this place called Raith. Claims she was sent here, by a madame, who she describes with an astounding lack of details. She said she was sent here to find help for her friend, Fionn. Her friend, who claimed he was a Fae of Danu, and helped train her to wield and fight the Fomorians that had taken over her world."

The Donn's gaze settles far more intently on my face as Gwen reveals her story.

His eyes are so rich a brown, slightly red—like a cherry-wood. They have dark circles beneath them, heavy with exhaustion.

His steps are slow, measured, and intimidating as he narrows the space between us.

It is slightly demeaning, having to tilt my head ever-so-slightly-back to maintain eye contact.

He takes in my appearance pointedly, still not a word uttered in response.

Flashes of him striking me into silence at the first word I speak run through my mind, clamping my mouth shut.

I rub my index finger over the rough, bleeding edge of my thumb, letting the pain center me, preparing me to argue for the Fianna's sake.

"There is nothing I wouldn't do to keep my people safe," his words are rough, his voice gritty, as if he hasn't spoken in a while. "There is no atrocity I won't commit, no world I would not cross, to protect them." He looks between my eyes. "Think about that before you lift a single hand against anything as small as a gnat in my home. Or utter a single word to anyone about us. If you do, it will be the end of you. I don't make idle threats."

I shiver, and nod, letting out a slow breath, keeping my mismatched eyes on his.

He waits until he's satisfied, still looking agitated at my presence. Then he abruptly turns around, prowling around the desk where Wyll awaits. "What is it you want, then?" he asks roughly, turning to level me with his stare again as he shuffles around pieces of parchment on the desk.

My thoughts are blown to the wind, like the shreds of Diana's notes, fluttering away in the breeze.

I squeeze my thumb in my fist.

What do I want?

"The woman who sent me—I don't know her name—all I know is she is… not a anything I've ever heard of." I grasp at the fluttering pieces of the story, desperate to find a direction. "She is tall and raven-haired, seems to know things—everything really—and she said that I may find allies under the mounds to help me with something. Do you know who I may be referring to?" I ask, searching for some credibility.

The Donn waves a hand. "The Banshee, Clio, I believe her name was. She paid a visit once, stalking through the territory. She found it ill-suited to her purposes. Too many beasts bigger and stronger than her, I suppose. Though she did say she would never utter a word of our presence here when I happened upon her." He grits his teeth before hissing out. "I suppose I have some threats to follow through on."

Banshee. The madame is a Banshee? A harbinger of death. She certainly brought misfortune thus far.

"Perhaps," I say, disappointed that my connection to her may hurt my plight. "I came to you because there are more of your people. In Suri." My eyes bore into his, hoping I look strong. "And I need help, to get them out—to get them back. Once they hear of this place, they will want to rejoin you. They've been searching for something like this, all of you, for a very long time."

"So you've said."

Every bit of me wants to go to him—wants to drop to my knees and beg. I would if it didn't seem like he would scrape me off his boot like a bug.

So I just start talking, never taking my eyes off his face. Snatching at shreds of paper in wild air.

I tell him about the Fianna, how they claimed to land and consequently be stuck on Suri. I recap our meeting in the clearing, not leaving out my failed thievery. I speak of my wielding, how it began and how Fionn trained me, our days on the road, that fateful day in Raith. I gloss over the imprisonment, the words stuttering and overwhelming. I can't speak of it, not with these strangers—not while I stand here, a walking corpse, from the days since then. And I do not tell him what the king told me about my heritage, not if it will worsen the likelihood of aid. I recall Fionn, spitting words of derision in my face at the revelation of my parentage. I just tell the Donn I was sent to Suri as a babe, a child hidden, and ferried away between worlds.

"I'm sorry, I tried. I really didn't know that the Fomorians would be there. It's my fault—" I choke, feeling tears burn, and hating them. "He wouldn't be there if it weren't for me, and I am trying to fix it. You can't leave him there. You can't. You have to help me. I lo—" I grit my teeth, closing my eyes against the searing pain that shoots through my chest. "He doesn't deserve to die like that."

When I open my eyes again the Donn is staring at me with a piercing intensity, having sat silently but intensely through my frantic rambling.

"And the others, where are they?" he asks quietly, gently, eyes flickering to Wyll, who at some point turned to stare out at the world beyond the balcony.

"Some… died that day. Two of them. Dealla and Deri." My heart stutters, so bruised but so determined to keep pulsing. I stare at the whirling patterns on the desk. "They fought, bravely, but they were killed. Dealla… one got her. It started… eating her soul, I think—I don't really know what it looks like. And then Deri—Deri just lost it, stopped fighting, just let them kill him—"

Wyll, as if unable to listen to more, passes behind me, and leaves through the archway with nothing but a light scuffling sound of his leather boots on rough stone. I look at either of the two left for explanation. They both look lost to their own agony.

"Did you know them?" I ask quietly, heart squeezing at the pain in the room.

It had been close to thirty years since separation, but I assume when you're immortal, that is a blip in time.

The Donn nods solemnly. "We thought everyone else dead. Finding out that some are not… or were not, however brief, then learning of their death, is horrible. Deri—It became apparent that the Deri you were talking about is my uncle's son." He gestures to the archway where Wyll disappeared. "He thought him long dead but… for a moment there… it didn't feel like it."

Sorrow washes over me. Deri's father. The resemblance is notable, now that I see the truth of it. The way they hold themselves is the same. Like noble stags in a wood.

"I'm sorry," I whisper, knowing the sentiment is so small, basically negligible. It only means anything to the speaker. It helps you ride through the palpable grief of others. It makes you feel better, not them. Suddenly, I feel bad saying even that.

The Donn nods in acceptance of my condolences anyways.

Deri whirls in my mind—his strong face, and fiercely protective loving. He had pulled me from the ground.

I cross my arms in front of me, my hand rubbing over the still burned spot on my arm.

A thought strikes me.

"Wait… You're Deri's cousin then?" I ask, recalling a night fireside, discussing Deri's cousin on his mom's side.

The Donn looks at me suspiciously before nodding.

"Erron is your name, isn't it? He talked about you one night. He told me you were his best friend." I smile solemnly. I want him to know that Deri loved him. That is worth something.

Erron, the Donn, looks at the floor to gather himself before meeting my eyes, face now stoic. "Yes, he was. I'm sure you need to rest and recuperate after your… ordeal." He swallows the last word. He turns to Gwen, who shadows me, not uttering a sound. "Gwen, if you will show our guest to a room and gather her some clothes. Make sure she eats and drinks." His voice is stern.

He's dismissing me?

"What about the Fianna?"

"We will decide what to do after you've eaten and rested." His tone leaves no room for argument.

I can feel myself tip, tip, tipping right over the edge of my limit.

"We haven't decided anything! Fionn doesn't have time for me to eat and rest!" He just heard everything I said and decided to leave it be?

He looks back up at me, his fist clenching around a page. "We haven't. There are risks to consider, outcomes to weigh.

I must discuss with the council."

I storm over to his desk, ice in my exhausted veins. Leaning across it, shoving his papers—maps, carefully illustrated and drawn to scale—to the floor. I can feel my sanity losing its footing, slipping on a sheet of ice. "You're considering leaving them there?" I await his justification, daring him to speak it. "You said you would do anything—" I lean across the desk and shove his absurdly huge chest, the force of it shooting back up my arm, like shoving a tree. "—for your people. And because you've spent some time apart you no longer claim them? How convenient." All my hopes are smashing into nothing. My disappointment is too huge of a chasm to face. "You're a coward. You sit here, in your stone castle, while Fionn rots away in a dungeon? While your niece is out there, an orphan, hiding from the very people who took everything from you?" I'm openly screaming now, my madness echoing across red stone.

He does not rise to my challenges nor my insults. "You need to calm down."

I'm already gone—lost to some manic haze that's been building for days—weeks—years, maybe. It has been building every moment I've spent looking at shadows that don't exist, or combing through every tiny detail, trying to find where everything went wrong.

"No! Do you know what they're doing to him right now? You want to wait? You don't know what they do! You left before you could find out. But *I* know!" It's a shattered sob, one of bone-trembling anger. One that only serves to make me angrier with myself, because now I'm crying and I look like a hysterical woman. "You don't deserve them!" I climb over his desk, ready to claw his eyes out.

It's like a dream where you're trying to warn everyone that something horrible is coming, but nobody will listen.

Gwen has me in a chokehold before I can reach Erron, dragging me off the desk though I scrape my fingertips down its polished face.

Erron's hands grip the edge of his desk. Eyes running over me, assessing the threat anew while I thrash.

"Shhhhh..." Gwen whispers in my ear over my noises. My nails are tearing at the skin of her arm across my neck, but with the state of my nails, I think it hurts me more than her. "He didn't say that. You're fine. He's going to help you."

The world is blurring at the edges, my fight rapidly dying out.

A snap of wood sounds.

Erron's stricken face is the last thing I see as he says firmly, "I'll help you."

It's like I finally have all the pieces of paper.

Chapter 41

Mariana

The fabric still waves in the wind. The sight clear in dawn's first light emboldens me. Mom would change it to the black cloth if something were amiss.

There are five today—too many for the three whipping posts in the center of the camp. They stand stock still, awaiting their torture, the red-head's rebellion from yesterday fresh in our minds.

Not everyone knows what's about to happen. I couldn't risk letting word reach the ears of the Crows.

We all gather, weary from the day, dirt and debris a crust on our skin. The Crows line the top of the wall, waiting for their favorite part of the day, watching the human guards shove us around, pulling the five people to the posts in the center of the space.

I cannot wait to make it more exciting for them.

They don't get a chance to tie a single slave to the post before I step into the center.

It must be a sight; some weak, thin girl, barefoot and

garbed in rags, stepping up, shoulders back, to a group of full-grown men, armed to the teeth. I almost wish I could view it from the outside. I should feel scared, but excitement thrums in my veins. I've waited for this moment.

I fear no man.

"Get back in line," one of them grunts.

I don't stop.

I do not falter.

The one I go for barely reacts quick enough to draw his broadsword.

But he has to blindly swing it as I gouge his eyes out with my fingers.

It's euphoric—the vengeance I've dreamed of these past weeks.

His swinging forces his comrades to step back from helping him. They step back into my two allies, Emris and Zarah, who divest them of their daggers and slit their throats.

Those two are the only ones with prior training.

Crows fly their roosts, racing to the rescue of their fellow monsters, racing down stairs and fleeing their posts.

As I assumed they would.

I engage with a guard that approaches me, slipping nimbly past his guard, nicking one of his daggers, and stabbing it straight between his helm and shoulder braces, in the side of the neck. It goes in easy there, popping through pipes and tubes in the neck.

The fray grows, my other few comrades jumping in, grappling and slaying. Exacting vengeance we've all dreamed of. And as more join us, the uninformed slaves stop fearing retaliation. They stop thinking about what will happen afterwards, they only see the tides and how they shift before their very eyes. Everyone craves justice. It's amazing how quickly humans tear one another to pieces under the right circumstances.

And as the Crows flood the space behind the troughs, I know we need to move.

"The gate!" I shout at the top of my lungs, snatching a longsword from the corpse of a fallen soldier. "To the gate!"

The troughs are toppled, thanks to Dierdre, blocking the Crows in, stalling them for a few seconds.

I stay back, facing the Crows as they make their way through the obstacles, knowing what the soon-to-be-free slaves will find at the gate: weapons pulled from supply carts that run to the capitol. There are far more slaves than there are Crows, guards, and slavers, and therefore blades.

I remember how strong these bastards are, but I also remember killing them. I'm just hoping they don't have other tricks up their sleeves. That the presence of human guards and slavers will keep them from showing themselves as the monsters that they are.

As my sword clashes with the first one, I think of days of heaving stone, fed on scraps. My arms tremble and falter, though I'm quick enough to feint and evade. That will only last for so long; they'll learn my moves.

Sure enough, the next time I dodge I'm met with another blade, almost falling to it.

I leap onto a trough, not daring to look to my right to see if the gates have opened yet—if my newly armed comrades are on their way to help. My new leverage allows me to land a blow, slicing through sinew and abdominal muscles, though not quite deep enough to eviscerate. Shame.

I fall to the other side of the trough, barely landing on my two feet. The only thing keeping me in this fight is years of training, skills pounded into my being with sweat and pain.

The divide between the Crow and me allows me a chance to glimpse my allies, and what I see robs me of breath.

The gate is still closed.

And they are crowded against it, pinned there between it and a group of Crows. I fear I'll never forget the look on their faces; gut-wrenching terror, and hopelessness. Disappointment—both in me and themselves, for believing. And in some, accusation—I started this. I led them to this doom.

The Crow leaps over the trough with inhuman grace and kicks out, straight in the knee. My leg buckles.

I try to recover, I really do.

But he is so damned quick for a huge man. So strong as he leaps on my fallen form, quickly pinning my hands to the rocky ground.

He wraps one meaty fist around my throat and squeezes.

He crushes and crushes me, the look on his face full of malice.

I gasp and thrash and beg for breath.

I try to scream for help, to no avail.

I plead with the sky and its giant black spots that now hang there, growing like clouds of doom.

But nothing I do matters.

Perhaps it never did.

The light pierces through my head like a blade, sharp and bright. The sunniest of days, but somehow also the darkest.

My hands are bound together, hanging from the wooden pole I lean my forehead against.

Thoughts of survival and betrayal begin to whirl as I gasp in a breath, wondering how I got here.

What happened?

Why did nobody come?

I'm still blinded, scrambling to understand what happened.

Hot air blows against the bare skin at my back. The skin there is hot and tight, as if it has been sitting under glaring sun for hours, burning. My smock has been split open at the back; I feel it hanging off my shoulders.

My eyes adjust to the bright white light. And what I see makes me want to die.

Deirdre, Zarah, Emris, all of the slaves I had worked with kneel in front of me, in chains.

Most are crying silently, which is the most striking, as I had thought we had all run out of tears.

How did my plan fail?

Why would they abandon me?

My mother would never have abandoned me while there was breath in her lungs.

Fear and betrayal mingle so bitterly. Was my group discovered up in the mountains? What could have befallen them while I was here? And without them, I am but another slave. Nothing more than another nameless face, another fruitless fight, another bland dying of the light.

My allies look at me in terror, their eyes flickering to something behind me.

"I must say, your timing is impeccable," a cool voice says over the tense silence. "I suppose I ought to thank you for that. Things around here are so dull most of the time."

A few deep chuckles sound behind me, all taunting, all deep and male.

Looking over my shoulder I see him—the most beautiful man I have ever seen.

A crown rests on his pale brow. It gives him away, even more than how pretty he is.

The king.

His blue eyes—chips of ice—pierce through me as sure as the sunlight. They entrance me. His hair, a rich brown, curls softly around his temples. He is garbed in the finest regalia, all emerald green and black, aside from his shirt: crisp, white, and billowing in the breeze, surely fitting the blazing heat.

This man ruined all of us.

This man rained terror down on my home.

This man is the reason my father is dead.

The reason I'm here.

"How heroic." He quirks a brow, staring so far into me, like he is rifling around in my mind. "You fought so well, I thought you would at least be able to speak."

His casual tone makes me long for things. Long for my blade through his chest. Long to crack open his rib cage, flaying him open for all to see the dead rotting inside of him. Long for the feel of his heart in my bare hands.

He must see it, because he cracks a smile.

His gaunt undertones… malice wafting off him in waves—something about him screams inhuman. And what a bitter humor it is that fills me.

Of course.

Of course he's not.

Who else would have let this happen?

I can't even crack a smile at the obviousness of it all.

I still haven't dropped eye contact, nor responded.

He walks up to where I'm bound to the whipping post, settling down on his haunches.

"Nothing to say? Let me guess. You're thinking that you'll be the death of me. Hoping, perhaps." He's all seriousness, eyes flickering between the two of mine. He's even more sickeningly beautiful up close, eyes starry, his features both masculine and delicate.

"I would never say something so cliché." The words come out rasping before I can stop them.

He laughs, cold but rich, a goddamn dimple flashing.

"Very well then. I can respect that." He stands back to his impressive height, eyes flickering to the rest of the slaves. The men behind him have eager glints in their eyes.

I take stock of them as the king moves amongst them, consulting them quietly. I don't recognize any of them from my time in the camp.

One stands with feet spread, observing with obvious disdain. Painted in brutality, powerfully built, with long dark hair braided down his back, he is larger than his companions, scarred and massive. The others flicker fearful glances at him. Another general, I assume.

Another gaunt man stands at his side, dwarfed by the former, though his eyes are far more assessing, more far-seeing. He wears a pendant around his neck, a symbol of the sun. He holds with him parchment bound in a book, charcoal for writing strapped to it. Perhaps an adviser. A scribe. Kings need such things. Though what he could be recording of this event, I haven't a clue. I cannot imagine it will ever make the official records.

The savage one addresses the king firmly, impatiently, without the usual formal niceties, "Kill her."

The statement, so bold, commanding, spoken to the king, sends silence rippling through the crowd.

The Pretty King shows nothing to indicate this enrages him.

His icy blue eyes cut to me for a moment before responding, "No. I don't think she deserves death."

The scarred Crow looks as if *his* inferior had just defied him.

"Death would be too quick," the king says before turning to address us all. "I am a tolerant man. I allow my people to live their lives how they wish. I allow them to be wealthy or be poor. I allow them to have as many children as they wish. Allow them to worship whatever god sways them. The same could not be said for every place in this realm. I allow you to work here, to work for what is fair, as opposed to seeing you hang from the gallows." He sounds like a chastising father. "What a waste of life that would be." He looks like he means it. "But I do not tolerate treason. I cannot. To betray your fellow countrymen—to betray those that would keep the peace—I cannot let that go unpunished."

The hypocrisy and delusion of his speech almost makes me laugh.

Almost.

I stare at him, daring him to look at me. Look at me as he condemns me.

He does.

Unflinchingly.

"And so, as instigator to this whole incident, I must punish you. But I will have mercy on the rest of you." He still stares at me as he addresses the rest of them, daring me to drop my own eyes. "And so you shall bear the punishment of all."

I do not waver.

I do not let him see the tremble of my limbs. Relief and fear wars for ownership of them.

He nods to a Crow, one that holds the whip.

I must speak my piece. I want it known.

"One day, when you die a young death, you will see me," I whisper. "When you breathe your last breath, you will know it was me, and what I worked for, that did it. I hope you choke on it." I don't look away from him as I say it over the gleeful muttering of his men.

I settle in, squaring my shoulders, my eyes not leaving his.

He looks surprised—at least there's that.

"That is quite the vow," he says, softly, settling in beside his advisors, maintaining eye contact.

A guard approaches in the edges of my view, a whip in hand.

Neither of us speaks as the lash first comes down on my bare back, slicing through skin.

I don't make a noise, even as my body screams.

My skin, then my muscle, splitting with every lash.

And I burn and burn.

Like being thrown into flames, forced to stay still as they consume you.

I do not falter.

My vision wavers with every strike.

I hear the whip, in the back of my mind, underneath everything else. How it whooshes through the air before cracking against wet skin.

I don't know, after a time, if I make any sounds. I must. But my eyes never waver. Not for a second. They just hold his, as his hold mine.

I can feel my knees, sitting in puddles of my own blood.

I don't look down at it. I keep looking at those starry, soulless eyes.

But before my vision goes black, I swear I see him—in his inhale.

The tiniest catch in his breath.

Only then do I close my eyes.

Only then do I *fall, and fall, and fall*.

And know no more.

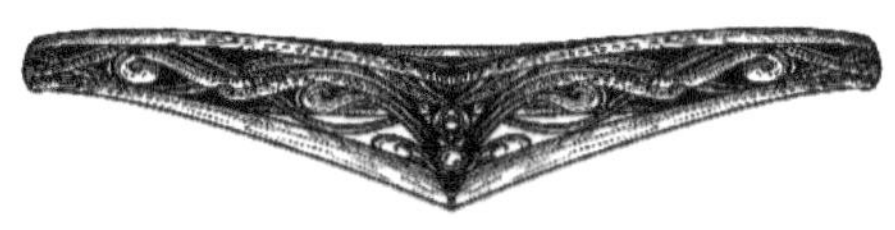

Chapter 42

Cloves and woodsmoke.

The scent is warm and welcoming. It weaves through my dreams, soothing their jagged edges. They warn of evil outpacing my flight, sang me songs of endings both violent and too soon.

My bleary eyes open to a world of red stone and candlelight. A plate of food sits on a short table beside the plush bed I lay on. The scent of the warm-spiced fruit tart on it makes my mouth water.

My joints ache as I push myself into a sitting position, trying to recall how I ended up here.

I'm wearing fresh clothes. A white tunic, lightweight and soft as a duckling, falls down over the top half of my thighs. My cheeks warm as I realize someone changed my underthings as well—I can only hope it was a woman. Dark trousers are folded on the chair across the room, brown leather boots sit on the ground beside them.

A light breeze, carrying the scent of woodsmoke, comes in through the darkened window opening. Night has fallen since my interaction with Erron.

The memory of it floods back, propelling me to my feet. I must go talk to the Donn. I've already wasted too much time resting.

How much time have I spent resting?

The thought quickens my movements as I pull the trousers on.

Has it been days or hours?

I shove my feet in the boots; they're soft like butter and fit a little loosely. The ones I came here in were probably discarded. So many holes covered them, they were hardly usable anymore.

I snatch the fruit tart from the plate as I flee the room, shoving it into my mouth as I open the door to the hallway. The flavors almost make me moan. I forgot how heavenly sweet fruit and cinnamon taste. How long have I lived on meat and root vegetables? I hadn't needed sweetness nor pleasure, I needed something to keep me alive—but this sweetness tastes like living.

Torches light the way as I trot down the hallway. This one could be any of the hallways we walked through on our way to speak to the Donn. I keep my steps quick and light as I take turn after turn with no knowledge of where I'm headed.

Could Gwen not have explained the layout of such a place as we walked? Was I too far gone to bother remembering my possible escape routes? We both had other things in mind.

My breaths are quick and strained as I quicken my pace.

The halls are a labyrinth, every turn bringing me to another hallway that looks the same. Finally, I round a corner that leads to a staircase. I go all the way down, my thighs screaming with the effort. I'm unsure if the muscle fatigue means I've been asleep for too long or not enough.

I had one goal, to get help. And as soon as I acquired said help, I rested? There will be time for rest when I have my people back, when everyone is safely on this side of the rift.

I kick myself for every second lost to my body's needs.

Whenever my mind brushes over Aine's smiling face, I feel sick. She's alone now. I hope she has Konan, Armund, and Elva looking out for her. Keeping her safe.

It's not the same.

It will never be the same. And I mourn for her.

I rage for her.

The hall near the entrance is at the bottom of the steps. A few Fae mill about, some seated at a great fire pit in the center of the great hallway. They cast me curious glances as I pass by, searching for a familiar face.

The light of more fire flickers from outside of the front entrance. Sounds of laughter and music sing pleasantly from outside, it mingles with the ever-present charge in the lifeblood of Annwyn.

As I round the corner, exiting the stone city, what awaits beyond steals the breath from my lungs and freezes me in my tracks.

Dragons.

Two of them, lounging amongst the fire and Fae. They tower over the scene, their scales and strangely feline eyes glittering in the firelight. They grumble and trill at one another, the sounds rattling over my bones. The larger one looks like the one who flew me here in its claws, with glowing green eyes and verdant scales. It puffs smoke at the smaller dragon. The smaller one is the color of bronze, with a crown of spikes that gives it a regal appearance, like a ruthless dragon prince.

Bronze bares its long, jagged teeth at Green in response,

shuffling its wings in agitation. Green looks away, seemingly bored of the interaction. Bronze stands to an impressive height and slinks away on all fours, the movement of it sounds like a herd of horses trampling through grass. Its tail, clubbed and spiked, trails over the ground behind its departing form before Bronze crouches slightly and leaps into flight, its wings booming with every beat—kicking dust up. I have to cover my eyes for a moment to keep it from getting into them.

The Fae that laugh and play around the roaring fire in the center seem unaffected by the dragon's interactions. They play lutes and stringed instruments, some engaged in close conversation. They're all long and graceful—beautiful. All twenty or so of them behave so familiarly with one another. They touch freely, playing with hair, heads laying on shoulders. Even the males cuff one another on the back of the neck or arm, sling arms over shoulders, lean closely in confidence.

I've never seen anything like it.

"Alyx!" a familiar voice calls from amidst the revels.

I spot her amidst the Fae—Gwen.

"Calm, Vyrain," Gwen runs a hand over Green's jaw affectionately before making her way to me. She is garbed head to toe in brown leathers, complete with matching gloves.

Green watches every step Gwen takes over to me, its serpentine neck snaking out over the group to get a closer look at me.

Vyrain.

I can't take my eyes from the predator sizing me up. The hair on my arms stands up and I freeze. I'm able to keep myself together enough to take the dragon in, with all of its lethal glory.

Vyrain peers at me with predatory eyes, giving a sinister growl.

Heavy scaled plating runs over its brows and crests over their nostrils. Spikes of lighter green begin at the pole of its head and snake down its entire spinal column in one long crest. Its scales glimmer in every shade of green, like a sunlit forest.

"She doesn't have much love for those that smell like human," Gwen says, coming to stand in front of me with a smile in her voice. "I wasn't sure how long you would sleep."

"How long?" I finally flick my eyes to hers.

"Two days. You must have needed it. Erron wanted us to let you rest for as long as you could." She eyes me concernedly.

My stomach turns. Two days. How could I have let that happen?

"You shouldn't have. We need to leave." I chew on the skin around my thumbnail, keeping Vyrain in my periphery.

The Fae around the fire shoot glances our way. Some are wielding fire at their fingertips, like one would fidget with a rolled smoke. The chatter has quieted somewhat.

"Erron has discussed your plight with the council. While they all believed that we should help the Fianna, some were hesitant to risk our hidden position here," Gwen explains.

I open my mouth to argue but she interrupts me.

"But between the two of us, we were able to convince them of the seriousness of the Fianna's position in Suri. They were placated with an increase in patrols at the rift. It is a bottleneck, making any force moving through easily picked-off. It would be near impossible to pose a threat from the outside of Annwyn." She pauses.

Does she think I plan to lead enemy forces here?

She goes on. "There is value in every Fae life. So, you and Erron shall go." She grins a feral smile. "And of course, myself. We are going for stealth rather than brute force. Just the three of us—along with Vyrain and Rignon."

Wary at the mention of an unfamiliar name I ask, "Who is Rignon?"

"An important member of the alliance. You'll meet him soon enough. Though I warn you, he has a foul temper." She smirks.

I'm glad she finds my ignorance amusing.

"We need to leave soon." I shuffle on my feet, casting the Fae at the fire a glance. They aren't even trying to look as though they aren't listening anymore.

She eyes the group as well. "I agree. I would not want to leave my kin a moment longer. I believe Erron has had the time to gather the provisions." She looks back at Vyrain, her eyes softening slightly. "Now to convince her this is a good idea." She grimaces.

Vyrain makes eye contact with her rider and puffs out a cloud of smoke, whipping her spiked tail back-and-forth like an agitated cat.

"I don't know that she will fit through the tunnels…" I whisper, not wanting Vyrain to hear.

The dragon in question screeches, high pitched enough for me to wince.

I suppose she has very good hearing.

I feel a prickling at the back of my neck, causing me to look back at the entrance to Tech Duinn. A dark figure strides out.

The Donn. I don't even have to make out his facial features to know it's him. The way he carries himself is quite distinctive.

He makes it to us in seconds, his long legs eating up the

distance quickly.

He looks the same, like perhaps he hasn't slept or changed since I last saw him. Since I tried to claw his eyes out.

"Ahh, the Donn decides to come out and join us. Finally, had enough of your scrolls, Erron?" Gwen teases, nudging him with an elbow.

He nudges her back, seemingly without thought, taking me in from head to toe.

Gwen looks at me with a glint in her eyes. "And about your earlier concern—we've thought about everything. Don't concern yourself with the details. We just need your knowledge of the castle and the Fianna once we arrive in this… Raith place." With that being her only dismissal, she strides gracefully towards her mount.

Gwen leaps onto Vyrain's foreleg, which is extended for her, and gracefully climbs her way up the beast, to settle between two spiked plates at the base of Vyrain's neck. The she-dragon clambers to her feet—her height easily twice that of the bronze dragon before. "Best of luck, Alyx. I'll see you two at the rift."

With a great running leap, Vyrain takes off into the night, the enormous trees nearly falling backwards with the might of her flapping wings.

I'm unsure if I could ever get used to the sight.

"How are you?" Erron's rumbling voice asks.

"You shouldn't have let me sleep so long," I say instead of answering his question. I couldn't begin to explain how I am.

"You would have been useless to me if you couldn't even stand. You were dead on your feet."

"They need us to have been there by now more than I needed to sleep."

He pauses, his rich brown eyes glowing nearly red in the firelight. How can he argue otherwise?

"We will get them back," he says, instead of arguing.

I nod, because I cannot voice the retorts in my throat. How could he know that? What was the price of my resting? Will I be able to bear it? Will they?

He puts his face directly in front of mine, capturing my attention. "Whatever we find, we will deal with it. Whatever has happened to them, they will cope. Just as you have. Just as I have. Just as they have before. We will do what we can, and we will move forward, together. There is nothing else to be done, Alyx. Don't let the rest of it consume you." He gives me time to absorb that before turning, gesturing back where he came from. "Come. Rignon is waiting with our supplies in the pit."

He waits for me to move first before setting off too. As I walk beside him, our steps in sync, I can't help but question myself: have my thoughts always been so plainly written across my face?

The entrance to the pit is a short walk away. The pit is the nest of dragons, Erron had told me. Their tunnels burrow deep into the stone.

Never could I have imagined the ominous feeling it incites. It looks like the site of some great battle. An amalgamation of ruined stone and whirling mystery, like power itself has nestled into the rock and made a dark home. It smells of cinders and dry stone.

As Erron leads me down the footpath that trails into the dark chasm, part of me debates running away. Surely, he doesn't need me to go in there and gather the supplies. Surely, I can meet Rignon out in the moonlight. Falling down the cliffside sounds more appealing than wandering into the dragon's lair.

Erron ignites a ball of fire in his leather-bound palm when we pass under the opening. The flame is bright enough to give us some visibility. Enough to see the yawning cavern before us, black soot lining some spots of the cave wall. Low trills and grumbles echo from the depth, though it's too dark for me to see the monsters that create them. They sound far into the cavern, though not far enough to make my heartbeat slow.

My feet scrape on gravel even though I try to place them lightly. Even my breaths are too loud for my comfort.

"Why are we meeting Rignon here?" I whisper. "Isn't there somewhere better?"

"No," Erron says, full voiced. It echoes. The sounds from beyond stir.

The sound of great leather wings moving echoes. Boulders tumble loudly.

Erron turns to me, firelight casting shadows across the strong panes of his face.

Growling rumbles so close I can feel it in my bones. Talons scratch across the cave floor.

At first all I see is light moving beside us.

A reflection of firelight in bone-white scales.

The dragon's head rises and fills the space behind Erron's shoulder. Blood-red cat-eyes bigger than my head glow in the flickering fire as they zero in on me.

"Erron!" I gasp, grabbing Erron's arm and pulling him away from the sword-like teeth, dripping with strings of saliva that glisten right behind him.

"Rignon." Erron's stern voice echoes out as he whirls around to face the dragon, holding the flame out before him.

The dragon's nostrils flare as it dips its head closer. A violet glow grows deep behind the cage of his maw.

Erron's leather-clad arm is still in my grasp, but he pulls away. With his one hand still holding the flame, his other reaches forward to meet the scaled snout of the terror in front of us, dauntless.

I'm plastered to the stone at my back, uncertain if this dragon will allow me to move from it. Its eyes are fixed on me in glaring suspicion, grumbling low in its chest.

"This is Alyx, Rignon. She is coming with us," Erron says.

"This is Rignon," I whisper. Of course.

"Yes. This is my dragon. He dwells here much of the time. He will be our mount. If he agrees to allow you to ride with me." He gives Rignon an assessing look.

I laugh slightly without humor. "Ride him?" I whisper.

Erron finally looks back at me. "It would take too long to travel on foot. Not to mention it would be a far greater risk to our mission on our way. On our way back, once they're safely with us, we will proceed on foot back to Annwyn."

I nod.

"Will he let me? Ride him?" I ask.

Erron turns back to Rignon; they communicate with a look alone. Rignon growls low in his chest.

No. There's no way.

There's also nothing I won't do to get to my people as soon as possible.

"What about in his talons? What if he carries me like that. Like Vyrain did?" I ask, my whisper slightly louder now.

"That's the contingency plan. Though I doubt you would enjoy it much."

"I doubt I'll enjoy either much."

"You would be surprised how quickly your fear gets swept away in the wind."

"You don't know my fear."

"I know fear."

"I'm sure," I say bluntly. I know that he knows fear. But he's giving me too much credit.

"Come here." He jerks his head. "Please," he softens the command.

I keep my fingertips on the wall as I lean forward, pulling my back from the cool stone.

Rignon's red eyes follow the movement.

I breathe deeply through my nose, smelling the charred scent of the pit.

Rignon growls again, lunging towards me threateningly.

I force my feet to stay planted where they are and pull one hand from the wall, lifting the back of it towards his bared teeth.

I'm going to lose a hand.

Rignon's nostrils flare slightly, and his exhale is like holding my hand to a roaring fire. His head jerks backward with a snarl.

My hand goes back to the wall.

Erron looks worried and confused, his harsh jawline flickering.

He knows. Rignon knows. I didn't tell them who I am, what I am.

My heart is pounding a hole in the front of my chest. It hurts.

I wait for the ruling beast to deem me a monster. Some flaw in nature—something that should not exist.

Rignon looks at me again, grumbling once more before pulling his head back.

Instead of making a meal from my flesh, he gives me his shoulder, leaning it into the wall below the walking path.

Now that his body and scarlet wing bones are exposed, I

see a black leather saddle there, right behind the space where his serpentine neck ends. The seat is slight, with large crests at the front to hold onto, and a large crest in the back to brace against. A mix of straps are all wound up around the bottom of the seat. Great big straps reach forward, strapping across Rignon's front, and more reach down, towards Rignon's barrel-chest.

Erron sighs agitatedly, shaking his head, like he's shaking the worry off. "Temperamental. You wonder why people call you that." He gestures me to follow him as he strides for Rignon's shoulder.

I slowly shuffle towards them. Erron seats himself in the saddle, bending his knees forward and belting straps around his knees on either side. He leaves a space in front of him.

"I can get on?" I ask, flickering my eyes between the two.

"I don't think he will eat you if you do," Erron says blankly.

At a glance, his dark eyes twinkle slightly.

I'm glad to see he is capable of joking.

"Do you two speak to one another?" I ask, placing a trembling hand on the hard leather saddle. It doesn't move.

Erron looks at Rignon, who eyes him back at the question. The dragon seems to have some understanding of our conversation.

"In a sense," Erron responds after a moment. "It's a vague sort of communication. More through feeling and incomplete thoughts. They do not speak as we do. Though their souls may communicate with their bonded rider's."

Erron is eyeing the distance between myself and my proposed seat with a hint of amusement as he speaks. Rignon's shoulder is still propped against the cliffside, waiting.

I take a deep breath and force myself to abandon the

apprehensive thoughts.

I clamber into the saddle in front of Erron. He lets out a huff as I accidentally clip him somewhere sensitive with an errant limb. Once I'm settled, back warmed by the proximity of the giant Fae male behind me, I inspect the leather straps near my legs.

"Let me do that," Erron murmurs.

His gloved hands adjust my legs forward a bit before moving onto the straps. He deftly wraps a strap around the distal part of my thigh, pulling it tight to the saddle.

I try not to pay attention to how close we are, though I can feel my face warming slightly. His strong thighs bracket my scrawny ones, despite me shuffling as far forward in the seat as I can. Through my apprehension about the parts coming up—particularly the flying bit—I note that Fionn would be displeased to see me pressed up against another male. I feel the guilt ping through my chest and scoot forward even more.

Or would he even care? The last interaction we had would suggest that, no, he wouldn't.

Though with a rested mind, I can no longer be sure what his plan was, or if he meant any of his words. What if he was trying to save me? What if he was trying to tell me to make the deal with the king?

I couldn't blame him if he did mean his scathing words— if his hurt ran too deep. If his feelings for me were too shallow to overcome the devastation of the truth.

Even if he hates me now, I'm not sure if I could un-love him. Perhaps it's a fitting penance, unrequited love.

He would be upset about many aspects of this situation I'm in.

His tales about the fire-breathing beast he defeated once seemed like a grandiose battle from folklore. I don't want to think about what sort of complications Fionn killing a dragon will have on his return. It may be a story best left buried.

"Are you ready?" Erron asks, having finished the strap on the other side.

I nod, lost still to my thoughts.

Rignon stands up, no longer leaning a shoulder against the wall. The rolling movement makes me lean forward and grip the saddle crest in front of me with both hands as hard as possible. My heart leaps to my throat. Rignon takes steps to the entrance of the cave, every movement giving moments of weightlessness that makes my stomach flutter.

"Keep your weight down in your seat as much as possible, try not to lean forward too much. The straps are sturdy, trust them." Erron's instructions are firm in my ear.

When Rignon perches on the ledge of the cave opening and basks in the moonlight. I lose my breath at the magnificence of it all. His bone-white scales are iridescent in the moonlight, his scarlet accents and crest points all shining, as if bloody. It may be the most beautiful sight I've ever seen.

And then it's over.

Because he leaps.

And I'm *falling*.

It feels like forever and the quickest second all in one.

I hear nothing but roaring wind in my ears. I see nothing but Rignon's long scaled neck and the world racing past in a free fall.

I feel nothing but icy wind everywhere, the straps digging into my legs keeping me in the seat, and my soul falling from my body.

And then the weight crashes down on me in one wing-beat.

I try to force it into my seat, but Erron has to grab me with one arm to keep my face from smashing into the saddle-crest in front of me.

My weight was too far forward, like he said.

With every wing-flap, my weight is forced hard into my seat. But eventually, we are soaring high, no longer gaining altitude.

Once I gather myself, I look over my shoulder at Erron, my face still fixed in shock.

"There was nothing I could have said to prepare you," he says with the smallest of smiles at the edge of his mouth.

Laughter bubbles up in my chest.

I press my hand over my heart and the noises burst free.

I can't make it stop.

Long, peeling laughter streams from me. The sound is so foreign from my mouth.

It's so shocking that I laugh harder.

So much that it dissolves to noiseless shoulder shaking.

There was nothing he could have done to prepare me. Truly.

I feel his chest shaking with laughter too.

It makes me laugh more, leaning over the saddle crest because I can't hold myself up anymore.

This is ridiculous.

I'm riding a *dragon.*

The thought makes me laugh harder.

Chapter 43

The mountain on fire glows in the starlit sky. Flames bleed down its side, clouds emerging from where the hot blood meets the sea and its light dims. The joining of worlds is nearby.

Smoke and ash rain down, even upon the dragon's back, soaring through the night sky.

Erron and I stopped laughing eventually. The laughter trickled out slowly, the seriousness of our mission bringing stillness to our mood and hardening the elation into resolve.

A keening cry echoes across the landscape. It sounds like part threat, part invitation.

Rignon responds with one of his own, vibrating my very being with its volume.

Rignon picks up speed slightly, tilting his body towards the noise.

"We have a mission, Rignon," Erron calls out firmly.

Rignon keeps his pace and direction.

"When we return," Erron reasons. A pause, then a grunt from both males.

Rignon banks right, back in the original direction, with a disgruntled shake of the head, like he's shaking off his primal urges.

In the distance, near the fields of black stone that cover red dirt, a brilliant green dragon perches on a cliff's edge.

"What was that noise?" I ask.

"A dragon that lurks in the lava tubes—the veins beneath the mountains—she patrols the space around the rift well enough that we don't have to spare many patrols out this far. I sent Gwen out there by chance the day she found you. My people have taken to calling the dragon 'the Dark Fury.' She has a distinct aversion to Fae."

"Was Rignon going to fight her?" I ask, unable to imagine such power used against something of equal measure. I shudder at the thought.

"No… The Dark Fury is his mate. He's spent much time traveling with me recently. He misses her."

"They only have one mate?" I ask dumbly.

"Strictly." There's a smile in his voice. "They bond like the Fae, though I think it's a bit more voluntary. They develop a sort of mind-soul connection. It came as quite a surprise when we found out that they have similar mental abilities to us. We thought the Fae were some of the only beings that could."

"That is strange," I say as we descend slowly, moving to land beside Vyrain and Gwen. "Humans don't do that. There is no mental link to other humans, nor to other living things."

"*That* is strange."

Rignon kicks up dust as he lands at a bit of a run.

I spot Gwen sitting regally upon Vyrain. She looks like a warrior princess. Her warm toned brown hair is pulled back in a long braid that brushes the rear crest of her saddle. Her tan skin is covered almost completely by leather, her sword sheathed at her waist.

Erron calls out to her, "I'm surprised you beat us here."

"I'm not." She dusts off the spotless shoulders of her leathers. "That beast of yours grows lazy. He's never as fast as Vyrain."

Rignon lets out a bone-chilling growl. Vyrain looks down her nose at him—even as he stands taller than her—preening at the praise from her rider. Gwen just smirks at Rignon, unfazed.

Seeing the two dragons beside one another throws their features into stark contrast. Rignon is significantly larger than Vyrain, both in bulk and height. His limbs are stockier. His legs and neck are proportionately thicker with muscle. Vyrain is slenderer of build, seemingly built for swiftness and agility.

"He has traveled many more leagues recently than Vyrain. He hasn't had as much time for midday naps as some have. Pardon him for pacing himself," Erron says to Rignon's defense.

"And many more lay ahead." Gwen gestures to the entrance of a cave large enough for even Rignon to fit through, barely. "This tunnel seems large enough for the dragons up until the rift. Shall we?"

The dragons shake out their crests, seemingly agitated as we approach the cave entrance. Vyrain leads the way, walking comfortably into it on four legs. Rignon must tuck his wings in and duck his head to enter, the darkness swallowing us all. If I stood in the saddle I could reach the ceiling of the cave with my hand. The dragon's steps on rough rock echo down the many tunnels that branch off in all directions.

Both Gwen and Erron light the way with flames. While Erron uses a ball in the palm of his hand—holding it at my side—Gwen creates lines of flame down the outside of each arm. I wonder if she does it because she looks amazing, or if she just wants to keep her hands free.

The air feels charged here, like wisps of energy caressing my senses. I feel as though I could cast out a net and harness enough power to live off for weeks. As it is, I reach out a psychic hand and feel the prickles of power all over my body. I cannot help but absorb some of it. It feels like drops of crisp water from an ice-cold mountain stream in a parched mouth. Gwen and Erron appear like blazing beacons in the night—their energy vibrant, though tightly shielded.

Rignon and Vyrain feel like angry masses of pure whirling power. It is swathed in spikes of adamant. To try to pull from them would grievously wound me.

As the dragons trek through the darkness, I feel it far ahead—that weaving of energy, interlocked hands of pure power. The fabrics of two worlds, intimately joined.

Vyrain's easy walk turns into a slink, her tail whipping across the rocky ground as she feels it too. Rignon grumbles unhappily.

"Their dislike of this place—or more the humans themselves—is inherited. The fact that these two are willing to pass through the rift is a testament only to our bond," Erron murmurs in my ear. His breath tickles.

"Why?" I ask, shrinking from the feeling, pressing into the curve of his arm on the other side.

"I'm not exactly sure. When we learned of the rift here, of where it led, our bonded discouraged us from exploring the other world. I take it that there have been relations between the two species before that went awry. Their feelings are that humans are fickle, greedy. That they know no loyalty and aren't to be trusted. Do you agree?"

The answer feels obvious, but it also feels like

condemning a whole group of people that don't deserve it.

"Are we fickle? I suppose we would seem that way to a people that are so long-lived and fixed," I say, pausing to consider how to make him understand. "We have such little time to grow certain of ourselves—of our paths. I think, on some level, maybe we worry that we are wasting our time. Feel that we won't have the time to experience all that we desire. It makes us… question ourselves. And at the same time makes us act without full thought.

"Are we greedy? The worst of us are, even when born under the best of circumstances. The best of us aren't, even under the worst. And there are many in the middle, who pick and choose when to reach for what they want—based on too many things to list." I think of Mariana's face as she warned me of what happened to Diana. She is loyal to her core, even to someone who did not deserve it. "There is loyalty among us. Great loyalty."

There is nothing but the rolling movements of Rignon beneath us as my companions in the tunnel absorb what I've said. The dragons have no protest to my words, to my surprise.

"You speak of humans as though you are one," Gwen calls back, her flame-lined arms flickering with Vyrain's steps.

"I do," I say. "I feel like one still, even after discovering my power. They shaped me as much, if not more, than my mother's womb did." Though I'll never fully belong to them, I don't say. I'll never fully belong with anyone. I'm painfully stuck between three peoples, to whatever end.

"It is a unique circumstance," Erron states quietly.

"Quite," Gwen says, with an edge. I see the rift up ahead, the firelight reflecting off it. "It is a miracle, that a Fae female was able to get her baby across the rift, without herself. And that you were able to settle with a family, one that knew nothing of you, or where you came from." Her voice reveals her suspicion.

Vyrain brushes her nose over the barrier before melting through it, like one would pass through the surface of water.

Erron says nothing to Gwen's blatant challenge. I don't know if he shares her suspicion. He only says, "Rignon will offer energy enough for both of us."

Rignon bristles and smashes his tail against the wall of the cave, seeming to work up the resolve to follow Vyrain. He eventually lowers his horned brow, first meeting resistance before the rift allows him through.

I fell through the last rift I crossed. This time, it is nearly as disorienting as that. I pass through the wavering barrier, my body feeling as though it goes through great pressure. My head spins and ears pop.

Coming out on the other side feels as though someone has thrown a blanket over my senses. My power feels as though it is wading through mud, requiring exponentially more effort to grasp onto anything.

The space on this new side is just as dark, different tunnels branching out in every direction. The dragons are both releasing low grumbles that echo ominously. Their crests are like hackles, raised and alarmed.

I look back at Erron to see him panting, looking as alarmed as I've seen him since that moment I crawled over his desk.

I place a hand on his knee beside mine. "It's fine. This is normal. This is what the others said they experienced as well when they landed here. You get used to it."

"Get used to it?" Gwen's voice is shrill and angry. "I'll get used to it just like I'll get used to being blind!" Her teeth are gritted as she turns to me, "If you have brought us here to trap us, changeling, I will butcher you myself."

The dragons both eye me viciously, making my heartbeat speed-up and palms sweat.

"No. I haven't. The worlds are different, and it feels wrong. I know. I didn't realize how wrong until now, otherwise I would have warned you. I'm sorry." I recall Gwen's words before the rift. "And I understand if the circumstances surrounding my landing in Suri are suspicious. It is something I have dwelt upon myself, to no end. I have no idea how I ended up there, or who brought me." The words feel so powerless I feel as though I may as well have stayed silent., but I'm flailing now, desperate to be believed. "I think it may have been Diana. She was from Danu, though I never saw evidence of any power from her. I didn't even know she was Danaan until we were separated. She was always just the healer in my village, but she knew a lot about me when I was a baby. She spoke of it once. She knew Fionn, but never joined the Fianna for some reason. She's the only explanation for how I got there, as she stayed near me my whole life."

They ponder my words for long seconds.

"I would like to speak to this Diana," Gwen states, still glaring.

"She's dead," I say, voice breaking.

"Convenient," Gwen says.

"I know. I know you don't trust me. I don't know how to fix that. But what if you turn back now, and I wasn't lying?" I plea. "There will be many chances to corroborate my stories."

"Not if you have an army of Fomorians waiting on the outside of this cave," Gwen pushes.

"Then go look. Keep me here. If you don't return quickly, Erron can kill me and turn back. Even if there were

Fomorians waiting out there, none would be prepared to take on Vyrain," I reason.

Erron tenses at my back.

I feel, more than see, Gwen sizing me up. "Fine. I will go." She dismounts Vyrain, falling to the rocky ground in one leap. She lands without injury. "Vyrain will stay. We cannot risk them knowing about the dragons. I shudder to think what they would do to harness such power."

Vyrain disagrees, very vocally. She snarls in Gwen's face, snapping her many teeth inches away from Gwen's nose.

Gwen stands her ground, saying nothing back. Presumably discussing mind-to-mind.

Vyrain roars loudly, scraping talons against the ground.

So much for stealth. Surely, the town of Dun heard that.

Gwen turns and darts away, ducking into a tunnel too small for Vyrain to follow. Vyrain scrapes at the rock with her talons, unhappy with her rider's decision, but unwilling to oppose her by following the larger opening before us that will surely take her to the outside.

Her tail whips against the cave wall as she turns to observe me, cat-eyes narrowed, teeth bared.

"She will come back," I say, hoping I speak the truth. What if the king sent men after me? What if they are waiting there, the king having let me be the bait to lure more out from their hiding place?

"She had better," Erron says, his first words since crossing the rift. He sounds just as rocked by this whole experience.

I turn to look at him. "I am not the enemy." I do not drop my gaze, even as he seems to peer into my very thoughts. "I promise."

His gaze seems to wander over the planes of my face. I

must look horrible, but I hope I look honest too. He looks jarringly handsome, even in the dim firelight he's managed to sustain.

Whatever he sees must satisfy, as he nods shortly.

We sit with bated breath until Gwen reappears, lit by flame, too stealthy for footsteps to preclude her.

She nods at the two of us atop Rignon, seemingly satisfied that no trap awaits outside the mounds. She approaches Vyrain who gives her an angry hiss, backing away. Gwen stops in her tracks, hands going to her hips. They engage in a mental argument we aren't privy too for a handful of seconds before Vyrain begrudgingly extends a foreleg, allowing Gwen to remount her.

We navigate the tunnels until we reach the dawning light. When we clamber out into the open air, we are on the coastal side of the mounds. The sea roars at us, some violent greeting to show the dragons they are not the most powerful beings in this world.

The dragon's scales sparkle more brilliantly in the dawn. Rignon's opalescent scales reflect rainbows as he basks in the light. Vyrain, in all her emerald glory, perches on a rocky ledge, head tilted towards the sun.

When we tear through the skies of Suri, for once I look down upon it and feel hopeful.

I soar upon the wings of changing tides and a wrathful new dawn.

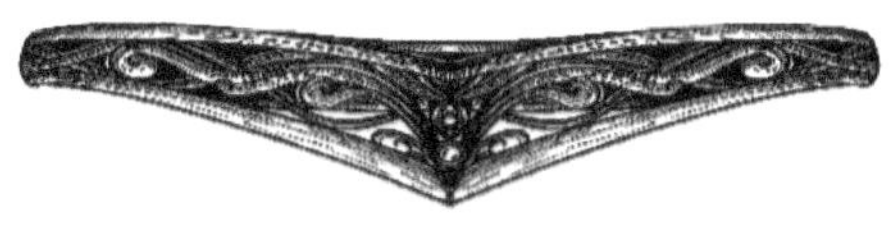

Chapter 44

"Are we sure there's no place to bring him? Have you no healers here?" Erron grunts as he finishes positioning the drunkard down a side alleyway between two residences.

The white linen billows in the twilight breeze, hiding the man from view of the street and the wraiths that would prey upon him.

It took us only three days to reach Raith from the rift all the way on the other side of Suri. It took me weeks on foot.

"You will be hard-pressed to find someone to take him in. Our healers don't bother with this sort of thing. This way he will be out of sight until he can sober up enough to awaken and stumble home," I say, aware suddenly of how terrible it all sounds.

Summer rains pour down on our three hooded figures, the passed-out man before us sleeping through the onslaught. The streets are near-empty at this time of evening, the Crows heavily enforcing curfew since I escaped. The once bustling city life is now a skeleton of its former vibrancy. The music wasn't playing on the king's road this afternoon as we took the madame's passage back into Raith. The stands at the market were thin of supplies. The carts near-empty and the people ravenous, enraged when the stands containing their only food source ran out. The children no longer play in the streets, the few that I saw were begging for food or coins that I didn't have.

The bodies of the starved or hanged were piled near the wall. I can still smell them.

After dropping us off under the cover of the mists that roll off the sea, the dragons had flown above the clouds and out to rocky outcroppings along the gulf coast. They are aware of the many merchant ships traveling through the gulf that may see them if they aren't careful, positioned amongst the rocks.

This afternoon, both Fae had walked stoically behind me as I led them through the entrance that I had fled through weeks ago. The madame's man had stood post, giving us a solemn nod before allowing us passage. She will soon be notified of our arrival, I'm sure. Neither Gwen nor Erron had uttered a word since we entered Raith, though I saw a tear roll down Gwen's cheek when we passed the piles near the wall.

We had traversed the outer edge of Raith until we saw this man, splayed out in the street. After so much death, it felt wrong to leave him to the mercy of the Crows in the night, even if his own carelessness was the cause of it.

"This whole place is wrong," Gwen grits out, voice trembling. Her eyes are scanning the rooftops.

Erron agrees with a nod, staring at the man. "What is there left to save?"

The question churns my stomach. I had not thought that saving these people was a thought in his mind. It was in mine, thought it felt too far-off to dwell on.

I'm not sure what it would look like; to save these people who have endured such things. When a wound festers, you cut it clean from the body. When it spreads too far, there is no amount of culling that can save the doomed. To try to save it is to prolong the suffering. What use is this effort when he will probably end in the same place tomorrow? What use is a fight against evil when evil already lives embedded in our very being?

"We don't have time to ask such questions. I doubt we will find any answers," I say, addressing Erron.

Erron looks at me, rage boiling in his eyes. It is the blood of the mountain as it falls into the sea. I fear this day in Raith may have forever tainted his view of humanity. I fear that, after today, he will think the same of humans as the dragons do.

"Let us go. Let us do what we can," I say softly.

What is there to do but what must be done?

It is the smallest thing, saving five people in a world where the bodies are piling up. It is standing up when you want to let the dust bury you. It is going to do your work when you can't stand for people to look at you. It is doing what you can, even if you only do it with the tiniest shred of hope. The kind of hope that feels like none. The kind that you only know exists because, if it didn't, you wouldn't have gotten up at all.

Erron nods, like he hears the weight of my words.

Gwen follows me first when I lead us down the last street. I hear Erron follow a moment later.

I open the manhole and leap down. Gwen jumps in after me and lands in a stream of sewage. Her shriek of rage is barely muffled by her clamped lips.

"I should have warned you about that," I say.

Getting out of the castle from the tunnels was one thing. Searching through the maze of tunnels that run underneath the entire city, hoping to find one specific sect of them, is another. The city itself is built on a slight hill, with the castle sitting regally at the crest of it. The tunnels utilize this to allow the waste to flow downward, out to the sea. I figure if we move against the softly flowing current, we are headed in the right direction.

Wrong.

Many pathways dead-end in the upper-class sect. The clatter of hoof-steps and the glow of oil-lamps lighting the streets above establish that we are below a luxurious area.

A luxurious area, but not the palace.

With every path blocked, my anxiety grows. Fionn is so close, and once we have him, we can find the Fianna. His position, imprisoned and probably subjected to torture, makes him the first task. Every second counts.

Every second counts and with every dead-end there are minutes wasted. I recall my fingers, shattering under Gyddeon's blade pommel. They were healed when I awoke in Tech Duinn.

I trudge faster through the water, my breaths coming faster.

I was healed while he was stuck here, at the mercy of Gyddeon, who knows nothing of it.

Eventually, I lead us to a path obstructed by iron bars.

"This must be the way. It would be foolish to allow such a way directly into every part of the castle. It makes sense they would block it off." Erron brushes past me as he speaks, grasping onto the bars with both hands, and attempting to pull them apart.

"How did you get past them on your way out?" Gwen questions behind my back.

"They didn't exist," I murmur, perplexed. Surely, I would recall such a detail.

Erron swears as he is unable to bend either bar with brute strength alone. He removes his gloves, tucking them into his cloak pocket.

His hands are broad and strong, like a smith's. They also have red ink covering the back of them, strong patterns and small symbols radiating from his wrist down over the tops of his fingers. The sight strikes a chord in me.

His shoulders rise with a deep breath as he grabs onto them once more, the patterns in his hand moving as he grips the bars.

The bars begin to glow red-hot under his palms. His arms shake with effort as the bars begin to bend, softened in their molten state.

I consider keeping up the search to find the exact way I came from, but the time it would take convinces me otherwise.

We pass through the grate and continue.

At our swift pace, the first manhole we come upon peers into a dimly lit room. As I peer up into it, the welcome smells of rosemary and warm bread fill my nose. I nearly groan, finally given relief from the sickening smells of the tunnels. I listen for some time, trying to hear the gentle movement of a cook bustling about in the kitchens.

"Anything?" I ask them.

"There's nobody there," says Gwen. Erron grunts in agreement.

I breathe deeply and push up on the stone circle, body straining under its solid weight.

Once the cover is slid over, I hoist myself up, glad of the rest and food I've consumed over the past several days.

The room is not what I imagined of the palace kitchens.

I expected fine meats roasting in ovens, great bundles of vegetables and exotic fruits ladening tables, and dishes of the finest making being prepped for the king and his company. What I find is quite the opposite.

The space is mostly empty of food, only a loaf of bread sitting upon the table, a few sausages hanging from twine. Barely enough food for the kitchen staff, much less an entire palace of guards and kingly guests.

Erron and Gwen join me in the room, looking around for danger.

"There's no food here," I state dumbly.

"They don't eat much," Erron says, eyes glazed as if in reverie. "Their taste skew towards souls. It's something my people noticed quickly, when we took them on as guests in the beginning. The fact that they did not eat much at all. We thought they were trying not to be a burden, but we realized they had some lewd practices quickly afterwards."

The thought of what has been sustaining these things for so long makes me sick. All those people, piles of them, for years.

"We should go," I whisper, afraid to speak too loudly. I cannot stare at this empty kitchen any longer.

The kitchens are on the same level as the cells, but we find they have no direct routes to them. We have to go up to the main level, where the throne room is, to get to the doorway that leads to the cells.

The castle is shockingly empty, the few guards present being human men. It is as if the king is away, and he brought his guard-dogs with him. Some soldiers stand at the top of the stairs. Gwen swiftly dispatches them, silently laying their unconscious forms behind a curtain.

We cross the entrance hall, the door on the other side sickeningly familiar.

My body breaks out in a sweat at the sight of it.

Erron notices when my breathing escalates, and I balk slightly before we reach the door.

It's as though my body can still feel the shivering that goes on until my body had no more energy to move. Starvation and thirst that made me feel as though I were going mad, like my hunger was gnawing on my bones.

The nightmares, the hound—I wonder if the Pooka guards the cells. I wonder if, this time, it will kill me.

"Alyx," Erron prompts gently.

I force myself to walk past his probing eyes—to walk the last few steps.

I pull breath into my lungs from the belly up, feeling that kernel of power. Letting it grow until it hovers just beneath my skin.

I wasn't ready last time. There is no other option but for me to be ready now.

The knob is cold under my hot hands as I open the door.

My thoughts scream at me every step down the staircase. I keep my eyes open, peering at the bottom, watching for Gyddeon to appear. Waiting for the Pooka to spot me with its glowing red eyes and spindly claws.

Erron and Gwen follow me down silently.

The guard patrolling the room where Gyddeon tortured me is distinctly Fomorian. No Pooka in sight.

He spots me a second too late.

A blast of air is all it takes to shove him back against the wall.

His shadows whirl with the wind and the sound of his armor clangs through the small stone room.

The time it takes to right himself afterwards is enough time for me.

I inhale once more, gathering a storm of power. The

flames in the sconces are snuffed out by my breath.
And with my exhale, he meets an icy end.

421

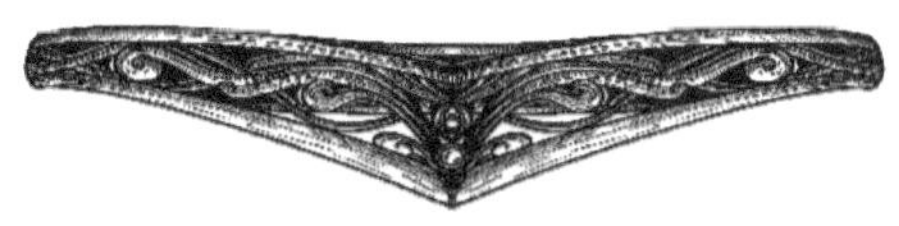

Chapter 45

His skin is tinged with blue, frozen in something akin to fear.

Gwen looks between me and the Fomorian with apprehension, like her entire assessment of me has just been proven wrong.

Erron keeps his expression schooled, though the clenching and unclenching of his fists gives away his nervous energy.

"Are there any others?" I ask, voice hollow.

"Not yet," Erron replies.

"The noise," I say, like asking a question.

"Might be a calling card to them. Gwen will stay here, ensure that we don't get surprised while we look for Fionn," he states.

Gwen nods in confirmation, gaze still flickering between myself and the frozen monster across the room.

I don't like the way they look at me, like they both no longer know what to think of me.

Did they think I was powerless? Did they think I should have left him alive? Did they think me a monster for killing him?

Erron stalks towards the guard, plucking the jingling keys from his belt. He looks back at me, checking to see if I'm ready to follow him into the depths of the dungeon.

This time, I let him lead the way as he traces his bare hand across the stone, each step measured and slow as we walk down the hall. We pass the cell I rotted in and I shove every panicked, useless thought as far down as possible.

"I can't feel anything," he says, brows drawn. "It's like running into a wall of the universe. It's as if nothing exists behind it."

I nod in acknowledgment, thinking of other ways to find Fionn in these long hallways of closed doors. To call out his name, hoping he's able to hear us, and hoping we find him before everyone else finds us, is equally as risky. I killed the only source of answers we had.

Opening all the cells one-by-one is a risk. Whoever is in them may be dangerous, if not directly to us, then to our mission, but I see no other way.

Erron nods, agreeing with the question in my eyes.

He uses a key to open the door in front of us, slowly allowing the light to flood the cell.

I clasp my hand over my nose as the smells of waste and decay assault us. The figure of a corpse huddles in the corner, face-down. Its flesh decays in shades of gray and brown. Dried blood pools beneath their face. They must have killed themselves by bashing their head into the ground.

I recall when I thought that was my best option, too. Letting my head go limp as Gyddeon bashed it into the ground repeatedly.

Erron shuts the cell firmly, moving onto the next.

Most of the cells we open reveal a similar sight. Not all self-inflicted, some probably died of neglect. A few were in states of desiccation, and I assume they were food for the Crows—but none are Fionn.

It is as if the Fomorians left and forgot their prisoners. Left them to starve and die.

Erron doesn't say as much, but his shoulders slump slightly at every door.

He opens another, not bothering to brace himself against the sight before him.

I would not recognize him if I hadn't run my fingers through that hair. If I hadn't played with those fingers as we held hands in stolen moments. If I hadn't been lit aflame by those golden eyes time after time, I would not know the bloodied and bruised, skeletal face that frames them.

He is huddled in the corner, head leaning on his shoulder, as if too weak to hold himself up.

Without thought, I bolt to him.

"Fionn," I whisper, voice trembling. My hands ghost over his hair, his face looking too painful to touch. Even immortals can be killed. It seems as if he is hovering in death's doorway. I need to get him out of here so I can see to his wounds. Make sure he's not bleeding inside.

"Alyx," Fionn whispers back, his eyes finally focusing on my face. He reaches up, half of his fingers twisted and broken. His eyes are finally focusing on my appearance, figuring out that I'm here to rescue him. He brushes back my hair from my face and the heat of his touch is like the most soothing of balms.

Maybe he didn't mean what he said in the throne room.

When his hands both go to my neck, I'm still not expecting it.

He has me on my back in a second, squeezing both hands tightly around my throat, crushing my trachea with his slight weight bearing down on me.

Frail he may be, but his immortal strength never fails him when vengeance is on the line.

"You're a fucking parasite!" he screams in my face, golden eyes maddened at the sight of me.

His fingers scrape across the side of my neck as he's suddenly pulled off.

Erron has him pinned on the ground before I can make any sense of what just happened.

I scramble backwards until I'm in the doorway, ears ringing, frantically pulling in air through by bruised windpipe.

Fionn thrashes weakly in Erron's grasp. "She's a traitor. A half-breed monster!" He cranes around Erron and shouts at me, "I'll kill you for this!"

The ringing in my ears grows louder.

"No. You won't," Erron growls, subduing Fionn with a firm shake. "Look at me. Look. At. Me. What am I?"

Fionn does finally look at Erron. Taking in his pointed ears and immortal grace. Fionn's thrashing dwindles to a stop.

"Fae. You're Fae," Fionn whispers, as if saying it too loudly will make Erron disappear. He looks hopeful for the first time. Like seeing the sunlight after months of darkness.

"Yes." Erron releases Fionn abruptly, lurching to his feet and coming to me.

He grabs my hand, his callouses sliding against my skin.

It's like the skin-on-skin contact jerks me out of my shock. A feeling like ice racing down my spine tears a gasp from me. Erron pulls me to my feet, and I feel adrift. Lost—somewhere far away, tethered to the present moment only by Erron's hand in mine.

I look at Fionn, still laying on the ground. He must have used all his residual strength trying to kill me. My voice is surprisingly calm, considering everything whirling in my chest, "We came to rescue you."

"How did you get out?" Fionn asks, looking as though he already knows the answer.

"Someone left the door to my cell, as well as an escape route for me. I didn't have time to get you out then, but I came back for you and the rest of the Fianna."

He laughs, cruelty twisting the sound. "Right. I've told you before, you're a bad liar. Do you know what the king said?" He looks at Erron beside me, whose gaze I can feel heavy on my face. "He said that you took his offer. He said that you betrayed me. He said that you were on your way to find him the greatest prize imaginable. He said you would find him the rest of the Fae of Danu."

Blood bleeds from my face.

It's like I've been in a trap this whole time. It felt like it, but I couldn't see how.

Why? Why? Why?

"No. No that's wrong," I say weakly.

I look to Erron, begging him to believe me.

He looks like someone just stabbed him through the chest, his eyes searching every plane of my face. He removes his hand from mine—it's like he's left me adrift.

I look back to Fionn. "He lied. He's playing you. He's playing some game, and I can't figure it out. He let me out, yes. He did. He left my cell door open and then forced me through the opening to the sewers before I could get you out Fionn. The rest of what he said—it's not true. I didn't make a deal with him. He told me to go and wouldn't tell me why. He just said that I had to go before he changes his mind. Please believe me. I would never betray you."

"Did she tell you what she is?" Fionn asks Erron.

It's like I'm holding on by a few fingers, dangling over

a cliff, and Fionn is prying them off one-by-one.

I knew that the things I've lied about would come out. I knew Fionn might do it. But for a few seconds there, when I first saw his face, I thought he might love me back.

I turn to Erron, but he's still staring wide-eyed at me, disbelief coloring his face. His eyes only flicker to Fionn before returning. "What are you?" he asks roughly.

"An abomination," Fionn says for me. "A Fae and Fomorian bastard. Just like the king." His tone turns imploring, "Brother, leave her here to meet her fate. There has been nobody here to check on us or feed us in weeks. We can leave, together. Get my Fianna and ensure nobody follows us back. We don't have to be the ones to kill her, but she shouldn't exist."

He wants to leave me here. In these cells. To die like the others.

"Erron," I say, steeling myself. Trying to shove back the shattering feeling in my chest. I can't look at Fionn again. I can't see his face say those words. I think it might live in my nightmares forever. "I lied to you, yes. I wanted to make sure we did not abandon this mission. It was too important that we get the Fianna back. I lied to you for the good of Fionn, for the good of my people. For the only people I claim." I'm not sure how else to convince him. I'm not sure that my words have ever been able to hold much weight. I settle on the truest thing that I can say. "I am not your enemy."

In between the horrible, caustic things burning my chest, there is a real, tangible resolution settling within me.

I will not be a prisoner again. Never. Either he lets me leave with them, or I go out fighting.

"Well, we do not claim you." Fionn's voice comes from behind me. It sounds like he's managed to stand.

It is like the final degree that sets the water to boil.

I don't even face him as I hiss, "I wasn't asking you to. Erron might not be so blinded by his own self-righteousness and need for vengeance. He might see past the basest of plans to sow seeds of distrust amongst our group."

"You are a poison," Fionn grits out. "I was a fool to think I could trust you. And I will not be made to look a fool again."

I finally look back at him.

"You would still be rotting here if it weren't for me. If I didn't accomplish what you never could. I found the Fae. I secured their aid." If I didn't know him, I would think the hits weren't landing. But I see the twitch in his lip. "If I am weak, what does that make you?"

Fionn's leash on himself snaps and he lunges for me once more.

His weakened state makes him fall for it, the defensive maneuver that he taught me. I had hoped I wouldn't have to use it. But I'm ready this time.

His own momentum helps me push him to the wall with one arm cranked behind his back. My other arm bars his torso against the wall.

I get in the last word, the only thing I really have left to say to him. "I would never have abandoned you as you have abandoned me."

I release him, stepping back right into Erron, who hovers near the two of us. He must have thought to intervene.

Sounds of conflict fill the hallway outside our door. Fionn's shouting must have alarmed the guards left on the main level.

Fionn turns to lean his back against the wall, wincing from his extensive injuries. He glares at me, ready to launch back into whatever tirade he has planned, when Erron interrupts him.

"We go now, or you stay here. It is decided. Alyx is not our enemy."

Fionn looks at him like he is an idiot. "You are—"

"I am the Donn. The heir of Maica, Queen of Danu. You will trust my judgment and come silently. I do not want to hear another word from your ungrateful mouth." Erron's voice is that of a king—unyielding and full of power.

The amalgamation of emotion that floods me at those words makes my knees waver. I would like to say it is all relief, but it mostly feels like I'm falling, and I don't know where the end is.

The noise in the hallway dims, blades clatter against the ground.

Fionn looks at him with both awe and defeat before nodding.

Erron looks out into the hallway, tension falling from his shoulders at what he sees.

Gwen fills the doorway, unscathed. "Are you about finished?" she asks, exasperated.

Erron helps Fionn stand and walk out of the cell. I quickly follow, unwilling to give anyone the chance to close the door on me.

Gwen falls in with me, the look on her face saying she heard our words. I lead us to the manhole where the king once forced me to abandon Fionn.

Gwen leaps down into the hole first.

Erron lowers down Fionn, Gwen helping him from the bottom.

"I'm sorry," I say to Erron, once he straightens. I'm unable to look him in the eye.

"I understand."

"I wish I hadn't. I think I could have trusted you."

He nods in the corner of my vision.

I feel like he doesn't forgive me. For some reason, I need him to forgive me.

"Go." He gestures down into the hole.

I hesitate, wanting to beg him more for his forgiveness. But maybe I don't deserve it, and I don't have the time to.

I jump, this time praying I never have to come back.

Chapter 46

We make it through the tunnels, the way back unbarred, just as I remembered it. I wonder if the king did it to ensure I could leave. I wonder if he waded in the waste himself to remove it or if he just knew that this path was clear.

Fionn shoots me distrustful glance after distrustful glance. I can see in his eyes he will kill me given half the chance.

It is silent until we reach a suitable exit, the light of dawn peeking through the holes in the lid stone.

As soon as we breathe the fresh air, I feel the need to run. To get away from Fionn and his looks. To run far from the castle and the horrible things that happen there. To get away from Erron and my betrayal of him and Gwen. To sail across the sea and forget my miserable life. I think it's the shock wearing off. I can only hope one day I'll stop feeling like this.

We steal some clothes for Fionn. A pair of dark linen trousers hanging from a windowsill and a dark blue lightweight tunic billowing from a line. Once he is passable, he dons a light cloak, drawing the hood up to hide his emaciation, the filth that lingers over him will have to wait. I admit begrudgingly to myself that he still looks handsome, even in such a state.

A familiar maroon door greets me, and I pass it to head down the alleyway, the group following behind me.

Facing the brick wall near where the madame stopped, I knock on the stone, feeling rather foolish. A few paces down, the stone wall moves, retracting backwards before moving aside as a head pokes out. The man says, looking befuddled, "Down here next time, miss. I almost did not hear you."

My face warms as I lead us down the stairs, down the hallway and into a familiarly garish office.

The space feels small with all of us in it. Gwen wanders about, fondling baubles and feeling the texture of fabrics. Erron still aids Fionn in walking. Fionn's leg appears to be broken after having watched him, though he won't let me close enough to really look at it.

The bookshelf-door swings open and there she is. The madame looks like the cat that ate the cream as she wanders in. "Well, well, well. Look who did it. I'm afraid I'm growing rather impressed with you, healer."

"Madame, thank you, for your help. We came to seek more information, if you will give it. We come to seek our friends. Would you have any more information about where they may have gone?"

"Ah yes, I do have something that belongs to you. It will be here any moment. You picked quite the time to show, the king has been gone since a few days after you left. My birds say he's coming back soon, with quite the company. I'm sure he will be delighted to realize he's missing one of his most prized prisoners," She says demurely, lighting up a smoke.

Erron speaks next, "I believe you have some answering

to do, Banshee. When last we met, I told you to keep the secret of my people. I believe I threatened to wipe you from the face of this realm if you so much as uttered a word about us. And yet, here we are, because you went back on your word."

She's grinning slyly, blowing a cloud of smoke out from between two red-painted lips. "Would that you had even half your power here, Erron. You're so handsome when you're angry. It almost makes me want to let you try. It would be nice to feel the warm hands of a Fae male again." She flickers a glance at me. "I thought you might let this one time that I broke our deal slide, my lord Donn. Considering what kind of prize I led to your den. You should really thank me."

Erron's jaw flutters as takes her measure. It's like watching a mountain lion and a wolf stare one another down. "Never again," he says, letting the offense slide like a slow, calculated surrender of a battle.

"I thought you might feel that way," she says smugly.

A shadow fills the doorway.

Not just a shadow. The Shadow.

Elva stands there, looking stricken.

I can't help but gasp her name in elation.

She's as beautiful as ever. Her midnight skin aglow in the candlelight. Her hood is down for once, revealing her closely shorn hair and elongated, pointed ears.

She rushes to us after a beat, murmuring our names in astonishment. She gets a good look at Fionn and gasps, "What has happened?"

"What happened to you?" Fionn growls.

His anger surprises me.

"You were gone that day. Just gone. What exactly, was more important than coming back that evening?" he interrogates.

The madame chimes in, "She was coming to see me, boy. She remembered me from our last interaction and couldn't resist."

Elva shoots the banshee a look. "I saw Alyx leaving. I remembered who ran this pleasure house and wanted to ensure nothing was amiss. Luckily, nothing was. Unluckily, by the time I returned..." She glances nervously at the madame. "Everything had fallen apart. I didn't know if you were alive or dead. Eventually, after finding nothing about anyone, I returned. I offered my services in exchange for access to her birds. I've been trying to find everyone."

She had been watching me—spying on me. The thought stings, but I suppose it may have been justified.

She sees the look on my face. "I just wanted to allow you your space, but I wanted to make sure your ignorance was not being exploited."

I nod, waving it off, though another thought occurs to me.

I turn to the Banshee. "Why didn't you say that she was working for you when I came by searching for help? It would have been helpful to have Elva when I was risking my life, racing across the country to get to the mounds. Was it just amusing to you?"

The Banshee's face darkens. "I don't appreciate being questioned, faeling. Your friend was already halfway to Gormes by the time you stumbled in. You did not seem inclined to wait. Neither does it look like your lover had the extra time."

"We aren't lovers," snarls Fionn. He looks at Elva. "You should know. Your little friend here isn't what she seems." He eyes me. Erron shifts more of Fionn's weight back on his bad leg. Fionn gasps in pain before snarling at Erron.

"Watch your mouth," Erron rumbles.

"She should know," I state, a lump in my throat. "Tell her Fionn. Let her decide."

He does. He spares no details of our time imprisoned while we were together. He tells her of that day in the throne room. He tells her the whispers the wicked king poured in his ears. He tells her of Gwen and Erron, who then introduce themselves stiffly. He tells her of what occurred in the cells just hours ago.

I wait for her judgment. When she offers none, I say "If you would like to hear my side, I could tell it."

She merely looks at me, stoic as always. "Perhaps while we are on the road. You're no traitor. Let us go."

The utter faith she has in me is like a balm to my abraded heart. She gives me the slightest of smiles as I walk up to her.

"It's good to see you," I say, softly.

A slow smile creeps onto her face.

"You too," she replies.

What else could I say to her? I've missed you. I was scared you would hate me. I was worried that I would never see you again.

All these things would make me sound like a child, but I feel them all the same.

Instead, I ask, "Do you know where they are?"

Elva nods. "I found them recently." She looks down, sighing. "They're a bit on edge. Have been ever since I found them. Konan won't leave Aine, but Aine is in no shape to go anywhere. Armund wants to stay with them." She pauses, then adds to both Fionn and I, "They thought you were dead."

Even Fionn has stopped glaring at the topic of conversation.

"What do you mean Aine is in no shape to go

anywhere?" I ask, my heart stumbling. "She wasn't hurt. She was fine." Besides what she witnessed.

"She's okay. You'll see. She is just… not as she was." Elva sweeps for the doorway, grabbing onto the crook of my elbow. "We shall go and get them. The sooner we are all together again, the better."

Fionn says, "All of us should go."

Elva eyes Fionn's legs. "You won't make it. Not on that leg. We will bring them back here and you can see them then."

"Either Gwen or I should go with you," Erron says. His surly expression says he's considering dumping Fionn on the ground.

"Sure. But be quick about it." Elva stops in the doorway. "Clio can get you to our meeting point." She indicates the madame. "I want out of this cursed city today. I crave the full weight of my power. I'm sure you all understand."

Gwen nods, wide-eyed in agreement. "I'll go. Erron, enjoy the cripple."

Fionn glares in protest at being addressed as such.

Erron looks like he wants to argue, but he lets her go with a pointed glance.

"As always, it's been a pleasure, Elva." The madame gives her a heated look before turning to me. "Alyx, don't forget our bargain."

"Why not just ask me now?" I ask.

"Because you don't know the answers yet."

I nod, apprehensive. I'm not sure how many revelations I can survive.

Walking out the door between Elva and Gwen, I'm eager to see the others. I'm eager to see my mission through. I'm eager to see Aine, and make sure she is whole. I'm eager to see her, to reassure myself of her resilience. To be able to reassure her that she never has to be alone.

As we walk, it feels like a hole is being slowly punched through my chest.

Elva was correct in saying that Fionn would not have made it.

Gwen and Elva's long-lived bodies are lithe and graceful, easily scaling the rocky wall. They now wait at the top, watching me in amusement.

If I'm part Fae, my body is not yet aware.

My every muscle tremors in fear and weakness as my hands grip onto the rough stone. I scrape my foot against the wall, seeking a hold that was so easy for the others to find. The noon sun beats down on my black cloak, heating me past comfort. Waves crash against the cliff below, only serving to worsen my fear.

I climb as Gwen chatters.

"Don't worry, Alyx. If you fall, we'll sing songs of your bravery," Gwen chimes from her place, seated at the edge, feet kicking happily. Her heels sometimes hit the wall, causing bits of rock to fall in my face. "I'm still impressed you got on Rignon." Elva doesn't flinch at the mention of the dragon. She was debriefed on our way here. She only watches me with her intent, midnight eyes. "I was betting he takes a bite out of you just for the mere fact that you thought he might let you. Erron will give me shit about that forever. Next time we make a bet about you, I'll be sure to bring you in on it. He is an unbearable loser, but an even more unbearable winner."

She pauses as I make another stride upward.

Turning to Elva she asks, "What are the odds she makes it to the top without needing help?"

Elva considers for a moment before she says, "Fair."

"Want to bet your bow on it?" Gwen holds her hand out in proposition.

Elva eyes it with disgust, "No."

I reach the top. Face level with Gwen's swinging boots. If I wasn't so sure I would fall, I would rip her boot off and throw it in the sea.

Hauling myself over the edge takes every modicum of residual fear-fueled strength.

Elva swiftly stands, holding her hand out to bring me to my feet.

No rest for the weak.

The rest of the narrow path along the rocky cliffside is pocked with crumbled rock and drop-offs. The waters in the Gulf of Ashri dance in the late-summer sunlight. The ship-docks along the outside of Raith are just around the bend, out of sight. Merchant boats sail in the distance, the noontime sun bearing down on boats of various sizes flying flags of varying colors and symbols. I recognize some as belonging to the high houses of the eastern continents. Theirs is a collection of many small countries, ruled by the wealthiest families of each country. They tend to stand peacefully with one another and the other countries across the sea.

Amidst the boats is an eerie specter, the Isle of Tori. The dark protruding isle is abandoned, due to the lore of its accursed land. Some people say ghosts sing there day and night, and you can hear it when the city is quiet. They say that the soil is all ash and the ground more likely to crumble beneath your feet than draw forth life.

As our boots tread the crags, I search for a cave or an outcropping. None appear.

A scuffle behind me freezes me in my tracks.

Looking back, Gwen is grappling with a large, pale-haired figure.

Only when the knife is locked between their two hands do I recognize him.

Konan.

"Who are you?" he growls.

Gwen growls back, words lost to the animalistic need to defend one's life.

"A friend. One of yours. A Fae woman from Danu," Elva shouts, leaving them to their skirmish.

Gwen's rich brown hair falls back in their struggle, revealing her ear's pointed tips.

Only then does Konan pause, his eyes flickering over her face, catching more than once on her ears.

"How?" he asks, still holding her on her back foot.

"I went and found them. The rest of the Fae of Danu. If you'll release her, we can discuss it further. Hopefully in the company of Aine and Armund," I say, hoping to deescalate this before Gwen rips his throat out with her teeth. I see her eyeing it.

He only lingers a moment before disengaging with bared teeth.

"Aine felt you coming," he says, looking to Elva.

She jerks her chin in acknowledgment.

Elva keeps on, leaving the rest of us to follow.

Konan advances to walk behind me, leaving Gwen to the rear. "Where have you been? Where is Fionn?"

Where have I been? Dying. Coming alive again. Crossing worlds. Dealing with kings.

"Fionn is alive. Injured, but alive. That is why he couldn't come with us. I'll wait to explain until we are with the others, the story is too long."

He grunts in annoyed acquiescence.

His brutish form used to intimidate me. Now it's a small

sort of comfort when my shoulder brushes his chest.

Elva ducks into the side of the rock, an opening I would never have caught.

I follow her.

The cavern it hides is sizable, large enough to fit all of us standing or laying. The space is lit with a modest fire in the center.

"Alyx." My name is a gasp from across the fire.

The lighting is still playing tricks with my eyes because I don't see him until he wraps me in his gangly arms.

"Armund," I say with a smile, squeezing him back.

"I thought you were dead," he whispers into my hair.

"It would never be that easy," I reply lightly, pulling out of the embrace. Never mind how close that came to being true.

"You were never going to fall off that wall," comes a small, halting voice from across the flames.

A voice both familiar and foreign.

I walk slowly towards the voice, feeling the heat from the flames as I circle around the fire.

"I might have," I reply warily.

Aine sits on a piece of driftwood, not looking towards me, but towards dancing flames in shades of violet and orange. Her hands cupping her elbows, she leans into the warmth in front of her.

I want to go to her. I want to reach out a hand, but she seems so distant.

"You were sturdy. Like a mountain in a storm. The only thing that wavered was your breath."

I look at the others, scattered around the cave. Armund leans against the cave wall, arms crossed. He gives me a small, encouraging smile. Konan hovers behind my shoulder. Elva and Gwen linger at the edges, observing us.

I wish we didn't have such an audience.

"How did you see that?" I ask.

"I see everything now." She pauses. "And nothing."

I take the seat beside her. She turns her face towards me when she feels my arm brush hers.

Her eyes.

They're the same beautiful hazel set in an almond shape, but now they only look towards me—look through me, unseeing. Moving back-and-forth slightly, like when they're closed and you're in a deep sleep.

She looks lost. Like she's been wandering for some time and is on the brink of accepting that she will never find her way back.

She's blind. How, I'm not sure. But my insides are shrieking in outrage. I'm one big knot of destructive vengeance at the thought of what she's lost. Of how scared she must be. How she lost the people she should be able to depend upon, always. And then lost her sight as well.

I close my eyes against the onslaught of emotion.

I don't realize my reaction until her hand settles on mine, burning warm against my frigid skin. I look at her.

"It's okay," she says.

Her comforting me in this moment causes my rage to flare, the air turning so cold that I can see our breath. I grip her hand tightly in mine, unable to bear not holding onto her in some small way.

"No. No it is not okay. Who did this?" I hiss, jerking around to look at Konan.

Elva speaks up when Konan looks too angry to speak the words, "Nobody, specifically. It is a soul-wound. Sometimes, with the Fae, we experience something so traumatic it manifests in physical symptoms. Those wounds are unlikely to heal—she is unlikely to see again. It occurred after that day, in the alley…"

Just the mention of that day makes my stomach bottom-out.

It was my fault really, that we were all there in that alley.

I want to beg her forgiveness. I want to tell her I'm sorry for the rest of my existence. But somehow it feels wrong to make this about me, in any way. To all but force her to forgive me in front of an audience. To force her to think about that day for even a moment more than I'm sure she already does. I swallow my shame, breathing deeply.

Instinctively searching for my center, I pull my power back into me. The air warms slightly.

I look at her. She's waiting on my words. I feel like they have weight now—too much weight.

I drape my arm across her small shoulders that carry so much and say, "I've missed you."

She smiles, brilliantly. Just as brilliantly as always.

I think it might kill me.

"I've missed you too."

I'm thankful she doesn't see the tear I shed. Pulling her firmly under my arm, I squeeze her until I have to force myself to stop before I hurt her.

As the others begin quiet talk, full of inquisitions and updates, I interrupt, "We are going to get out of this place."

Chapter 47

It takes time to relay all the information. About myself first—then to argue with Konan as to why he should not kill me outright. He seems to share Fionn's stance about my trustworthiness, unsurprisingly. He eventually stands down, unwilling to upset Aine. His eyes follow where I go now.

Armund takes it in stride, seeming to take every scrap of information and file it away for later study. I notice him observing me more often now. I try to ignore it. I try not to think too hard about what he's thinking.

Gwen steps in for the rest, briefly discussing Annwyn, and how we are planning to go back. Nobody takes much convincing. The many years spent in this realm seem to have no sentimental value to them as they rapidly pack up their measly belongings and we set out to meet the others.

We walk along the sea-cliffs, Aine walking along them without effort or fear. Something about her blindness allows her to 'feel' the world around her more keenly. She reaches out with her mind, like when I reach out to things with my mind, but on a grander scale.

"I should warn you, we in Annwyn have some new companions," Gwen starts. "I have a feeling you will be charmed. They will be traveling back with us. They can be a little… disconcerting, at first."

"That's what that was," Aine gasps, unseeing eyes wide. "They're across the bay. They feel… like power. Like more power than anything I've ever felt."

I pretend this comment doesn't set us all on edge for differing reasons. I assume the others have grown used to Aine's eerie comments, but I have not.

"Who?" Armund asks, sidling up beside me.

"Dragons," I state, watching his brows draw down and eyes blow wide.

"Dragons. Like—"Armund begins.

"—yes," I cut him off. Like the one Fionn fought. I won't be the one to let it slip to Gwen about Fionn's past with the dragons. Neither should Armund.

As the rocky cliffs change to crawling grass and soft, coastal dirt, I spot two figures, hidden within a thicket of trees. Erron and Fionn.

They've settled along the edge of farmland, the sheep flocking on the upper ridge of the property. Most of those sheep live to feed the king and his militia, the gates of Raith sit only a few leagues away from here. They are taken as taxes while their farmers live off their measly leftovers.

I had thought the Crows were a necessary evil in the beginning. They protected us, even if they also hurt us—killed us, on occasion. It was the lesser of two evils, or so it seemed.

Now I know better.

What does a king, with men that don't eat, need with all those sheep?

He needs to keep his people too hungry to fight back.

Keep them too desperate to survive the day that they're unable to worry about a year from now.

Now, I wonder how I never saw it for what it was. That their justifications were only a plight to establish a firm grip without too much push-back. It only succeeded because we were unable to stomach the idea that the worst-case scenario was the one we were in. Nobody wants to believe that they are sitting on the edge of destruction. Nobody wants to believe that their king seeks not to serve them, but to break them. Because if you believe that, what are you to do? When you're already feeling small, hungry, and powerless, what should you do when soldiers—armed to the teeth—traipse in and demand obedience?

We never were anything but a flock of sheep led to slaughter.

I can run. Escape to a world across the rift and hope to never be found.

What of the world that raised me? Can I leave them to their fate? And what about those across the sea, that won't be aware of what is happening when their soil runs dead and dry? When snakes begin to swarm in the grass, will they know to fight back while they still have the chance?

What am I to do?

That question haunts me as we step under the cover of trees.

When Erron catches sight of us, he squares his shoulders.

Fionn runs his eyes over our three recovered members, clearly reassuring himself of their wellbeing. I wonder what I could ever have done to earn such love from him.

The bruises around my throat are proof enough that I never had it.

Fionn struggles to his feet, unable to put weight on his left leg. When the males reach him, his face has risen to sheer amazement, like he never believed he would see them again. As he clasps arms with Konan first and pulls him into a one-armed hug, Konan freezes, never one for affection. Armund waits, eager and elated, before Fionn pulls him all the way in. Their reunion fills the air with sweetness, two brothers thanking god that the other lived long enough to embrace one more time.

They release, both handling one another roughly in that odd, male way of affection. Slowly, a sort of solemnity falls like a blanket over the joy. Aine approaches, having walked at the rear of the group this whole time.

Fionn staggers to her, pausing and leaning on a tree beside him.

He rubs a hand down her raven hair, settling his hand on the nape of her neck. She doesn't look up at him. I wonder if she's doing it consciously, trying to hide her condition. Or if she just sees no point in trying to aim her face up at him.

He sighs, seeming unsure of his next words.

"I'm so sorry." He flounders for a second, searching the tree canopy for words. "Your parents were the greatest and most noble of us. I should have—" He swallows harshly. "I should have done more. I should have protected us all. You paid the greatest price. And for my failure, I will never be able to atone. But I will spend every day of my immortal life trying to make this right for you. You will want for nothing. You have my word."

Her shoulders shrink with every word, surely the worst of her memories playing back in her head. Still, despite her anguish she looks up at him and whispers, "Thank you."

Fionn's brows scrunch a bit in confusion.

As if she can feel his confusion, she quickly explains. "I can't see. For now. Maybe forever. But I'm okay. I can still 'see' things, sort of. I can see their energy. I know what water is, ground, air, people. I can still see the light…" she trails off awkwardly, as if unsure what else to say.

The rest of us shift on our feet, pretending to be paying attention to other things, letting the two have their interaction. Everyone other than Konan, who's wandered to Aine's side.

I look over at Erron, who has yet to move towards the rest of us. He's staring at Aine like he's seen a ghost of someone he loved. He walks slowly, as if in a trance, coming to a stop beside me. "Deri's girl?" he asks solemnly, brushing his shoulder against mine.

I nod. "Do you want me to introduce you?"

He looks afraid of her in the moment before he looks down at me, searching my face for something, those dark eyes catching on the bruises collaring my neck. "Everything went smoothly?"

Caught by the changing of subject I stumble over my words. "Yes. Yes, everything went well." I think about Konan, his altercation with Gwen, and his siding with Fionn. "Well, Konan, the big pale male, he wanted to throw me off a cliff. He almost threw Gwen off a cliff, but we managed to sway his opinion." I shrug, making a joke of it. "He almost didn't have to; I almost fell on the way up. Elva wasn't kidding that Fionn wouldn't have made it."

Erron's face remains flat, perhaps even losing some color. Not finding it funny.

"It wasn't that serious. Gwen wouldn't have let him push her off a cliff," I clarify, feeling foolish for trying to laugh about it. Of course, he wouldn't find that amusing.

"I realize that," he says, nodding stoically. He looks at me seriously. "The greater danger is that Gwen would begin to chatter ceaselessly until he threw himself off a cliff. And then the others would never trust us."

His face remains so unchanged that it takes a moment to process that he's made a joke. I choke on a laugh, drawing the eyes of everyone else.

Erron finally acknowledges his own joke with a slight upturn at the mouth. When I look at my new audience, my eyes clash with Fionn's first. They darken as he looks between Erron and me.

I step away, creating more distance between the two of us before I introduce Aine, Armund, and Konan to Erron. Armund's eyes go wide, Konan grunts, unimpressed, and Aine tilts her head as if tuning into him.

"You're my dad's cousin," Aine states with all the bluntness of a child.

"Yes." Erron looks sick as he looks at her. "I'm glad to meet you, Aine." He pauses. "When we get back to Annwyn, as I'm sure Gwen explained, there is someone else I know who wants to meet you, when you're ready. Your grandfather. Deri's—your dad's—father. He still lives, back in Annwyn. He is one of my most trusted councilmen."

Her eyes grow wider.

I step in beside her, feeling the current of hatred directed at me from Fionn, who still stands near her. "Only if you want to," I state firmly, flashing Erron a glance.

"Of course," he says gently.

Elva melts out of her place in the shadow of a tree as she says, "There are things we should discuss before heading back. Things I've learned of when I was in Clio's employ."

We turn to listen. Armund comes to stand between Fionn and I, slinging an arm around my shoulder. I'm relieved that he hasn't completely abandoned me, even when he knows that Fionn hates me.

Even with the hateful glances falling my way from Fionn, being back with all of us together feels as though a piece has finally clicked back into place. Like there was something grating on my nerves for however long that I never noticed, and now it has been set to right.

"In exchange for use of her birds in the palace, Clio sent me to follow the king. To Gormes, where he is overseeing the mines. He had received some visitors in Raith just before he left. They went with him. Two of them looked familiar." She looks to Erron as she continues, "You are the Queen's son. As the ambassador of my people, I had met with her days before the fall of Danu. Met with her and some of her visitors. Surely you remember their leader."

Erron's face is dark in remembrance. Looking every bit the avenging prince, the shadows of the grove falling ominously over his face. "I do recall a few of their faces. And names."

Elva nods darkly. "Ethalor was with the king. Along with his advisor, the pious piece of shit that always follows him around."

Hearing such language come out of Elva's mouth is shocking.

"Balor," Erron says his name like a promise of retribution.

Fionn speaks this time, steeling himself first, "They were there. They brought me to him again. In the throne room. They were there. They watched."

Nobody has to ask what they watched. Fionn's broken and bruised body is enough description of what was done to him after I left.

His words dig into my open wounds. His pain like salt burning in fresh cuts.

Armund's arm squeezes a bit around my shoulder.

"He seemed to… answer to them," Fionn finishes, blinking rapidly to clear his mind of memories that ring pain.

"It was like he was trying to please them."

I add this new information to the puzzle that is the Pretty King.

I wonder if I'll ever discern his agenda. I try to reconcile the seemingly benevolent act of releasing me—seemingly without a tail—with everything else vile he is a part of. Nothing fits together.

"Well, he probably was trying to please them. He is their agent. Perhaps, given what Alyx and Fionn claim he said to them, he is one of their offspring. That will build-in the need to please," Elva hypothesizes. "Whatever the case, we have a much larger issue. They didn't kill them all."

The silence is heavy.

She continues, "The Fae. They're still alive. They're still in Danu. They're enslaved. Many died during the initial takeover, but most were kept alive, to this day."

My mind whirls, trying to piece it all together. I knew that a few were still alive, but most of them?

Gwen is the first to speak, blinking back astonishment, "Why would they do that? What are they doing with them?" Her eyes jump to me. "Didn't you say that the king said there were only a few of you? They can't have kept them all for breeding. Right?"

I search mine and the king's conversation, looking for answers. "I—I don't know. He made it seem like there were some who lived, for a time. But he only spoke of my mother—of how she was killed. He gave very little away about the state of Danu. He wanted me to join him before he gave me the details."

Erron looks as though the ground beneath his feet gave way. "They've been there—all this time. And we just left them. I thought they were doomed."

Elva continues, "Whatever the case, they are establishing

a foothold here, with the king and the Crows. But Ethalor and Balor remain in Danu most of the time. Which means there is a rift. Between here and Danu."

"Or they walk through worlds like you," Armund suggests.

"They don't," Elva says firmly.

"How could you know that. They came from seemingly nowhere," he argues.

"Because, boy, I would know."

They bicker while I search through my memories. I watch a bird soar high above the bay.

Aine whispers something to herself.

"What?" I ask.

"Are they going to try to kill us?" she asks, quietly.

"Who?" I pull out from under Armund's arm to lean closer to her. Surely, she isn't referring to the Fomorians who, she's aware, are going to try to kill us.

She only points out, at the sky over the bay.

At the bird.

No, not a bird—a dragon.

I can just barely make out their four limbs and clubbed tails as they soar far over our heads.

"No. They didn't try to kill me at least," I say, mostly telling the truth.

"Why do you sound like you're lying?"

"They're not going to try to kill you," I say firmly, craning back my head as they soar past us.

"We should be going." Erron steps up to my side, following my gaze. His voice is that of a king as he addresses us all, "We must return to Annwyn. Discuss with the council. I will not sit in my home while my people live in chains."

Fionn is ghostly pale. Not taking his eyes off the sky as the others begin gathering their packs.

I bump into him on purpose, drawing his eyes, which quickly narrow. I shake my head at him, wide-eyed. Don't tell them about you and the dragon.

He swallows and jerks away from me.

"Would you let me set your leg before we leave?" I ask.

He laughs bitterly. "No. I would rather not have the hands of a leech touch me again."

The name is like a hit, but one I was expecting. My heart only stutters a little

Erron snatches his hood, jostling him roughly. He snarls, "Remember my words, faeling. I'm not above putting you in your place, even if you are crippled."

Fionn snarls back at him, flame licking up his hands, which burn into the tree behind him. It's his first show of strength since we rescued him.

Erron quirks a brow. "Adorable. Maybe once we get you back and healed you can learn how to wield correctly. Until then, watch your filthy mouth when you talk to her. She's the only reason you weren't left to rot in that cell."

Erron shoves Fionn away with more force than necessary, causing him to suck in a pained breath.

Fionn's eyes, glazed with agony, find mine. The agony melts into a glare. I'm not sure he will ever let this go.

Armund wraps his arm around Fionn's waist and helps him limp away.

Erron rubs his chest, hard, as if ridding himself of the aggressive energy, then heads to the front of the group without looking at me, clearly eager to get moving.

He says something to Gwen who heads back to us, addressing the group, "Rignon will fly ahead and scout. He'll let us know if anything is awry. They cannot carry everyone, so we will have to walk. Fionn, you need to see a healer. You and I will fly ahead to Annwyn."

Before Fionn can protest, we all hear it. The billowing flaps from above.

The dragon.

Vyrain, in her verdant glory, sweeps down, agile as a dancer, landing in the field in front of us. The wind she creates throws leaves and branches and flattens the grass.

The Fianna shuffles backward, nervously eyeing the creature before us. Aine stays beside me, mouth agape.

Fionn scrambles away, peeling himself away from Armund's arm, and falling onto his back, wide-eyed.

"No," he says. "No, I'll walk. It needs to be re-broken and set by now anyways."

"I'm afraid you'll slow us down too much," Gwen says blandly as she walks up to her dragon, running a hand down her scaly nose.

Vyrain's claws flex into the ground in a feline show of pleasure. One that destroys the ground beneath her claws.

"I cannot get on her," Fionn protests again, staying on the ground even when Armund offers him another hand.

Vyrain's green eye opens, zooming in on Fionn. She inspects him closer, sniffing at his boot. She lets out a bone-chilling growl that can be heard across the plains.

Fionn's face drains of blood.

I thought I had seen Fionn afraid, but it had been mere echoes of this very real fear that now consumes him.

I think I should be enjoying it, but I don't. I know that fear, and just watching it play out is painful.

"I doubt she would let you anyhow," Gwen says. "But she will carry you in her talons; you just have to try to hold your leg still."

Gwen takes a running leap onto Vyrain's saddle, her brown hair tossing in the coastal wind.

Fionn only has time for a muffled shout before Vyrain

grabs him with one talon and leaps for the sky. Her wings, beating in the air, carry her high enough to pass for a bird in a matter of seconds.

To his credit, he doesn't scream.

The others stare after her in awe.

The sheep in the pasture bleat and run for cover.

I find myself longing to fly again, even if it is terrifying. To escape this doomed place on the wings of freedom. I fear the thought is a lie.

Ever since that day when Diana died, I've been running. Trying to find safety. Trying to find peace in a peaceless world.

I fear that evil has legs, and it's coming for us—in every world.

Rotting flesh in the body of our world, it cannot be outrun. You either succumb, or take a blade to it.

I can think of no greater purpose for a bastardization of nature, such as myself, than to be the blade that removes it.

Book 2 coming soon.

<u>*Acknowledgements*</u>

Writing this novel has been the thrill of a lifetime. I never thought I would be a writer—only ever a veracious reader with a head full of ideas and no words with which to express them. So, thank you to anyone who took a chance on this book and made it all the way here, to this back page. You've made my dreams come true, and made me feel like my words are worth something. The list of people that have been bright points of inspiration and support throughout this process is long, and surely, I cannot name them all—but I'll do my best.

Firstly, I would like to thank my husband, James. I'm a bit ashamed to say I'm not sure if I would have believed in myself enough to finish this if you hadn't believed in me first—so thank you, for that. Thank you for tolerating my vagueness and ramblings that make no sense. Thank you for being the first person I run to tell my dreams to, and for never making me feel silly for them.

Thank you to my family—all of you. Even though I didn't tell any of you I was writing a book, I felt your belief that I am capable of whatever I put my mind to. I hope you can forgive me for keeping everything under-wraps.

Special mention to my grandma, Vickie. You gave me your love of books. It has been the greatest gift that you could have passed on. I love you, I admire you. Thank you for your endless support.

Thank you to all of my friends. If I've ever spoken a word to you about this book, just know you're special and I appreciate the space to share this delicate, little piece of myself.

Thank you to my team that worked on this book with me. Kyla, my cover designer and illustrator—you came into this project with excitement and dedication that rivaled my own,

I could not be more grateful. Your art is beautiful and the friendship we developed along the way is too. Lizzy, my editor— I appreciate your gentle honesty and dedication to making this story better. Becca and Tessa, my beta/proofreaders—you were my best cheerleaders. You gave me the confidence near the end of this process when I needed it most. Thank you all for giving your time and expertise to me.

Love,

Wrylie

Wrylie Parks' somewhat maladaptive tendency to bury herself in fantasy romance novels is what inspired her to write her debut novel, *Promise of Dusk.*. She can frequently be found wandering the mountains of Colorado, where she lives with her husband, James, and their dog, Zoey —who is definitely a human in dog skin.